The girls who live in the

"STEW ZOO"

The posh Manhattan apartment building where the stewardess relaxes—and partys—between flights.

BETSY had been going with a young avant-garde artist until she got tired of his violent temper and his acid trips. Now she is gradually losing her heart to the aloof pilot she flys with on the New York to Paris run, but he doesn't seem to know she's alive.

LEE always seems to fall in love with the wrong man. She's dating a married man on the rebound from a brief affair with a flight engineer who is a notorious ladies' man.

LINDA's reputation proceeds her on every flight. She will go out with anyone—airline personnel or passenger—to fight off her horrible fear of being alone.

Julia Percivall

The Stewardess

AVON
PUBLISHERS OF BARD, CAMELOT, DISCUS, EQUINOX AND FLARE BOOKS

This Avon edition is the first publication
of *THE STEWARDESS* in any form.

AVON BOOKS
A division of
The Hearst Corporation
959 Eighth Avenue
New York, New York 10019

First Avon Printing, April, 1973.

AVON TRADEMARK REG. U.S. PAT. OFF. AND
FOREIGN COUNTRIES, REGISTERED TRADEMARK—
MARCA REGISTRADA, HECHO EN CHICAGO, U.S.A.

Printed in the U.S.A.

DEDICATION

This book is dedicated to all cabin attendants flying
the air routes of the world

and also

To Nicholas
Who,
Several years ago
(At the age of two,)
Travelled solo to London
From Lima, Peru,
Making the trip
Unforgettable.

Part 1

Flightway International 410

JFK/LHR

1

The twenty-one floor apartment building on the East Side of Manhattan, referred to by the young neighborhood set as the "Stew Zoo," stood bathed in the pale yellow sunlight of a late November afternoon.

The building had obtained its nickname because of the many teams of stewardesses it housed. On one of the high floors a Pan Am stewardess was fast asleep, exhausted from the transoceanic trip she had just completed. Her roommate, also with Pan American, was halfway across the world; the two had not seen each other in weeks, due to uncoordinating schedules.

On the floor below, in a bigger apartment, four girls were pooling information and money. They had just signed the lease, and were in the early stages of settling in. Two of the girls were with TWA, the third was with Eastern as a new-hire and the fourth was with United. Former roommates' marriages had caused the regrouping among them; tentatively, they meted out living space and discussed the sharing of closets.

In various apartments on other floors of the building, the lives of the girls who flew for a living were chronicled in unmistakable ways. The regulation luggage stacked in easily accessible positions; the art objects, found and bought in far-away places and now gracing Manhattan coffee tables; the uniforms hanging clean and ready to go in closets or lying crumpled across a chair back, scheduled for the cleaners'—these were just a few of the signs of a stewardess household.

Not all the tenants of the "Stew Zoo" were stewardesses, however. Mrs. Shumway, an elderly widow and long-time tenant who was the building gossip, had at first been alarmed by their arrival but had later softened her opinions. Growing families also occupied the block, and occasionally complained when airline parties kept their children awake. Fortunately, friction was infrequent, due to the expert arbitration of Mr. Kelly, the otherwise incompetent building superintendent. On this particular November afternoon, Mr. Kelly was in his cubbyhole apartment on the ground floor clearing some empties off a small table and wondering when he'd have to "babysit" for that damn turtle again. The tank just fitted at one end of the table; no sense in cluttering the place up meanwhile. He drained the final drops from one of the half-pint bottles before throwing it away with the others. Meanwhile, the turtle, known to his owners as Thomas, was up on the sixth floor in his tank in front of the living room window. He was stretching his neck toward a morsel of raw meat. Flightways stewardess Sharon Roberts gauged his movements and released the meat from between her fingers; Thomas took off for the deep end of his tank to devour his prey underwater and Sharon returned to fixing supper in the kitchen.

As she cracked some eggs into a bowl, an alarm rang in one of the apartment's two bedrooms. She decided she'd give Betsy a few minutes to wake up and wash her face before making her an omelette.

While waiting for her roommate, Sharon checked the kitchen cabinets and began a grocery list. Her shortness made it difficult to see the back of the shelves. Nobody, she thought with annoyance, gets an extra can of *anything* unless I make the list or do the shopping. Well, she amended silently, Betsy does, sometimes. But Lee . . . Lee's just impossible.

"Hi." Betsy Blair, wrapped in a white terry bathrobe, was standing barefoot in the doorway. "I'll be back in a moment. Just want to try waking up my face a bit." She disappeared into the bathroom, her long hair a tangled red rope against the white bathrobe.

I don't know how she does it, Sharon thought, compar-

10

ing Betsy's untameable mane with her own carefree short dark hair. Still, she had to admit that Betsy's hair was beautiful, even if it was impractical for a stewardess.

When Betsy returned to the kitchen, Sharon had most of the light meal almost ready. She enjoyed cooking and preparing the meal gave her a full opportunity to check up on the kitchen supplies.

Sharon poured a cup of coffee. "Here." She handed it across the kitchen table to Betsy. "Have some of this. It'll help you wake up."

"Thanks." Betsy's eyes still looked sleepy, and her hair, although pulled back and tied with a ribbon, still was not under control. She yawned, pushed an escaping wisp off her cheek and sipped the steaming coffee.

"Ohhh, that tastes good. What really helps is having a thoughtful roommate."

Sharon smiled and began the omelet. "Depends on the roommate," she remarked. "Last year, when I was sharing that other place, there was one girl whose coffee was like dishwater." Flipping the eggs into the pan, she changed the subject. "So it's London for you, at last."

"Yes, and I'm really looking forward to it." Betsy's tone brightened visibly. "I wasn't at all sure I'd get the bid. I didn't think I had enough seniority. There's so much I want to do and see in London, I don't know if a month's worth of trips will be enough."

"The shopping's marvelous." Sharon flipped the eggs expertly in the pan and remembered her own recent trips to London. "If you're planning to sightsee on your first trips, maybe you could pick some things up for me." There were still a lot of things Sharon wanted for her trousseau; a roommate's empty suitcase on a return flight was an opportunity she did not wish to pass up.

"I'm afraid not, Sharon. I want to get Christmas presents," Betsy said apologetically. "And I do intend to go shopping for myself."

"Is there anything special you're looking for?" Sharon asked. "I know some great buys. Cashmere, for one."

She handed Betsy the finished omelet and reached for the pad on the counter.

"Here, let me give you the address of the place where I got some sweaters and skirts last month. They have discounts that are really worth while."

"Thanks, I want to get some clothes," Betsy said between mouthfuls. "Suddenly, I feel like my whole winter wardrobe needs revamping."

"The prices are much better than in Paris," Sharen continued. "Of course, the couturier clothes are fabulous to look at. Did I tell you that last trip I got a ticket to the Dior fashion show?"

"Yes, you did."

"Well, this time, I won't bother. I mean, I have so many other things to get."

Betsy smiled and asked after Sharon's fiancé.

"Tom? He's picking me up tonight. We're going to look at some unfinished apartments. Not that we intend getting one of them, but we want to see what the layouts are like."

"I thought you did that last week."

"We did. This is another building. The only way to be sure of getting what we want is to do a little comparison shopping, you know."

Betsy reached up and felt her hair experimentally. "I really must get going. It'll take me an age to get my hair to stay up."

"If you'd use some spray . . ."

"I hate using spray."

Sharon sighed. "You and Lee. I swear, if there weren't rules and regulations, you two'd go out on flights looking like something out of the East Village." It was an old argument.

Betsy smiled and said, "Oh, come on now, Sharon, we're not that bad, are we? And by the way, where is Lee? I haven't seen her in weeks. Our schedules never seem to coincide."

Sharon frowned. "It's not just her schedule—although it's true she's doing that crazy double Rome trip. You know, the one with the trip back only as far as London and then out to Rome again before returning here."

"Yes, I knew she'd gotten that. It wasn't her bid, but with her low seniority . . ."

". . . she got stuck with it. I don't think she minds much, though. Sometimes I don't think she cares about *anything*. And that includes her private life. This time the guy's married, and she's spending her free days over at his place. That's why you haven't seen her."

"A new one?" Betsy sounded puzzled. "But what about Carl? And anyway, if the new one's married, how can Lee be spending time at his place?"

"The new one's married but recently separated, and has a place in the city. So he plays with Lee, and fights with his wife in Hastings, I think he said. He was here last week when Lee left for Rome."

"I see," murmured Betsy. "And what about Carl? I thought he and Lee were serious."

"It was only serious on Lee's side." Sharon shook her head disapprovingly; she had told Lee more than once that Carl Masden would let her down, but Lee hadn't listened. She never did.

"Poor Lee." Betsy was sympathetic.

"It wouldn't be 'poor Lee' if she'd show even a grain of sense," Sharon answered sharply. "I told her what Carl was like, and so did several other people. Anyone who's flown with him knows what he's like. He isn't called Casanova Carl for nothing. But no. She had to find out for herself."

"Still, she must've been hurt."

"Well, there's this new one now, Hank something or other." Sharon rose and began clearing the table. "Speaking of men, how's Mike?"

"Very busy. He's preparing for a new show," Betsy said.

"Is he taking you to the airport?"

"No, of course not."

Sharon shut off the faucet. "What do you mean, 'of course not'? Tom always takes me when I go out on a flight."

Betsy sighed. "You know Mike never goes to the airport if he can help it. He says it depresses him."

Sharon also sighed, but for a different reason. "You know," she said, "you're almost as bad as Lee when it comes to men. You both let yourselves be pushed around . . ."

"Mike doesn't push me around."

Sharon turned away from washing the dishes, and looked straight into Betsy's dark brown eyes.

"Well, I've yet to hear of him doing anything for you."

"Well, he's an artist."

"As if I didn't know! What with him telling me, and

13

you telling me. . . . and anyway, Betsy, where on earth did you meet Mike? I've been meaning to ask you for ages. He's not the kind of person you usually find in our crowd."

"At a party."

"What party?"

"One that was held when you were out on a trip." Betsy's voice was slightly muffled, and she rose from the table. "I must get going now, or I'll never make the bus. Thanks for the omelette, Sharon. It was delicious, as always."

Sharon turned back to the sink, and her thoughts returned to her own plans. If Tom came around six, they could eat in before going on to see the new apartments. That way, they would have more time and maybe they could even take some measurements. It would be easier to compare the new apartments to the others they'd seen, if they knew the measurements.

She put the milk back into the refrigerator and noticed that they were low on butter. She pursed her lips and made a note on the counter pad. Tomorrow she would stock up on groceries before her flight to Paris.

Another kind of shopping list began forming in her mind.

2

Betsy went into the bathroom and stepped into the shower.

By the time she emerged she was pretty sure Sharon would have forgotten her questions about Mike. She did not want to be asked any further questions; her answer in the kitchen had been a lie.

Betsy remembered very well the day she met Mike.

It had been during the summer, on the same day that she had turned down Jay Marshall's umpteenth proposal of marriage. This time, Betsy had tried to make it clear that her refusal was definitely final.

"But Betsy, we have everything going for us," Jay had said.

She had heard it all before—their friendship since early childhood, the hometown and background they had in common, the joy with which their parents would view the match—theoretically, the perfect marriage. She really was fond of Jay, and proud of his achievements. Jay Marshall, M.D., the pride of his parents and the most popular young intern on the staff of a well-known New York hospital.

But still . . . no. No. There had been a highly emotional scene, right there in the apartment. Jay had stormed out, hurt and angry, and suddenly she had felt unable to stay in the still-charged atmosphere of the apartment. Both her roommates were out on flights and there was no one to talk to. She left the apartment and walked several blocks in the hot summer night.

The humidity was oppressive and Betsy became aware

of a strange feeling of weakness and dizziness. I wonder if I'm going to faint, she thought, more with surprise than alarm. Betsy had never fainted in her life.

She spied a coffee shop and went quickly inside. The air-conditioned interior was an immediate relief, and as soon as she sat down in one of the several empty booths, the fuzziness in her head cleared. She began to feel better.

"Coke, please," she told the student who was playing at being a waiter for the summer.

She sat and absentmindedly stirred the ice-cubes around in the glass with the straw, thinking about how difficult life could get without your meaning it to.

She did not know how long she sat there, but when she eventually came out of her reverie she felt as though she were awakening from a long sleep. And that someone was staring at her.

It was a tousle-haired young man sitting at a table on the other side of the room. When he caught her glance, his concentration did not waver. He looked down at the pad he held in one hand and quickly sketched in some strokes with a crayon. Then he rose, and without any hesitation, came over to her booth and sat down.

"Want to see?" he asked. "Most people do."

She felt irritated. All she wanted was to be left alone.

"No, thank you," she said coldly.

"Most people are interested in seeing a sketch of themselves." His hazel eyes were inquiring, but his whole being exuded confidence.

"Are you trying to sell the sketch to me?" she asked.

"No. But it's an idea." He grinned, pleased at the thought.

Betsy picked up her purse, ready to leave.

"You've hardly touched your Coke," the young man commented. Then, seeing she was intent on going, he said: "Stay for just a little longer. Please."

She did not know why she stayed. Nor why she looked at the sketch, admitted she liked it and answered the young man's questions.

"What made you think I was trying to sell you the sketch? Do I look like a hustler?"

"I've seen artists working in cafés in Paris. They do on-the-spot portraits and mostly people are so intrigued

16

that they buy them. I guess it happens more often in Europe than here."

"I couldn't do that." His statement was decisive. "I only sketch faces that have some quality that attracts me. So I'm not real hustler material, after all."

He was still staring, taking in every detail of her face. His gaze was intense, yet curiously impersonal.

"Then you know Paris?" the young man inquired.

"I've been there quite a few times."

"On vacation?"

"Not exactly."

"As a student?"

She shook her head and her long hair swung about her shoulders.

"Do you ever wear your hair up?" he demanded, apparently losing all interest in Paris.

"Sometimes." She smiled and thought of the countless times she pinned up her thick hair, using what seemed like a million pins in an effort to comply with airline regulations about neat hairstyles.

"I'd like to see you with it up. It would give you a sort of Latin look. Have you any Latin blood?"

"My grandparents were French."

"Your coloring's unusual. Very attractive. It's not often you see genuine Titian-red hair. It would be a challenge to paint."

"I really have to go."

"Your nose is genuine, too, thank God." And the disconcerting young man gave another of his wide grins. "It has line, and substance."

She felt as though her nose had suddenly become a beacon, claiming everyone's full attention. But no one had heard her unwanted companion's comment.

"Noses—they're fascinating," he went on. "Their proportions are essential to the rest of the face. Women so seldom seem to know that." He still sketched as he talked. "Take all those females who go and have them fixed. *Fixed*, for God's sake. Sure, they're fixed. With all the wrong proportions—too much upper lip, and an endless jawline. Then you get that pushed-in look, like monkeys have. . . ."

"You're very critical."

He didn't even bother to look up. "So's every artist."

17

Betsy rose. There was no point in her staying. He stopped sketching and looked up.

"I'm not being critical of you," he said. "You're beautiful. But I imagine you know that. You must have been told so plenty of times."

Then he, too, rose, and looked at her solemnly across the table.

"My name is Mike," he announced. "Mike di Falco. I live and work in a loft in the East Village. Now, what else can I tell you about myself? Oh, yes, that I believe in following beauty wherever I find it." He gave an exaggerated bow. "Now, is that enough of an introduction to allow me to escort you back to wherever it is you live?"

And that was the way she had met Mike.

It had seemed only natural to tell Sharon she had met him at a party. It sounded so much more respectable that way. Sharon did not approve of girls who let themselves be picked up by strangers.

Oddly enough, before she met Mike, she would not have approved, either.

There was much about Mike that was fascinating to Betsy, and she was shrewd enough to figure out why. He was the only person she had ever known who was really free. He lived without schedules, without obligations, with no regard for appointments or possessions. Most of the things that loomed large in the life of an average person simply had no meaning for Mike di Falco at all.

Ironically, the very life she herself had sought because of its many freedoms—the flying life—was guaranteed, any time it was mentioned, to draw abuse from Mike because of what he saw as its restrictive conformity.

"I'll bet you people even *think* on schedule," he jeered on one occasion. And, on another: "Hey—d'you have to check with the captain before you can go to what I'll just bet you call the *little girls'* room?"

"We don't. They're called blue rooms," Betsy had answered quickly, only to be stung by the yell of delighted laughter from Mike.

"You see? That's *just* the kind of crap I mean."

It was better not to mention Flightways, or her schedule, or anything connected with her job if she could possibly help it. Once it was a reference to needing some sleep before going out on a flight that set off one of Mike's tirades.

"My God, you're not to be believed! Just listen to yourself, will you? Planning your sleep, like some middle-aged, middle class nag of a wife!"

"But Mike, I have to."

The phrase *have to* was always a red flag.

"*Have to?*" Mike yelled. "Man, like you don't *have* to do a fucking thing in this life except shit, piss and die. And you don't even *have* to live, if you want to close it down."

"Aren't you over-dramatizing?" Betsy asked. "All I said was I need to catch up on some sleep—and here you are, discussing suicide."

Mike stared at her, his temper subsiding as quickly as it rose. He shook his head in disbelief, but his manner remained calm.

"But you let it ride you, that's the hang up," he told her. "You just don't dig the way freedom can be. Should be. Is."

On another occasion, after she had inadvertently mentioned her desire to go to London, Mike said, "So you go to a whole load of foreign places—but d'you really know where it's at?"

She learned a lot about real life from Mike on his own home ground.

For, despite his temper and his moods, Mike was exciting to be around. His involvement with art was total; its importance for Mike enveloped Betsy from time to time, and she began looking at paintings in a different way, and enjoyed the discoveries that he enabled her to make. Mike, usually an impatient teacher, nonetheless found her an apt pupil.

And then he painted her. For Betsy, the experience was unique.

After a session, stiff to the point of numbness, she would watch as Mike the artist became Mike the man again. She was almost frightened the first time she saw him disappear behind his easel, silent and concentrated, totally removed from her as a person and intent only on form, light and color. For what seemed like hours, he would not say a word. Then, abruptly, as though on signal, she'd hear a defeated grunt escape him and she was

19

grateful for the sound. It meant she could move again. With any luck, it could also mean they'd at last go get something to eat. Mike could go for extraordinarily long periods of time without eating or drinking at all; in fact, Betsy found his physical needs something he could apparently turn on and off like a faucet. There seemed to be no balance, no normal routine of any kind.

"There you go again," he said once when she mentioned it to him. "You want to eat on schedule, drink on schedule, fall into bed on schedule—come on, Betsy, tell me how you'd set up a perfect sex schedule."

But she had only laughed in answer, and they hadn't quarrelled. In his good moods, Mike laughed often. In his worst ones, he refused to see her.

"When I'm like that, just go away and leave me alone," he told her after the first time it happened. "It has something to do with the way I am, not the way you are."

Betsy learned to accept Mike as he was in this respect. With the passage of time she began to suspect he was not able to accept her in the same manner. There were times when their worlds clashed, and it became routine for Mike to hold her responsible for the inevitable collision.

"You just keep hanging onto that dumb-ass job of yours to drive me out of my skull! Your goddam schedule, it's ruining my work. I never know when the fuck you'll be around."

"You really are the classic egomaniacal artist!" Betsy retorted, having learned to give as good as she got.

Mike backtracked. "Come live with me."

"I can't. My schedule. . ."

"Then leave that miserable airline and come live with me," Mike said. It was not the first time he had brought up the subject.

"I can't."

"Why the hell not? You can move in here any time. And I could sure do with a resident model. All the best artists have them. Think, Betsy, you could be famous." His wide grin appeared.

She smiled, too, but shook her head. "No, I wouldn't. People only remember the artist, not the model. And besides, I don't want to give up my job."

His anger returned. "Piss on your job!"

Betsy controlled her voice. "But I like it. I happen to

enjoy flying, and seeing different places, and meeting lots of different people."

"Jesus, you're so unbelievably *bourgeois!*"

"You're always saying *'bourgeois'*, but I don't think you even know what the word means. You just use it for anything you don't like."

They argued often. He sneered at her job and her friends, he taunted her about her admission that she wanted, eventually, to marry and have children. And Mike didn't do any of the things that a boyfriend was supposed to do, according to girls like Sharon. He did not give her flowers or presents, he did not escort her to the airport, or meet her after a flight, nor did he show any interest in where she had been or what she had done.

In spite of everything, Betsy could not free herself of the fascination he had for her. He was exciting, and she could not bear to lose him, although she was aware that for as long as they were tied together, they would both suffer through the constant friction between their entirely different outlooks. There had never been anyone like Mike in Betsy's life before, and he fulfilled a need which she had not even known existed. There was a quality in their relationship that held her captive and, from the time Mike appeared, demanding and arrogant and irresistible all at the same time, Betsy forgot all about Jay and his proposals of marriage.

She turned off the shower and wondered if what she felt for Mike was love. Betsy believed in love. Mike, of course, did not.

"The attraction between us is purely physical," Mike was fond of saying. "I love your beautiful body. You love my body and what it can do to you."

Betsy had protested. No one had ever spoken to her so crudely before. She was attracted and repelled at the same time. In all the facets of her relationship with Mike, she was aware of the double pull of conflicting feelings.

Abruptly, Betsy pulled off her shower cap. No more time to think about Mike now. She had to finish packing, get into her uniform. Then down to the terminal and the bus out to Kennedy Airport.

As she went about her routine tasks, thoughts of Mike gradually faded from Betsy's mind. The familiar pre-flight feeling crept over her. She began to wonder who else would be on the flight, what sort of a trip it would be. In winter, you never knew with the weather . . .

What would London be like? It was a new city, and that made it exciting.

As always, it felt good to be getting on her way.

get ready...in....

3

Betsy finished packing with the speed of long practice. Already in uniform, and lacking only the jacket of her pants suit and her fake fur hat to complete the outfit, she moved methodically through the motions she had gone through so many times before, preparing for her trips.

Shoes were tucked well into one corner of her suitcase. Underclothes were lodged in another. Two bras, two camisoles, a slip and two pantyhose; a third pantyhose went into her overnight bag, more out of habit than actual necessity, for since she was wearing the pants and not the skirt of her uniform, it was unnecessary to safeguard against getting a run on the flight.

The third set of underwear was the set she was wearing; Betsy, like so many of the other stewardesses, always flew with a minimum of three sets. One on, one ready, one washed-and-drying, was the rule of thumb while actually on a trip. She'd rinse out the set she had on when she got to her hotel in London. That way it would be clean, dry and ready for either the return trip or any unexpected extra days off that might occur. To expect the unexpected was a good attitude in airline circles, and a self-sufficient laundry system was commendable, too.

She didn't plan to take a coat. If it was that cold, she could always use the uniform cape with its fake fur collar, even though airline regulations discouraged the use of uniform garments when off-duty. But to take a heavy winter coat . . . no, it was really not worth it. Betsy de-

23

cided on a skirt and jacket set; that should take her through her free day in London. She laid the garments flat at the bottom of her regulation-sized suitcase, added a turtleneck sweater and a pair of pajamas.

Sharon came into her room and leaned down to get the telephone.

"Okay if I take this back into the living room?" she asked.

"Oh, sure. I'm not expecting any calls before I leave."

Sharon began coiling the long extension cord as she walked toward the door again. Glancing at Betsy's choice of pajamas, she said, "I'd take another pair, if I were you. You'll be cold in those."

"Why? Is it really that cold over there? Or doesn't the hotel have central heating?"

"It's supposed to have, but I wouldn't count on it. They don't heat places the way we do. I have a bed jacket that might fit you," Sharon offered.

"No, thanks, Sharon, I think I'll manage with this," and Betsy drew a long-sleeved granny gown from the drawer and replaced the pajamas.

Pronouncing it perfect, Sharon left, taking the telephone with her. Betsy packed the nightgown and closed her suitcase. She finished her minimal makeup and put her cosmetic kit into the overnight bag on the edge of the bed.

Betsy zipped the bag shut and reached for her hat. She watched her motions in the mirror as she placed it on her head careful not to dislodge the French twist holding her long hair up and in place, well above her collar. The hat fitted snugly and felt light and warm and was a godsend in windy airports on cold winter days. Then came her uniform jacket; her cape would be the last thing she put on.

"You're off, are you?" Sharon appeared. "Well, have a good flight, and if you have time, don't forget that cashmere place. It's really worth trying."

"I won't. Thanks for the address, and everything."

As she talked, Betsy carried her bags into the living room. The living room was unusually neat, due to Sharon's compulsiveness. When Lee, whose bed was the convertible sofa placed in the shallow alcove, was in residence, the apartment tended to be somewhat messy. Betsy was midway between her roommates in neatness.

The telephone was on its table next to a chair. Betsy grinned and said "I see you've tied up the extension cord. Do you think that will prevent Lee from tripping over it?"

"Not really," was the rueful answer. "But maybe she'll miss it the first two or three times she walks by."

Just before she went to the hall closet for her cape, a thought struck Betsy. "What about Thomas the Turtle?" she asked. "Shall I take him down to old Kelly?"

"No, I'll do it tomorrow."

"Okay." The cape slipped into place over her shoulders, and Betsy stuck her arms out through the side slits to reach for her handbag, the overnight bag and her suitcase. "See you when I get back."

And Betsy Blair, stewardess for Flightways International, left the apartment for the airport and Flight 410 to London.

4

Flightways Inc., the huge, sprawling airline with both international and domestic flights, had a sizable number of its stewardesses based in New York. Only a practised traveler or another member of Flightways could tell which girls flew the domestic operation and which the international, for the uniforms were identical. The giveaway signs were the bags they carried; the girls flying for the division known as Flightway Continental, with routes within the United States, carried dark blue overnight bags. Those carried by stewardesses in the International division were a bright and pleasing red.

Betsy, her red overnight bag well in sight, scanned the crowd in the East Side Airlines Terminal in search of a splash of similar color. None was visible inside the building, and at first, all the other stewardesses she saw were in the uniforms of other airlines. Eventually, she spotted a group of Flightways girls, all with dark blue bags; they were on their way to another bus and smiled as they went by.

Betsy went out to the ramp where the Kennedy bus was parked, and there a girl in a Flightways pants suit was carrying a bright red bag. The girl turned around and saw Betsy.

"Hi," she said. "Are we scheduled out together?"

Betsy knew her to be Linda Kesnik, although they had never actually been introduced. Linda was senior to Betsy, although Betsy judged her to be roughly her own age. She was a tall girl with an air of worldly fragility and a wary expression in her light grey eyes.

"I'm on four-ten to London," Betsy answered.

"That's it," the other girl answered. "I'm Linda Kesnik."

Betsy introduced herself, and the two stewardesses boarded the bus together.

"This your first time over there?" inquired Linda. "I don't think I've seen you listed on four-ten before."

"Yes. I've been flying Paris and Frankfurt. Then I figured it was time for a change, and so I bid London."

Betsy, who had heard plenty about Linda from Sharon, among other people, was not overjoyed to find herself teamed on the flight with her. It was said that Linda was difficult to work with and apt to take unnecessary advantages. She was also said to be one of the sleepers—the kind of cabin attendant who, in defiance of all the rules, caught a nap whenever possible on a long flight. Particularly on night flights, and Flight 410, with its evening departure from Kennedy, was exactly that.

There were other rumors about Linda, too, but what she did in her private life, Betsy figured, was, after all, her own business. And anyway, insofar as she knew, they were only rumors, a thing Betsy had found out early was very much part of airline life. Rumors about personnel, company policies, tactics, new openings and routes, rumors about everything were a shadow-like constant in every airline. Naturally, she knew the Flightways rumors best. Sometimes, some of them even proved to be true. The others were usually swiftly forgotten and just as swiftly replaced with new ones.

Betsy and Linda placed their suitcases in the luggage space up front, chose seats a few rows behind the driver and settled in to them after shoving their overnight bags underneath. Betsy took the window seat, Linda having made it clear she wanted the aisle one.

"It's my legs," she explained. "They're too long to be comfortable in the seat space, so I usually extend them into the aisle if I can."

"My roommate, Lee Pickering, has the same problem," Betsy said, opening her handbag and retrieving her commuter ticket.

27

"Oh, yes, Lee Pickering, of the *Massachusetts* Pickerings. I've met her."

Betsy looked up in surprise. Linda's sarcasm was undisguised.

"She doesn't go around making a big issue of it," Betsy said in defense of Lee, who never mentioned her family background, although it was well known.

"She doesn't have to. *Everyone's* heard of the great Massachusetts family."

"Well, that's not her fault. Besides, they're nice people."

"Oh, I'm *sure* they are."

Betsy decided to stop reacting. She didn't want to have a stupid argument; after all, they'd have to fly together for the rest of the month. And if Linda didn't like the fact that Betsy's roommate came from a well-known family, well, that was Linda's problem. It seemed a waste of time to try explaining to her that Lee, the product of divorced parents, had enough problems of her own. Linda would no doubt think up some snide remark to make about that, too, so silence seemed the best way until a safer subject of conversation was found.

Silence worked. Linda took off her cape and rearranged her overnight bag and took her time about settling into her seat; Betsy, glancing at her from time to time, began noticing unmistakable signs of fatigue. Linda, thin to the point of being emaciated, had the kind of high-cheekboned good looks that made her almost stylized, but the dark smudges under her eyes drained her face of vitality. Her fine-boned features suggested a refinement quite at odds with the reputation she had on the airline and Betsy wondered whether the rumors she had heard were true, or merely rumor-rumors.

Finally, Linda settled into her seat. "I hope it's an easy flight," she remarked, examining her long nails for no apparent reason. "Do you have any idea about the rest of the crew?"

Betsy admitted she had none at all. "I got my own bid, and didn't bother looking at the board."

"Well, we'll find out soon enough."

The bus, whose engine had been vibrating for some time, began to slide forward. Betsy settled back in her seat; the well-known ride lay ahead of her.

Betsy smiled at Linda vaguely and then turned to stare,

28

unseeingly, out of the window. The mesmeric movement of the bus lulled her into a pre-flight daydream. It was restful, and she almost forgot about the stewardess sitting next to her.

Almost, but not quite. Betsy hoped the rest of the crew would be somewhat more compatible.

5

The red European sports car slid to a stop in front of the tall lean man in the airline uniform. He waited for the garage attendant to get out from behind the wheel and then, leaning down, threw his suitcase on the back seat and wedged his flight kit close behind it.

"She's a beauty, Captain Fleming—the best you've had yet."

The attendant gave the sports car's windshield a last loving swipe, and David Fleming got in behind the wheel. Checking the instruments on the panel before him, he pressed down on the accelerator. The attendant listened with pleasure to the sound, and the two men nodded with satisfaction when their glances met through the window.

"Okay, Captain. Have a good flight."

The low-slung car stopped roaring, but even when it idled, the engine breathed power. Then its driver eased it into gear and started forward.

For a moment the attendant watched as the car cleared the rest of the ramp and came to a stop at the street-level exit of the garage. Then the roar mingled with the sounds of the traffic of Manhattan, and the attendant turned to his next customer, who was parking a Ford.

"Where's my goddam flight kit?" Larry Johnson shouted, glaring around the bright yellow bedroom of his suburban home.

30

"In the hallway with the rest of your bags," shouted his wife Myra from the kitchen downstairs.

"What?" Johnson yelled back, finishing the clumsy knot he had managed to make in his tie. To attempt another did not even occur to him, and he made his way down the stairs humming and content.

"You're getting deaf," Myra said, "just like all the others. You only hear when there's a jet engine roaring close."

Her husband ignored her words and asked, "What's that?" He moved closer and peered into the pot of sauce she was stirring with a long-handled wooden spoon.

Larry Johnson took the spoon from her and dipped a finger into its bowl, scooping up some of the mixture and licking it off his finger.

"Hmmm, not bad at all."

"It's time you left. Come on, out of here! As I remember it, Flightways International doesn't approve of co-pilots who are chronically late."

"Flightways doesn't approve of co-pilots, period. We're just trained monkeys in uniform, but I've told you that before."

He sighed, allowing his wife to push him toward the door. Myra surveyed his large bulk as he picked up his suitcase and said, "You know, I'll bet you're the only man in existence who looks more untidy in uniform than out of it."

"I always told you I was unique." Co-pilot Laurence A. Johnson reached for his flight kit.

"Don't forget what I told you, Larry."

"The list is in my billfold."

"Well, remember to *look* at it, Larry. I'll really be mad if you don't bring back the things I need."

Her voice followed him as he went to the garage. "So don't spend all your time just eating and sleeping, or you'll come home empty-handed, and with none of the things I've asked for."

"I won't, I will, I won't." He got into their elderly automobile and started its recalcitrant engine.

Johnson blew an exaggerated kiss as the car swerved down the driveway.

"Pilots, the world's worst drivers," Myra Johnson said to

herself, a sadness tinging her goodbye smile. She turned back into the house and went straight to the kitchen and began to stir her sauce vigorously. The house always felt far too empty when Larry was on a trip.

6

When Betsy and Linda arrived at the Flightways Building at Kennedy Airport, they went straight to Operations on the lower level and signed in for their flight. Both examined the list of the crew with the usual interest, but it was Linda who made the first comment.

"Oh, we have the Loner!" she exclaimed, pointing a long finger at the name David Fleming inserted in the captain's slot. "What's he doing on this flight, I wonder?"

Betsy, who had never flown with Fleming, and had only vaguely heard of his nickname, asked, "What's the matter with him? And why shouldn't he be on this flight?"

"Well, in the first place, he can be pretty hard-ass. A very gung-ho gentleman is Captain David Fleming." Linda's tone indicated quite plainly she did not like him. "And in the second, he's a senior captain. So what's he doing on four-ten? It's not exactly a senior flight."

But Betsy, who had caught sight of another name on the crew list, paid little attention to what her co-stewardess was saying. The Flight Engineer was Carl Masden, Lee's ex-flame. Poor Lee might be upset when she realized he was on Betsy's flight. Well, it couldn't be helped; Betsy hoped the new and unreliable-sounding Hank would be enough to make Lee forget Carl. It was, however, a very small hope; Betsy knew Lee had really fallen hard for Carl Masden.

"Oh, hell," Linda muttered.

"Now what?"

"Of all the godawful luck. We have Rudi as purser."

This time, Betsy knew what was upsetting Linda. Rudolf Becker, a Swiss national who had been flying with Flightways for several years, was generally no better and no worse than most other pursers except for one thing. Rudi spoke five languages fluently and he did not like having cabin staff working with him who only spoke English. At first, this had never happened, for all stewardesses and pursers who flew the overseas flights were required, by company regulations, to speak at least one and preferably two foreign languages. But during the last year the company had relaxed its rules, and now those with enough seniority were allowed to bid the international runs even if they spoke no other language but English.

When the company changed its policy, Rudi had protested strongly. He had pointed out that it was discrimination, that the young men hired as stewards were still required to speak more than one language, and that it didn't matter whether they were referred to as pursers or stewards, the job was supposed to be on a par with that of the female cabin attendants. He also stressed the resulting extra work load on the foreign speaking, suggesting that perhaps extra languages should then be recompensed with extra pay.

To all this the company had listened politely, but their policy remained the same. Rudi was furious. When he discovered his protests had been of no avail, he proceeded to vent his anger on those with whom he flew who had no second language.

From her companion's reaction, Betsy guessed Linda to be English-only, remembering that the senior girl had indeed only transferred to Flightways International in the months since the policy change had taken place.

"Look, if we work together, we should be okay," Betsy told Linda. "I speak French, and my Spanish—well, I can get by. So if we work it right, we shouldn't have any problems."

Linda gave her a hard look. "Ol' Ridin' Rudi *knows* I only speak English. We've flown together before. An unforgettable flight." Linda grimaced. "He'd harass me even if we were carrying nothing but chimpanzees."

Betsy laughed. "Let's see who else is on." She read down the rest of the list. "Second officer Laurence A.

Johnson—oh, that must be Joker Johnson. He's nice. I've flown with him before. Marianne Lund. Judy Fransella." She looked up at Linda. "I know Marianne. Who's Judy Fransella?"

Linda shrugged. "New, I guess."

"Then it looks like we get first class," Betsy commented. "If you want to bid it, that is."

"I'd be out of my mind not to," Linda said. "Who needs the cattle back in tourist? There's never anyone worthwhile back there, or at least so seldom it's not worth taking the chance."

Betsy opened her mouth and then closed it abruptly. What was the use of saying that she knew girls who preferred working the coach section? It was sure to sound prissy, or like a put-down. Well, perhaps it *was* a form of put-down; in any event, Betsy was sure it would be taken as such, and in Linda's ears would have the prissy sound for which Mike so mocked her. If there's one thing he's done for me, she thought to herself, it's make me self-conscious about sounding prim. But that's not fair to Mike. He's done a great many things for me. I don't shock as easily as I used to.

A small smile escaped her at the thought.

Linda, misinterpreting the smile's source, grinned and said, "Well, they do trample all over one like a herd," and, putting down the pencil attached to the signing-in board, added, "we might as well go through and see if anyone else is here."

The two girls went from Operations into the crew lounge. Here, in the quiet no-man's-land between the busy, voice-filled offices and the jet-roar of outdoors, Betsy and Linda found that Rudolf Becker had arrived before them.

"Hi, girls," he greeted them, only the faintest trace of an accent sounding in his voice. "I hope you're ready to work hard this trip. We have a company executive along, and you know what that always means—service has to be perfect *plus*."

His washed-out blue eyes looked meaningfully at Linda, and Betsy noticed that his skin was very pale even for someone with his kind of light blond hair. She decided it was probably the black uniform. The harsh contrast was very hard on the purser's complexion, and even the white of his shirt did not form an adequate barrier.

A door behind them opened, and two more girls in uniform entered the lounge where the pre-flight briefing would be held. Rudi introduced them, although Betsy had greeted Marianne Lund as she entered, and Linda had nodded to her, too, in unenthusiastic recognition. Marianne, a round-featured, shapely brunette, had on her uniform skirt rather than slacks; the second girl was, like Betsy and Linda, in the pants outfit.

"Betsy, Linda, this is Judy Fransella."

"Hi, there."

"Hi."

She was short—probably even shorter than Sharon, Betsy reckoned—and fresh-faced. Her smile was wide and genuine, and she had the kind of stance and build Betsy always associated with bouncy energy.

"Shall we start, girls?"

The four Flightways stewardesses gave their flying seniority date. Linda proved to be the most senior; Judy, it turned out, was on her first flight.

"Yes, that's right," she smiled, a vivacious dimple appearing low on one cheek. "And I'm *very* nervous."

"But you had a training flight, didn't you?" Rudi asked.

"Not on this run."

"Never mind. You'll get the hang of it soon enough."

"I guess." But Judy sounded dubious.

The selection of posts started.

"Linda?" Rudi looked at the senior girl.

"I'll take first class galley."

Betsy was surprised by Linda's choice. She had expected her to want to work the first class cabin. That was the one with the closest contact with the passengers and if, as she had insinuated, she was on the lookout for someone "worthwhile"—which obviously had to mean a man, presumably eligible—the choice of first class cabin work was ideal. First class galley meant doing all the cooking and much of the setting-up procedures, getting the bar cart into shape, the serving trolley, and all the tray set-ups that could come at any time, to say nothing of meal preparation and oven-watching. All this kept the galley girl in the galley and, for the most part, out of passenger reach and contact. Perhaps Linda, who looked tired, figured she'd have an easier time in the galley? Maybe try to sneak a nap sometime? With Rudi on board, Betsy didn't think the chances were too good.

". . . but perhaps if you don't answer to Betsy, you'll answer to Miss Blair instead?"

Rudi's harsh voice sawed through Betsy's train of thought. She felt her face flood with color and murmured a hasty apology. As second senior girl, she had to make a choice.

"First class cabin," she decided.

"Then I'll take coach cabin," Marianne spoke up.

Rudi eyed her speculatively. "I don't think it will divide up quite so neatly," he told her. "Remember, Judy's new, and . . ."

"Oh, but I think I'd *better* stay back in the galley," the junior girl began.

"You may need some help there, too," Rudi interrupted. "And a bit of cabin experience is a good idea on a first flight. Anyway, I'll be coming back more often than usual, keeping a close check on both of you. There's a light load, fortunately, so I don't think you'll have any trouble."

Marianne smiled vaguely at no one in particular, and Judy said it made her feel better to know she could call on Rudi for help.

"You won't have to call, he'll be breathing down your neck," Marianne told her, but she said it sweetly and without further comment. Rudi had turned back to Betsy.

"Betsy, as first-class cabin girl, you'll be in charge of a child traveling alone."

Betsy smiled; she liked working with children. They were usually so enthusiastic about flying. It made a pleasant change from the blasé attitudes of so many of the adult passengers. Children traveling alone were usually very well-behaved, and if they were not—ah, dream of every stewardess: *you could tell them to behave themselves.* It made up for the times a difficult adult could not be handled in the same way. The children—those few she had ever had to admonish—always heeded her instantly. It was probably a combination of the uniform and the position of authority in the cabin, Betsy decided. Little rebels always managed to quickly metamorphase into Betsy's little helpers.

"Boy or girl?" she asked.

"A boy. His name is James Murray, and he's deplaning at London. His father will be at the airport to collect him."

"How old is he?"

Rudi frowned at the paper in front of him. "Only six. Seems very young to be traveling alone. You'd think parents would go along, too, or send a nursemaid, or something. You'll have to keep close tabs on him, Betsy, and check to see you have some toys up front."

The session was soon over. Linda lit a cigarette and murmured, "It's not going to be an exciting flight, is it? No one in first."

Since there were a half-dozen passengers listed for the first class section, this number including the young James Murray, Betsy knew that what Linda meant was no one famous or important was going to be on board. No movie star, no television personality, no eligible male. According to the passenger manifest, there were two married couples, the little boy and a man traveling alone.

"He might be a millionaire in disguise," Betsy suggested, pointing to the last name.

"I doubt it." Linda looked at the name. *"Armand Bressanovitch.* I've never seen it in the columns."

"I guess it'll be a quiet trip."

Linda gave a yawn. "Just as well, anyway. I'm pooped. If it's quiet, maybe I'll get a chance to catch up on some sleep."

The door from Operations opened, and the black-uniformed cockpit crew members walked in. She recognized the second officer, Larry Johnson, and the engineer, Carl Masden, who had come to the apartment several times with Lee. He was walking right behind the tall man who led the group. Bringing up the rear were two men in civilian clothes; they would soon be introduced, Betsy knew, and were this trip's air marshals.

But it was the tall man with the four gold stripes on his sleeve who commanded her attention. So this is the Loner, Betsy thought, watching him look around the room with an air of quiet authority. His gaze rested on her for a brief moment, then continued its all-encompassing sweep. Those eyes don't miss a thing, Betsy realized, and she continued looking at the man as he and the other new arrivals entered the crew lounge and came over to the flight attendants.

It was the tall man who, quite at ease, made the introductions.

"I'm Captain Fleming," he stated. "This is First Officer Johnson, and this is Flight Engineer Masden." Betsy saw Larry Johnson mouth a "Howdy" at her and Marianne, and Carl smiled and nodded at all the girls in general.

Fleming then indicated the men in civilian clothing. "These gentlemen are our sky marshals for tonight's flight. Mr. Hadley will be traveling in first, and Mr. Skarp in tourist."

Both men nodded at the crew in general, and got down to business.

"I'll make it quick, because I know you've all heard this before." It was the man named Skarp who was doing the talking. "We're on as anti-hijacker protection, and that is our only business on board."

Betsy heard Judy whisper something behind her, and realized that, dull as it might be to hear the same thing over and over again before each flight, there *was* a reason for repetitive briefing: new crew members, like Judy, had not heard it all before.

"Both Mr. Hadley and I are carrying thirty-eights. The bullets we use are low-velocity. They are also soft-nosed. If a hijacker gets funny, we can pump one into him without penetrating his body. That makes it certain that there is no risk of punching a hole in anyone else, or in the fuselage."

Well! Mr. Skarp certainly had a knack for combining the facts with graphic phrases. Betsy remembered other briefings she had attended in the early days of the sky marshals. The airlines, outraged at the increasing incidence of skyjacking, had hired with less discrimination than was later the case. Even now, there was only cool civility between cockpit crew and marshal team; earlier, Betsy remembered pilot outrage on many occasions.

"They're nothing but a gang of gun-happy goons," one had said.

"Who the hell does he think is in charge here?" This from an irate captain who wanted the marshal on board removed. The marshal in question had been a far cry from the plainspoken Mr. Skarp. Indeed, Betsy remembered that briefing as a series of grunts and phrases linked together with an occasional "dem" and "dose."

But no, Mr. Skarp was a far cry from the remembered marshal of a flight long past. He was now discussing the subject of signals.

"Got that?" he was saying, and the usual murmur of assent answered him. "As to the buzzer system, let's run through it just for practice," and he enumerated the cockpit to galley buzzer signals should trouble break out on the flight deck.

"Then any of you girls, or you," he nodded at Rudi, "will contact either me or Mr. Hadley," and he went on with the tactics to use in case of such an emergency. "Remember, we might not get the chance or have to use weapons at all, but maybe it will make you relax if I tell you Mr. Hadley's a black belt, and I don't do badly at karate myself."

Betsy saw Johnson frowning at the marshal, but Captain Fleming appeared to be as impassive as before. Skarp continued to outline tactics, and when he had finished, the group dispersed. The two marshals went back through Operations and into the waiting halls of the Flightways terminal itself: the flight crew made ready to go out to the waiting aircraft. Betsy fell into step as they walked along the lower level, the concrete corridors already giving hints of the outside wind.

"So this is your first flight ever," she remarked to Judy Fransella. "Is it also your first time overseas?"

"Yes." Judy gave one of her infectious grins. "And I'm really looking forward to it. I've always wanted to see Europe. My grandparents came from there."

"So did mine." But Betsy guessed Judy's to have been Italian, rather than French.

Linda, just a step behind them, said to Judy, "Well, if you've never worked a trip before, you'd better watch out. They'll probably try all the old corny gags on you."

"Who's *they?*" Judy wanted to know. "And what gags?"

"*They* are the pilots. All they need to see is a new stew on board, and all of a sudden their heads fill up with silly putty. Or maybe that's what's always in there. But it gets worse, it kind of activates, with a new girl. And then they go into their silly question routine. So if anyone asks you to do something downright ridiculous, come and check with me or Betsy before you do it."

"Or me," Rudi's voice said behind them. Betsy turned to let him join ranks and noticed that Marianne was trailing far behind.

"Captain Fleming doesn't look to me as though he's the kind who stands for much fooling around," Betsy commented.

"But there's Joker Johnson," Linda reminded her. "And that Masden doesn't look like a guy you could trust."

You can say that again, Betsy thought fiercely, remembering Lee.

"But what sort of things will they ask me?" Judy persisted. "Tell me. I'd rather be prepared."

Rudi sniggered. "Well, they might ask you whether you belong to the Mile High Club."

"Oh." Judy sounded perplexed. "And do I?"

He sniggered again. "You'd have to be initiated . . ." Leaving his sentence open, Rudi smiled at the new girl, who regarded him questioningly.

"Oh, come on, Rudi, now don't you start being a pain in the ass, too," said Linda with irritation. "Belonging to the Mile High Club," she explained to Judy, "means having gotten laid on a flight. When the plane was flying over a mile high, obviously."

"Oh. I see." Judy considered this a moment and then asked, "Do they have many gags like that?"

"They do, but we won't have time for any." Rudi was all business again. "You'll be quite safe if you stick to your work." He gave Judy a malicious smile.

They reached the outer corridor and the aircraft lay just beyond. The gleaming flight of steps reflected the lights of the Flightways building, and several vehicles moved around beneath the plane. Betsy felt the wind buffet her as she walked across the open space to the bottom of the stairs, and the empty feeling she associated with being out on the flat field of an airport came to her again as it always did. The hollow bowl of sky, now darkening with the autumn night, was clear and star-marked, auguring a cold and possible frost. She shivered as she reached the steps, and hurried quickly up them. At the top, the empty feeling struck her strongly.

Then she walked inside, into the warm and brightly

41

lighted cylinder of the Boeing 707 that was about to occupy the efforts of the whole flight crew, each in his or her individual capacity. Betsy was immediately aware of the distinctive smell; part metal, part food and part recirculated air, it was unmistakable and all pervasive in an airplane's interior. She breathed it in and welcomed it, glad to be on board.

It was good to be about to take off again.

7

The Flightways building at Kennedy Airport, a structure with the sweeping lines of a double-tiered boomerang, stood in the light of the floodlamps that crowned it. The building, renowned for both its daring architecture and its efficiency, housed both the domestic and the international Flightways operations.

Two passenger levels and a series of swooping walkways within the terminal made passage of the heavy traffic swift and easy. Tickets, baggage, passengers, crew, freight and farewell parties flowed smoothly along channels that had been years in the designing.

From the road, passengers were able to disembark from cars or buses at certain points along the concave side of the boomerang. From there, their paths were directed by both signs and uniformed personnel, depending on their destination.

"San Francisco, sir? May I see your ticket, please? Yes, that's right . . . right this way, sir—and have a good flight . . ."

"Over to your left, ma'am, and straight down to the end of the wing. You'll see the passengers arriving from Miami coming through Gate 12 . . ."

"Flight four-ten? Yes, certainly. May I have your name, please?"

The blonde woman in the full-length fur coat said, "No, I'm not going. Just James. Here's his ticket, and do you think you could take him over now? They said you would

43

at the office downtown. I simply must rush to my appointment."

The ground hostess accepted the ticket and looked at the child at the woman's side. He stood watching her impassively, his face unsmiling but seemingly unperturbed. The hostess reached under the counter and pressed a calling button. If they were going to be saddled with a child traveling solo, she wanted another counter girl to come up.

The woman was talking to the small boy.

". . . and you'll behave yourself, won't you, darling?"

"Yes."

"You don't mind if I go now, do you?"

"No, Piero told me you would. He said he wanted you to go to dinner with him."

"Yes, well . . ." His mother appeared flustered, the ground hostess noticed. "Be good on the flight over, darling, and, and . . ."

"Shall I tell Daddy you say hello?" the small boy suggested politely.

"You promise me you'll be good, darling." The mother swept down to embrace the child. Then, with a wave, she was off, and the ground hostess noticed with relief that her buzzer call had been answered.

At another counter, a family of four were piling their bags onto the scale.

"Phew! Just under the wire," the father noted with relief, and he watched while the family luggage with its London destination tags slid off the low metal weighing platform sunk through the counter and was placed on the moving belt behind the uniformed ground personnel. It made its way along a panel and disappeared behind a wall. More bags, belonging to other people, followed at uneven intervals, all mechanically making their way down to the loading pallets waiting at the lower level. From there, the luggage went out to the plane.

The streamlined 707, already visible through the convex glass facade facing the airfield was the center of a swarm of activity.

Among those moving beneath the aircraft's metal bulk was Flight Engineer Carl Masden, who was making his pre-flight check. The small trucks and battery carts throbbed and revved around him; flashlight in hand, he went about his inspection with absorbed care.

Up in the forward section of the passenger cabin, the commissary representative greeted the stewardesses as they came in through the front entrance. He then turned back to checking the food trays, slamming them in and out with practised ease. Several storage cartons were still standing on the floor; Rudi stopped and looked at them, then addressed the other man.

"I hope you've given us something decent," he remarked. "We've got a company VIP on board this trip, and everything had better be good."

"Listen, you always get the best, and you know it. So quit complaining."

"It's not me who complains. It's the passengers," Rudi sighed. "And like I just said, company personnel flying in first are always the biggest pains in . . ."

"Take a look for yourself. There. Does this satisfy you?"

Rudi glanced at the tray pulled out from the freezer compartment. "Hmm. Ice cream gateau," he commented. "Not original, but it's decorative. How about the cheese board? That's usually a favorite with male passengers."

Linda and Betsy hung up their capes, slung their fake fur hats into the overhead rack and stashed their overnight bags under the coat rack.

"Guess we'd better get going," Linda sighed, stifling a yawn and briefly stretching her arms over her head. Betsy only smiled in answer, and the next minute both girls had plunged into the pre-flight checking that was almost second nature to them.

Magazines, pillows, oxygen bottles, blankets, extra masks, first aid kit, gum. . . . Mechanically, Betsy made the movements that took her from one point of the cabin to the other, methodically noting the equipment on board. The metal clicks and thumps coming from the galley meant that Linda was also checking her equipment. Ovens, operative; coffee maker, hot cup, water supply, table linen, cutlery, cups . . .

"Hello, gorgeous," the commissary man greeted Betsy as he passed her on his way to the back galley.

"Hello." Both her response and smile were instant, automatic. Her mind was busy checking toys.

45

"Rudi," she called, "there doesn't seem to be a model airplane . . ."

The Swiss purser was at her side almost at once. No matter how hard he might ride his co-workers, Rudolf Becker himself was among the best on the line.

"Here." He handed her a small silver plane.

"Oh, for heavens' sake, and I thought I'd searched through everything! Where on earth . . ."

But before Betsy could finish her question, Rudi was gone, his quick steps taking him down the aisle into the coach section.

"Marianne!" His voice came sharply from the rear of the plane. "If you paid as much attention to the passengers as you do to your hair, you'd be the best stewardess on the line. Now let's get this cabin checked over. Never mind your hair. No, leave the galley checking to Judy. She's got to learn."

Linda emerged from the front galley and sank down onto a seat. "Oh, great. It sounds as if Rudi's in a lovely mood," she said. "That's all I need this trip. Rudi riding me all the way. God—I'd give anything to be back in bed instead of waiting to take off for Europe."

"Oh, I don't think he'll ride you. Marianne's probably asking for it," Betsy said, continuing to check through the contents of the equipment chest which held, among other things, the children's toys and the stationery tablets. "She needs someone to chase her, and Rudi knows it's the only way to get her going. If he doesn't bring her back to reality now and then, she drifts off into her dream world."

"Don't I know it," Linda replied, sounding irritable. "You only have to fly with her once to catch the act. Marianne Lund, famed star of stage, screen, television—and center aisle."

Betsy giggled. "I once heard someone say she lived in a permanent state of rehearsal. She thinks she's going to be discovered on board."

"Yeah, well, you'd have to be blind and deaf to miss her act, but I don't know whether it'll get her discovered, or fired. I did some domestic trips with her, and she gave a wonderful impersonation of a stewardess all the way to the West Coast. *She* did the impersonation, I did the work."

Linda's voice trailed off. Betsy pushed back the metal

equipment container, locked it into place and stood up, and as she did so she gave Linda a searching look. Linda looked pale, and the shadows under her eyes seemed darker than ever.

"Are you feeling all right?" Betsy asked. "You look sort of frail."

Linda gave a grimace that was meant to be a smile. "No, I'm okay. I'm just tired."

"Watch it! Here comes Rudi."

At Betsy's warning, Linda rose smoothly and swiftly from her seat and disappeared into the galley.

"Have we got everything we need up here?" Rudi inquired.

"As far as I can see."

"Well, double check, because with this company guy on board, I don't want any slip ups. His name's Connell, by the way. I'll signal to you when he comes on; I've met him before."

"Top echelon?" Betsy asked. Although she had heard the man's name, there were so many executives in the vast complex of Flightways that it was impossible to know all of them by heart. "I mean, I know he's not the president, but . . ."

"Nah, he's one of those section heads, with a title that probably says *assistant to,* but means nothing. A middle exec, and that's the worst kind. Top men are always better."

Betsy nodded. "I know."

"Anyway, Connell's traveling with his wife, so that will probably make him even more difficult and apt to throw his weight around."

"I know what you mean. I'll look out for them," Betsy promised.

Rudi disappeared off toward the rear of the plane again.

The metal ramp outside clanged with footsteps and Captain Fleming came through the entrance. Larry Johnson was right behind him.

"Hey, Betsy," he called. "About that marshal."

Betsy came up the aisle in answer. Linda had momentarily disappeared.

"Which marshal?"

"Hadley. The guy you'll have up here in first."

47

"Oh, yes. The one Mr. Skarp said was a black belt, or something."

"Yeah. That one. And I don't care if he's a *chastity* belt—you keep that goofball out of our hair."

"Yes, of course." Betsy had no idea what the co-pilot meant, other than that he did not like the marshal. Johnson hastened to explain; David Fleming appeared to be listening as intently as Betsy.

"I've had that guy on before, and he's a stand-in for Wyatt Earp. Spelled U-R-R-P. So don't let him come up front, okay?"

Fleming entered the conversation at this point. "I'm sure Betsy knows better than to let anyone come forward without permission."

Johnson shrugged. "It's just this guy tries to get persuasive around girls."

"I know what you mean, Larry. Don't worry about it."

The two men went through to the cockpit up front. Betsy looked around for Linda to tell her what Johnson had said. The restroom door slid open, and Linda emerged.

"Do I look better now?" she asked.

Betsy gave a start of surprise. The dark circles under Linda's eyes had disappeared and though her skin was still pale, there was now a delicate pink glow across her cheekbones.

"Don't look so surprised," Linda smiled. "It's easy to get the effect, once you know how. And with the dim light in the cabin, it looks quite natural."

"Certainly does," Betsy agreed. "Why, you know how to use cosmetics like a professional."

"I thought of becoming an actress, once. Even did a stint in drama school."

"Like Marianne?" Betsy glanced towards the other cabin where the pretty stewardess was flustering about, trying to keep up with Rudi's commands.

Linda laughed. "Oh no, not like Marianne at all. When I saw that I didn't have much chance of making it, I decided to give up the whole idea. Permanently. It's a tough life and all the odds are against you. I soon saw that. And then, my mother . . ." Linda's voice trailed away. Betsy listened with interest. Linda had not mentioned her family before.

48

"Your mother didn't approve?" Betsy prompted.

"No, it wasn't that." Linda turned away. "She—she had ambitions to be an actress when she was young. It didn't work out for her, either. So I figured I should go into something more—stable."

While they talked, both girls continued working. Betsy repeated to Linda what Larry Johnson had said about the air marshal, and Linda said. "Oh, one of *those*, is he?" and Betsy said she supposed he was. Neither girl expected anything other than a possible passing annoyance with the man; he was, after all, on board to do a job, and a gentle reminder of this out of the other passengers' hearing was all it usually took to calm a boastful and over-eager marshal down.

Carl Masden appeared in the entrance and went up front. As he opened the flight deck door, the mechanical sounds of a cockpit gearing into action sounded through to the cabin, the crackle of a radio interfering with the multilevel electronic whines.

The captain and co-pilot were already in the left and right seats respectively. Flight Engineer Masden settled himself into the seat at right angles to Johnson's back and surveyed the panel in front of him. Fleming looked back and saw Masden, then glanced across at his co-pilot.

"Ready?" he asked.

"Just a minute," came an answering grunt. Co-pilot Johnson was adjusting his seat belt.

"You're getting too damn fat, Larry. Better look out, or you won't make it through your next physical."

"There's nothing wrong with me, and it's not fat. It's all solid muscle," Johnson grinned.

Masden's voice broke in from behind the two senior pilots. "If you develop much more muscle, Larry, you'll be a natural for the jumbos."

There was a strained silence, during which a smile twitched at the corners of Fleming's mouth. He did not, however, offer any comment.

Johnson turned around and looked at Masden who returned his stare with a quiet smile.

"Just remember I'm senior to you," Johnson told him. "And around here, *I* make the funnies. It's one of the few privileges I get in this miserable seat." With that he turned to face the front again, cranking the check list into pre-flight.

"Ready?" Fleming's voice asked again.

The checking started.

"Crew oxygen?"

"On."

The radio crackle sounded through the cockpit.

"Equipment blower? Pitot press?"

"On."

"AC power?"

"Check."

"DC power?"

"Check."

"Battery switch . . . galley switch . . . fuel heaters. . . ?"

"Check . . . check . . ."

The door behind them opened and closed; Rudi Becker was on his own final check the whole length of the plane. He turned to the two girls in the first class galley and announced, "The passengers will be boarding in a few minutes." Then he looked more closely at Linda.

"You look better," he told her.

"Thank you, kind sir," Linda retorted. As soon as the purser was out of earshot, she muttered, "Lousy little creep."

"He's okay if you don't take everything personally."

"But he means it personally!" Linda protested. "Betsy, you are so naive."

Betsy felt color rising in her face and she turned away to hide her sudden anger. Linda was echoing Mike's very words. Was she really naive? Was it so terribly obvious to everyone who met her?

Linda gave a sudden cry. "Oh my God—I forgot!" She grabbed for her shoulderbag.

"What's the matter?"

Rummaging furiously, spilling the contents of her bag over one of the seats, Linda finally found what she was looking for—a white and gold compact. She opened the compact and Betsy saw that it contained small pink pills, set in plastic in a neat pattern.

"I nearly forgot to take my pill!" Linda wailed. "I should have taken it this morning. Oh God, that's twelve hours, do you think it will make any difference? Do you think it would be a good idea to take two now?"

50

As Linda gulped down the pill, Betsy saw Rudi signaling that the passengers were about to board. She moved forward towards the cabin door.

Behind her, Linda was saying in a worried tone: "Do you think I should take two? What would you do, Betsy?"

Betsy, who had had the workings of the pill explained to her by Jay Marshall, turned and said briskly, "No, just take another one the regular time tomorrow morning."

"But supposing . . ."

"Linda, the passengers are coming on."

The next moment, Betsy was smiling at the middle-aged couple stepping into the plane. Out of the corner of her eye, she saw the discreet hand-signals Rudi was giving behind his back. The message registered. Company personnel: the name was Connell.

"It's a pleasure to have you aboard, Mr. and Mrs. Connell," Betsy said. She was relieved to see that Mrs. Connell, at least, returned her smile.

8

As she distributed pillows, newspapers, answers and smiles up and down the cabin to the first class passengers, Betsy was also making mental notes: tattersall, red, grey, blue striped bow . . .

Betsy identified male passengers by their ties. She had discovered, right at the beginning of her career when she usually had to deal with a large cabin full of passengers, that the easiest way was to remember the ties, forget the faces. The ties were more distinctive.

Women were invariably easier to identify. Betsy could spot something to trigger her memory every time— clothes, jewelry, hairstyle. But with men, it was simpler to stick to ties.

Tattersall, red, grey, blue striped and bow. Company Executive Connell was wearing the tattersall number. Not that she was going to have to worry too much about him. Rudi was attending him unctuously. The red tie belonged to the elderly man who was traveling with his wife, who had blue-rinsed hair and was wearing real pearls.

Grey tie was the man traveling alone. It was silk matching the well-tailored suit and the thick, well-cut, grey-at-the-temples hair. This, Betsy realized, had to be Armand Bressanovitch, and she wondered whether Linda might not change her mind after all, even if she had never seen his name in the gossip columns.

He appeared to be in his late forties or early fifties, and he had an abstracted air that made him seem remote. He had only nodded in response to Betsy's "Good evening," and he had not said a word since he boarded. Grey tie, grey man, Betsy thought, and went on to the next one.

Sky marshal Hadley was wearing a blue striped, she had noted out of habit, but she did not need to remember his tie to remember who he was. As always with the marshals, she greeted him as the total stranger and paying passenger that he was pretending to be. Only in case of actual emergency did any of the crew members ever acknowledge the marshals on board. Hadley, she was glad to notice, had settled into his seat. He looked as the marshals often did—slightly too large for the seat he was occupying, and somewhat ill at ease. Well, better that than chasing up and down the plane after the stewardesses, which was what Johnson had implied in his warning. But that sort of behavior seldom happened on overseas flights, and Betsy knew it. As a last thought, before moving further down the aisle, she hoped Hadley knew it, too.

The bow tie belonged to six-year-òld James Murray. He had been brought on board by one of the ground hostesses, who had escorted him to his seat. He was now comfortably ensconced in it, reading the emergency regulations from the flight pack with a very grown-up air. Betsy stopped by his side and bent down to talk to him.

"My name's Betsy," she told him with an encouraging smile, "and I'll be looking after you for this flight. If you want or need anything, you just call me. I'll be walking up and down the cabin most of the time, but if you can't see me, just press this bell, okay? Then I'll know it's you that's calling, and I'll come and see what you need."

"Thank you very much." The boy looked up at Betsy with eyes that were a deep cornflower blue.

"Shall I fasten your seat-belt for you? It can be a bit complicated the first time, I'd better show you how it's done."

"Thank you," the boy said in a tone of patient politeness. "I can manage."

He lifted his arms and Betsy saw that he had the seat-belt already neatly fastened across his lap.

"Why, that's very clever of you! Did you work it out for yourself?"

"I've flown lots of times before."

This boy was as blasé as any adult she had encoun-

53

tered, Betsy thought. She had to keep reminding herself that he was only six years old. He was an unusual child and he intrigued her.

"Have you traveled alone before?"

The boy blinked. "I nearly always fly alone," he said.

Betsy put the model plane on the seat beside him. "This is a model of the plane we're in," she said. "I thought you might like to have it."

"Thank you." He glanced at the plane, but made no move to pick it up. Betsy was perplexed. Small children usually seized them immediately and prized them as souvenirs of their trip.

Satisfied that her young charge was safely buckled into his seat, Betsy turned to the other duties that remained to be done while they were still on the ground. Above her the music playing over the public address system ceased and Rudi's voice announced, "Good evening, ladies and gentlemen, welcome aboard Flightways International . . ."

While he went through the speech in English and French, she finished checking her passengers, then went forward to get out the demonstration life jacket. Linda already had hers on and was in position at the top of the first class cabin; Betsy walked back to the divider between first and coach where the curtain was still half open for the demonstration's purposes.

When Rudi's first speech had finished, she heard Judy's voice begin. Her Italian was flawless, despite her initial nervousness.

"*I passagieri sono pregati . . .*"

Then Rudi took over the microphone again, and the demonstration started. Betsy coordinated her movements with the purser's measured sentences; the aircraft was taxiing smoothly along to take its position at the end of a runway.

". . . and under no circumstances are the jackets to be inflated inside the aircraft . . ."

A few more phrases, some more indicative gestures, and the demonstration was over. Betsy took off the life jacket and put it back in its pocket up front. The pitch of the engines had changed now; she glanced at her watch and saw that they were leaving right on schedule.

The plane was about to take off when Betsy decided not

to use the jump-seat assigned to her. She checked with Rudi, then went to sit next to James.

"I thought I'd keep you company while we take off."

The boy's lips moved but Betsy could not hear what he said above the roar of the engines at full power. She could have guessed, however, that the answer was another of his polite and automatic thank-yous, delivered in his mid-Atlantic accent.

As the 707 lifted off the ground and began climbing, Betsy was glad to see James peering out the window. Well, at least he was showing some interest. Betsy leaned across and asked, "Are you called Jimmy at home? Or Jamie, perhaps?"

A shake of the fair-haired head.

"What would you like me to call you?"

"James, please. I'm always called James."

"I see. And do you remember what I'm called?"

"Betsy."

"It's short for Elizabeth."

"Yes."

Betsy had the uncomfortable feeling that she was appearing childish to this solemn boy. She unbuckled her seat-belt and stood up. Smiling, willing James to smile back just once, she said:

"Don't forget, I'm here to look after you. Anything you want, you let me know. All right?"

"Thank you." A polite smile appeared on the small mouth, but the blue eyes were serious as ever.

"See you later."

In the galley, Linda and Rudi were setting up the bar trolley. Seeing the orders for cocktails gave Betsy an idea. She turned to James and saw, with an inward sigh of relief, that he had picked up the model plane and was looking at it with some interest.

"Would you like a drink, now?" Betsy inquired. "A glass of milk, or soda, or juice?"

"No, thank you."

"Look, can I fetch you a headset? Even if you don't want to watch the movie, you can listen to the music. All kinds of music. There might be something you liked."

I'll pay for the headset myself if necessary, Betsy thought. Maybe he would like one, but didn't have any money. You never knew with kids, they could get themselves into such tangles over a simple thing like not having change.

"Try it, just for fun."

Without waiting for James to turn down her offer, Betsy fetched a headset. James fumbled in his jacket pocket and brought out some crumpled dollar bills.

"I have to pay for it," he said.

Betsy felt she had made a difficult situation worse. As she searched for something to say, she heard Linda's voice.

"Hi. What kind of cocktail can I give you? Orange juice on the rocks? Tomato juice stinger?"

Linda stood behind the bar trolley, looking very tall and glamorous. Betsy again could not help but notice the difference between Linda now, and the fatigued-looking girl who had signed on for the flight. She should have been an actress, Betsy thought, as soon as the passengers appeared as an audience, she switched on her stewardess performance perfectly.

"Peanuts, potato chips, stuffed olives?" Linda went on.

For the first time, James smiled. "Orange juice. Please," he said.

"Fine. How about some potato chips to keep you going until dinner time?"

James shook his head. After Linda had wheeled the trolley away, Betsy said, "I guess potato chips are a bit difficult for you right now."

James turned his head sharply.

"I saw the gap when you smiled," Betsy said.

A moment of hesitation, then as if making a big decision, James gave a deliberate grin—one that exposed all of his teeth. Or those that had not yet fallen out. There was a large gap where the two first upper front teeth had been.

"Did you put them under your pillow, when they came out?" Betsy asked. "When I was a little girl, I used to put mine under the pillow and get a dime for each tooth."

"Yes, I put them under my pillow."

"Did you get a dime?"

"No, I got ten dollars."

"My!" Betsy disguised her surprise with a quick laugh. "Those are valuable teeth you have."

Ten dollars for a child who had lost a tooth? Betsy

wondered. And paying first-class fare for a six-year-old? The boy was hardly likely to benefit from the free cocktails and wine and champagne, while the gourmet food served was more likely to upset a child's stomach than please him. Not to mention that there were rarely children in first-class, so the boy had little chance to make friends. It occurred to Betsy that whoever James' parents were, they didn't have too good an idea of what was good for small boys.

Later, in the galley, Betsy couldn't resist telling Linda about the ten-dollar teeth.

"Spoiled little brat," Linda said.

"He's not spoiled, not really."

"Listen, any kid who has that kind of money lavished on him has to be."

"No, I don't agree. It may sound weird, but I almost get the feeling he's kind of neglected!"

"Neglected! Oh boy, it's obvious you've never seen kids who are honest-to-God neglected!"

Rudi, his usually pale face flushed, appeared in the galley.

"The Connells are *waiting* for dessert! Mrs. Connell will have grapes, Mr. Connell wants gateau, the cheese board afterwards. For God's sake, make it snappy. You're acting like you've got lead in your ass, Linda. Count yourself lucky Betsy and I are working this flight—and I mean, *working.*" He went back to the cabin.

"I'd give a lot to tell that s.o.b. what I really think of him," Linda muttered. "What does he know? Oh well." She took the gateau out of the freezer, slammed the door angrily.

Betsy put the grapes on a silver dish. Then she added a ripe peach and an orange, and arranged the grapes over the other fruit.

"Rudi said she only wanted grapes," Linda commented.

"But they look prettier arranged with the other fruit." To her surprise, Betsy saw that Linda was furious; she was suddenly aware that at that moment, the other girl disliked her intensely.

"Look, maybe it will put Rudi in a better mood, if he sees the dish looking pretty," Betsy said.

"Oh, gee-willikers, thanks!" There was no mistaking the

heavy sarcasm in Linda's voice as she picked up the tray and swept out of the galley.

Betsy filled a paper cup with water from the spigot. The atmosphere on the plane was so dry, she always felt thirsty while working. She tried not to think about the wave of intense dislike she had felt emanating from Linda. She was going to have to work the flight with her for the next month. She couldn't afford to have hassles right at the start.

It was safer to think about young James. Betsy didn't agree with Linda about him. Even at ten dollars for a tooth, she didn't believe that James was spoiled. For reasons which she could not define, the small boy had caught her interest. She wanted to know more about him. Why he was traveling alone. Why he was so solemn. And why, at six years old, he was so unnaturally self-sufficient.

"Taking a rest, dear?"

Rudi was back in the galley, depositing a trayload of silver and china with one hand, expertly pulling out the next tray with the other.

"Sorry." Betsy crumpled the paper cup and stuffed it into the over-full refuse bag.

There was no time for idle speculation now. There seldom was during a flight. Sometimes she might wonder about the passengers afterwards, but there was rarely much chance to get to know anyone properly.

There had been men who had wanted to date her, to become more than just friends-for-a-flight. She had gone out with some of them; but between those who had turned out to be married, and those who lost their charm on terra firma, it had never worked out. She knew it worked for some of the girls, but so far, it hadn't for her. When she thought back on the passengers she remembered clearly, and with that spark of special interest—they were the ones she had said goodbye to at the end of the flight, for good.

Betsy sighed. Flying was fun, of course, but it left an awful lot of loose ends that could never be tied up.

For instance, she really would like to know what went on with young James Murray. But experience had taught her that she wasn't going to find out. That was the way things were, and she had learned to accept it.

9

"Food," Larry Johnson said. "Chow. Chop Suey. Take your choice."

"Uh?" Fleming looked up from a concentrated examination of the gauges. "What's that?"

Linda watched the copilot gesture toward her. She was standing between his seat and Fleming's, but until Johnson pointed her out, she was pretty sure the captain had not noticed her presence.

"The pretty lady is here to take your order for dinner," Johnson said. "Captains, apart from being highly overpaid, are also rumored to have special stomachs. So, being renowned for the delicacy of their constitutions, they get first choice. Sir," he added, with a forward-motion salute.

Fleming gave him a slight smile and turned to Linda.

"Steak, if there's any on board."

"There is. How'd you like it?"

"Rare."

"Anything else?"

"Just coffee, thanks."

"A philistine," muttered Johnson, making his large bulk shudder. "No daring, no *savoir faire*, no sense of gastronomic adventure. Steak and coffee. Faugh! That you can get at Schrafft's. This is Flightways International, where every meal can be a thrill . . ."

"Or a shock," Carl Masden interjected. "Just wait, Joker, till you hear what else is on the menu."

"Okay, I'll fall for it. What other offerings are there tonight?" Johnson demanded.

"Shish-kebab," said Linda.

"Ye gods!" The first officer stared reproachfully at her. *"Shish-kebab.* You aren't a spy from Middle Eastern Airlines, by any chance, are you?"

Linda laughed and said, "It's lamb, and it looks very good."

"I don't believe a word you're saying but, because I am a very brave man, I'll try some. Later, of course," he added in a normal voice. "But David never takes long to eat."

Well aware of the rule that prohibited captain and copilot from eating at the same time, Linda asked the flight engineer whether he wanted food, too.

"Not yet." Carl Masden smiled up at her. "So you're Linda Kesnik." The smile shifted expression. "I've been wanting to meet you."

"Oh?" Linda felt the quickened interest she had felt on other occasions, too.

"That's right. I keep hearing all these interesting things about you."

Like I'm an easy lay, Linda thought to herself, and what would you say, buster, if I told you I go out with the guys because I hate to be alone? And that I don't put out nearly as often as they say I do.

But she knew Carl Masden would be the type to boast of scoring whether he did or not. She also felt he'd ask her out in London. And that she'd go.

Aloud, she said, "That's nice," and went back to the first class galley where she quickly set up a tray for Captain Fleming with the limited meal he had ordered. It certainly left the field open for Johnson, she realized. Despite his bitching about the kebab, he'd be able to sample any of the many things that Fleming had not chosen. The only things he could not have were those the captain had elected to eat, in this case, only a steak. The ruling, an implacable one, was carefully observed by all the cockpit crew; food poisoning, should it ever occur, could thus never affect the pilot and copilot at the same time. Linda knew for a fact it had never happened on a Flightways journey, but all the same, the rule, like all vital safety regulations, was religiously observed.

When she took the tray up front and handed it to Captain Fleming, Joker Johnson made a big show of slavering over the sight.

"Steak," he groaned, "steak, my kingdom for a steak."

"You wouldn't want it, Larry. It's only for philistines."

"David!" bawled the copilot. "Tell that cheap engineer back there to get off at the next stop! He's stealing my lines. Next, he'll be stealing my roll of Tums."

Linda felt Carl Masden's hand on her arm. She looked down.

"Tell you what," he said. "You can bring me my chow when you bring Larry's up later. I'll take steak and whatever else is going with it."

Linda recognized Carl's type only too well, the perennial lady-killer, all dash and charm and insincerity and double-timing. Oh, yes, he was sure to ask her out in London.

". . . and I'd like my coffee at the same time," Masden was saying, "Heavy on the cream, okay, hon?"

Johnson's voice cut in, booming effortlessly over the insistent sound of the engines.

"Drinking coffee with your meals gives you gas," he announced authoritatively. "It says in the latest C.A.B. bulletin that flight engineers are not entitled to fart on duty."

"Larry," Fleming's voice broke through, "hand me the log book, will you?"

Linda wondered whether the captain's interruption was a form of rebuke and a way of ending the light banter. But nothing in his expression indicated he had heard or even been listening. As she left the cockpit, she shot him another quick glance and saw he was absorbed in making calculations even while chewing his steak.

Back in the galley, she told Betsy, "I get the impression that this captain wouldn't even notice if you forgot to serve him dinner. He's one of the non-eaters, that's for sure."

"Joker'll make up for that."

"And how. I'll bet that man thinks about food all the time."

"Well, that's better than what some of them think about all the time," Betsy smiled.

Linda, thinking of Carl, made no answer. She set up

61

trays for him and Johnson. Fleming was sure to be through in a very few minutes, and then the other two would be able to eat. Larry had asked for mineral water; she uncapped a bottle and poured half of it into a china cup. Betsy, beside her, commented, "I always think it looks funny."

"What does?"

"Things like soda and milk being served in cups instead of glasses."

"You would." Because, Linda added silently to herself, you've probably never had to drink anything out of anything that wasn't the *right* kind of glass, or cup. Bet you've never had to use paper napkins over and over again in your life.

"But of course, I see the point," her working companion was saying. "It wouldn't do to let the passengers see liquid-filled *glasses* going up front. Why, they might get the impression that pilots *drink!*"

In spite of her former flash of anger, Linda laughed, Betsy's remark triggering memory of the old airline saw that, owing to the no-drinking rule before and during flights, pilots felt obliged to catch up on their liquor during their days off.

"I suspect the Loner doesn't drink much, anyway," she observed. "Not even on ground. There doesn't seem to be much to that man. Hardly says a thing—certainly not more than is necessary. Not what you'd call the friendly type."

"With Joker Johnson and Carl on board, that's probably just as well."

"Oh, do you know Masden?" Linda kept her question casual.

"Sort of. He's been dating one of my roommates for some time."

"Lee Pickering?"

Betsy nodded. She did not, however, offer any further information. Linda tried prying.

"You don't sound as though you like him much."

Betsy shrugged. "He's not my type. And I don't care for. . . ." She broke off in mid-sentence. "If you want my advice, which I'm sure you don't, don't get involved with him."

"Are you trying to protect your friend Lee?" Linda

could feel her resentment heating her face and coloring her cheeks.

"Partly. I guess I'm also trying to protect you."

"Gee, thanks!" Now the anger flared. "When I need your protection, remind me to send you a postcard."

Careless in her irritation, Linda accidentally knocked over an open cream container, splashing its contents over the metal counter. She grabbed a paper towel and muttered, "Shit!" angered even further by the intake of breath she heard beside her.

"I suppose you don't approve of swearing, either," she snapped at Betsy as she mopped up the cream.

"It isn't that, but suppose a passenger were to hear you?"

Linda said "shit" again and finished cleaning the counter. Wordlessly, Betsy reached for another cream container and placed it on the tray that Linda was setting up for Johnson.

"Thanks." Linda only just managed to make herself utter the word. Instead of thanking Betsy, she felt more like kicking her. Mealy-mouthed little prig. Girls like that always got on Linda's nerves. The type who wouldn't say shit if they had a mouth full of it. And then they always made out they were so unshakable, so superior.

The cockpit bell signaled that Fleming had finished his dinner, and Linda took the other two trays and headed up front. At the flight deck floor, she paused, and then took a deep breath. She had several more hours of the flight to get through, and there was no point in working herself into a nervous state. If she could just exercise some control, and be a bit more calm, everything would be perfectly all right. One thing at a time. Right now, the crew meals. One thing at a time. There would be hours to sleep later.

On her way back out with Fleming's empty tray, she was accosted by the flight marshal. He caught up with her as she reached the galley. Betsy's relayed warning came to her mind at once. But Hadley didn't make any requests to go to the cockpit; instead he seemed to want her to pay attention to him.

"Come on, at least some coffee together," he wheedled unpleasantly. "You'd do that for any passenger, surely you would."

As she glanced down the aisle in search of Betsy or Rudi, Linda noticed that the man traveling solo was staring at her. When he saw he had her attention, he gave a faint smile. Betsy, she saw, was sitting next to the little boy traveling alone.

Linda took the opportunity to get rid of her pest.

"Excuse me, a passenger is calling me," she murmured to the air marshal. "A *legitimate* passenger, buster," she could not help but add as she swept quickly past him and down the aisle toward the man in the grey tie.

10

Rudi had already started the movie, Betsy noticed, seeing the light flickering on the watching passengers' faces. She finished tidying the trolley and put away the cheese board. Mr. Connell wanted more coffee, and she set up a coffee service to take to him.

Rudi appeared by her side and asked where Linda was.

"Up front with crew meals."

"Do you want to eat now?"

"No, thanks." Sharon's omelette was still sustaining her. It seemed unlikely, but then, she usually chose to eat sparingly on flights.

"Then I'll have my dinner and go through the paperwork at the same time. I'll take it up here on the jump seat." Rudi moved with quick precision, selecting the choicer offerings of food available in the compact galley fittings.

"I'll hand it to you."

"Thank you, Betsy."

He took the document briefcase and sat on the forward jump seat reserved for the cabin attendants, which was by the front entrance. Betsy carried his food over, and Rudi settled down. Seeing he had all he needed, she left and took Mr. Connell his coffee. Then she continued down the aisle, checking to see whether anybody needed anything.

She stopped when she reached the man wearing the grey suit and the grey silk tie. He was sitting back in his seat, apparently relaxed. He might have been asleep except for the fact that his eyes were wide open.

"Everything all right, sir?"

The man continued staring ahead for a moment as if unaware of his surroundings. Then, with a start, he came out of his reverie. He blinked.

"What did you say?" he asked.

"I wondered if there was anything I could fetch you. Would you like a magazine? Or a drink?"

"No, nothing, thanks." The man had a quiet, well-modulated voice. He leaned back in his seat again, and resumed staring straight ahead. Betsy felt she had been dismissed.

A small figure bumped into her in the narrow aisle.

"Excuse me!" It was James.

"Where are you off to in such a rush?"

"I have to go to the bathroom," James announced.

"Will you be okay on your own? You know how everything works?"

"Of course. I told you—I've flown lots of times before. I know how to manage."

For a moment Betsy felt irrationally cross. What a bunch of self-sufficient people! She might as well sit and twiddle her thumbs, what with everyone being so darn sure they could manage everything perfectly well without any help.

"I don't feel sleepy." James was standing in the aisle, staring up at her with wide blue eyes.

Betsy sat down so that they could talk on the same level.

"Well, if you don't feel sleepy, we'll have to find something to amuse you. What would you like to do?"

Something close to a smile passed over the boy's face.

"Will you be here when I come back from the bathroom?" he asked.

"Yes, I'll be here."

"Good. Then it won't matter about my not being sleepy."

The boy trotted off along the aisle, towards the rest-room. Betsy moved back to where James had his seat. She thought of possible things they could do. There were maps, with the plane routes marked; there were coloring pens and a pad, if he wanted to draw. Maybe he enjoyed playing card games.

She was glad the boy was becoming more friendly. His aloofness had been rather worrying. A quick professional glance around the cabin told her that there were not likely to be calls for service while the movie was running. That meant she had some time to spend with James. She felt it would prove to be really worthwhile.

11

"I like to draw," James said. He examined the colored drawing pens Betsy offered with interest.

"Do you have art lessons in school?" Betsy asked.

"I don't go to school. I have a tutor."

"I see. Well, do you have art lessons with your tutor?"

James grinned. "He can't draw—he's hopeless."

"But you can draw very well."

Betsy watched as the small boy covered the first page of the sketch pad with outlines. He drew a car, a plane, a small sailboat. The car was red, the plane black, the sailboat blue. Betsy noticed that James drew outlines only, he didn't fill in colors. But the outlines were skillfully done for such a young child.

"Which color is your favorite?" Betsy asked.

"I like red best, and blue best and green best."

"You can't like *all* those colors best, only one can be your favorite."

James' blue eyes regarded her indignantly.

"*I* like them all best." It was stated with certainty. Turning a page he began drawing what Betsy thought at first was an orange. But the orange circle sprouted hair and eyes and a nose and a mouth.

"That's you," James announced. "Do you like it?"

"Hmmm. Do I really look orange?"

"You're more of a yellow color," he said finally, with the devastating frankness of a child, "but the yellow pen is too bright for drawing people."

Looking at the crude face, Betsy commented, "You draw cars and planes better than people."

"They're easier. Faces are very hard. Grown-up artists say that faces are very hard to draw. I know because my mother told me so."

"Is your mother an artist?"

James considered for a moment. "Not really," he said. "She draws pictures and she paints. But not, not . . ."

"Not professionally?" Betsy suggested.

"Not—professionally." James pronounced the word with great care. "She calls it her hobby."

"Are you going home to your parents now?"

"I'm going to visit my father. He lives in London. He has a big house there."

As he spoke, James was drawing a house. He outlined the building in black and it filled a whole page of the pad. At the bottom of the page, he drew a small door.

"How about windows?" Betsy suggested.

"I'm *coming* to those." James' voice was impatient.

"Sorry."

The black pen was busily outlining rows of very large windows.

"My father bought this house and then he had it changed. It was an old-fashioned house. My father told the man to make it new. He has lots of new windows. Big windows, with lots and lots of glass."

A frown appeared on the boy's face and he stopped drawing.

"What's the matter?"

"How—how can I draw the glass?"

"Leave the paper white," Betsy suggested. "It will look like a window."

"No it won't."

"Well, it's very difficult to make it look like glass." Betsy was getting interested in the drawing project. It took her back to the time when she had made her first efforts at drawing pictures and had pondered the enormous problems of making sky look like sky and glass look like glass. But as far as she could recall, these problems had not bothered her when she was as young as James. At his age, she had been content to fill in blue for the sky and just leave space for a pane of glass.

"Your mother must have taught you a lot about drawing," Betsy remarked. "You seem very advanced."

"Yes I am," James agreed, "everybody says so."

There was a silence. Betsy stood up and glanced around the cabin. The passengers were all apparently watching the movie. Betsy was about to walk through the cabin, when she saw Linda starting down the aisle. Linda gave a small okay signal with one hand so Betsy sat down again.

The house was now drawn in more detail.

"Does your mother like the big house in London?" Betsy asked.

With great concentration, James embarked on drawing a tile pattern on the roof of the house. Quite a while after Betsy put her question, he replied,

"My mother doesn't live in London. She lives in Connecticut. My parents are divorced. My father lives in London. I stay with him six months every year."

Betsy felt the need to say something but she was afraid of treading on delicate ground.

"You certainly do plenty of traveling," she said eventually.

"Yes. I travel more than grown-ups. I like it."

"Good." Betsy examined the picture of the house with a critical eye. "Isn't there any lawn?"

"Not much. There is a garden, but it's at the back. There is a tree in front, though."

Seizing the green pen, James drew a small tree in the corner of the page.

"The leaves are green, but perhaps the tree-trunk should be brown," Betsy commented.

"I don't like brown. Brown is my most horrid color."

Abruptly, the page was turned and James began drawing cars again, red ones. "I like cars best," he explained, "that's why I draw them best."

"I have to go and see if everything is all right," Betsy told James.

"Why?"

"It's my job to make sure everyone has what he needs. How about you? Would you like a drink, or a snack?"

"No, thank you. I'm going to do some more drawings. Why don't you stay and see me draw?"

"I'll be back later. Why don't you try to sleep a little

70

now? If I make up a cosy bed with a blanket and pillow, will you lie down for a while?"

"No!" The boy was definite. "I don't want a bed. I want to sit up."

"You'll be tired when we get to London."

In a tone of complete indifference he said, "That doesn't matter."

"All right. I'll be back later on to see how you are."

Moving silently through the dimly-lighted cabin, Betsy noted that the Connells had made themselves comfortable with blankets and pillows and seemed fast asleep. The other middle-aged couple were tucked up in blankets, the man sleeping and breathing heavily, the woman lying back but wide awake. When she saw Betsy, she sat up.

"I can't sleep," she complained. "This is not at all comfortable."

"If you like, I could make up a bed for you, there is plenty of room . . ." Betsy offered, but the woman cut in crossly,

"I don't want to move now! Can't you give me something to help me sleep?"

Betsy decided her best tack was to appear knowledgeable.

"I'll bring you a drink of hot milk. That always helps," she said.

"Huh! It doesn't sound like much use to me."

"Give it a try," Betsy murmured, "I've known it to work wonders. We once had Evelynne Gray, the film actress, on board, and she said she could *never* sleep on a plane, but I gave her some hot milk and she slept for most of the flight. She couldn't believe it when I woke her up with breakfast the next morning."

"Oh, really?" Her blue-rinsed head settled back against the pillow. "Evelynne Gray? Well, I guess I might as well try it."

Before the woman could change her mind, Betsy moved off towards the galley. On her way, she glanced over to where the grey tie was sitting.

The grey tie wasn't sleeping at all, he wasn't even lying back listlessly, as he had been ever since the flight started. He was sitting up and talking nonstop to Linda. Betsy watched for a moment with interest. The man had been uncommunicative in the extreme, before. Whatever he

71

was saying held Linda spellbound. She seemed to have forgotten her tiredness and was listening attentively to everything the man was telling her.

Wondering if Linda's interest was genuine or faked for the occasion, Betsy went into the galley. Rudi was now working on the bar accounts, muttering to himself as he did so.

"Who's the man Linda's talking to?" Betsy asked. The scene in the cabin had aroused her curiosity.

"Which one?"

"The man traveling alone. About fifty, grey suit, grey tie, looks like a businessman."

Rudi thought for a second. "His name's Bressanovitch. That's all I know about him. He's not on the VIP list. Why, are you interested? Does he take your fancy, dear?"

"No, but he has taken Linda's."

"That's not difficult!"

Betsy prepared the milk for the wakeful passenger.

"That for the kid?" Rudi wanted to know.

"There's a woman who can't sleep."

"Who?" Rudi's voice was sharp.

"Relax, it's not Connell's wife." Really, Betsy thought, Rudi overdid things at times. Good service was one thing, obsequiousness was another.

"I don't know how people are supposed to sleep at all, with this terrible noise all the time," the woman complained, as she took the milk.

"Some passengers find the engine noise kind of soothing," Betsy murmured. "There's a kind of rhythm to it."

"The lights are disturbing, too. Why some people . . ." The woman turned and glared across the cabin to the spot where Linda and the businessman were sitting, "have to keep the reading lights on all the time, I can't think." She nervously fiddled with her strand of pearls.

Betsy was pretty sure the pearls were worth a fortune, they had a beautiful luminous glow that was exceptional. The nervous fingers played with the pearls as if they were mere worry beads.

"Would you care for a snack of some kind?" Betsy suggested. "I can get you some cookies."

"No, thanks," the woman snapped, "I don't want to ruin my digestion, as well as lose my sleep."

"I'll dim the lights," Betsy said, moving quickly away, "that should help."

Betsy snapped off a reading light that had been left on by mistake, then glanced across the cabin. Linda and the grey tie were now sitting in shadow. She would have given a lot to know which of the two had turned off the light that had previously spot-lighted them.

In the galley, Betsy felt a sudden tiredness.

"I think I'll eat now," she told Rudi. "Okay if I take a cigarette break up front after I've finished?"

Rudi nodded, pushing his paperwork slightly to one side so that she could reach the food compartments better. Then he went back to muttering over the accounts. "You'd think after all this time, Marianne would have learned how to count cordial bottles. I'd better go and see what's happening back there, anyway. If she's running true to form, Marianne's probably sneaking her beauty sleep in a corner, and leaving the new girl to watch over everything."

Betsy felt relieved she was not one of the hapless girls in coach, about to encounter Rudi's bad temper and unfinished bar accounts. As he left the front galley, she managed to attract Linda's attention discreetly. After a few minutes, Linda excused herself to her companion and came over.

"What's up?"

"I'm going to eat, and then go for a cigarette break up front. Rudi's just gone aft, and he's in a foul temper. Could you watch things here?"

"Sure. Go ahead." Betsy saw Linda do an inspection tour up and down the aisle, and then go back to talking to the grey tie. Meanwhile, Betsy settled herself in the jump seat, a food tray in her hand. She balanced it on her lap and ate quickly, without interest. She wasn't all that fond of shish kebab, and was more attracted to the way it was served on long skewers than to its taste.

When she finished her meal, she returned to the galley and scraped the leftovers into the refuse, stacking the utensils in with the other used equipment. Then she took her handbag and went up front.

"Hi, beautiful," Carl Masden greeted her, looking up from the newspaper spread on his table. "Where've you and the other girls been all this time? We could do with some pretty company up here."

Betsy smiled politely at him and took her cigarettes out of her bag. Masden's lighter was quick to appear.

"Thanks, Carl."

"Anything for you, hon. I haven't seen you smoke in an age. Thought you'd given it up."

Betsy shook her head. "No, but I've never smoked much. You know, one or two here and there."

"That makes you one of those irritating people who can smoke five cigarettes a week and not yearn for more," he commented. "I hate you," he added, his grin belying the statement. "It's people like you who make me feel I'm an addict."

Turning in his seat, Johnson said loudly, "You *are* an addict. Smoking ruins the palate."

"Eating ruins the waistline," Carl rejoined, well aware of his own lithe build and lean-muscled frame. Betsy suspected privately that he was almost as vain of his well-proportioned physique as a voluptuous starlet might be of her body. Carl Masden had always struck her as being overly pleased with himself but then, he wasn't her type. She had never liked overly handsome men. And he was extremely good-looking, there was no denying it. Lee had once told her she used to get upset when they went out, because she felt sure every woman was looking at him.

Larry Johnson turned to face front again and busied himself with a radio checkpoint. The squawking static-ridden sounds grew louder; Betsy smoked silently, staring at the blackness of the windshield, which was relieved only by points of light reflected from within the cramped cockpit itself. Then she shifted her gaze and, for the first time, got a good look at Captain Fleming.

Close up, she could see that, though the brown hair was still thick, it was beginning to show a lot of silver. He had to be close to forty, she reckoned. He looked younger when he smiled, she remembered, but he didn't seem to smile much at all. He had the sort of understated good looks that Betsy felt were genuinely attractive in a man— a direct contrast to the almost pretty-boy features of Carl Masden. Fleming's fine-drawn features were well-shaped and forceful.

74

However, the captain's personality impressed her more strongly than his looks. He seemed cool, capable, determined—yet somehow withdrawn.

Johnson finished his checkpoint, replaced the radio mike on its hook, said, "Ah, shit," under his breath and finished filling out the form clipped to the board on his lap.

"Not good, eh?" Carl asked.

"Bloody limey fog. We may yet find ourselves in Paris or Frankfurt," he added for Betsy's benefit.

"There's no need to jump to conclusions," Fleming said. Betsy was surprised when he entered the conversation; he had seemed miles away from his immediate surroundings.

"Yeah, but considering they're almost down to minimums, and it *is* November . . ." Johnson said, lazily.

"It can change in an hour," Fleming remarked. "And we have more than that to go before we even start letting down."

"Okay, okay, Cap'n, suh," the copilot muttered. "I was just hoping for a Paris landing. Think of it," he turned to Betsy. "Me and the new Orly runways—why, I could've given them a real Johnson Special, one of my more bounce to the ounce creations."

"If he gives you the landing, I'm getting off," Carl announced.

"It'd be worth trading my roll of Tums to get that threat activated."

Again, Betsy got the impression that Fleming was quite unaware of the banter between the other two crew members. He was leaning forward, tapping a gauge. When he leaned back and put his hand back on the wheel, she noticed that his hands reflected the same personality traits as his appearance and behavior. They were well-shaped and they rested on the wheel with the quiet calm and determination that seemed to be Fleming's entire persona.

She stubbed out her cigarette. "Would anybody like coffee?" she asked. "Or a sandwich, or something?"

It was Fleming who answered first. He turned to look at her, gave one of his rare smiles, and said, "Coffee'd be great. Black, no sugar."

"Now about a sandwich?"

"No, thanks. Just coffee."

"Gallons of cream and tons of sugar for me, sugar." Johnson emphasized. Carl also wanted coffee.

Linda was in the galley when Betsy got back.

"How're things up front?" she asked.

"Okay. But the weather's closing in at Heathrow. We might have to divert."

Linda shrugged. "So what else is new, on a winter schedule?"

When the three coffees were ready, Linda said, "I'll take those. I want a cigarette break, myself."

"Oh. Okay." For reasons she could not define, Betsy felt disappointed.

Linda picked up the tray.

"I'll give your love to Carl," she said, in a silly, teasing tone.

Carl? Betsy wondered. Oh, that was it. She laughed quietly to herself. Linda was on entirely the wrong tack if she thought she was interested in him. But that remark revealed who attracted Linda's interest.

Yet a short time before, Linda had been raptly listening to the businessman passenger. She certainly believed in playing the field. Betsy had heard that Linda aimed to get off every flight with a man in tow. Maybe Betsy was seeing her in action.

She wondered who it would be in the end—the businessman or Carl. For Lee's sake, she hoped Linda would settle for the passenger, although second thoughts told her it probably wouldn't make any difference.

In the cabin, Betsy saw that everyone was now dozing, even the woman with the pearls who had declared it impossible to sleep. She almost wished someone would wake up and ask for something. The dimly-lighted cabin and the blanket-wrapped passengers made her feel sleepy. She was tempted to sit down. But she was afraid that if she did, she might drift off. With Rudi in his present mood, that would be unwise.

No, Betsy thought, it was better to keep going. Apart from the fact that sleeping during flights was against all regulations and there would be trouble with Rudi, she had found that when she did try to snatch a short nap, she woke up feeling worse, not better.

At the back of the cabin, Betsy found that James had fallen asleep with the model plane clutched in his hand. He had his feet up on the pillow and his head was wedged against the corner of the seat. He looked uncomfortable but he was deeply asleep.

Best not to disturb him, Betsy thought. She took down a blanket and covered him gently. She adjusted the blanket over his slight form, looking down at him for a while. The boy appeared so vulnerable, lying there, so terribly young to be so alone. She wondered how parents could let such a young child travel on his own.

She remembered his serious manner of talking, the surprising sophistication. Sometimes, his self-sufficiency made him rather unappealing. But he was asleep, she thought, he looked helpless, and altogether different.

12

Balancing the trays with care, Linda Kesnik made her way into the Boeing's cockpit. The bright light of the winter morning sky entering through the windshield made her tired eyes smart briefly, and she was glad she'd used eye drops when she'd redone her makeup before preparing the breakfast service.

Rudi and Betsy were handling it in the cabin while she brought up the two requests up front. Fleming had declined any breakfast and had finished a cup of coffee sometime before.

She handed Johnson the tray with the two rolls, eggs and fruit juice. Carl Masden got the one with a roll and coffee. As she stood between the two pilots' seats, Linda avoided looking straight out into the glare and glanced down, earthwards, instead. There wasn't much of anything to be seen, and the cloud mass below them looked suspiciously familiar.

"The last time I saw it looking like that, we ended up in Frankfurt," Linda remarked to no one in particular, trying to see Fleming's face as she spoke in order to catch his reaction. There was none, but Johnson took her up on the subject.

"I prefer Paris," he said, his mouth full of scrambled eggs. "Let's make it profiteroles and coquilles St. Jacques rather than knockwurst on rye, okay?"

"Should I tell the passengers there may be a diversion?" Linda asked, knowing Rudi would be getting on the public address system soon. For announcements, it had been one of the quietest flights she had known; Fleming had only spoken once shortly after they'd left New York. She presumed he'd come on the air again before landing, but there were some captains who never seemed to stop talking the whole way across. Fleming apparently left all talk to the purser on duty and, if there was going to be heavy fog at the airport in London, it might be wise for the passengers to be told now.

"It'll be Heathrow," said Fleming calmly. "We're going to attempt it, and I see no reason to believe we won't get down."

Larry Johnson looked at him in amazement. "You don't, huh? Well, how about that pea soup they say is lying all over the field, for openers?"

"They're not below limits," came the flat answer.

"No, they're just sitting on them, that's all." Johnson's come-back was a mutter, and he concentrated on his breakfast.

Linda went back into the cabin and found Betsy working on the coffee seconds. She joined in immediately with unconscious ease.

"Looks like we really may not get into Heathrow after all. There's fog." And she went on to describe the exchange between the pilots.

Betsy groaned. "Well, I only hope it's the captain who's right this time. The thought of diverting somewhere, instead of getting to a hotel bed makes me feel exhausted. I don't know why, but I'm beginning to fold."

Linda watched her go off down the cabin with the coffee refills. When she came back, Linda suggested, "Maybe you'd feel better if you re-did your face. It helps. Or, anyway, it always helps me."

"Yes, so I see." Although Betsy's tone was perfectly polite, Linda thought she heard an implied rebuke in the remark. But she hadn't taken so long to change her makeup; Betsy had only begun to arrange the breakfast service when Linda had come out to take over. And she'd done all the work a galley girl was supposed to do before taking up the pilots' breakfasts. So what was this redheaded Miss Priss insinuating?

Betsy was saying, "But I haven't the time, right now.

Rudi wants me to help back in the coach galley. That new girl, Judy, needs a hand."

"Then why doesn't he . . .?"

"Because he's too busy riding Marianne. He's really hounding her now, working the cabin with her."

"Why? What'd she do this time?"

Linda saw Betsy's face go blank as she said, "Spent too much time in the restroom, re-doing her face." And again she walked off, leaving Linda with a strong desire to kick her where it would hurt the most. Furious, she busied herself tidying away the rest of the trays and crammed the trash into the already loaded bins. She had been feeling just fine, until this run-in with Betsy. Now she felt all edgy again. Why was it that Betsy, and all girls like Betsy, always make her feel as if she were in the wrong?

The flight engineer appeared in the galley.

"Hi. Any more coffee?"

"Sure." Linda poured a cup and handed it to him. He smiled his thanks and drank some, eyeing her over the rim of the cup.

"You look pretty good, for so early in the morning," he remarked.

Linda smiled. Now she felt vindicated, and was glad she had taken the time and trouble to freshen up, never mind what Betsy thought.

"Have a cigarette." Masden proffered a crumpled pack.

"Thanks." Linda bent her head to light the cigarette from the lighter Masden offered. She was aware of the young engineer's eyes examining her closely.

"Do you have any special plans for London?" he asked.

"The usual thing—rest, then some shopping. Not much time for anything else."

"I don't know about that." Masden grinned. "Layover is 25 hours minimum. That's time to do—quite a lot."

"Depends what you want to do, I guess," Linda remarked. She had a feeling that the conversation was following so familiar a pattern, that she could hardly be bothered to say her part. She knew that Masden would continue working up to his proposition, and that she would go along with it.

Suddenly, Linda pushed her cigarette towards him.

"Quick, take it!" she hissed. Rudi came into the galley.

"No room to move in here," Rudi commented, staring

from Linda to the engineer with pale eyes that were beginning to look bloodshot from fatigue.

"I'm just going. You can't say I don't know where I'm not wanted," Carl retorted. He swallowed the last of the coffee and put the cup down on the counter. To Linda, he added, "Thanks, sweetheart. Be seeing you."

He made no attempt to ease past the purser, but elbowed his way saying, "Oh, *excuse* me, I didn't mean to push," with a sneer. The moment he had left, Rudi turned to Linda.

"Does that son of a bitch normally smoke two cigarettes at a time?" he demanded, his face pink with annoyance.

"You'd better ask him." Linda feigned a nonchalance she was not feeling. On the contrary, a tight band of anxiety was pulling in around her.

"You'd better be careful, Linda." The purser's voice was low pitched. "May I remind you that we have Mr. Connell on board? All we need now is for him to see you smoking."

"But I'm not smoking!" Linda snapped.

Rudi gave her a bloodshot look. "You know exactly what I mean. And if you want to get a lousy report— *another* one, from what I hear of your record—that's up to you. But don't work on it when you're flying with *me*. I don't want your troubles laid on my back."

Trouble, trouble, Linda raged, not listening any more to the angry spate of words. Why did all the trouble have to head her way? Why couldn't Rudi go off and pick on Betsy for a change? How did the Betsys of the world always manage to avoid trouble so neatly? They seemed to float through life, as if protected by magic. Her angry thoughts made her clumsy, and in her fury she dropped a sheaf of cutlery to the floor.

"Goddam it!" she muttered, bending to pick up the scattered pieces.

As she did so, a card fell out of the pocket of her working smock. Linda shoved the knives and forks onto the counter, then straightened up, holding the card in her hand.

"Do you need help in here?" Betsy was back.

"No thanks!" Linda snapped. She stared at the card. Then she muttered, "The nerve of some people!"

81

"Meaning me?"

Linda looked at Betsy and noticed the flush rising on her cheeks. It looked like Miss Priss had a temper, after all.

"Meaning the guy who slipped me this card," Linda said, holding it up for the other girl to see.

Betsy scanned it, began laughing.

"What's so funny?" Linda demanded. "Plenty of guys slip you cards."

"I think the same man passed me one, too."

"Oh, no!" Linda exclaimed. "You mean the old guy, the one with the wife with all the pearls?" She saw Betsy nod, her eyes bright with laughter.

"Well, that takes some beating! At his age and with his wife sitting right beside him!" Now Linda was laughing, as well. "I thought I knew all the ways a guy could slip you his card, and all the messages they could write, too. But somehow, I didn't expect it from him, not with the blue-haired dragon lady keeping guard beside him."

"How about the other man?" Betsy asked. "The one you were talking to for so long."

"Not talking to, *listening* to," Linda said. "Oh, he just wanted someone to tell his story to. Frankly, I think he's a bit of a weirdo."

"Really? He looks normal. I mean, typical conservative-type businessman and everything."

Linda shrugged. "He struck me as kind of oddball."

"Interesting?"

"I don't really know. You know the stories some people tell, when they're on a plane. I don't know why, but because they're flying, they come across with these strange tales. I think my friend of last night is one of the story-tellers, that's all. How about your kid? How's he doing?"

The laughter died out of Betsy's eyes. "He was fine last night but now he seems to be getting nervous. I'm not sure what it is. He is used to flying so I don't think he's afraid of the landing."

"What does he say?"

"He asked me to stay with him at the airport."

"That's the job of ground-staff," Linda commented. "Once we've landed, you hand the kid over to them. That's the extent of your responsibility."

"I know. But he seems such a lonely kid—and all he

wants is for me to stay with him until his father arrives. It's not much to ask."

"Suit yourself." Linda slopped some coffee into a cup and drank it down quickly. She became aware that Betsy was watching her. "Oh, you want some coffee?" she asked, reaching for a second cup.

"Thanks." The voice held something very like sarcasm.

God, Linda thought, I hope I'm not working the line when Betsy makes it to Chief Flight Stewardess, she'll be a real doll to work for.

13

Uneven fingers of fog stretched out from the thickening sea of grey that lay beyond. The Flightway 707, already down from cruising altitude was following its descent clearance. In the cockpit, Larry Johnson repeated the instructions coming from London Center.

"Flightway four-ten, maintaining ten thousand . . ."

Fleming, frowning with concentration, had command of the wheel; Carl Masden, sideways behind them, vectored his panel now set for landing. The three men's voices called and answered each other in the detailed checking off of descent gauge positions.

Their dovetailed duties continued uninterrupted by the entrance of Rudi Becker and his equally fast departure. The purser was making his last checking trip on which he always made a point of overseeing the full length of the plane. He picked up a discarded snack tray next to the flight engineer's feet before returning to the passenger cabin and shutting the flight deck door behind him with a firm jerk.

On his way back down the aisle, he passed Linda Kesnik, finishing the last clearing away necessary in the built-in confines of the first class galley. Further along, Betsy Blair was checking an alien landing card filled out by the woman with the long string of pearls.

"Yes, that's right," she was saying. "Just keep it with your passport, and they'll ask you for it on ground."

Becker picked up a blanket lying over the back of an

inner seat, folded it twice and threw it into the overhead rack. Going through to the coach section, far more disorder met his eye. He worked his way steadily down the aisle to the rear galley, where the flushed face of Judy Fransella looked up at him in dismay.

"I can't get this to lock into place!" she wailed, struggling with a tray module out of line with the wall unit. Rudi grasped it with her and slammed it into place. Beyond the back galley, emerging from the left side restroom, Marianne Lund avoided yet another lecture by being in the company of two small girls.

"They needed help," she explained, leading them back to their parents. The family of four was sitting midway up the cabin where most of the tourist class passengers had grouped themselves the night before.

The plane dipped down, and Rudi knew they were about to make the final descent for the landing. His practised eye gauged the fog; with Fleming, they'd probably make it . . .

Betsy strapped herself into the seat next to James and said, "Well, we're almost there. Aren't you glad to be nearly home?"

"Yes." But he didn't sound it, and Betsy looked at him carefully. That nervousness he'd begun displaying was still bothering the child.

"You will stay with me?" he suddenly asked, turning to her.

She smiled. "Well, I can't exactly get off the plane right now, can I?" Then, seeing his expression, she added, "Of course I'll sit here with you while we land."

"No, I mean afterwards. After we've landed."

"But your Daddy's coming to get you."

"Yes, but till he comes," James persisted.

"Okay."

"Do you promise?" The little face looked anxiously into hers. It seemed so important to him that Betsy found herself saying, "Yes, James, I promise."

They were descending rapidly and were in the fog now. The light thumps that came with the change in the atmosphere around them knocked against the sleek sides of the plane. Betsy leaned back in her seat, enjoying a last short breather. But there wouldn't be much more work to do, and then the hotel, and blissful bed . . .

"But I *promised*," Betsy repeated, putting her suitcase down on the pavement. She shivered and pulled her fur-collared cape closer around her.

"Oh, for God's sake, you'll miss the crew car if you go running after the kid now," Linda said crossly. "Stop the mother hen act. There are plenty of ground staff who can take care of him just as well as you can."

Betsy shivered again as she stood between Linda and Rudi, with Judy and Marianne a few paces away from them in the cold damp air of a foggy London morning. Technically, her work was through; not only had the cabin attendants finished their duties when they handed over the plane to the oncoming crew, but Betsy had gone all the way into the terminal with the self-possessed little James Murray. There she had handed him over to a ground hostess in uniform, after which she had returned to the aircraft to finish her job and wait for the cabin attendants boarding at Heathrow.

She found them on board, and, after the usual greetings had been exchanged, it only took them a few minutes to get the changeover effected. She and Linda put on their hats and capes and picked up their overnight bags. Rudi, already in his overcoat, was waiting for them on the ramp. Marianne and Judy, having descended by the coach door ramp, joined them at the foot of the metal stairs. Together, the deplaning cabin attendants of Flight 410 walked across to the terminal building and through the usual formalities.

But all the time she was saying good morning and showing her passport and collecting her luggage, Betsy was thinking about James and the worried look in his deep blue eyes. The ground hostess said that no Mr. Murray had checked at the Flightways counter as yet, but no doubt he'd be there any moment, probably by the time she got James through the required authorities.

"May I have your passport, James?" she had said, bending down to him, and had helped him take it from the case in which he carried it.

"You will come back and stay with me, won't you?" he had whispered, just as Betsy was about to leave, and she

86

had smiled and nodded. Now, waiting for the crew car to take her to the airport, she realized she had not checked to see whether James had been fetched or not.

"Well, you didn't see him in the terminal, did you?" Linda demanded.

"No, but he might have been in the Flightways office, or in the bathroom," Betsy countered.

Linda snorted.

"Look, dear," Rudi put in, "I understand your feelings, but you *know* the boy is being adequately looked after. Be reasonable. You've been working all night, you need some rest, and the car'll be here any minute now."

"And anyway, what's so special about that spoiled brat that he gets so much attention?" Linda muttered.

"But the pilots aren't here yet," Betsy persisted, "and it'll only take me a moment."

"There they come," Linda said triumphantly, pointing to the three figures walking towards them: Fleming, tall and straight; Masden, shorter but lithe and neat; and Johnson, bulky and rumpled.

"Where's the wagon?" Johnson demanded as they reached the waiting group.

"Coming in a moment," Rudi told him. Johnson looked unconvinced.

Edging away from the group of crew-members, Betsy spoke quietly to Rudi, "I won't be long, but I must check and see that he is all right." She wished she had slipped away without telling anyone about James, or had made another excuse for disappearing.

Rudi gave a loud and elaborate sigh of exasperation.

"Don't blame me if you find yourself stuck at the airport. And please don't come to me tomorrow with stories about being tired, when you have to get back to work."

"I *promised* . . ." Betsy began, but the captain's voice interrupted her. "What did you promise? What's the problem?"

Betsy looked up at Fleming. There were lines of tiredness on his face and she was afraid he would not prove very sympathetic.

"The little boy on board," she explained. "He specially asked me to stay with him until his father picked him up."

"How old is he?"

"Only six. He seems awfully lonesome."

Fleming said, decisively, "No reason why you shouldn't wait with him, if you want to." Turning to Rudi, he added, "She can get a bus from the airport later. Won't hurt her to do it the hard way."

Betsy smiled her thanks and the captain's face relaxed into a smile, too.

"Don't stay all day," Rudi grumbled, "remember you're here for work, not for running after waifs and strays."

To Linda, Betsy said, "Look after my luggage for me, will you? There's my case and the overnight bag."

"Okay, I'll see that it gets to our room."

As Betsy turned to leave the group, Johnson demanded loudly, "Where's the goddam car?"

A British-accented voice replied, "Sorry sir, bit of a hold up this morning. It's the fog."

"What fog?" Johnson shouted.

"What fog?" The British voice echoed. "It's pretty thick everywhere. Haven't you just come in through it?"

"Nah. Clear as a bell up there," Johnson said, staring up into the damp greyness overhead.

Betsy walked away from the argument, back into the terminal building. The atmosphere was cold and empty. Betsy shivered again.

She found James sitting beside a ground hostess. When he saw Betsy, he jumped up to greet her.

"Oh, good! I knew you'd come back. This lady said you wouldn't." The blue eyes gave the disbelieving ground hostess a scornful look.

"Has your father arrived yet?" Betsy asked.

James sat down again, suddenly dejected. "No, he hasn't."

To the ground hostess, Betsy said: "This little boy came in on my flight. I'm going to look after him till his father comes. I'm Miss Blair, you can check me with Flightways, if you like."

The girl looked doubtful. "I have instructions to remain with this child," she said. "I can't leave him like this."

"That's all right," James broke in, "you can go, Betsy is here and she's going to look after me."

"Maybe it would be a good idea for you to keep in touch with the information desk," Betsy suggested to the other hostess. "Then as soon as Mr. Murray arrives, you can page us on the P.A. system."

"I suppose I could do that," the girl said, reluctantly.

When the ground hostess was finally convinced, Betsy took her young charge over to the nearest counter.

"Let's have something to drink," she suggested. "I could do with some coffee."

James decided he wanted orange juice.

"Will my father know where we are?" James asked, in a small voice.

"Yes, of course. As soon as he goes to the Flightways desk, we'll be called over the system."

"Oh." James sucked orange juice through his straw. When his glass was half-empty, he paused, then blew an experimental bubble or two. Betsy smiled. That was more like small-boy behavior. It bothered her that James was so serious most of the time.

After two cups of strong, black coffee, Betsy felt her post-flight tiredness receding. When she had turned back into the terminal to rejoin James, she had literally been aching for bed. Keeping her promise to James had been an effort, but now she was glad she had made it.

They sat at the counter for twenty long minutes. There were few travellers about, the handful of people drinking tea and coffee were mostly airport employees.

Betsy looked at the change in her purse.

"This money is new to me," she told James, "do you understand it?"

"Yes." James carefully selected the right coins from the purse. "You need one like this, and one like this."

After they had paid their bill, Betsy went over to the Flightways counter. There was no news of Mr. Murray. No message had been received regarding James. Frowning, Betsy looked at her watch. She began to wonder how long their wait was going to be. She had an uneasy feeling that she could not define. Perhaps it stemmed from the fact that she believed that a father who cared for his son would have been there at the airport when the plane landed, fog or no fog.

Trying to sound cheerful, she said, "I expect your father is being held up in traffic. The fog must be causing delays everywhere. He'll probably arrive any minute now."

"I don't know." The boy's expression was blank. "He's often late."

"Even when he's supposed to be meeting someone?"

"Yes."

James was mechanically kicking the counter in front of him. The right foot kept swinging and kicking, swinging and kicking.

"You'll spoil your shoes," Betsy said. The boy appeared not to hear her and went on kicking.

"Come on, let's go find something to do," she suggested, taking James' hand. "It can't be long now."

"What shall we do?"

"Oh—well, we can look at the souvenir shops. And the newsstands. Do you like comics? We can get some, if you like."

"No thank you."

For a moment, Betsy was afraid there was going to be a sulky rebellion but in the end, James quietly accompanied her to look around the shops. Furtively glancing at her watch, Betsy spent as long as she could, examining the shop-windows in detail. Before long, James announced, "I think these old souvenirs are *boring*. My father says it is all rubbish, anyway."

Betsy sent up a small prayer for the arrival of Mr. Murray and headed back towards the information desk.

"Perhaps my father has forgotten I'm arriving today," James remarked, in a casual tone.

"What?"

"He forgets things, sometimes."

Shocked, Betsy could think of nothing to say. The girl at the desk was quite definite.

"There is no news and no message has been received. I've double-checked, as you asked me to."

James was kicking the counter again, his foot moving rhythmically, swing, kick, swing, kick.

Suddenly, a male voice demanded, "What's happened? Why are you still here?"

Betsy spun around to find herself facing Captain Fleming.

"Oh! You took me by surprise, I didn't expect to see you here," she exclaimed.

"I could say the same thing." Fleming's shrewd eyes

went from Betsy to James and back again. "I take it the boy's father hasn't turned up yet?"

"No. I guess he must be held up some place. Though I wonder he hasn't tried to call."

"Have you tried phoning his home?" Fleming asked.

"I didn't think of that!"

Fleming crouched down beside the small boy. James looked at the man in uniform and stopped his kicking.

"What's your father's telephone number?" Fleming asked, in a quiet voice.

James began rummaging in the flight bag he was carrying. He produced a much-creased card and handed it over. Betsy looked at the card as Fleming placed it on the desk counter. It was smeared and crushed now, but originally it had been white and elegantly engraved with the name ANDREW MURRAY. A telephone number was hand-written in large figures under the name.

"Call this number at once," Fleming told the girl.

After dialing several times, the girl said; "Sorry, sir, there's no reply."

"James, is your father usually at his home address on Monday morning?" Fleming inquired.

"Yes. Um—yes, if he didn't go away for the weekend."

"Keep trying the number," Fleming told the girl. To Betsy, he said, "I guess the guy must be held up in traffic. Though why he doesn't call, is beyond me."

They spoke quietly, not wanting James to hear their speculations.

"Hell, this fog has been bad locally all night. You'd think he could have made allowances and started out earlier. Or arranged for a message."

Betsy recognized anger in Fleming's voice.

"Leaving the kid to wait like this . . . It isn't right . . ."

Out of the corner of her eye, Betsy saw that James had gone back to kicking the counter. She didn't have the heart to tell him to stop. She didn't want the boy to be upset by Fleming's anger, either.

"How come you're here, Captain?" she asked, trying to divert the discussion. "Is there something you have to do here? I thought you were going to the hotel with the others."

Fleming's mouth tightened.

"I was—then you mentioned the boy. I figured it might

91

be a good idea for me to see what was going on. I just had a hunch—that's all."

"No good pilot ever dismisses a hunch," Betsy said, quoting an airline maxim. "But you don't have to feel responsible, I can look after the boy until . . ."

"Don't tell me what I'm responsible for!"

Betsy started. Fleming gave a rueful grin.

"Sorry, Betsy, I guess I'm angry at this guy and it sort of rubbed off on you! All the same, I do feel responsible. I was responsible for the child while we were in flight—now I don't feel like walking away and leaving him when we're on the ground. I don't care who else is around to take charge, it simply doesn't feel right."

"My sentiments, exactly," Betsy murmured. She knew that she was not responsible for the boy's welfare any longer, either. That still did not permit her to feel justified in handing him over to yet another temporary guardian.

"He's being tossed around like an unwanted package," she said, "it's not right. Someone has to stick with him and care what happens."

"Don't worry," Fleming said, "that's exactly what we're going to do."

14

It was cold and damp on the outdoor observation deck, but it was the one place that interested James. The fog had lifted sufficiently to allow normal traffic and the boy stared out over the airfield, watching planes landing and taking off, asking endless questions.

Captain Fleming patiently supplied the answers in a kind of running technical commentary. Both Fleming and the boy seemed oblivious to the chill.

Behind them, Betsy stamped her feet and walked briskly back and forth in an attempt to keep warm. She pulled her fur hat down and the collar of her cape up, and still shivered.

Funny, she thought, the male disregard for physical comfort when involved in some specifically male pursuit. Such as watching planes. Or playing football. Betsy kept walking and stamping. It all reminded her of the times she had put up with similar discomforts in order to watch Jay Marshall play on the college football team.

"Come and see!" James called out.

Betsy moved over to the rail.

"A 747 just landed," James said. "Did you see it?"

"Oh yes, sure."

"You can wait inside if you prefer," Fleming put in, with an amused smile.

"But there's nothing interesting inside!" James exclaimed.

Fleming laughed and gave Betsy a quizzical look.

"I guess I'll keep you two company," Betsy said. "If I go back into the warmth I might fall asleep."

But Fleming was already pointing out another plane. "Look, James, the one just coming in on Runway ten left . . ."

It seemed as though they spent hours on the observation deck. Betsy was surprised at the patience Fleming showed, in the way he treated James. Yet perhaps it wasn't a question of patience, she thought. He seemed to be really enjoying himself, talking to the boy and explaining things. He was more relaxed than she had seen him before.

When, after what seemed an age, Fleming said: "Come along, everybody inside, that's enough for one day," Betsy remarked quietly, "You certainly helped take his mind off the fact that his father hasn't turned up to collect him. I think he's glad of the wait, now."

Fleming shrugged, made no answer.

"Do you have children of your own?" Betsy asked. "You act like you're used to . . ."

But before she could finish her sentence, Fleming said "No!" in a curt tone that cut off further discussion.

He *is* touchy about anything that might be regarded as personal, Betsy thought; no wonder he has a reputation for being a loner.

James announced: "I have to go to the bathroom."

"Right over there," Betsy told him. "We'll wait for you."

As soon as the boy was out of earshot, Fleming said, "I'm going along to the office to tell them to check with the police, on all accidents. Something must have happened to the boy's father. He couldn't possibly have forgotten. And even if he had, there should be an answer from his home phone. The fog has lifted considerably now, so traffic holdups can't be the reason for the delay any more. I've got a feeling this has to be an accident case."

"Oh, no!"

"Accidents happen all the time." Fleming's face bore its tense lines again, his mouth was set.

"Poor James, he seems such a bad-luck kid."

"I agree with you there. And I, for one, have had enough of seeing the kid kept waiting and wondering. It's time to put a stop to it. I'm going to have the accident check made. We'll wait a while longer, to see if there are any results. If nothing comes through, we'll think again."

"It's weird. I don't begin to understand how all this could happen."

"Like I said, an accident would explain everything. This morning was a logical time for it to happen. Thick fog, heavy traffic on the road, a man trying to hurry to get to the airport . . ."

Betsy shook her head in mute protest.

"That's the way it goes, whether you like it or not." There was a steely quality in Fleming's voice. "It's better to face the worst."

"I guess you're right. Oh—here he comes."

To James, Betsy said: "Captain Fleming has to go on up to the office, on business. We'll go get ourselves a hot drink, okay?"

"I don't want a hot drink! I don't want anything." James glared defiantly. His face was pale now and his fair hair lay damp against his head.

For the first time, the small boy looked close to tears. He muttered, in a fierce little voice: "I'm tired. I want to go home."

Fleming bent down and seized hold of James. With one swift movement he swung the boy up onto his shoulders. Striding along the airport corridor, he said, "You are going to do what Betsy says, young man. First thing, you both have a hot drink. Captain's orders, you understand? Then you keep out of mischief and wait for me. Everyone got that?"

"Yessir!" Betsy said.

"Yes—sir," James echoed.

Thank God Fleming decided to stay around, Betsy thought. I don't know how I would have managed the child without his help. He really is great with kids. It's so unexpected. She glanced up at Fleming, and smiled. The captain's face remained grave.

James was persuaded to drink some hot tea, English style, with plenty of milk and sugar in it. Betsy tried to get him to eat as well, but the boy refused all suggestions of food. Betsy drank more black coffee. The airport coffee was not the world's best but she told herself that it should at least help combat the tiredness that was beginning to creep over her again.

Without thinking, Betsy gave a huge yawn. She became aware that James was watching her with a worried expression.

"I'm sleepy, it's always like this after a flight," Betsy said.

"Didn't you sleep on the plane?" James wanted to know. "I thought everyone did."

"The crew members don't—it's against regulations."

"Why?"

"Because we're on the plane to work, not to sleep. And it's our job to look after people while *they* are sleeping."

"But supposing you're very tired?"

"You shouldn't be very tired. You see, we know what time we are going to start work and so we sleep during the day, so's to be fresh for the night-flight."

Betsy glanced at her watch.

James looked at the watch, then he stared up at the airport clock.

"You haven't changed the time," he said, reprovingly. "I changed my watch when you told us to, on the plane." He held out his wrist and displayed a gold watch, set to the right local time.

"We don't change our time," Betsy explained. "We stay on New York time while we are over here."

"Why?"

"Because we're scheduled to go home tomorrow. There isn't time for us to adjust to European time. It's easier to stay as we are, for a short period like twenty-four hours."

"I see." James appeared to be giving the matter careful thought. After a while, he asked, "What time will you go back tomorrow?"

"Our return flight is scheduled for tomorrow afternoon, just about the time you'll be having more English tea."

A voice sounded behind her. "I'm afraid that's not so."

Betsy jumped at the sudden interruption. Fleming was standing beside them.

"I've just gotten a long-range weather forecast," he said, "and it looks like more fog on the way. I stopped off in Operations and they said there's a distinct possibility of a change in schedule. There's bad weather all over Europe, and there may be a hold-up of equipment. You know how it goes. We should know definitely what's going to happen by this evening."

"What about—the other thing?" Betsy asked, keeping her voice low.

"All under way. We should hear something soon."

Time crawled. James fell asleep, lying on a bench. Betsy covered him with his coat.

"He must be exhausted," she told Fleming, "he didn't sleep much on the way over."

"You must be pretty exhausted, yourself."

Betsy was aware of Fleming's keen gaze on her face. She looked at him. The steady gaze made her feel slightly uncomfortable.

"It's a long wait," she murmured.

"Too damn long. If I get to meet this boy's father, I plan telling him a few home-truths."

"You must be tired, too."

"We should both be at the hotel, catching up on our rest. And James should be at home, where he belongs. But I'm not going to let this situation drag on much longer. Enough is enough. Ten more minutes, and if there's still no news of any kind, we go into town to the hotel."

"What about James?"

"If his father hasn't turned up, he comes with us, if he wants to."

Betsy blinked. "I don't know that the company will go for that."

Fleming passed a weary hand over his forehead. "Betsy, I don't give a goddam what the company will go for, I'm not letting this kid be tossed around any more. If there's nowhere else for him to go, he stays with us."

Fleming made his words come true. The Director of Passenger Relations and several other company functionaries who felt themselves concerned in the matter of James Murray, uncollected child passenger, found themselves listening to what Captain Fleming had to say.

"It's not your responsibility or Miss Blair's," one executive said. "We will provide a qualified nurse, a hotel room if necessary, every care will be taken."

"Much as we respect your devotion to duty, of course," put in a smarmy character from company personnel.

"It's not devotion to duty, it's plain concern for a child!" Fleming snapped. "The boy doesn't need a *nurse*. He's not sick! He needs someone to care what happens to him."

Listening to the argument, Betsy thought, Fleming speaks with such conviction, almost passion. Surely, he must have children of his own, to care like this? It was hard to imagine a man without a family arguing so fiercely for a child. In the end, Fleming had the last word.

"We are going to the hotel. The boy comes with us. You can phone the hotel now and tell them to have the extra room ready."

"But supposing Mr. Murray arrives at the airport in the meantime and the boy isn't here?" wailed the Passenger Relations man.

"Listen to me." The captain's eyes were icy, the tone sharp and hard. "We have waited far too long already for this man to turn up. If he is so late in coming to pick up his son, then one of two things applies: either he doesn't give a damn, in which case, I don't give a damn for him either, or else there's been an accident. In the event of an accident, which presupposes Mr. Murray can't get to the airport personally after all, as long as the boy is safe and his whereabouts are given to his father, it doesn't matter too much exactly what the location of those whereabouts is."

Eventually, a demoralized Passenger Relations department behind them, with executives moaning about "legal responsibilities" and other things the captain had swept aside, Betsy, Fleming and James were promised a car to take them to the hotel.

"I have to make a phone call," Fleming announced suddenly. "I'd almost forgotten."

He strode off. Betsy saw that he went to the pay-phones in the public lounge instead of returning to the company offices. Did he simply want to avoid any more hassles with company executives, she wondered? Or was he making a very private call?

"I don't want to stay with a *nurse*," James was saying, "that's silly. I'm not a *baby*."

"Well, they meant a person who could look after you properly. Not a baby-nurse."

"I don't want anyone like that."

Through the glass-panelled door of the phone booth, Betsy could see the captain in profile. She saw him throw back his head and laugh.

"I'm glad I'm staying with you. And with Captain

Fleming." James' voice brought Betsy's attention back again.

"We're glad to have you with us," she said. She reached out and put her arm round the boy's shoulders. Instead of protesting at such baby treatment, as he had done on a former occasion, the boy leaned against her arm. He was looking tired; his face had a pinched expression.

Betsy noted the signs of fatigue, but a corner of her mind was still registering the way Fleming had thrown back his head and laughed. She had not seen him laugh like that before. A few minutes before, he had been in no mood for hilarity. Who could change his mood so quickly, get through that stern exterior with a few words on the telephone?

I'd give a lot to know, Betsy thought. Then, swiftly, she corrected herself. No, perhaps she wasn't so anxious to know, after all.

15

Betsy woke with the heaviness of insufficient sleep, looked at her watch on the night table and decided she had better make an effort. By the sounds coming from the bathroom, Linda was taking a shower. Getting ready, no doubt, for dinner and the evening; Betsy closed her eyes again and wished she could sleep the night through.

But no. It would be better to get up for a while, eat something, and then return to bed. She sat up and stretched, hoping movement would help her wake up.

The sounds of running water stopped and in a few moments, Linda appeared from the bathroom, draped in a bed-sheet.

"Oh, you're awake," she remarked. "I thought maybe you'd sleep right through."

"No, but I feel the temptation." Betsy stretched again and swung her legs out of bed. "Wow—but I'm exhausted . . ."

"I told you not to waste your time on that kid," Linda observed. "You look pooped. Well, I suppose you think it was worth it. When did poppa finally turn up to collect his little boy?"

"He didn't. We've still got the little boy. He's right here in the hotel."

"Oh, for chrissake . . ."

Betsy watched as Linda crossed the room. The other girl was known never to pack either a nightdress or a robe in her luggage. She slept nude and mostly, she walked around nude. If she wore anything at all, then it was a sheet from the bed. Betsy could not help but admire the skill Linda had acquired in draping the sheet around herself, she ended up looking glamorous. If I did that, Betsy thought, I'd look as if I were rehearsing for a ghost routine . . .

Briefly, Betsy recounted what had happened at the airport during the day.

"Captain Fleming stayed with you all the time?" Linda asked, in amazement. "What was there in it for him?"

"He stayed because he felt he should!" Betsy retorted. She went on: "He's certainly different from the way I had imagined. I figured him for a real cool character. But he was so concerned for James, you should have seen him. He fought for the kid, too. The Passenger Service people wanted James fixed up with a professional nurse, the whole bit, but Fleming said if the boy wanted to stay with us, then he should stay with us, and that was the end of the argument."

"Sounds like Captain Fleming impressed more than the Passenger Service people," Linda commented.

Betsy ignored the barb; she gave a huge yawn. "I'm so tired."

"You were stuck at the airport for *hours*, it's no wonder. What are you going to do now—sleep?"

"No, I'll get up and have dinner first."

"You'll be eating about the same time as the rest of us, then."

"Linda . . ." Betsy propped herself up on one elbow. "Fleming really has a way with kids. It was kind of unexpected. Does he have family of his own?"

Linda let the sheet drop back onto the bed. Betsy saw that the other girl was more than slender, she was becoming downright thin. Her ribs and hip bones showed clearly through the pale skin.

"Fleming doesn't have any family," Linda replied. "He's a loner in private life, as well. So far as anyone can find out, that is."

"He's not married?"

"Nope. You see. . ."

Linda's reply was interrupted by a knocking at the door, and James' voice calling, "Betsy! Betsy!"

101

"Darn." Linda grabbed the bedsheet again and wrapped it around her.

"Just a minute, I'm coming," Betsy called. She grabbed for her cape which lay untidily on a chair with all the rest of her uniform clothes, and slipped into it.

"What is it, James?"

"He can come in, I'm respectable," Linda called out.

James stepped into the room, looking about him, round-eyed.

"I wondered—where you were," the boy said. "I sat on the bed, but then I woke up and I wasn't sure what was happening. I mean, I didn't know if I was asleep ... I came to see ..." his voice trailed off, uncertainly.

Betsy was alarmed by the child's pallor and state of confusion.

"Back to your room," she said, steering James through the door. "Maybe I should put you straight to bed and order some food from room service."

By the time they were in James' room however, the boy seemed to have recovered some of his usual aplomb.

"I don't *want* to go to bed now," he announced. "I want to have dinner downstairs, with the grownups."

"Okay." Betsy went into the bathroom. "I'll run the bathwater for you. Can you bathe yourself all right?"

"Of course I can!"

"Then while you're having your bath, I'll go back and get showered and dressed. Then I'll call for you and we'll go down to dinner together. How does that sound?"

James looked thoughtful.

"Don't worry." Betsy knelt beside the boy. "I'll only be a few doors away if you need anything."

Back in her own room Betsy went straight to the shower. She let the water rush over her, first as hot as she could bear it, then cool, finishing off with a brisk cold spray. Her tiredness seemed to run off her body with the water. She rubbed cologne over her skin and felt refreshed. When she returned to the bedroom Linda was dressed and putting the final touches on her makeup.

"Going out this evening?" Betsy enquired.

Linda grimaced. "I doubt it. It looks like it's shaping up to be a dull trip. But I keep hoping." She stuck a row of false lashes on one eyelid with the precision of long practise.

"I thought you were planning to see Carl," Betsy said.

"So did I!" Linda gave a hard laugh. "He was talking about going out to dinner. But just before you got here, he called me and said he 'has' to go out some place. I guess that means he has another date lined up. Which leaves me stuck here, all by myself. God, I *hate* being left alone for the evening."

Betsy watched as Linda applied the second strip of lashes, admiring the deft way the delicate job was done. Betsy had tried wearing false lashes but she could never get them to stick on straight. She had ended up looking squint-eyed, instead of like a sultry beauty, I guess I'm not the sultry type, she thought. Linda was, though. Even now that she was looking tired and a mite too thin, she still had a kind of glamour.

Linda was saying in a sharp tone:

"I guess you're glad that Carl ratted on me. You were so concerned over your precious roommate and her affair with him. . . ."

"No, really, I. . ."

But Linda was not listening. "If it's any satisfaction to you, I get the impression he stood me up deliberately."

"Surely not! You're so ready to see insults, all the time."

Linda brushed mascara over the false lashes.

"You're better off without him," Betsy said, "he's not exactly reliable. I don't know what you girls see in him."

"Oh, for heavens' sake—stop talking like Dear Abby!" Linda retorted. "And for your information, Carl *is* good-looking, has charm—and he *is* single."

Betsy gave up the argument and applied her attention to brushing her hair.

The door slammed and Linda was gone. Betsy put the hairbrush down and regarded herself in the mirror. A month of working and sharing hotel rooms with Linda was not going to be much fun, she thought. But then the way things were shaping up, this trip wasn't much fun in any respect.

Not for young James, certainly. For herself—well, she felt badly on account of the small boy, and she was having trouble with Linda. On the other hand—Betsy did not entirely regret the time spent waiting at the airport. Getting to know David Fleming had been intriguing. She was sure that had things not turned out the way they had, she would never have had the chance to know him at all. He was by nature an intensely reserved man, and it took something like a child in trouble, to bring out his real character.

Linda had said that he wasn't married. She had been going to say more, Betsy remembered, when James had interrupted. She supposed that meant Fleming was divorced. At his age, it would be unlikely he was unmarried. Funny, though; she found it hard to think of him as divorced. He didn't seem the type.

Fleming's last words to her as they parted company in the hotel lobby, had been: "I'll see you and the boy at dinner."

Betsy glanced at the clock, gave an exclamation, hurried with her dressing. She tied a wide scarf around her head, letting her hair flow down her back. She made a final examination in the mirror. Her skin looked all right, she couldn't be bothered to use anything other than a trace of foundation. At the last minute, she decided to apply mascara to her thick lashes. A quick spray of duty-free perfume, and she was ready. She hurried out and along the corridor to see how James was getting on. He was ready, and they went downstairs.

The hotel dining-room was almost empty. Betsy stood in the entrance-way, looking for Fleming.

"Oh!" The exclamation broke from her lips before she could suppress it.

"What's the matter?" James asked.

"Nothing." Betsy could feel the color rising in her face. She stared at Fleming, feeling both angry and resentful. He was seated at a small table in a corner of the room. Across the table from him sat Linda.

Trying to appear completely unconcerned, Betsy took James' hand and walked with him away from the captain's direction. At a larger table on the other side of the room, Johnson was sitting alone.

"Mind if we join you?" Betsy asked.

"A pleasure, sweetheart. Who's your beau?"

Johnson was on his feet, holding Betsy's chair, shaking James' hand, introducing himself to the boy.

"Where is everybody?" Betsy looked around the dining-room. "Where are the other girls, and Rudi?"

"I gather the girls have plans for seeing the town. Rudi disappeared on highly mysterious 'business.' I'm beginning to wonder if our Rudi isn't a spy in disguise. Like, the James Bond of the air. Young Carl is out, presumably getting laid. Oops, sorry, shouldn't have said that in front of the kid. I'm not used to kids." Johnson looked abashed.

"That's all right. I know how grown-ups talk," James said.

"Do you, now?" Johnson's eyebrows shot up.

Betsy could not help glancing at Fleming's table. Linda was talking and the captain seemed to be engrossed in what she was saying.

"That's an interesting combination," Johnson said, seeing the direction of Betsy's gaze. "When I got down to the dining-room, David was already here. I went to join him, but he told me he was expecting company. I can take a hint, so I moved off. Then Linda turned up, made a beeline for our handsome captain and *voilà*—a brand new friendship was born."

Betsy made a point of showing James the menu, explaining what he might have.

"As a matter of fact, I was surprised when Linda joined him," Johnson went on, "I'd figured he was waiting for you."

"Really? I can't think why."

After the waiter had taken their orders, Johnson asked James: "Is this your first visit to London?"

"Oh no, I've been here before. My father lives here."

Betsy saw the puzzled expression on the pilot's face. Johnson was well-meaning, she thought, but tactless to a fault. The last thing she wanted was Johnson upsetting the boy with references to his missing father. She kicked Johnson's leg under the table, in warning. The pilot said "Ow!" and then, "What have I done this time?"

Betsy smiled at him sweetly. "Nothing yet. To make sure you don't *upset* anybody, don't ask too many questions."

"You girls have no respect," Johnson grumbled, "you wouldn't kick David, that's for sure!"

"I don't know about that," Betsy muttered. Turning to James, she said: "Mr. Johnson is our First Officer. He'll be happy to tell you anything you want to know about planes, and flying."

Johnson leaned toward James, a confidential grin on his face.

"You want to hear the real truth about co-pilots?" he asked in a conspiratorial whisper. "Well, don't tell anyone I told you, but—we're all really trained monkeys. In disguise, of course, co-pilot's disguise," he added with dignity. "They zip us into our suits, and tell us 'Monkey see, monkey do.' And so that's just what we do; whatever the captain says—ours is that nice man over there . . ."

"I know him," James said.

"Do you indeed?" Johnson's heavy eyebrows raised in admiration. "Well, he's the big boss, and after he leads me up front to my seat. . ."

Betsy hardly listened to the words that followed. She toyed with her food, her mind an angry turmoil. Fleming had seemed so concerned about James. And he had definitely indicated that they would have dinner together. Betsy was sure James had been looking forward to it. He had taken a liking to the captain. She couldn't understand how Fleming could have a tete-a-tete dinner with Linda instead, without so much as a word of explanation.

"Isn't it, Betsy?"

She surfaced from her jumble of thoughts. "What?"

"I was explaining to this young man that it's really lunch-time for us. It's evening here, but back home it's mid-day. We stay on New York time while we're away, it's easier."

"I know that already," James stated. "Betsy and the Captain told me about it."

"Looks as if something is happening," Johnson commented, nodding his head in Fleming's direction.

Betsy looked up in time to see Fleming striding out of the room.

"The waiter brought a message, looked like he was wanted on the phone," Johnson said. "Guess it's Operations, about equipment."

Betsy could feel her heart thumping. Supposing it was news for James. Would it be good or bad? Supposing the police enquiries Fleming had insisted upon had led to news of an accident? She looked at James, who was busily

106

spooning up ice cream, and for a moment she could not speak.

"He's a cagey character," Johnson was remarking, "but a great guy when you get to know him."

"Who?"

"David. David Fleming."

"Have you known him long?" Betsy asked.

"Years. He's one of the best. He's had a rough ride, but he comes through everything on sheer guts."

Betsy supposed Johnson was talking about Fleming's professional experiences as a pilot. This prompted her to inquire:

"Why is he flying this route? He's a senior pilot, but this isn't a senior route."

Johnson grinned and shrugged. "I daresay David has his reasons. That's not to say he's going to tell anyone what they are. But you'll find he rarely does anything without a darn good reason for doing it."

"Must be something special, for him to accept this junior trip."

"I doubt he *accepted* it, he must have *asked* for it."

"Do you have any idea why?"

Johnson gave an elaborate wink. *"Cherchez la femme,"* he said, grinning foolishly.

It was no use expecting sense from Johnson, he was a specialist in silly answers, Betsy thought crossly. She looked across the room. Fleming had not yet returned and Linda sat alone at the small table. On impulse, Betsy stood up.

"Come along," she told James, "we're going to wait for Captain Fleming and see if he has any news for us."

"You haven't had your coffee," Johnson protested.

"I don't want any, thanks."

Linda's greeting was not enthusiastic.

"Oh, it's you," she said, as Betsy pulled a third chair up to the table.

"Right the first time," Betsy replied.

The girls glared at each other. James said: "May I have more ice cream?"

"No," Betsy snapped. "You've eaten more than enough. You'll be sick if you have any more."

James was so surprised by the sharpness of Betsy's reply that he accepted her words without protest.

"Wasn't Larry good enough company for you?" Linda asked, looking sulky.

"He was very sweet. He made James laugh a lot."

"I always knew that his jokes were meant for six-year-olds," Linda muttered.

"I decided we should wait for Captain Fleming, to see if he has any news for us. We might as well wait here—unless you're telling me that we're not *allowed* at this table."

Linda did not reply. She lit a cigarette and blew a long stream of smoke into the air.

Suddenly, Fleming was back at the table.

"What news?" Betsy asked, anxiously.

"Good news," he said. Addressing James directly, he went on: "Your father has telephoned the company to say that he has been—uh—unavoidably delayed—that was why he couldn't get to the airport—but now he's back in London."

"Can I go home now?" James was all attention, the bright blue eyes fixed hopefully on Fleming.

"When your father was told that you had been brought to this hotel he—uh—he said that you could go home in the morning. He said that would be more convenient. He's sending the car for you tomorrow."

"Why? Why not now?"

"It seems that your father had a small mishap ... nothing serious ... but I understand he was thrown by a horse. He's home now, resting. It'll be better for you to go home in the morning, son."

James nodded, his head drooping. He was silent for a while, then he looked up at Betsy.

"*Now* can I have more ice cream?" he asked.

"You're sure it's not serious," Betsy queried the captain, "about Mr. Murray's accident, I mean."

"No, the guy I spoke to said that Murray himself spoke on the phone and he sounded okay." Fleming signalled to a waiter. "Bring some more ice cream for this young man," he said.

Linda said, in a sulky tone, "Now that all the excitement is over, maybe we can all relax and think about something else for a change."

Fleming's clear eyes stared at Linda, who stared back

108

at him, defiantly. He turned his gaze to Betsy. Despite herself, she felt the color creeping up her face.

"I'm glad ... it's all working out," was all she could think of to say.

"One other thing," Fleming said. "While I was on the blower to the company, they confirmed that our layover has been extended by a day. Operations have had to do some re-scheduling due to bad weather and lack of equipment. We're scheduled out the day after tomorrow at 9 a.m. That'll give you girls time to shop to your hearts' content. Have fun!"

Fleming stood up. Linda asked, in surprise: "Do you have to rush away?"

"Yes. I have an appointment. Now that I know the boy is okay, I'll be getting along. See you tomorrow."

He patted James on the shoulder, said "Goodnight, son, sleep well," turned abruptly on his heel and strode out of the room.

"That's great!" Linda muttered.

"What's the matter?" Betsy asked.

"Don't play innocent with me." Linda's eyes were flashing fury. "You came over deliberately to break things up. Well, it looks like you've succeeded—and I hope you're satisfied."

"Ssssh," Betsy warned, glancing towards James.

"I'm not going to hush up on account of the kid! You seem to think that everyone is your personal property. First, you acted offended because I get friendly with Carl, then you bust in on Fleming and me. . . ."

"Fleming and you?" Betsy echoed.

"And why not?" Linda demanded, her voice high with anger. "He's a free man, isn't he? Why shouldn't he and I get along together? Have you got *him* marked down as your personal property, too?"

Betsy got up from the table, her face flushed. "Come along, James," she said. "Time for bed."

"I don't want to go to bed. . . ."

Ignoring the protests, Betsy said to Linda: "I think you're over-wrought. What you need is a good night's rest."

For a wild moment, Betsy actually thought that Linda might throw something at her. Then the tension seemed to pass and Linda's shoulders dropped. She sat staring down at the table.

"But I don't want to go to bed," James was still whining.

Betsy took his hand and almost dragged him out of the dining-room.

"If you want, you can watch TV for a while," she promised. "How about that?"

An hour later, Betsy closed the door of James' room behind her. The boy was tucked up in bed, one lamp left lighted so that he would not be frightened if he woke during the night. James had been so docile about going to bed that Betsy suspected he planned to get up and turn the TV on again, as soon as he figured she was out of earshot. She just hoped he wouldn't watch a program that would give him nightmares.

When she reached her own room she found all the lights on, the radio blaring, and the air heavy with wafts of perfume. Linda looked quite different than she had at dinner; she was wearing a blonde wig and had changed into a black pantsuit.

"Are you going out?" Betsy asked.

Linda smiled, said "Yes" and went back to applying blusher to her cheekbones. She seemed very pleased with life, apparently having quite forgotten the angry words that had passed between her and Betsy a short while before.

Betsy had an uncomfortable thought: could Linda be going out with David Fleming? Trying to sound casual, she asked:

"Who are you going with? I thought you were complaining about being left alone tonight."

"Carl called and said he was free after all. His plans had changed, or something. So we're going out on the town."

Betsy blinked. "I see," she said. "Carl. But he practically stood you up only a while ago—you said yourself you thought it was deliberate!"

"Hmmm." Linda regarded herself in the mirror, tilting her head at various angles. Then she turned round, seized her purse, said "Bye, don't bother to wait up for me," and headed for the door.

"Hey," said Betsy, "wait a minute! Linda—how can you let Carl pick you up again so easily, after what happened? Honestly, haven't you got any pride?"

Linda paused in the open doorway, facing Betsy. There was a strange expression on her face.

"No—I guess I don't have much," she said. She gave a brilliant smile, and was gone.

"Come and join the family breakfast table," Larry Johnson said, waving cheerily. "How did you sleep, young man?"

"All right, thank you," James replied.

Betsy sat down beside the boy. "What do you want for breakfast? Do you like cereal?" she asked.

There was a groan from Rudi, who sat at the table looking paler than ever, sipping black coffee.

"Debauched again," Johnson announced, jerking a thumb in Rudi's direction. "He goes green, every time someone mentions the word 'breakfast.' He almost swooned clean away when I ordered three courses. Personally, I think one of the benefits of this trip is the chance to enjoy a real English breakfast. I started with Scotch porridge, then I had kippers, now I'm finishing up with toast and Oxford marmalade. Very civilized."

With a look that was pure poison, Rudi picked up his coffee cup and moved away to a small table where he sat down alone with his back towards his fellow crew-members.

"He believes in a three-course breakfast, too," Johnson told young James, in a stage whisper. "Do you know what it is?"

"What?" James asked obediently.

"A cigarette, a cup of coffee and a good cough." The pilot laughed heartily at his joke. James smiled politely.

"Larry," Betsy warned, "not everyone can face your jokes so early in the morning."

"Hi, James, hi, Betsy!" Fleming appeared at the table and sat down next to Johnson. He looked round. "Where are the others?"

"Rudi's having the vapors in the corner," Johnson said. "What he gets up to that leaves him in that state in the morning, I hate to think. The two junior stews were down here at crack of dawn. I gather that the extended layover has led to wild plans for sightseeing. That accounts for everyone—except Carl and Linda." With heavy sarcasm, Johnson added: "I hardly think we need call in Sherlock Holmes to figure out why those two haven't yet appeared . . ."

He looked enquiringly at Betsy but she smiled blandly back at him, giving nothing away, and busied herself ordering her and James' breakfasts.

After he had disposed of his third slice of toast and his fourth cup of coffee, Johnson announced himself fit for the day. Fleming asked, "Off on the gourmet trail again? Eating your way round London?"

"I may sample some of the local cuisine." Johnson frowned. "If I have the time and energy, that is. My wife has given me a shopping list as long as my arm. Just *reading* it is hard work. I shall definitely need sustenance at frequent intervals throughout the day if I'm to get to the end of it."

"Very sensible of Myra to give you something constructive to do," Fleming commented. "All that activity might even get your weight down."

"Why don't you come along? With two of us, we could finish off the goddam shopping pretty fast, then dump the stuff and go have ourselves some fun . . ."

"No thanks." Fleming shook his head. "I'm booked up today."

"I'm never appreciated, wherever I am." Johnson leaned across the table and extended a large hand to James. "Pleased to have made your acquaintance, young man. Remember, next time you're on Flightways, ask if Larry Johnson's up front. I'll show you the cockpit, give you a flying lesson if you like!"

After Johnson had made his noisy departure, Fleming smiled at Betsy. "The kid looks none the worse for his adventures," he said. "You've done a good job, taking care of him."

Betsy smiled and poured herself some tea. She noticed that Fleming was sticking to his usual black coffee.

"A car will be sent to the hotel to pick the boy up, according to the office. Around ten-thirty," he went on.

"Is his father coming for him?"

Fleming shook his head, making a small grimace. "I was given to understand that the chauffeur would take charge of James."

The boy had obviously been listening to the conversation because he piped up suddenly: "It will have to be the chauffeur. My father can't drive now. He lost his license, I think. My mother said something about it."

The captain's shrewd eyes rested on the boy for a moment. Then he turned to Betsy. "Look, I don't know what plans you have for today—but I figure it'd be a good idea for you to take the boy all the way home. After what has just been said, I feel *sure* it would be a good idea ..."

Before Betsy could answer, James broke in: "Please, Betsy, come home with me. I want you to."

"What can I say?" She shrugged in mock-surrender. "The decision seems to be unanimous ..."

"James, would you go find the waiter for me?" Fleming asked. "I need more coffee and the guy seems to have disappeared." As soon as the boy left the table, he bent towards Betsy and said quietly: "This is confidential. The reason I'm asking you to go with the kid, Betsy, is that I have a nervous feeling about the whole set-up. After the fiasco at the airport yesterday—well, this time, I'd like to know the kid is truly and safely home. If you go with him, then at least we'll know that he really is with his father. Who sounds less and less like a father all the time ..."

"Yes, of course I will."

"I trust you, Betsy, I trust your sense. God knows, that kid needs someone like you around, someone he can rely on."

Betsy looked up, with a feeling of happiness—and saw Linda sitting down at the table, right opposite her.

"Hi, everybody!" Linda smiled sweetly in Fleming's direction. "It's kind of nice to have an extra day to relax in, isn't it?"

James came back to the table, followed by a waiter bearing coffee.

"Are you going home today?" Linda asked the little boy.

"Yes. Betsy is coming with me."

"That's nice." Linda spooned sugar into her coffee, then gulped down the black mixture. "Now I feel more human," she remarked.

Fleming was looking thoughtfully at Linda. He said, slowly, as if choosing his words: "Linda—I wonder if you would mind going along with James and Betsy? I've been explaining to Betsy that I would be easier in my mind if I knew for sure that he got home okay. With the two of you along there's be no room for doubt at all."

The two girls spoke simultaneously.

"I can manage fine by myself . . ." Betsy began.

"Oh, I was planning to . . ." Linda started.

"Listen to me, girls." Fleming was speaking in an authoritative manner. "This isn't an order, you don't have to go if you don't want to. However, I believe it would be in the boy's best interests if you went with him. Remember, you are representing Flightways while you're over here . . ."

"Okay." Linda gave a sulky pout.

"Good, that's settled. Let me know how it goes, won't you?" Fleming stood up, said a special goodbye to James, nodded to the girls, and quickly left the dining-room.

"Of all the nerve," Linda muttered. "I have a million things to do and he starts giving orders on rest time!"

Betsy said nothing. She was struggling to maintain her composure. It had been a shock to her, when Fleming had insisted on including Linda in the morning's activities.

She felt it meant that Fleming did not trust her. He had to send Linda along too, to make sure everything went all right. *Linda!* Betsy thought resentfully. Hardly the person she would have chosen for reliability . . .

Other questions formed in Betsy's mind. If Fleming was really so concerned—why didn't he accompany the boy himself? He said he had things to do. It seemed he had made arrangements that were so important they could not be changed, even over the small boy whose welfare supposedly concerned him much.

Betsy and Linda eyed each other warily across the table.

"The car is coming to pick James up around ten-thirty," Betsy said.

"Oh, that's great!"

Linda lit a cigarette. Betsy turned to James. "Come along, we'll go pack your things," she said.

The boy gave an unusually bright grin, revealing all the gaps in his teeth.

"I'm glad you're coming with me," he announced. "This is going to be a super day."

Linda coughed. Betsy put her hand on James' shoulder as they left the table.

"Of course it is," she said, "of course it is."

17

The poker-faced chauffeur led the way to the highly-polished Rolls-Royce limousine. He held the door while Betsy, James and Linda stepped into the spacious interior.

Linda ran her hand over the smooth leather upholstery. "This is my idea of luxury," she commented.

James was wriggling with excitement, showing his gappy teeth in a happy grin.

"Where do you live?" Linda asked him.

"Belgravia."

"Where's that?"

"Don't bother him," Betsy said. "You'll soon see for yourself."

Linda looked out the window. They were in a busy street lined with department stores whose windows displayed a tempting variety of goods.

"I don't know when I'll get my shopping done," Linda remarked. "Fleming has nerve, ordering us around during our rest time."

"I *wanted* to come," Betsy replied.

I bet you did, you goody-goody-two-shoes, Linda thought. She didn't know why it was, but everything about Betsy irritated her. She seemed so smug, so darned sure of herself. Linda went back to staring out the window. It was a typical London winter morning: grey, damp and chill. The sidewalks were crowded with people in heavy coats, carrying packages and shopping bags.

The car suddenly swung off into a narrow side street,

and they were in a residential area, with tall town-houses on either side of the road.

"Oh, it's so attractive," Betsy exclaimed. "I love all those trees and shrubs—it's so green, for winter!"

"It's so expensive, too," Linda said. "This is one of the most exclusive areas in London, if I'm not mistaken. Is this where you live, James?"

The boy nodded.

The Rolls slid to a silent stop before a large house with a cream-colored stucco facade. The chauffeur opened the door of the limousine and mounted the stairs to the entrance.

"My—home, sweet home," Linda said, looking up at the house. It was an imposing building, with black ornamental wrought iron railings and balconies that contrasted strongly with the cream walls.

"Linda!" Betsy exclaimed.

Linda shrugged. She didn't believe in pretending the house was the kind of place she was used to visiting, when it certainly wasn't. If Betsy wanted to pretend she wasn't impressed, then she could go right ahead.

A man-servant opened the door. The chauffeur murmured something, then hurried back down the steps to the Rolls.

"He can speak, after all," Linda murmured into Betsy's ear, "I thought he was a robot in uniform."

They stepped into a high-ceilinged entrance hall. Linda's immediate impression was a myriad of gleaming surfaces; they were surrounded by polished wood and gilt-edged mirrors.

While the two girls looked about them, James scampered straight up the wide stairway to the second floor.

"Master James!" the servant called, to no effect. The man turned to Linda and Betsy. Solemnly, he said: "I will inform Mr. Murray that you are here. Would you care to take a seat?"

He gestured toward a carved oak settle against the wall. However, before the girls could sit down, James came running pell-mell down the stairs again.

"Come and meet my father," he shouted in excitement, "he's in bed with a 'normous bandage round his head. He wants to see you."

"I can hardly wait to see *him*," Linda murmured.

The servant preceded them up the carpeted stairs. Linda noted the large portraits that hung along the hall at the top of the stairs. Family portraits, she supposed. She wondered what it would be like to see your own ancestors staring down at you from the walls, every time you passed by.

"Come *on*," James called out, "in here!"

Linda saw a man in his mid-forties, sitting up in a big bed. The man had small striking blue eyes and a ruddy complexion. The crown of his head was completely swathed in white bandage. He was studying the girls with considerable interest.

"How nice to have visitors," he said, in a plummy accent. "Do come in—this is exactly the kind of company I need."

He extended a well-manicured hand. Linda thought it seemed strange to be shaking hands with an unknown man who was sitting up in bed, but James' father appeared to find nothing strange about it. Linda felt that the shrewd blue eyes were not missing any detail of her appearance or Betsy's.

"Now that you're here—who *are* you, precisely?"

Linda giggled. Betsy looked surprised.

"James told me your names, but I'm not quite sure . . ."

"You don't remember anything," James put in, crossly. "This is Betsy who looked after me on the plane. She took care of me at the hotel, too."

Mr. Murray took a good look at Betsy and seemed to like what he saw. Then he turned to Linda. "And this lovely young lady?" he enquired, addressing himself to Linda directly.

"My name is Linda Kesnik. Betsy and I are stewardesses with Flightways International," Linda said. "We had your son on board our London flight."

"Lucky boy!"

Murray, Linda thought, had all the attributes of the practiced, middle-aged charmer who didn't realize how passé he had become. It was all there, down to the heavy-handed compliments. She was willing to bet that he was a drinker, too. There was something about the eyes, and the flushed complexion . . . all the symptoms she knew so well . . . She caught sight of a cut-glass decanter and soda syphon standing on a silver tray on the bedside table.

119

An empty but used glass also stood on the tray; the decanter was three-quarters empty. One accurate guess, she told herself.

" . . . and it's most kind of you two girls to escort James home like this," Murray was saying.

"We wanted to be sure that he got home safely, this time." Betsy looked steadily at the man in the bed, as she spoke, with the kind of expression that Linda found intimidating. "It was a very bad experience for James, finding no one had come to meet him at the airport yesterday, and no message to let him know what had happened."

Atta girl, Linda thought. Betsy believed in speaking her mind and in this instance, she showed courage in saying what she did. The house, with its obvious signs of wealth, the man in the bed, who was obviously used to getting his own way, all conspired to overwhelm the visitor from outside. At least Betsy wasn't letting the atmosphere of wealth and privilege throw her. Linda felt a grudging admiration.

Murray did not reply at once, merely lay back on his pillows and looked faintly bored.

"I was told that you were involved in an accident," Betsy persisted.

After a pause, Murray lifted a hand and touched the bandage round his head. "I have a nasty head wound," he said, "which required some stitches. The quack also diagnosed concussion. Well, probable concussion."

"I'm sorry to hear that," Betsy said, in a formal tone.

"How did it happen?" Linda queried.

"I'll try to explain what happened, though it was all very *complicated*." His voice was petulant. "You can't imagine what a *bore* the whole thing was. Anyway, I was at my country place for the weekend . . . went out riding. The damned horse threw me. I took quite a toss, must have lain unconscious for a while. When I came to, I was lying in a field and it was getting dark. Luckily for me, a farmer came across the field. He fetched a cart and took me to his farmhouse, and then went to get the doctor." Murray paused briefly for breath.

"The doctor said I should not be moved. So I stayed the night at the farmhouse. It had no telephone, of course. The next day, the farmer took me back to my own place.

There was a real panic started, by that time. I had been missing over twelve hours . . . no one had the slightest idea where I was. My housekeeper had called in the police the previous night . . . she became alarmed when I didn't return home, but my horse did!"

"Sounds like something out of a movie," Linda said.

"It was pretty dramatic for a while." Murray looked pleased with himself.

"An old thirties movie on TV," Linda added *sotto voce*, so that only Betsy could hear. She saw the signs of a suppressed grin twitching at the corners of Betsy's mouth.

"What with all the panic and my head feeling as though it had been *stamped* on . . . well, it was latish yesterday before I remembered James. I was in pain, you realize . . . my head was giving me merry hell. Then it was a question of getting up to London. I was driven up slowly . . . couldn't phone the airline until I reached town because I didn't have the number at my country place . . ."

Linda watched him, unconvinced of both the seriousness of his injury and his concern for James. After all, he could have gotten the Flightways International phone number from Information, or whatever it was called here in England. Directory Inquiries, yes, that was it. Plummy voice or no plummy voice, Mr. Moneybags Murray had hardly tried very hard to do anything about reaching his son. Until he himself was back in town and comfortably in bed in this mini-palace of his. It always seemed that the wrong people had the money. And all the hired help . . .

The thought of the butler downstairs reminded Linda of something.

"We rang here when we got in from the flight," she told the bandaged man, recalling Betsy's description of the Flightways ground girl dialing the number handwritten on the card in James' possession, only to get no answer. "And no one answered the phone . . ."

She let her sentence hang between them, accusingly. Andrew Murray looked surprised.

"You did?" he puzzled. Then his face cleared. "Ah, I know. You must have used the number on that card that James has . . ."

"Yes, that's right," Betsy confirmed.

"My private number," the man in the bed explained with a dismissing wave of the hand. "The servants *never*

121

answer that telephone. I'm the only person who does. There's another line for *ordinary* use. I suppose you'd better have that, too, James." He glanced at his son.

Linda realized from Betsy's tense attitude that the other girl was reacting the same way she was to Murray's story. She wondered if Betsy would say something. However, Betsy kept silent, and Linda didn't blame her. Instinct warned that it would be unwise to speak too bluntly to Murray, he was the kind of man who lived as he pleased and didn't take reproofs from anybody.

James was hopping about the room, very excited.

"Do be quiet and keep still," Murray said, putting a hand to his head. "You don't do a thing to improve my condition. My headache is getting worse by the minute."

"I'm afraid we must be tiring you, Mr. Murray," Betsy said. "We really shall have to leave now."

"Please—don't go just yet." A smooth, much practised smile appeared on his ruddy face.

"We don't want to bother you, Mr. Murray," Linda said. In spite of her effort to be formally polite, she could not quite keeping the mocking tone out of her voice.

The small blue eyes looked reproachfully at Linda. "Company makes me feel *better*," he said. "The company of pretty girls that is."

"Mr. Murray, I really think we ought to go." Betsy looked determined, now.

"Don't keep saying 'Mr. Murray'—call me Andrew, for God's sake."

"Well, much as we'd like to stay, we both have a lot to do," Betsy said. "Don't we, Linda?"

"Ah—yes, I suppose so." Linda was making mental calculations. She needed time for shopping, of course. On the other hand, she didn't see why they had to rush away so soon, when Murray was making friendly overtures. She hated to waste an opportunity and Andrew Murray was the only really rich man she had met in an age.

"Stay and have lunch with me," he was suggesting. "What do you say to that—Betsy, Linda?"

"Perhaps ..." Linda began, but she was interrupted immediately by Betsy, who held out her hand, decidedly: "I'm sorry, but we must get along."

"You too?" The blue eyes held Linda's gaze.

She wavered for a moment. As though he sensed her

dilemma, Murray murmured: "Perhaps you would be good enough to spare some of your precious time to visit me on another occasion? When I'm more in a condition to play host. I should be delighted to see you any time you're free."

Linda smiled and inclined her head non-committally. They said their goodbyes and all shook hands again.

"Don't forget—you must visit again," Murray said to Linda, giving her hand a squeeze.

"I will," she murmured.

James held Betsy's hand all the way downstairs. Linda said goodbye to him at the door and went on down the steps to the sidewalk. The Rolls was waiting to take them back to their hotel. The chauffeur opened the door. I could get used to luxury very easily, she thought, as she stepped into the car.

She looked back for Betsy. She was bending down, talking earnestly to James. A minute later, she got into the limousine and Linda saw that her eyes were very shiny. She's in tears, Linda thought with surprise. Who would have expected Betsy to get sentimental over a kid?

"You'll see him again," she said, trying to be comforting.

Betsy looked downcast. "I don't know if I will. I don't like his father much. I don't want to go to the house if he's going to be there."

"Tell you what—if you're so keen on seeing the kid, we'll both go visit. Then you can talk to James and I'll talk to his father. How about that?"

Betsy stared. "Did you like Andrew Murray?" she asked. "I thought he was horrid."

"No, I didn't like him much." Linda grinned. "But you know me, I'm always ready to sacrifice myself for a good cause . . ."

18

Betsy felt her eyes clear of the tears that had welled up, and leaned back against the comfort of the limousine's back seat. Beside her, Linda said, "Well, one good thing—we can claim cab fare for this jaunt and make a dollar or two on the deal. The company'll never question taking the kid home. I'll split it with you even, okay?" and she turned to look out of the window.

Deals, Betsy thought, not bothering to reply. It seemed to her the world was divided between those who dealt in deals all the time and those who wouldn't recognize one if they fell over it. Betsy felt she definitely fit into the latter category; she would never had thought of claiming cab fare as a company business expense on this occasion.

And yet, she knew Linda was right. The company would certainly pay them fare along, perhaps, with giving them a commendation report for having handled the situation on their free time. Still, it took a Linda to see it as a deal. Rudi was another one of the deal people, but Rudi, Betsy felt, never had a relaxed moment in his life. He always seemed to be peddling merchandise back and forth across the Atlantic and was, in fact, well-known for it with the company. *Ask Rudi,* was often the answer to a question on where to get any one of a wide variety of goods and services. Almost as soon as the Rolls turned out of the sidestreet, it got caught in a traffic jam. The two girls sat silent for a while. Finally, Betsy remarked: "I guess we'll have to tell Captain Fleming that James is okay. He's back home, and even if we don't think much of Andrew Murray as a father, there's nothing more we can do."

"Maybe it'd be better not to say too much about the father," Linda said.

"Why not?"

"Oh—like rubbing salt in old wounds, I guess."

Betsy felt her curiosity aroused.

"What do you mean by that?"

Linda countered with another question. "Don't you know about David Fleming? I thought everyone knew."

Betsy sighed, impatiently. Really, Linda could be exasperating.

"Look, all I know is what you told me. You said he's not married and that he doesn't have any family. I remember asking you about the family, particularly . . ."

"He used to be married," Linda said. She paused, then added rather dramatically, "He used to have a son, as well."

Betsy felt a little shock. "Do you mean he's divorced?" she queried. She was remembering Fleming at the airport, the way he had behaved towards James, seeming to know exactly how to look after a small lonely boy. She was remembering, with dismay, her own questions to him about children . . . and his curt denial.

"There wasn't a divorce." Linda sounded unusually serious. "Fleming is a widower. His wife and son died in a car crash."

"Oh, no!"

"It's a tragic story. It happened before I joined the airline, but one of the senior stewardesses told me about it. Larry Johnson has mentioned it, too. He knew Fleming's wife and child, you see.

"It happened four or five years ago. The Flemings had one child, a son, and they lived—oh, I don't know exactly where, out in the suburbs some place. You know, like lots of the married pilots do. Sometimes, Mrs. Fleming used to drive to the airport to meet her husband when he came in from a flight.

"The last time she did that, she brought the little boy with her. They were on the highway, there was an accident—and Mrs. Fleming and her son were killed."

"It's too awful to be true," Betsy whispered.

"I don't know the details," Linda said. "Naturally, no

one asks Fleming about it. I only know that there was this crash and as a result, his wife and son died."

Betsy looked numbly out of the window. She wasn't seeing the store-windows, the crowded sidewalks, or the crawling traffic any more. She was seeing Fleming's face. The fine features with that suggestion of inner tension and control . . .

"Larry told me that Fleming never speaks about it, not even to his friends. Since it happened, Larry says, Fleming has really withdrawn. He was the quiet type before, apparently, but after he lost his wife and child, he withdrew completely. Now he buries himself in his work as if that's the only thing that matters."

Betsy said slowly: "But James drew him out. He was different—with James."

"It's not hard to see why. He would obviously identify James with his own son."

"How old was his son?"

"I'm not sure, but I think he was pre-school age. He could have been around four, five years old. Like the Murray kid."

"Oh my God." Betsy twisted her fingers together. "When I think of some of the things I said . . ."

Linda put a hand on Betsy's arm.

"No use worrying about that now," she said gently. "Anyway, Fleming probably knows that you aren't aware of the tragedy. He can't blame you for anything, knowing you're ignorant of the truth."

Betsy held back her tears, with an effort. First, there had been the parting with young James, which had been harder than she had expected; now, the story of the tragedy that had wrecked David Fleming's life. She tried not to start crying because she was afraid that if she started she would be unable to stop.

"It's all too much," she whispered. "So much unhappiness . . ."

"Now look, hon," Linda sounded concerned, "you mustn't take it to heart like this. My Lord, everyone has their problems. We all have rough times to go through. You can't suffer for everyone else, kid, honestly you can't."

In a taut voice, Betsy said, "Some people just seem . . . to have much rougher times . . . than others."

126

"You can say that again, kiddo."

The Rolls began gliding forward. It proceeded a few yards, then halted once more in the solid traffic.

"Hell, I'm never going to get anything done at this rate." Linda drummed her fingers on her knee. She stared out the window.

"I guess I might as well jump out. I'll do my shopping here. If I don't get the stuff then the whole trip will have been wasted."

Betsy hardly registered what Linda was saying.

"Do you want to shop, too?"

Betsy jerked her attention back to the present.

"Shopping? Oh—uh, no thanks. I don't need anything."

"Okay. I'm off. See you later." Linda had the door of the Rolls open. She called back to Betsy, "At this rate, I'll probably get back to the hotel before you do!"

Betsy saw her, laughing as she picked her way through the jammed traffic to the sidewalk. Linda ran to the nearest department store entrance and quickly disappeared from sight.

The pressure of her emotion affected Betsy physically; she felt as if a heavy weight rested on her chest. She wondered at Linda being able to recount such a tragic story and then run off, laughing, on a shopping spree. Didn't she have the same emotions other people did? Perhaps it was simply that Linda wasn't as involved as she was.

Betsy had always tried to be honest with herself. She felt it was much easier to cope with things if you didn't fool yourself. Well, she wasn't trying to fool herself now: she had gotten emotionally involved with David Fleming. Fool, she told herself, to feel like that about a man intent on being a loner. A man who had deliberately withdrawn from everything except his work.

Of course, Linda's story had explained many things. It explained the reserve that at times verged on coldness, the withdrawal that would otherwise appear unnatural. But the story did not explain the real warmth and sympathy that had emanated from David Fleming during the time they had spent together at the airport. Such feelings could only mean that he had not succeeded in withdrawing completely, after all. There were times when circumstances weakened his control over his buried emotions.

127

But with a background like his—what price did he have to pay for those emotions? And would he be prepared to go on paying the price of admitting to them?

She was developing a headache. There had been too many things happening in too short a time. She wished she were back home, where she could rest and relax, instead of being alone in a foreign city, with a long working trip ahead of her in a few hours' time. She wished . . .

"Here we are, Miss."

With a start she realized they had reached the hotel. The chauffeur was holding open the door of the limousine.

Betsy stepped out and walked into the hotel, barely seeing where she was going. The lobby was crowded with people chattering in strange languages. Tourists, she thought dimly, tourists even in November. She asked for her room key, moved to the elevators. Everything was like a dream.

In her room, Betsy took some aspirin to ease the thumping in her head.

After she had swallowed two tablets, she lay on the bed. Her thoughts returned, inevitably, to Fleming. Now that she knew about his tragedy she understood a great deal. But she still wanted to know why he was flying to London on this particular schedule. Why was he interested in making frequent trips? Was London where he had finally found—well, someone who made him change his mind about being a loner? Was there a woman he came to see? Johnson had said "*cherchez la femme*," but he was always fooling; you never knew whether he was serious or not. Betsy buried her face in the pillow. Fleming had mentioned an appointment for the previous evening, and for today. What kept him so busy?

Everyone else had an obvious reason for bidding for London. Linda wanted to make money with her darned shopping. Rudi had some kind of racket going. Larry Johnson was there by order of Mrs. Johnson. As for herself, she had always wanted to visit London and had seized the first opportunity. They all had their reasons. They were all open about them—except Fleming.

Betsy stared up at the discolored ceiling. Why was it, she asked herself, that she always managed to get interested in impossible men?

128

19

An insistent tapping began breaking into Betsy's consciousness, and she suddenly woke with a start, sitting bolt upright on the bed, her heart pounding, until she realized she was in London and someone was knocking on the door of her hotel room.

"Who is it?" she called out.

"It's me—Marianne. Can I come in?"

"Oh, yes, sure."

The door opened and Marianne's face peered in. "I hope you're not busy. At first I thought you might be out."

Betsy rubbed her face, trying to assemble her thoughts.

"No. I was out, and then when I came back I had a headache. So I lay down for a while. Guess I must've fallen asleep."

Marianne went across the room and sat down in the easy chair near the window. She crossed her legs, showing off shapely ankles. Betsy observed that all Marianne's movements had a kind of deliberate languor, and she supposed they had been learned in drama school.

"Larry told me you were taking the little boy home," the girl in the chair said. "How did it go?"

Betsy told her, getting up from the bed and tidying her hair. It was now mid-afternoon; if she wanted to see any of London, or the stores, she would have to get going. Since there was really so little time, she decided to take a sight-seeing bus.

"I know it's corny," she said to Marianne, "but it's a pretty good way to get a general idea of a city one has never been to before. Then, next time, I can make a separate visit to someplace that especially interests me."

"What about tonight?"

"Tonight?" Betsy echoed. Marianne leaned forward.

"That's why I came by—to see if you'd be interested in going to the theater. I asked Judy, but she says she'll be too tired. She went sightseeing this morning," Marianne added, "and then shopping right after lunch."

"If she doesn't watch it, she'll wear her feet out," Betsy smiled.

"Well, she's working galley this trip," Marianne explained. "I'm the one doing all the walking up and down the cabin."

"In that case, why don't you come with me this afternoon?" Betsy asked. "We can both just sit comfortably in one of those glass-topped sightseeing buses, and watch the sights of London go by."

Marianne shook her head; she knew London quite well, she explained.

"And besides, I want to do some shopping before the stores close," she added. "But how about tonight? Will you come with me?"

Betsy considered the question for a moment. Then she said, "Yes, why not? I certainly don't have anything else to do tonight."

"I always go to plays when I'm in London," Marianne explained. "It's a passion with me, and there's such fabulous theater here. That's really why I bid for London in the first place. And this time, I persuaded the guy at the desk—the one who gets the tickets—to get me two seats for a new play at the Royal Court Theater. It's hard to get in but I'm friendly with this guy and he got the tickets as a favor."

Betsy examined the ticket Marianne handed her.

"I haven't heard of the play, or the playwright," she commented.

"The playwright is comparatively new, but he's well known to those of us who follow theater," Marianne said, a trifle sententiously.

"It's not going to be one of those weird plays with people in garbage-cans, is it?" Betsy asked. "I don't mean to sound square, but that stuff doesn't interest me. I guess I don't understand it."

Betsy remembered being taken to a couple of off-off-Broadway plays by Mike. One had consisted simply of a darkened stage, with two people sitting in a spotlight, cursing at each other. The dialogue had consisted mainly of every foul word Betsy had ever heard, with a few new ones she hadn't known existed until that night. Mike had called the play "invigorating." Betsy had found it intensely depressing.

Betsy decided to reserve judgment on this play until later. She glanced at her watch.

"Okay. I tell you what we'll do. Supposing I meet you down in the lobby before theater time? That way, we can each get our afternoon plans done."

They set a time, and Marianne left. Betsy went downstairs and inquired at the desk about sightseeing tours. She was informed that the travel office handling them was less than a block away.

"Leaves every hour on the hour, miss . . ."

It was, Betsy decided later, the perfect way to spend her first free afternoon in London, considering that she was tired from the combination of her out-of-kilter schedule and the emotional strain of the past twenty-four hours. She sat back in easy comfort high over the city streets. The wide-windowed sightseeing bus trundled smoothly past the famous buildings and historic sites. Up front, the guide talked into a microphone as the driver wheeled the vehicle in the traffic; all around her, tourists of all nationalities stared and talked to each other while the tour was in progress. She preferred to remain silent and was glad that no one sat in the seat next to her.

Big Ben . . . the Houses of Parliament . . . St. Paul's Cathedral . . . Threadneedle Street . . . the Tower of London . . . the names and the sights rich in history further stirred Betsy's interest now that she was actually seeing them. It was one thing to say "Buckingham Palace" and imagine a building where royalty lived; it was quite another to drive by the sprawling complex of buildings whose pale stone sharply contrasted with the bright red uniforms of the guards. It had always sounded like a storybook, and yet here it all was, and it was real.

And then there were the parks, where evergreens offset

the bare branches of the deciduous trees that stretched against the sky. More buildings, and then Chelsea, and the colorful shops along a winding road, and more parks and more sights, until it was almost too much.

Just in time, the bus turned back and headed for its starting point. The daylight had faded some time before, and the street lamps made the same streets she had seen earlier look completely new. London at night was another London. Walking back to the hotel she decided she liked it, too.

As she entered the lobby, she almost collided with Marianne; whose arms were full of packages.

"Did you have a good time?"

"Yes, lovely. Here, let me help you with those." Betsy took two of the parcels out of the other girl's arms.

"We have to hurry, if we want to get to the theater on time," Betsy said, as they waited for the elevator. "What time does the show start?"

"I don't intend hurrying," Marianne said, calmly. "There's plenty of time. The play starts at eight."

There was not that much time, Betsy thought, but she knew it would be useless to try and hurry Marianne. She lived on her own time and remained blissfully unaware of everybody else's. How she managed to turn up for flights and get through her work, Betsy could not imagine. Then she remembered the constant stream of complaints from Rudi about Marianne's slowness and "laziness." It wasn't really laziness, Betsy figured. It appeared that way because Marianne had a different time-system from the rest of the world.

Betsy called room-service and had a sandwich and a glass of milk brought to her room so that she could eat while she changed. There was no sign of Linda, apart from the packages and shopping bags strewn all over her bed. She had obviously come in, dumped her shopping and rushed out again. Probably with Carl, was Betsy's guess.

Back downstairs, while she waited in the lobby for Marianne, Betsy asked at the desk for Captain Fleming.

"Captain Fleming is out," the clerk said, after checking the room-keys.

Betsy had not seen him at the hotel since she returned from Andrew Murray's. He didn't seem the type to go out on the town. But you never know, she reflected, still waters . . .

She scribbled a quick note. "James Murray arrived home safe and sound. Mission completed. Betsy."

The clerk put the message in the pigeon-hole and promised to hand it to Fleming as soon as he came in. Betsy waited another fifteen minutes, watching the hands of the clock creep nearer and nearer eight o'clock. She scanned the people passing constantly to and fro, but the tall figure of David Fleming was not among them.

"I'm not late, am I?" Marianne was sauntering across the lobby, quite unhurried.

Betsy saw her surreptitiously admire her reflection in a wall-mirror and it somehow made her want to laugh. For all her so-called sophistication, there was something naive about Marianne. She was wearing a plain white wool dress, that, on her, looked anything but plain. Marianne had a well-developed figure and clothes clung in a way that was definitely eye-catching.

"Betsy, do you think I've put on weight?" Marianne demanded. "I'm sure I've gained at least a couple of pounds."

"Hurry, we'll be late."

"Seriously, I have such a weight-problem. If I so much as *look* at food, I put on a pound! I've hardly eaten a thing since we got here but I'm sure I've gained over the last couple of days." ‾

In the cab, Betsy said: "Tell me about this new playwright, you mentioned you'd seen other plays of his."

Marianne launched into enthusiastic description, diverted from her weight problem for the moment.

The play was better than Betsy had dared hope. By intermission she admitted, "It's really good! It's off-beat, but it's interesting."

Marianne was fluttering her false eyelashes at a man who was staring intently at her from the other side of the theatre bar, where the two girls were having drinks.

"Do you suppose he has anything to do with the theater?" Marianne whispered, "he seems to be very much at home here."

Betsy cast a look in the man's direction.

"I think he's at home in bars," she said. "He looks like a

133

typical businessman, he probably only comes here to pick up girls."

Marianne gazed soulfully about her with luminous green eyes.

"I don't know why I go on hoping, in such a difficult *metier*," she breathed.

Betsy observed that Marianne was succeeding in creating quite an effect, without seeming to do anything very much. Most of the people in the room now appeared to be watching them. She was not sorry when it was time to return to their seats.

When the play was over, the two girls lingered in the foyer, looking at the posters on display. A man's voice suddenly said, "What did you think of the play? Did you approve of it?"

Betsy looked up to see a young man with long hair, very casually dressed, standing next to her.

"Why yes—I liked it," she said.

"Ah—you're American," the young man commented.

"Are you both American? What are you doing over here?" another voice broke in.

Betsy saw that there were two long-haired young men.

"We're both American," Marianne replied, her gaze going from one to another of the strangers. "Are you connected with the theater at all?"

The first young man laughed. "Depends what you mean by 'connected'."

Marianne turned to Betsy. "I guess we'd better get a cab," she said in a tone that dismissed the young man completely.

"Let me introduce myself," the young man was walking beside them, refusing to be overlooked. "I'm Toby, and this is my friend . . ."

But the two girls were already out of the theater. "Those two are looking for a pair of idiots," Marianne murmured in Betsy's ear, "I know the type. They think all American girls are rich, and that they're easy pickups."

"What's the rush?" The young men had joined them on the sidewalk. "Why don't you let us invite you for a drink some place?"

"We have to be up very early tomorrow morning," Marianne said. She had stopped projecting her charm and her prettiness, her voice was sharp and she looked bad-tempered.

"Since when do tourists have to be early-risers? Come off it, girls!"

"We're not tourists," Betsy snapped.

"Then what are you? What are you doing over here?"

Betsy saw a cab approaching with its "For Hire" sign lighted. She waved her arms vigorously. Behind her, she heard Marianne saying briskly:

"We are school-teachers and we are on an educational tour with a group of fifty school-children. Tomorrow morning, we are off bright and early to the British Museum, with all fifty of the students."

In the cab, the two girls fell into fits of helpless laughter.

"Fifty school-children!" Betsy groaned, "oh my God! However did you dream up that one?"

"It cooled those two off considerably," Marianne remarked, "you should have seen their faces!"

"Whatever made you think of it?"

Marianne said, serious all of a sudden, "I never tell characters like that I'm a stewardess. They think all stews are good-time girls. They don't believe we work at all. We're ready, willing and eager, according to them, to go out on the town all night, every night."

"You're right," Betsy agreed. "It's hard to convince people that being a stew is a serious job and we really have to *work* for our living."

"Fifty kids." Marianne started to laugh again. "Oh, Betsy, I *wish* you could have seen the look of horror . . ."

As they collected their room-keys, Betsy saw that the note she had left for Fleming was still in its pigeon-hole. The two girls said goodnight and went their separate ways. Betsy saw that Linda was still not back. The packages lay undisturbed on her bed.

They had to be up early in the morning to check-in at the airport by 7:30. That meant leaving the hotel at 6:45. Betsy picked up the phone and asked for a 6 a.m. call. She undressed, packed her suitcase and rinsed out her underwear. Before getting into bed, she tied her long hair back to prevent it from tangling while she slept.

She switched off the bedside lamp. How late would Linda be? It would be typical of her to stay out late, Betsy thought crossly, before an early-morning start. No wonder Rudi kept warning her. Linda was heading for trouble if she didn't straighten out.

It would have been much better if she had been teamed with Marianne, Betsy told herself. Marianne seemed lazy but she worked all right providing she was not harassed, and she was a lot easier to get along with than Linda. Betsy felt she and Marianne had quite a lot in common; she couldn't think of any interest she shared with Linda.

Betsy lay awake for what seemed like a long time. She tried to stop the thoughts buzzing around in her head, but the more she tried, the less sleepy she felt.

"I have to be up early," she muttered fiercely, punching her pillow and settling down determinedly. "I must go to sleep now."

She tried the old trick of deliberately making her mind a blank. She imagined she was looking at black velvet: there was nothing but soft blackness, soft blackness, everywhere ...

Part 2

Flightway International 411
(delayed)
LHR/JFK

1

The Flightways airport limousine stood waiting outside the hotel. Uniformed crew members hurried out into the cold misty morning, their breath making vapor trails in the chill air.

"Okay, let's get the bags in here . . ."

"Let's hope the heater's working in this bus—or we'll all be frozen solid by the time we get to Heathrow . . ."

"Hi, Betsy!" Johnson shouted, "Where's the ball-bearing stewardess?"

"The who?"

"Becker."

"In the lobby. He'll be right out."

Betsy got into the car just as Fleming emerged from the hotel. Johnson greeted him and they climbed into the limousine's front seat together, talking as they did so. Turning to shut the door, Fleming caught sight of Betsy. He smiled and broke off his conversation with the co-pilot long enough to say, "Thanks for the note, Betsy. I was glad to hear the kid is okay."

"Well, I . . ." Betsy began, but Fleming had already resumed his conversation with Larry Johnson.

Rudi appeared, followed by Linda and Judy. More bags were piled in the back of the car. Masden came out of a side entrance, looking sleepy and carrying his suitcase. He greeted the rest of the crew and slung his bag on top of the pile.

"Where's Marianne?" Rudi asked.

"She was right behind me," Judy said, looking back at the hotel entrance. Rudi clicked his tongue with impatience. There was a slight pause. Only Fleming and Johnson continued their conversation without interruption.

" . . . and he brought it in on two without any trouble," Johnson was saying. "Never thought I'd hear anything like that about that flying brick . . ."

"Where *is* that girl?" Rudi was saying.

"There she is!" Judy exclaimed. "I told you she was right behind me."

"Come on, Marianne, you're keeping everybody waiting," Rudi called out.

Marianne got into the car, apologising for being late.

"That's all right," Fleming cut her short. "Are we all here now? Good. Then let's go."

The driver behind the wheel started up the engine. Moments later, the crew for Flightways International's delayed flight 411 was en route to Heathrow Airport.

Having dispensed with their on-ground duties with a maximum of speed, the cabin crew watched the silver 707 taxi toward its assigned parking space on the ramp.

"It's good that we got here early," Rudi Becker remarked. "They're in ahead of time."

He and the girls stood waiting while the passengers deplaned and disappeared into the building. When everyone was off, Rudi led the way across to the plane and the five cabin attendants climbed into the parked 707.

"Hi, there . . ." "Hi . . ." "Hey—you're here early . . ." ". . . if you don't count the day's delay . . ." The fresh crew greeted the purser and stewardesses inside the cabin, then all ten of them got together for the handing over.

"Here's the intransit seating chart." . . . "No, not too many . . ." "Five A's a pain in the ass, but coffee'll keep him quiet . . ." "Two babies here, so try to give her another seat, will you? Believe me, with those kids, that poor woman needs all the room she can get . . ."

As they exchanged paperwork and information, one set of cabin attendants picked up their cases and put on their capes and hats while the other set peeled off their outer layer of clothing and settled into the 707 for the flight across the Atlantic.

They were still all talking in a group in the first class

140

section when the deplaning purser said, "No official V.I.
P.s aboard, but you've got one, anyway. She's over there"—
he indicated a window seat—"and her secretary and agent
and his wife are all travelling with her. Their seats are
over there,"—again, he waved a hand—"but they wander
back to her pretty often.

"She's travelling as Mrs. Olga Jones, and has particularly asked for no publicity."

"But who is she?" Marianne interrupted.

The deplaning purser smiled. "You'll recognize her as
soon as you see her, all of you. It's Kara Lane."

"Oh, I wish I were in first!" Marianne moaned. She
looked imploringly at Betsy.

"No deal," Betsy said, firmly. She had no intention of
offering to change places with Marianne, however stage-
struck she might be. Betsy wanted to see Kara Lane herself.
She had seen the actress many times in movies and on TV
and admired her very much. Miss Lane came over on the
screen as a beautiful, intense woman; she played difficult
dramatic roles that had won her two Oscars. Betsy wondered what she was like as a private person. It was hard to
imagine Kara Lane as an ordinary passenger, after seeing
her playing so many complex and troubled characters.

"She boarded in Rome," one of the stewardesses said,
struggling into her cape and plopping her hat on her head.
"And she seems very upset about something, but she didn't
say a word."

"D'you have a mob getting on here?" another of the
deplaning girls asked.

Rudi shook his head. "No, a light load, thank goodness.
Maybe people switched to other lines because of the
delay."

"Not a chance," said the other purser. "Everyone's late.
You should've seen Fiumicino. It was a madhouse, with
all the planes on ground."

"You know, I think Kara Lane's whole trip must be
very hush-hush," said the girl in the hat. "Now that I think
of it, there were no paparazzi popping flashbulbs at her
when she came on board. And that's strange, because she's
been making a movie at Cinecitta, so you'd think she'd
want the publicity."

"Come on, gossip-column," said one of the other girls.

141

"I'm dead-beat. Let's get to the hotel." They all said good-bye and clattered down the metal ramp.

"I wish that were us," Linda murmured.

"Well, it's not," Rudi snapped, "and we'd better get going. Now, then—where's that luncheon service?" and he started for the galley.

The homeward bound trip for the crew had started in full earnest.

2

When the station agent announced the passengers were about to board, Betsy moved to the front entrance to receive them. Linda was halfway down the first class cabin aisle, on her way to the divider; beyond, Betsy imagined that Rudi was probably chasing Marianne down to the galley area, for he was in his usual perfectionist mood and was not yet sure of Judy's efficiency.

Betsy turned her attention to the people coming up the stair. It was not hard to recognize Kara Lane, alias Mrs. Jones. She wore a scarf on her head, babushka-style, over-size dark glasses and a full length mink coat with the collar pulled high. She may not be instantly recognizable as Kara Lane, Betsy thought, but she certainly looks just like an actress trying very hard to disguise herself.

Miss Lane was accompanied by a man and two young women—the agent, his wife and Miss Lane's personal secretary. It took Betsy some time to get the group seated to their satisfaction. Miss Lane insisted that she wanted to sit alone. After some argument, the agent and his wife agreed to this and sat down together, while the secretary took a seat by herself.

"Do you want a pillow, or a blanket?" Betsy asked.

"I'm so cold," the actress murmured, in a low voice, "bring me two blankets."

Betsy noticed that she was shivering. When Betsy brought the blankets the actress seized them as if desperate for warmth.

143

"Can I get you a hot drink?" Betsy enquired.

Kara Lane removed her large dark glasses and it was clear that she had been crying.

"I'll take some coffee," she said. Betsy had to strain to hear her. She spoke as if too tired to raise her voice.

"I'll bring it immediately after takeoff," Betsy promised.

"God, I don't know if I'll live till then."

Betsy promised her she would, and went on with her pre-take-off duties.

As she walked through the cabin towards the galley, Miss Lane's agent stopped her.

"You gotta take care of her," he said, jerking his head in the direction of the actress. "She's very upset. It's bad family news, and she's worried sick."

"I'll do everything I can," Betsy responded.

In the galley, Linda asked:

"What's it like out there?"

"One potential hysteric, otherwise okay. We're going to need coffee as soon as we've taken off, lots of it."

"What's Kara Lane like?" Linda wanted to know.

"She's the potential hysteric. I think we'll have to watch her. She's obviously in a state over something."

"What about the drunk?"

"What drunk?" Betsy asked in amazement.

"The guy sitting up front. Fortyish, very neat, with horn-rimmed glasses. He's high as a kite."

"Oh—he seemed so quiet. I didn't realize he was drunk. Are you sure about that?"

"Betcha life. You're naive, Betsy, if you don't know a drunk when you see one. We get enough on board, God knows. I guess it must be something to do with being nervous about flying. A little too much Dutch courage before boarding, and that's it."

"I thought he was just tired. I couldn't smell liquor, either."

"He's on vodka, you idiot. You wait, he'll be ordering more the minute we take off."

Marianne's voice sounded through the cabin.

"Good morning, ladies and gentlemen . . ."

Betsy noticed the careful diction. More evidence of drama school, she thought.

" . . . welcome aboard Flightways International. In a few minutes, we shall be taking off for Kennedy Airport in the

U.S.A., and we therefore want to take this opportunity
..."

Marianne enumerated the services available, and all the
routine phrases of the announcement sounded fresh and
new as she spoke them. Betsy, busy with her own tasks,
wondered briefly whether Rudi had given her the job of
the announcement in an effort to speed up her cabin work
later on. Rather like a prize in advance, or a carrot,
dangling, in the shape of more announcements later on.

The plane took off and lifted through the moist layers
of cloud with effortless grace. Betsy was already in the
galley, helping to set up the special food service arranged
because of the flight's unusual departure time, when the
intercom phone from the cockpit buzzed. She lifted the
receiver.

"That you, Betsy?" It was Fleming's voice. "Would you
come up front, please?"

"Now, what does he want?" Linda asked. "Tell him I'll
be bringing crew coffee as soon as I can."

The cockpit was full of brilliant sunshine. Betsy shaded
her eyes with her hand. The pilots were all wearing
sun-glasses against the glare.

"How did things go yesterday?" Fleming asked,
abruptly.

Betsy looked at him but his expression was masked by
the dark glasses. Feeling he was treating the matter too
casually, she queried, "What things do you mean?"

Surprised, Fleming said, "The boy, of course. When you
and Linda took James home. Was his father there? Was
everything all right?"

Betsy longed to make a sharp retort and it was on the
tip of her tongue to tell the Captain to "ask Linda" but
common sense prevailed. On board, the Captain was God.
This was accepted by everyone, crew and passengers alike.
No stewardess who wanted to keep her job told the
captain what she thought of him in front of other crew-
members and while she was working under his command.
Biting back the sharp words, Betsy said in a constrained
voice, "There was no problem getting James home. We
arrived at his house, spoke to his father and then we left.
That was all. It was over in about twenty minutes."

Fleming frowned. "What impressions did you get of the
set-up? What sort of man was Murray?"

145

In level tones, Betsy said, "My impression was that if luxury is all that a child needs, then James has everything. As for his father—I found Andrew Murray both urbane and charming."

Fleming was staring at her but Betsy still could not make out his reaction to her words on account of the dark glasses that shaded the pilot's eyes.

"I see." He was curt. "Well, Betsy—thanks for looking after the boy. You did a good job."

Unable to resist one small stab, Betsy said, "If you want to know more, you can ask Linda. I'm sure she would love to give you *her* impressions of the Murray household."

"Why? Are they different from yours?"

Betsy managed to swallow the "Ask her," that sprang to her lips. Instead, she smiled sweetly and replied, "I think they might be."

The exchange with Fleming left Betsy angry. If the captain cared as much about the boy's welfare as he claimed to do, he could have asked about him before this, she thought. Let him ask Linda, if he wanted more details. After all, it had been at Fleming's insistence that Linda had gone along.

After the first-class passengers had been served their late breakfast, Rudi told the girls that he was going aft to check on things in tourist.

"Thank God," Linda sighed, after the purser had disappeared into the second cabin, "let him chase Marianne and Judy for a while. I've had enough."

The morning sun was brilliant, too brilliant for comfort. Betsy moved down the aisle, adjusting window-curtains so that the glare did not bother the passengers. She found that Kara Lane had already pulled the curtains. The actress was leaning back in her seat, swathed in blankets. She had removed her dark glasses and her eyes were closed.

As Betsy turned away, Miss Lane's low voice said, "Please, don't leave me. Sit here for a while."

Betsy smiled and sat down.

"Is there anything I can get for you?" she asked. She looked at the actress and observed that she was very pale. "Are you feeling sick?"

Kara Lane shook her head. There was a look of pain in her large, dark eyes that belied her action.

"We're all set for a good trip," Betsy said, feeling foolish but wanting to fill in the silence. "There's good weather ahead, and we should make good time."

Seen close up, Kara Lane was beautiful, Betsy thought. She had fine, magnolia-white skin, against which her dark hair and long-lashed dark eyes showed in stunning contrast. She was wearing no makeup and though Betsy could see lines around the eyes and mouth, these only seemed to make the actress's beauty seem more fragile and delicate. Betsy got the feeling that Miss Lane was every bit as intense in real life as she appeared on the screen, if appearances were anything to go by.

A tear rolled down the white face, followed by another and another. Kara Lane lay back in her seat and let the tears roll unchecked. She did not seem to be aware that she was crying, her features remained passive and immobile, only the tears moved, in a steady flow.

"Please let me get you something," Betsy urged. "Are you in pain, do you feel ill?"

Kara Lane gave a weary smile. "You could get me some tissues."

When Betsy returned with a box of tissues, the actress took a handful and clumsily mopped at her face.

"I need someone to talk to," she said.

"Would you like me to call your secretary?" Betsy asked. "Or your agent?"

The dark head shook. "No, I don't want any of them. I'm tired of them—they are always around. Everywhere I go, they go. I'm never alone."

First, she complains she needs company, someone to talk to, Betsy thought, then she complains about never being alone!

Kara Lane made a grimace that could have meant anything.

"I'm feeling confused," she murmured, almost as if she could read Betsy's thoughts. "But then—I lead a confusing sort of life."

"It seems a wonderful life, to me," Betsy ventured. "I've seen your movies and lots of your TV performances, and I think you're the best actress there is."

"The best actress there is. I guess you could say that." Kara Lane looked at Betsy, her dark eyes very serious. "My whole life is a performance. I don't only act on the

147

screen or on the stage. I give a continuous performance—
Kara Lane, glamorous actress. The woman who has such
a wonderful life."

There was a silence, until the actress suddenly demanded,

"How old are you? Twenty-one, twenty-two?" Without
waiting for a reply, she went on: "I'm forty-nine. Does
that surprise you?"

"Yes! I thought you were—well, about thirty-five. You
certainly don't look older than that."

"It's all part of the performance. I *act* thirty-five. Luckily for me, my face hasn't let me down—yet. Do you
know that every morning when I wake up, the first thing I
do is look in the mirror, to see if my looks have gone?
Sounds funny, doesn't it? But I always think that it's going
to happen all at once, overnight—that one morning, I'll
look in the glass, and it will have happened. My looks will
have gone, and I'll be an old woman."

Kara Lane was fumbling with a gold cigarette case.
Betsy took the gold lighter from the actress's shaking
hand, and held it for her while she lit a cigarette.

"But that's only *one* of my worries," she continued.
"Perhaps it's even the least of them. After all, an estab-
lished actress can go on getting parts. She doesn't have to
look young forever. Or so my agent keeps telling me."

Betsy observed Miss Lane's hands. The fingers were
long, the knuckles unexpectedly prominent. The nails were
bitten down to the quick.

Kara Lane spoke in a low, monotonous tone. The
words seemed to spill out unbidden, the same way the
tears had flowed, one after another, over the still face.

"I'm going home," she said. "Home—that's Brooklyn. I
haven't been there in thirty years. Did you know I was
born and raised in Brooklyn?"

Betsy shook her head but she was not sure that the
actress saw what her response was. She felt that Miss
Lane was talking compulsively, that she would go on
talking even if Betsy moved away.

"I was born Klara Landauer. How about that? What a
name for an actress. It got changed to Kara Lane, in
Hollywood. Kara Lane: my first agent dreamed that one
up. He said I couldn't call myself Klara Landauer, it was

148

too Jewish. In those days, it wasn't fashionable to admit to being Jewish.

"Well, I doubt many people think of me as Jewish, now. I've had three husbands—all of them genuine Wasps. I've even got a Wasp son—isn't that hysterical? I haven't seen him in years, it's true, his father got custody. But I'm darn sure no one mistakes him for a Jewish boy. He's a Wasp through and through—his father has made sure of that." The actress paused. "I wonder if he even knows that his mother is Jewish? It would be just like my ex-husband not to tell him.

"So, finally, I'm going home. After all these years and all the disasters—back home. My father is dying. I got a message from my aunt Sophie. 'Your father is dying' she wrote me, 'come and make your peace with him before it is too late.' People always worry about it being too late. I don't worry about it any more; I *know* it's too late. For me, anyway.

"I can't go back to Brooklyn and be Klara Landauer again. And that's what my father would want. He doesn't want to see *me*—he wants to see his little Klara again, the nice Jewish girl. The pretty little girl who was so good to her momma and poppa—before she went away to Hollywood and became a whore.

"Oh yes, they think I'm a whore. I've heard that, via certain kind friends who felt it their duty to pass on the information. Of course, my parents thought it was immoral to marry outside the Jewish religion, outside Brooklyn, even. Let alone travel to Hollywood and marry a goy. Three goyim, to be accurate. Though by the time I got my third husband, I wasn't in touch with my family any more. They had long since resigned themselves to having lost their daughter. Their Klara was dead, as far as they were concerned. *They* preferred death to dishonor!" The actress gave a half-sob, half-laugh.

Betsy became aware that the agent was with them, leaning over the seat in front.

"Kara," he said, "don't upset yourself, sweetheart. It's all going to be okay. I promise you. Look, take your tablets, then you'll feel better. There's a good girl."

Kara Lane protested. The agent said to Betsy:

"Get a glass of water. Mineral water. Miss Lane has to take her medication."

Betsy brought the glass of mineral water. Kara Lane was persuaded to swallow two blue capsules. When Betsy tried to leave, the actress said sharply, "Don't go away! I want you to stay with me."

"Now, Kara, there's no need to get all upset ..." The agent was using soft, persuasive tones.

Kara Lane gave him a look of hatred.

"Fuck off," she said, with real venom.

A muscle twitched in the man's face, he hesitated for an instant, then without another word he returned to his seat.

"People," the actress ground out, "I'm surrounded by people—but I don't have a soul in the world to *talk* to."

Rudi was standing nearby. He raised his eyebrows, questioningly. Betsy moved next to him and murmured in his ear, "She's very upset. She seems to be going through some sort of nervous crisis. She wants me to stay with her."

"Then stay," Rudi hissed back. "You take care of Miss Lane, Linda and I can handle the rest. Call me if you need anything."

Betsy sat down beside the actress again. She took the blankets and wrapped them more securely around the older woman.

"Are you feeling more comfortable?" she asked.

The dark head nodded. "It's warmer now."

As if there had been no interruption in what she had been saying, Kara Lane went on, "My aunt Sophie was the only one in the family who kept in touch with me. She used to write, care of the film studios, to tell me the family news. Who had married who, who had died, who had the biggest bar-mitzvah. That sort of thing. When my mother died, I was on location, overseas. I couldn't get home for the funeral—I asked aunt Sophie to send flowers in my name. Even Sophie didn't write to me for a few years after that ...

"Then she started again. A note came once or twice a year. She said she saw all my movies, she watched me on TV. She never mentioned my father, until her last note. Now she tells me he is dying. That's not surprising, he must be well into his eighties. An old man ... and I bet ... I just bet ..."

The voice trailed off into a yawn. The dark head

150

dropped, the eyes closed, and Miss Lane gave a fluttery sigh and was silent. Betsy was alarmed.

"Miss Lane?" she said, loudly. "Are you all right?"

"She's okay." The agent had appeared again. "She's gone to sleep. It was the pills. They calm her down, send her off to sleep."

"Are you sure?" Betsy felt uneasy. The actress had fallen asleep so rapidly that it seemed unnatural. It was more as if she had suffered a collapse.

"Sure, I'm sure." The agent gave a confident smile. "Don't worry, kid. She's a very high-strung woman. But I'm used to looking after her and I know she'll be okay. Relax, she's all right. Just tired, that's all."

In the galley Betsy recounted what had happened, to Rudi.

"I hope to God she's not going to have a nervous breakdown before we land," Rudi commented.

"What's this?" Linda came into the galley. "Who's having a nervous breakdown?"

"Kara Lane, she's very disturbed about something."

"Do we have a doctor on board?" Betsy enquired.

"Yes," Linda said, with a wry smile, "he's the one who's drunk."

"Christ!" Rudi snorted.

"Oh, it's all right, he's reached the paralytic stage," Linda went on, cheerfully, "he is at least *quiet*. We should be thankful for small mercies."

"For the moment," Rudi commented darkly.

"I need coffee," Betsy said. She quickly poured herself a cup of lukewarm coffee.

"What was Kara Lane talking about all that time?" Linda wanted to know. "You were with her for hours! I could see her talking and it looked as if she was crying, too."

"She was reminiscing. Talking about her family—that sort of thing." Betsy felt she did not have the right to reveal exactly what she had heard. It had seemed too personal and painful to Kara Lane, to be relayed as casual gossip.

"Were you kept busy?" Betsy asked, to change the subject. "I rather lost track of what was happening in the cabin."

"It's an easy flight, no sweat. Last time I went up front,

151

Fleming said we should be right on time, it's clear weather all the way."

"I shan't be sorry to get home. It's been a busy trip, one way and another."

"I'm not so sure about that. I feel better for getting away for a while. I can't say I'm in any rush to get home." Linda felt in the pocket of her tunic top. She brought out a card and handed it to Betsy. "See this. Our drunken doctor."

"John Dennis, M.D." Betsy read. The address was Park Avenue, New York.

"He managed to slip me his card, like they all do!" Linda said, with a brittle laugh. "The first time he tried, he handed me a $20 bill by mistake. Then he spilled everything out of his wallet, all over the seat. Finally, we got all his junk together and he managed to pass the card over. I'm glad he's not my doctor, I tell you!"

When Betsy made her routine check of the cabin prior to landing, she found Kara Lane still in a deep sleep. She fastened the seat-belt across the actress's lap and the woman did not so much as stir.

The plane taxied to the designated ramp and the cabin staff took up their positions as the passengers prepared to disembark. Betsy, standing near the open doorway, saw Dr. Dennis stop and say something to Linda as he came lurching through the cabin. After the doctor had left the plane, Betsy caught Linda's eye.

"I still don't know if he's making a pass, or looking for a patient," Linda hissed, with a grin.

It took a long time for Kara Lane and her entourage to disembark. They had refused all offers of help; in fact, the agent and the secretary had insisted that they, and they alone, would assist Miss Lane.

"She gets upset if too many people fuss around her," the agent had said, when Betsy tried to be helpful.

Now the group was leaving the cabin. Betsy was alarmed at the extreme pallor of Kara Lane's complexion; she moved like a woman in a trance, her dark eyes staring dully ahead, seeing nothing. The agent supported her on one side, the secretary on the other. The agent's wife followed behind, her arms full of hand baggage, which she insisted on carrying herself.

152

"Good-bye Miss Lane, it was a pleasure having you on our flight," Betsy said, as the group reached the exit.

The dark eyes stared at her, unfocused. With a completely blank face, Kara Lane looked away as if she had never seen Betsy in her life before. Without a word, the actress allowed herself to be half carried all the way into the terminal.

"Wow, she's a strange one," Linda exclaimed. "Looks as if she's drugged, or something."

"I guess we'll never know . . ." Betsy murmured.

She collected her overnight bag, ready to leave. She felt disturbed by what she had seen and heard of Kara Lane. More disturbing was the knowledge that she would never know the end of the story. It was as if she had witnessed one small scene in a lengthy drama—enough to arouse her interest and involvement—and then the stage had gone black. Flying, meeting people on a plane, she told herself, leaves an awful lot of loose ends.

Marianne appeared. "What was Miss Lane like?" she demanded. "Did you get a chance to talk to her, Betsy? Do tell me all about her . . ."

Betsy smiled. "There's nothing to tell. She slept most of the trip."

"Oh, what a shame." Marianne looked crestfallen.

Betsy shrugged and walked slowly off the plane. She was struggling against an immense sadness. On the outward trip, there had been lonely little James; on the return trip, the equally lonely Miss Lane. Betsy was glad that the flight was over, but the sadness lingered on.

3

"I'm so glad this delay hasn't affected our schedule for the rest of the month," Betsy murmured, using the banal remark to cover up her delighted confusion. Sitting next to David Fleming in his zippy red sportscar was something that had come at her out of nowhere and she was still off-balance.

The tall captain had brought the low-slung automobile to a halt in front of her as she was leaving the Flightways Building. The other girls and Rudi had already left; Betsy, after completing her tour of Immigration and Customs, had gone to the Flight Service section and filled out a report on James Murray.

Tiredness had dragged at her when she finally left the building; she was glad to see there was a bus at the stop.

And then the red sportscar had slid to a stop in front of her.

"Hey, Betsy! Can I give you a lift?"

"Why—er—yes, if you're going to Manhattan."

"Sure am. Hop in."

Betsy looked uncertainly at the suitcase in her hand.

"Oh, yeah, that's right. I'll throw it in the trunk."

While he dealt with her case, Betsy eased herself into the automobile, stunned with pleasure and the comfort of the bucket seat. David Fleming got in beside her, shifted the car into gear.

Betsy did not speak until they were out of the airport and on the expressway, heading for Manhattan. The captain drove with concentration, steering skilfully through the traffic that was heavy at that hour. Her eventual remark, about their unaffected flight schedule elicited no response. And yet, his offer of a ride had been so totally unexpected. Really, Betsy thought, he is a most unpredictable man.

"You're very quiet," Fleming commented.

Betsy looked at him. The clear, grey eyes glanced from the road ahead to Betsy, then quickly back again.

"You're not exactly noisy, yourself," she replied.

A smile appeared on the captain's face.

"I guess you're wondering why I hustled you into the car," he said. "Well, I'll be frank. I wanted the chance to talk to you, privately."

Betsy waited, her heart thumping.

"We haven't had an opportunity to talk properly," Fleming went on, "and I want to know a lot of things. First of all, I want to know what you really thought about the situation with the little boy. It bothers me, I can't stop worrying about it."

"James?" Betsy felt the old anger rising. For a moment, she tried to curb it, but it was too much for her. "Why don't you ask Linda?" she snapped, not hiding her hostility.

Another quick glance from Fleming. "I'm asking you." His voice was very cool.

"Look, *you* wanted Linda to go along," Betsy burst out, "you didn't trust *me* to take James home safely. Well, if you feel Linda is so trustworthy, you'd better ask her for the details. I'm sure she'll be delighted to supply them."

There was a pause. Then Fleming said, in a different tone of voice, "Listen—there's something I have to explain. But it's—kind of—uh, difficult."

Betsy could see from his profile that he was frowning.

"It's about Linda," he continued. "You've gotten the wrong idea. It wasn't that I didn't trust *you*, Betsy. It was because I didn't trust *Linda*."

"It didn't look that way to me," Betsy retorted.

"I can see that. But—well, to be frank, the reason I sent Linda along with you that day, was simply because I wanted her out of my way. Out of my hair. Do you understand?"

"You mean—she was bothering you?" Betsy asked.

Fleming gave an embarrassed laugh.

"I felt she was—sort of hanging around too much. Everywhere I went, she seemed to be waiting for me. That first night, I was waiting for you and James to join me at dinner, when Linda came in and sat down at my table and started telling me a long story about some theory she had about what might have happened to James' father. I realize now that it was a load of garbage but at the time I was so darn worried, I was willing to listen to anything that seemed to have some bearing on the situation. Then, when you and James appeared, you went right over and joined Larry . . ."

"You looked as if you didn't want to be disturbed," Betsy murmured, remembering the scene of Linda and the captain, sitting at the table, deep in conversation.

"That wasn't quite the way it was. I—uh—tried to catch your attention—but you weren't looking my way." Fleming was beginning to look very embarrassed. Betsy made an effort not to smile too openly at his obvious discomfiture.

"Anyway, I figured that the best way out of the situation, was to send Linda off with you."

"Thank you for letting me know." There was a note of irony in Betsy's reply.

"Listen, I don't mean—hell—I wanted you to know that I *am* concerned about James. And it was obvious that you thought I'd more or less washed my hands of the whole problem, and the kid, and that got to me."

The car drew to a halt at traffic signals. Fleming looked at Betsy. It was an intimate look and she felt herself flush. Tension was building between them the way it had built during the hours of waiting at the airport . . .

"Tell me about James," Fleming said quietly, "I've been thinking about that kid ever since."

Betsy recounted all that she could remember of her brief visit to the Murray household.

"Mr. Murray invited you to come back?" Fleming enquired. "Are you going to accept?"

"I might. It depends—on a lot of things. I'd like to see James again, he begged me to come see him. But I think Andrew Murray might prove—difficult."

"I see."

Betsy said: "It's a paradoxical situation. In a material

way, James has everything any child could wish for. In another way, I'm not so sure he doesn't come under the category of deprived."

"Poor kid." Fleming's knuckles were white, as he gripped the wheel. "It's a lousy life."

Fleming guided the car in and out of the traffic. Betsy was remembering what she had heard about the captain's own personal tragedy. She didn't want to talk too much about James for fear of reviving memories. It was clear that Fleming was experiencing some kind of pain through James and his inability to alter the child's situation. Betsy wanted to say something to change the subject of conversation, but her mind was frustratingly blank.

She had told Fleming all he had wanted to know about her own movements, Betsy thought. She wondered if he was prepared to give any information about his own activities. He had, after all, claimed to be busy with various 'appointments.' Betsy recalled seeing him making his private phone call, and later on, telling Larry he was 'busy' for the day.

"I went to the theater in London," Betsy remarked, innocently. "It was great. Did you get to the theater—or anything—while we were over there?"

"No."

"Movies? D'you like the movies?"

"Sometimes."

Fleming was master of the final, uninformative answer, Betsy thought. She wondered why he felt the need to keep everything so intensely private. Was he afraid of revealing more about himself? She was trying to think up a way around Fleming's aversion to answering direct questions, when she became aware that he was speaking.

"What street do you live on?"

She told him. Progress was still slow through the heavy morning traffic, and it got slower the further they got into Manhattan.

She knew that Sharon would be away, she was on the Paris run. However, Betsy had quite lost track of Lee's movements. The chances were high, though, that even if Lee was home, she would be 'home' in some other apartment. That was the way Lee's life seemed to run. It crossed Betsy's mind that in all probability, she would have the apartment to herself that morning.

157

4

The car came to a halt outside the tall apartment building Betsy had indicated.

"Thanks for the ride," she said.

"My pleasure."

Betsy glanced at Fleming. He was smiling politely.

"I'm glad we had a chance to talk," Betsy said.

"There were a few things that needed straightening out." Fleming's tone was cool, non-committal.

Betsy took a deep breath. "Would you like to come up for coffee?" she asked. "I'll be fixing some for myself as soon as I get in."

"That's sweet of you, but . . ." Fleming hesitated.

Betsy waited for the inevitable excuse, bracing herself for it. Then she heard him saying, "Okay—I'd be glad to take you up on your offer."

Betsy felt a mixture of surprise, relief, and pleasure: surprise that Fleming should have changed his mind, relief that she had not, after all, made a fool of herself in extending the invitation, and pleasure that he wanted to accept it. They rode up in the elevator in silence, each one absorbed in private thoughts.

As she went into the apartment, Betsy called loudly:

"Lee! Lee? Are you home?"

There was no reply. Betsy walked through the small hallway into the living room. The divan in the alcove where Lee slept when she was home looked as if it hadn't been used in a long time. The apartment was very tidy, very empty.

"Shall I leave your case here?" Fleming put down the suitcase that he had carried up for Betsy.

"Oh, thanks. Do sit down. Anywhere. My, it seems kind of stuffy in here. You know how a place gets musty if it's empty for a few days." Betsy could feel herself beginning to get flustered. She tried to retain her normal composure.

"Would you prefer coffee or tea?" she asked, to cover up her confusion.

"I'll stick to coffee, thanks." Fleming sat on the sofa, watching Betsy with his shrewd eyes. His gaze made her feel slightly uncomfortable.

"I'll go grind the beans," she said.

"Need any help?" Fleming said following her to the kitchen.

"No, thanks. It doesn't take a moment."

"Where did you get the grinder? Looks like a genuine antique."

Betsy smiled. "Sharon brought this back one trip. I think she got it in Italy. She was dying to get a real old-fashioned grinder, so now we have to work at grinding the beans by hand, instead of using an electric machine like sensible people do."

"Who's Sharon—your roommate?"

"Yes. I share with two other girls. Sharon Roberts and Lee Pickering. Do you know either of them?"

"I may. The names don't mean anything right now."

"There are quite a number of stewardesses in this building. Mostly, we live two or three to an apartment, it's cheaper that way. Some girls share four to an apartment but that's too crowded, I think. I like company, and it's handy to have someone sharing the rent. But you want some privacy, as well. I have my own room here, and that suits me fine."

"This building must be the one they call the Stew Zoo," Fleming commented.

"Yes, it is. It's awful, the way people talk about stewardesses." Betsy pulled a face. "We must be the most maligned group ever."

Fleming gave a short laugh. "You should hear what they say about pilots."

"I guess people outside the airline world don't really

159

understand what it's like at all," Betsy remarked, thoughtfully.

"From the outside, it looks a lot of fun and travel and excitement. From the inside, well, you know how it is . . ." Fleming's voice trailed off.

The percolator was bubbling on the stove and the inviting smell of coffee began to fill the kitchen.

"Do you live alone?" Betsy asked.

"No."

Another question cut off, Betsy thought. She began pouring out the coffee.

They returned to the living room, carrying their coffee cups. Betsy sat down on the sofa, next to Fleming, and heaved a big sigh. She leaned forward, unzipped and pulled off her boots. She wiggled her toes, stretched her legs, then sat back against the cushions.

"Oooooh, it's good to be home," she murmured. "I feel I want to sit for a long while, doing nothing in particular, just relaxing."

"It's always that way after a flight," Fleming said. "You stay keyed up even after you leave the plane. It's not until you're through your own front door, secure in the knowledge that Operations can't call on you for a few hours at least, that you feel you're really off-duty and free to let go."

"Some girls go straight to bed as soon as they get in," Betsy said, "but I can't do that. I need time to unwind. It usually takes me a couple of hours, before I'm ready to go to bed. Sometimes longer. I like to have someone around to talk to, while I'm unwinding. If one of my roommates is home when I get in, we have a long gossip, catching up on all the news and showing what we brought home from the trip. That's fun. And it relaxes you so that you're ready for a nice long sleep."

Fleming was silent. Betsy stole a look at him. His expression was serious. Betsy took a cigarette. She offered the pack to Fleming.

"No thanks, I don't," he said. He took the book of matches out of Betsy's hand and lit the cigarette for her. "You girls all smoke too much," he commented.

Betsy decided to risk a snub.

"If you don't live alone—maybe you live in a hotel?" she queried.

Fleming looked at her, a faint movement around his mouth. For a moment, Betsy thought he might smile, or even laugh at her nosiness. Well, if he thinks I'm prying—he's right, she told herself, trying not to blush under his steady gaze.

But the moment passed, and when Fleming spoke, he said, "As a matter of fact, I live with my sister and her husband."

"Oh!" The exclamation was out before she could stop herself. Betsy could not hide her surprise.

Fleming grinned. "Didn't expect that, did you, Betsy? Did you imagine me with a bachelor pad, Playboy style, with wall-to-wall stereo and broads by the yard?"

This time, Betsy could feel the blush rising in her face.

"Well, no, not really, but I thought you might be sharing a place with another pilot."

"I'm too old for that sort of thing. That's okay for the youngsters. When I was in my early twenties, I shared an apartment with another guy. The place used to be long on dust and beer and short on food and clean glasses, as I recall. That kind of life's no good when you're my age."

"Some men think a bachelor apartment of their own is exciting," Betsy murmured.

"Oh yeah, sure—the swinging bachelor life." The tone of disdain in Fleming's voice was unmistakable. "Well, I've seen what that's like, Betsy—and believe me, it's not my style. I've seen those so-called swinging bachelors, pushing their shopping carts around the supermarket," he screwed up his face, and made his voice go high and imitative, "twittering over whether to get the prune or the apricot yoghurt, fussing about the laundry and the dry-cleaning. All that household stuff gives me the creeps. So do the guys who indulge in it."

Betsy laughed at the expression of disgust on Fleming's face.

The captain shrugged his shoulders. "Since I'm not the domestic type, I don't make the grade in the cosy bachelor-pad stakes. Guess I'm not house-trained enough. I make my home with my sister and brother-in-law and the arrangement works out fine. They have a large apartment, so we don't get in each other's way. And they respect my privacy. I am free to come and go as I please. They're casual people, I like that. I feel the place is my own. It's the ideal set-up for me."

"Your sister must be a very understanding person."

"Frankly, she's a nut. So's my brother-in-law. A couple of kooks—but nice kooks. My brother-in-law is my sister's third husband. I like him. I hope he's going to stick."

Then Fleming smiled and said, "I guess he will, at that. Eric Rasmussen's been able to hold out for the last ten years, so I figure they'll make it all the way."

Betsy smiled. She was thinking how totally different Fleming was from anything she had expected. Beneath that cool exterior, there was an interesting personality.

"Do you have a regular boyfriend, Betsy?" Fleming asked suddenly.

Betsy gave a start. "Uh, well, there is someone . . ." she began.

"Sorry, maybe I shouldn't have asked." Fleming didn't look particularly sorry, Betsy noted. "I guess a girl like you is bound to have plenty of fellows waiting around."

The memory of Jay Marshall flashed through Betsy's mind, and then she thought of Mike. The memories of her affair with Mike made the color rise in her face.

"Yes, I can see there are," Fleming said. "You're running through the list, right now. Tell me—anyone serious?"

"Depends what you mean by *serious*?"

Fleming gave her a long steady look. Then he leaned forward, put his hands on her shoulders and pulled her towards him. He brought his mouth down on hers and kissed her hard.

"I've been wanting to do that for quite some time," he said, his voice very low, as they broke apart. "You're beautiful, Betsy. You do things to me."

She sat looking into the grey eyes, wishing she knew what went on inside Fleming's head. He put his arms around her. At that instant, the telephone shrilled. They both jumped, then grinned self-consciously at the way they had been startled.

"Hello?" Betsy grabbed the receiver, hoping that whoever had chosen to call at that moment would be promptly struck by lightning for his sins.

An unknown male voice asked: "Is Lee there?"

After she had hung up, Betsy said, "It was someone for Lee."

"But you're expecting a call, aren't you?" Fleming asked.

"Why, no. What makes you think that?"

"You leapt so quickly for the phone. I got the impression that you were waiting for somebody."

Betsy stayed silent. It had crossed her mind that the caller could have been Mike.

Fleming was picking up his uniform cap and overcoat.

"I guess I'd better be getting along," he said. "The tiredness is beginning to hit. I'd best get home to bed."

Betsy stood up, reluctant to see him go though she, too, was feeling more tired by the minute.

"Will your sister be expecting you?" she asked.

Fleming threw his head back and laughed. "She's far too disorganized to ever expect anybody. Sometimes I wonder if she even notices that I've been missing for a few days."

"She must be very easy-going, not to worry at all about the times you come and go."

"Yeah. There's only one tiny snag in the whole set-up. Just one little thing that stops it from being perfect."

"What's that?"

"Every so often, when my sister doesn't have enough work to keep her busy, she gets around to remembering her only brother. And that means trouble. It's always trouble when Margaret starts thinking. Because the next thing I know, she's rustling up all these single, available women for me to meet. The kind of women who want to get themselves a husband."

"I'm sure you manage to fend them off without any trouble," Betsy said sharply.

Fleming shot her a quick glance.

"Thanks for the coffee," he said. He came close, took hold of her again. "You're sweet. You made the trip something special."

He kissed her, lightly. At the door, he said, "Be seeing you," and his tall figure strode rapidly away down the corridor.

Betsy went straight to her room and lay down on the bed. She could still feel the pressure of Fleming's lips on hers. It was a feeling she wanted to hold on to for a while.

She just lay on the bed, thinking. It had all been fine until the telephone had rung. It was as if the shrill ring of the phone had snapped something special that was just beginning to build. Then, it had seemed for a moment or two that the feeling would be re-established. But for some reason she could not fathom, Fleming had started giving her the speech about women who wanted to get husbands. She hadn't known whether to laugh at him or throw him out. Had he been making idle comments about his life with his sister—or had he had the colossal nerve to warn her off? If that was the case, he could go to hell, she thought angrily.

The post-flight fatigue was dragging her down into sleep. She closed her eyes. The veil of tiredness lifted momentarily, as Betsy wondered what Fleming had meant by his parting words. "Be seeing you." Did he mean on the next trip? Or—before that?

She could resist the tiredness no longer. She turned her face into the pillow and pulled the blanket up over her head. In this snug cocoon, she fell into a deep sleep, in which puzzles were resolved in distant dreams.

5

It was late evening when Betsy woke up. Fuzzy with sleep, she pulled on her robe and went into the kitchen. She made a cup of instant coffee, feeling too tired to start grinding beans for the percolator. It was tempting to go right back to bed and sleep right through till morning. Betsy gulped down some of the hot black coffee and it helped to strengthen her resolution. After all, it would not take her long to unpack, and then enjoy a nice long bath and maybe eat something. Then she'd have all the chores done and out of the way, and a good night's sleep would erase the post-trip tiredness.

"Hi! Anyone home?"

Lee's voice called from the apartment door.

"Lee!" Betsy was genuinely pleased. "I haven't seen you in an age."

The matching suitcase, overnight bag and shoulder bag were all dumped just inside the door. Lee, tall and very slim, was in the act of dropping her cape and fur hat onto the floor, to join her luggage. Pulling off a scarf, Lee came into the living room. The scarf wafted to the carpet. Before she got to the divan, Lee had discarded her boots.

"Any coffee?" she asked.

"Sure, if you dont mind instant."

Betsy went back to the kitchen. It had been so long since she had last seen Lee that she had forgotten her slapdash ways. She had even forgotten the strip that Lee

165

invariably performed, shedding her uniform piece by piece, starting the moment she stepped inside the door.

By the time Betsy had the coffee ready, Lee was lying on the divan, in her pants and bra, with her clothes scattered all around.

"Good thing Sharon's not home," Betsy observed. She picked up her roommate's uniform jacket and slacks from the rug and draped them over a chair. Miraculously, Lee's body-shirt was on the chair already.

"It was a pig of a trip," Lee said. She reached to her head and tugged at her elaborately coiffed red hair. The wig came off and Lee threw it across the room. She rubbed her ears, sighing with relief. "Those things are killing if you have to wear them for long," she said.

Her short blonde hair was pressed close to her head, giving her a very young, slightly boyish look. Lee stretched long, slender arms and legs and indulged in a mammoth yawn.

"You're on the Rome double-shuffle, aren't you?" Betsy asked, referring to a Flightways set-up in which cabin attendants did over a week's duty out of home base, flying the Atlantic there and back only once and doing flights out of Rome in between.

"That's my bid, for my sins," Lee finished stretching, and contemplated her long fingers and elegant nails. "We had delays everywhere; I'm a day late getting home; the weather was godawful in Europe; there was hardly time to do anything except sleep in Rome—and to cap it all, I broke two nails on the way home."

"Sounds like a great trip." Betsy picked up the empty cups.

"Oh, yes, and another thing. They made us take off our wigs," Lee pointed at the one she had just discarded, "every time we got back to Rome. Seems some girls smuggled stuff in packages under their wigs."

"On Flightways?" Betsy exclaimed. Smuggling of any kind was of course absolutely prohibited, but to smuggle narcotics of any kind was asking for trouble on an international scale.

Lee shook her head. "No, no one on the line," she said. "The scag's apparently been going in several directions— up from Africa, across from the Middle East and I think they pinned down one girl who came in from India, but

166

I'm not sure. Anyway, the heat was on, and so wigs were off. Actually, I only put mine back on again for the flight home." Again, she ran her fingers through her short hair.

"Well, after all that, I imagine you're hungry, aren't you?" Betsy eyed Lee speculatively. "How about some spaghetti? That's easy and quick enough, and I could rustle up a sauce."

Lee smiled. "That'd be great. Wow—but it's nice to get back when there's someone home to do the cooking!"

They went into the kitchen together, Lee trailing after Betsy, and she watched while Betsy looked at the shelves.

"There're all sorts of goodies," she finally announced. "Sharon must've laid in some staples. There's also a batch of extras she brought on her last trip. Those dried mushrooms she gets in Paris, for one. I could use them to make the spaghetti sauce."

She busied herself while Lee watched her from her chair at the kitchen table.

"And how was *your* trip, Betsy?"

Betsy told her. At least, she told her about young James and his rich father, her clashes with Linda, her trip to the theater with Marianne and the strange meeting with Kara Lane on the flight home.

"Quite an action-packed few days," Lee commented. By the time Betsy finished her account, they were sitting at the kitchen table, forking up spaghetti.

"Who else was on the flight?" Lee asked, a little too casually.

Betsy replied, "The fourth girl was someone called Judy Fransella. She's new, so you wouldn't know her. The captain was David Fleming."

"And?"

"The other two pilots were Larry Johnson—and Carl."

Lee's blue eyes were very narrow.

"Did Carl give you any message for me? Did he ask after me?"

"Not exactly," Betsy murmured.

"Hell!" Lee pouted. After a moment's thought, she asked: "Were there any calls for me?"

"Oh, yes!" Betsy suddenly remembered. "Some guy called this morning. Not long after I got home. But he didn't leave his name and he rang off before I could ask him."

167

"But it wasn't Carl?"

"No, I'm pretty sure not."

"Could have been anyone. Maybe Hank. Not that it matters." Lee pushed away her empty plate. "I've been thinking a lot about Carl while I've been away," she said. "I've come to the conclusion that he's a no-good bum. But I can't stop feeling the way I do about him."

She paused, and went on, "I wish I'd gotten your bid, Betsy. You'll be flying with him for a whole month. If I could do that, then maybe we'd be able to reach some kind of understanding."

"Maybe," Betsy said, doubtfully.

"Would you trade with me?" Lee looked up, flashing a wide smile. "It might mean a lot to me."

Betsy picked up plates from the table and took them over to the sink. She rinsed them under the faucet.

Anticipating Betsy's answer, Lee said, her smile gone, "I guess you're right. It wouldn't make a darn bit of difference, really."

Betsy stacked plates in the dishwasher.

"Betsy . . ." Lee's voice was hesitant. "Who . . . that is, who was . . . Carl dating . . . on the trip?"

"I don't know if he was 'dating' anyone seriously."

"You don't have to play with words. I know that Carl must have been dating someone. As to his being *serious*, I guess he's not serious about anyone. Tell me—who was it this time?"

Betsy lit a cigarette before she replied. You had to be careful what you said to Lee. She seemed dumb in many respects but where instinct counted, she had a way of getting straight to the true meaning of what was said.

"I think he went out with Linda while we were in London. Of course, I'm not certain."

"How do you mean, not certain?"

"Well, that's what Linda said. She's not reliable, though, and it wouldn't be a good idea to believe everything she says."

There was a brief silence, during which Lee propped her elbows on the table and cupped her chin in her hands.

"Trust me, to fall for a guy like Carl," Lee said. "I know perfectly well that you and Sharon don't approve of him. Or of any other of my dates, come to that. Well, I have news for you. I don't approve of 'em either!"

168

"Then, why. . . ?" Betsy enquired, raising her eyebrows.

"Because I don't seem able to help it, that's why! It sounds so easy, for women like Sharon to talk about security and all that stuff—but I think I'd *die*, if I had to live with someone like Tom! He may be okay for Sharon— but as far as I'm concerned, he's strictly dullsville. All that virtue can be an awful goddam bore, when it comes right down to it."

Betsy drew on her cigarette. Lee was unusually talkative; she had never heard her voice so many of her opinions before. She supposed it must be Lee's way of winding down after a hectic flight. Maybe throwing off her inhibitions as she tossed off her clothes, helped her relax, until her tiredness took over completely and she could sleep.

"You should understand that, Betsy. Otherwise, you wouldn't have turned Jay down—or taken up with a character like Mike. You agree with me, don't you?"

"I guess so. Certainly, I couldn't take Tom as a fiancé. But he's perfect for someone like Sharon, you've got to admit it."

Lee frowned. "That's what I don't understand," she said slowly. "How come Tom is perfect for Sharon and so he makes her happy—but the guys I think are perfect for me, don't make *me* happy?"

"Write Dear Abby," Betsy advised. "It's too complicated a question for me."

"Don't you feel that way about Mike?" Lee persisted.

"I feel it's time I took a bath," Betsy said, trying to evade the question.

"Are you in love with Mike?"

Betsy considered. She stubbed out the cigarette in an ashtray, taking a long time over it.

"I think I just fell out of love with him."

A gleam of interest immediately appeared in Lee's eyes.

"Oh—who's the new love?" she inquired.

Betsy cursed herself for a fool. She shouldn't have underestimated Lee's ability to pounce on what lay behind the remark she had just made so carelessly.

"No one," Betsy said. "Now, I *must* get into that bathtub."

She hurried to the bathroom and turned on the water so

169

hard that the noise drowned out whatever Lee was calling after her.

When Betsy emerged from the bathroom, she found Lee asleep on the divan. All the lights were on and Lee was still wearing her pants and bra. Betsy turned off the main lights, leaving one lamp burning. Then she found Lee's robe and draped it over her.

Lee, Betsy thought, managed to live like a permanently displaced person. She drifted through the apartment and then left without anyone being really aware that she had been there. She slept on the divan bed, the most tangible sign of her presence being the discarded clothes she scattered around. Lee didn't even have many possessions; a few clothes and her regulation luggage seemed to be the extent of her belongings.

Suddenly, the blue eyes opened.

"Oh, did I fall asleep?" Lee murmured.

"Sorry, I must have disturbed you. Go back to sleep again."

Lee stretched. "I don't know—I don't feel like settling down for the night, somehow. Maybe I'll nap for an hour or two. Then I'll think of something to do."

"Like what?" Betsy asked. "You're just off a flight, for heaven's sake, you need your sleep."

"Not me, I'm the original cat-napper, remember?"

Betsy had, in fact, forgotten that Lee rarely slept more than a few hours at a time. It was so easy to forget things about Lee.

She was sitting up now, looking at Betsy. "Tell me—who did you meet in London? Someone must have made your feelings change towards Mike. You were pretty well hooked on him last time I talked to you. Come on, tell—who was it?"

"It wasn't Carl!" Betsy was on the defensive.

Relief showed on Lee's face for a fleeting instant. Then her expression changed to one of interest.

"But there is somebody?"

For a wild moment, Betsy actually considered telling Lee about David Fleming. Then her natural caution prevailed. After all, what was there really to tell? She knew so little about him. They had not even gone out together. She didn't even know whether they ever would. His parting *be seeing you* was as ambiguous as most other things were about him. No, there was nothing she could say. Her relationship with Fleming, whatever it was, was a new and very uncertain thing. She didn't feel she could talk to anyone about it yet, not even a gentle friend like Lee.

She turned away and stared around the room, pretending she had not heard her roommate's last question.

"Where's Thomas?" she asked, looking in vain for the turtle's glass tank.

"Sharon was the last one out, wasn't she?" Lee answered. "She must've taken him down to Kelly's apartment."

"I'll go get him," Betsy replied and, after returning to her bedroom to slip on a sweater and some slacks, went down to the superintendent's apartment.

Mr. Kelly was in his customary alcoholic stupor as he handed Thomas over. Mrs. Shumway, already in the elevator when Betsy entered, smiled at the girl and peered into the tank.

"Oh, it's a turtle," she said in disappointed tones, as though a turtle, innocent in its habits, denied her a critical opinion.

Betsy, stifling a desire to say, *no, it's not, it's a tarantula*, smiled back innocently and said, "Yes. His name's Thomas."

"Thomas?" echoed the building's bespectacled busybody.

"Yes—because we figure he doubts we'll ever feed him."

The elevator stopped at the sixth floor and Betsy smiled at the woman muttering "Doubting Thomas" under her breath in the stationary car. She was still smiling as she reached the apartment door at the memory of Mrs. Shumway's near-sighted stare.

Lee was sitting up, smoking a cigarette, her robe draped over her shoulders.

"How's the pet monster?"

"He seems okay." Betsy regarded Thomas critically. "But I don't think all those whisky fumes can be too good for his health."

Lee laughed. "He must be used to that by now, with all the time he spends down there with ol' Kelly."

Betsy put the tank back in its customary place, gave him some turtle food and went back into the kitchen.

171

When she emerged she noticed that Lee had gone to sleep again.

She picked up the telephone and took it into her bedroom, and turned off the lights. If nothing woke Lee, she might get a decent night's rest.

Betsy pulled her door to, leaving only a minute gap for the telephone's extension cord. She had just climbed into bed when the telephone shrilled. She leaned over to answer it.

"Hello?"

"Betsy?" It was Mike.

"Yes, Mike."

"Thank God. I thought I might get Sharon, that prissy roommate of yours."

"I just got in from my flight today," Betsy told him. "I'm in bed."

"I'll be right over." Mike's laugh echoed over the line.

"Nothing doing." Betsy was firm. "I'm exhausted. I've just worked my way across the Atlantic. Not to mention that it was a pretty tiring trip all the way round."

"So?" Mike sounded bored.

"So what I need now is sleep. Hours and hours of it."

"You could get some sleep here. Why don't you come over?"

"Now?"

"Yes, now."

She did not want to go all the way down to the East Village. It was late and she was exhausted.

"No, Mike. I'm too tired."

"Shit." It was more statement than criticism. "Tomorrow morning, then? I've got a whole load of things to show you."

In the end, she agreed. She would be down the next day.

"But tomorrow evening, Mike, there are chores I *must* do."

"Oh, sure," his voice mocked. "All on schedule, eh? But okay, tomorrow evening. Anyway, I gotta go to the gallery tomorrow during the day. It works out fine." He sounded pleased with himself, and cheerful. "See you tomorrow."

Betsy put the phone down and reflected that she had given Mike almost no thought all the time she'd been

172

away. Until recently she'd thought about him a great deal. But this last trip, she'd gotten involved with James, and then there had been David Fleming.

Why had she agreed to visit Mike? Did she have a guilty conscience? It didn't make sense; she hadn't done anything. Yet, as soon as Mike phoned, she had been ready to fall in with his plans. Sharon would call that "running after" him.

Betsy lay back and smiled to herself. Sharon so thoroughly disapproved of Mike. Most people she knew, disapproved of Mike. Had that been his attraction for her? Was it that corner of herself that wanted to be different, to go against the stream, that felt the attraction of Mike?

It was always difficult to understand one's own attractions. Betsy always found other people's entanglements easier to analyze than her own. Well, almost always, Sharon's for instance. As she had told Lee earlier, it was easy to see why Sharon and Tom suited each other so well. Lee's attractions were more complex. Privately, Betsy thought that Lee seemed to be seeking some form of punishment, because the men she inevitably fell for were the type who would let her down. And Lee knew it, Betsy was pretty sure—knew it even when she first went out with them. Certainly she knew that Carl Masden was called Casanova Carl.

Oh, go ahead, Betsy told herself. Be smug and smart about everybody else. But how about yourself, Elizabeth Ann Blair? What makes you fall for someone like Mike di Falco?

And as the words went through her head, she knew it was all over. All over between her and Mike.

She also had the immediate suspicion that he was not going to take to the idea gracefully.

6

"Were you up all night?" Betsy called to Lee, surveying the collection of cups littering the kitchen counter.

"Just about," came the answer, shouted from behind the sofa. "And now I can't find my blouse."

"It's on the chair. You put it there last night."

"Oh. Oh yes, I see it. Thanks."

Betsy finished preparing breakfast and went to the shower. Both girls were tackling the usual post-flight tasks. Parts of uniforms had to be washed, others taken to the dry cleaners; boots and shoes got a thorough polishing, usually home-administered, although every so often Betsy would treat herself to a professional shine, usually when the pair in question needed re-heeling. And there was household laundry to be done as well as grocery shopping.

"Are you sure you're not too tired?" Betsy asked as they began dividing the chores between them. "You didn't sleep much at all."

"I never do," Lee smiled. "And anyway, I can always take a nap later."

"Well, if that's okay with you," Betsy said dubiously.

Lee decided to do the laundry; Betsy said she would go to the dry cleaners' and the store.

When Betsy returned from the store, Lee greeted her with news of a party in the building that evening.

"Up in 20A. We're both invited, of course."

"Thanks, but I'm going to see Mike."

174

And Betsy told Lee about his late phone call while they put away the groceries.

"Well, you could bring him."

"He doesn't like parties."

"And he doesn't like airline people," Lee finished. "I remember now."

Betsy smiled. Mike's few visits to the Stew Zoo had not been happy ones.

"Well," Lee went on, "you could come up to 20A when you get back from the Village. It's sure to be an all-night affair."

"Maybe, I'll see."

"I'm so glad it's right here in the building. I feel like a party, but I don't feel like going out very far. It's too cold."

"I think you feel it because you're still tired," Betsy commented. "Why don't you get some rest?"

"Maybe later," Lee murmured, sounding insincere. Betsy let the subject drop; Lee was gentle and pliable up to a point, but if she wanted to tire herself out, that was her business.

The first thing Betsy noticed was the number of new canvases in the loft. Before she took her coat off, she ran from one to the other, looking, comparing. Mike watched her, waiting for her comment.

"You've done so much!" Betsy exclaimed. "When did you find time for all these?"

"Do you like them?"

"Yes, yes, I do. You've got a real feeling of New York in these street scenes. They—they really convey the atmosphere."

Mike lit a cigarette, trying to look nonchalant.

"I hit a good streak," he said. "Been working like a madman these past few weeks."

"While everything else went to hell," Betsy commented. She looked around the loft. There was a thick layer of dust everywhere, debris littered the floor, unwashed pans and dishes stood piled in and around the large, old-fashioned sink, together with paint-brushes and rags and old paint-splattered jars. Mike himself was dressed in dirty, paint-blotched jeans and a sweater; his hair was dirty and there was stubble on his face.

The violence of Mike's reaction to her remark caught her unaware.

"You bitch!" he burst out, "you narrow-minded, petty, stupid . . ."

"Hey! Wait a minute! What did I do?"

"I've been working my goddam ass off, achieving Christ knows how much real work, worthwhile stuff. And you come in and all you can do is stand there making prissy comments about the way the place looks! Christ—why don't you get out to suburbia, where you belong, along with all the other stupid chicks who don't know a work of art from an asshole."

"Listen, I told you I like the paintings!"

"I like the paintings!" Mike did a cruel parody of Betsy's voice. Then he stamped off to the end of the long room, throwing himself down on the battered old couch.

Betsy began fastening her coat. She picked up her woolen scarf.

"What are you running away for?" Mike's voice demanded.

"I'm not staying here for you to put me down," Betsy replied, "and I'm not 'running away' as you put it. I've decided to leave."

With as much dignity as she could muster, she made for the door.

Mike was at her side almost immediately.

"You can't go now," he said.

"Just watch me!"

"Look—I'm sorry if I sounded rough. But you don't understand—I've been through a hell of a working bout. I've run myself ragged. Literally. I feel like a man who's been on a royal bender and who's just beginning to wake up. No kidding."

The sincerity in Mike's tones made Betsy stop. She looked at his face. She saw the stubble on his pale skin, and the bloodshot eyes.

"You look horrible," she said.

He laughed. "Sure, I believe you. But I'm not asking you to admire my manly beauty. I'm asking you to understand about my work."

His work. Betsy turned back into the loft, taking off her scarf and coat. She knew that there was nothing in Mike's life that really mattered to him besides his work. She

176

should have remembered how oblivious he was to every-thing else, how touchy he became when he wore himself out with a prolonged painting bout. She wondered how she could have forgotten in such a short time.

"Have you anything to eat?" she asked. She poked in the closet that served as a food cupboard. There was some moldy bread, a can of beans, and a jar of instant coffee. The small ice-box next to the sink held a carton of milk and a withered orange.

"When did you last eat?"

"I've no idea." Mike was lighting another cigarette. "Oh, yeah—I had some crackers at the gallery this morn-ing."

"You'd better call the deli, have something sent up. Otherwise you'll starve right in front of me."

His good humor apparently restored, Mike dialed the number of the delicatessen down the block. He ordered pastrami sandwiches, pizzas and beer.

When the food was delivered, they picnicked on the floor. Though Betsy hadn't thought she was hungry, she managed to eat some pizza and drink some beer. From the way Mike wolfed down the rest of the food, she could tell that he had not really eaten in a long, long time.

They lit cigarettes. Mike gave a long, smoke-filled sigh of satisfaction.

"I feel more like a member of the human race, now," he remarked. "God, but these past few days have been something! I wish I could describe how it feels—but I'm hopeless with words. I can only talk with colors and form and stuff you can *see*."

Betsy leaned back against the couch.

"Do you see any *advance* in my latest work?" Mike asked. "You see, I feel as if I kind of took a step forward. I'm not sure—it's so goddam difficult to judge your own stuff, but I definitely have the feeling that I've progressed in some way or other."

Betsy shivered. It was cold in the loft. The only means of heating the huge room was an electric heater and an old wood-burning stove that was unusable because Mike was out of wood.

"Kev was here the other day and he said that *he* thought there had been a definite development in style ... I guess I ought to let Lenny see this lot, he's the best critic

177

I know ... but there's been a show uptown and everyone's been tied up for a while."

Art is the only thing that exists for him, Betsy thought. She pulled her coat round her shoulders, trying to keep warm. Mike either didn't care that she had been away for days or else he hadn't noticed. Betsy suspected it was the latter. All he could think about was what was happening in his own narrow world. He didn't ask about her trip, or how she liked London, because he simply had no interest.

He was prowling about the loft, looking critically at his new canvases.

"Come here," he called over his shoulder, "tell me what you think of this one."

The painting was a scene in a Village coffee-house. Betsy knew the place well; it was always jammed with students, artists, and unemployed actors and actresses. She and Mike had often been there together. Mike had obviously been spending some time there on his own. She scanned the scene; in the foreground was a very pretty girl.

"Who's she?" Betsy asked, pointing at the girl.

Mike gave a huge shout of laughter.

"Christ, but if that isn't just like a woman!" he exploded. "You ask for an opinion on a painting and she fixes on the nearest female that she doesn't know."

"You don't have to say anything if you don't want to," Betsy said stiffly. She was beginning to feel that she could do nothing right as far as Mike was concerned.

"I'm not worried about telling you about her," he said with relish. "She's a cute chick I met in the coffee-house one night. I sketched her, got to know her. And since you're looking so suspicious Betsy, my love, I'll put all your suspicions at rest, right now. Yes, she did come to the loft, so that I could finish drawing her. And yes, I did sleep with her. Does that satisfy you?"

It took an enormous effort, but Betsy controlled her impulse to wheel round and hit Mike across the face as hard as she could. Something told her that that was the kind of reaction he was trying to provoke. She had had enough of being provoked by Mike. She waited a few seconds and when she was sure she could keep her voice steady, she said, "It's really nothing to me, whether you sleep with her or not. You're free to do what you like."

Mike laughed again. "Sure am, baby."

"And so am I," she finished. "That's the way we both want it. That's the way it is."

There was a silence.

"Who you been sleeping with?" he demanded, suddenly.

Betsy walked away. She picked up the debris of the picnic and tried to cram the used paper plates and napkins into the already overflowing garbage pail.

"Leave that," Mike ordered. "Stop playing housewife, it gets on my nerves."

"Stop ordering me around—that gets on *my* nerves," Betsy countered.

Another silence. The expression in Mike's grey eyes was one of pure surprise.

"What's got into you, tonight?" he asked. "You're in a kinda funny mood. What gives?"

Betsy rinsed her hands at the sink and dried them slowly.

Impatient for an answer, Mike persisted, "Are you mad about the chick I told you about? If so, then you're out of your cotton-picking mind. Look, I can't stand the jealousy-bit and we'd better get the whole thing straight, right now."

"Oh, I've got it straight," Betsy said, coolly. "We're both free and it works both ways. That suits me."

"So you've met some other guy? Okay, big deal. I suppose you want to tell me all about him, that the idea?"

"No, I don't. And there isn't necessarily another guy."

"Come on—there has to be. That's what this is all about, isn't it?"

Betsy took a deep breath. "No, Mike, it's not. It's not about anyone you might be sleeping with, or I might be—interested in. It's about you and me."

Mike narrowed his eyes. "Are you working up to the marriage scene?" he asked. "Telling me I've got to make an honest woman of you, something crazy like that?"

"Heaven forbid!" Betsy looked round the loft and the squalor of it struck her forcibly. "No, as a matter of fact, Mike, I'm trying to tell you that—it's all over."

"What's all over? What's all this melodramatic stuff?"

Betsy spread her hands in a gesture of helplessness.

"Mike—I'm telling you that our affair is over. Finished. I don't feel the same way I used to. I suspect that goes for

179

you, too. There's no point in dragging it on, when it's already dead."

After a long and thoughtful pause, Mike said, "So you have met someone else. And you think you're in love with him. Right?"

Betsy smiled; she couldn't help it. She was thinking of David Fleming. How ironic that Mike should assume she had met someone and started an affair. He would never believe she was interested in a man she had not yet gone to bed with.

"I suppose you've fallen for some robot in uniform— one of those uptight pilots," Mike sneered.

"Mike, it doesn't matter whether there is or is not another man in my life. That's beside the point. The point is, that I feel there is nothing going for *us* any more. Why, you don't even know that I exist! I come here—at your orders, practically—and you don't bother to ask if I had a good trip. I've been away, damn it—I've been thousands of miles away. And you don't want to know how it was, you don't ask anything about my life, all you talk about is yourself, and your own interests . . ."

"Listen, I'm an artist, not a suburban husband. I don't go for that had-a-good-day-dear routine, and you know it."

"Mike, you don't go for anything outside yourself. You're totally selfish."

"I'm an artist! That's all that matters to me!"

"That's your excuse." Betsy looked Mike straight in the eye. "You use it like a club to get your own way in everything. Okay, if that's how you want it. But I can't take it any more, Mike, and that's the truth. I'm telling you it's all over. I'm through."

"You stupid bitch!" Mike shouted. "You don't know what the fuck you're talking about. You sound like every bourgeois, husband-hunting chick I ever met! All you're worried about is keeping things neat and tidy, asking the right, polite questions, making the social scene. Well, I don't go for that shit. So if you don't like it, then you can clear out and good riddance."

Betsy picked up her scarf and looked around for her purse.

"That's right—run away!" Mike was still shouting. "Run away from anything that disturbs your tight little world, with its up-tight little ideas."

"Mike, I'm sorry . . ." Betsy began.

"Sorry, hell!" He was really angry now. "You simply can't face the truth, the real world, that's what it's all about. You want to live in a phony set-up where things run on phony schedules, where there's a goddam routine for every goddam thing and life runs according to a set of rigid rules. Outside of that framework you fall to pieces, you haven't the guts to try and really live."

"That may be so." Betsy spoke quietly, trying to calm Mike's rage. "I'm not saying it's not. I'm only saying that I can't live your way. I have to live the way that feels right to *me*."

He seized hold of her arm. "Jesus, to think that I tangled with a stew!" he sneered. "You live your whole life by the rules, don't you? And how about the new fly-boy lover? I suppose he's the same, huh? All fixed ideas, and up-tight, gung-ho, can't see further than company regulations. Christ, what a bunch of goddam hypocrites you all are."

Goaded, Betsy snapped, "It's easy to sneer, but you know absolutely nothing about it!"

"I've seen some of those pilots. Neat uniforms, short hair, square heads and square ideas."

"There is nothing especially virtuous about having long hair and dirty clothes," Betsy raged. "You may think so, but I'm telling you there isn't!"

"Why, you . . ." Mike's fingers tightened on Betsy's arm so that his grip hurt her.

"Listen—those guys do an important job, too," she flared. "They are responsible for other people's *lives*! Every time they take a flight, they hold the lives of a great many people in their hands. Pilots aren't up-tight, Mike—they're *responsible*!"

"That's a load of bullshit." Mike's angry face was staring right into Betsy's. She could see the stubble that covered his cheeks and chin.

"Try thinking about it next time you take a flight," Betsy said evenly. "And when you're sitting in your seat, just ask yourself who you'd rather have up front flying the plane. Some crazy artist, who doesn't give a damn about anything and believes in playing everything by ear—or a well-disciplined man who knows his job, who's trained to follow the square regulations you sneer about, who understands that keeping rules is a matter of life and death." Her anger was roused to full pitch. "I don't know how you have the nerve to make such cheap cracks! You don't understand anything about airline life, you don't know the responsibilities we carry or the importance of what we do! We don't follow the rules for fun, you know—we do it for the safety of idiots like you!"

For a moment, Mike hesitated. Then, he seized hold of Betsy, pulled her roughly towards him and kissed her hard. She struggled, but Mike had a firm grip on her.

"Let me go, let me . . ." She tried to wriggle out of his grasp, to escape the strong arms.

Mike laughed. He kissed her again, a long voluptuous kiss. Then he pulled her with him towards the couch.

"No, no, I won't!" Betsy was screaming. She beat against Mike with her fists, kicked out at his shins.

"Ohh! You dirty bitch!" Mike stumbled as one of Betsy's kicks hit home. In a second, she twisted out of his grasp. He grabbed for her, and got hold of her coat.

Betsy felt herself being pulled down onto the couch. She fought desperately, flailing with arms and legs. Mike threw himself down on top of her, managing to pin her beneath him so that she was helpless. Betsy struggled for a while, then suddenly went limp.

"You give in?" Mike was grinning.

"No, I don't." She was furious. Furious at her own helplessness.

"I bet your pilot doesn't make love to you this way," Mike said. With one hand, he pulled at Betsy's zipper.

"Stop!" Suddenly, Betsy found that Mike revolted her. He was dirty, his clothes smelled, his body smelled. His unkempt hair and unshaven face were physically repellent. Desperate to escape, Betsy gave a sudden heave of her body. Mike was caught by surprise and tumbled off the couch.

Betsy leapt to her feet, swept up her coat and holding her open dress against her, ran for the door.

From the floor behind her, Mike said, "Okay, okay. I get the message. Rape's not my bag. No need to run out of here half-dressed, screaming for the cops."

Betsy stopped, watching Mike warily from the far end of the loft. He picked himself up, sat down on the couch.

She began zipping her dress up, keeping a close eye on Mike as she did so.

He said, in almost a conversational tone, almost as if he was talking to himself, "You needn't think I'm so hard up for a lay that I have to rape you. Jesus, it's not worth the effort! Your pilot is welcome to you. Prissy little bitch. That chick I painted, she knows what it's all about. She knows how to give a guy a good time, without any crap."

Betsy moved quietly toward the door. Mike's voice continued its catalogue of insults. She hesitated a moment. There was no pause in Mike's vicious speech.

Without another word, Betsy walked out of the loft. As soon as the door closed behind her, she ran down the stairs as fast as she could, stumbling several times in her haste.

Outside, it was cold. Figures were lurking in the shadows against the building. They spoke to her, one tried to touch her, but she pushed him out of the way in her headlong flight.

She was on the avenue where there were lights.

"Taxi!" She shouted, standing in the street waving her arms frantically. A cab screeched to a halt beside her. She heaved a sigh of relief and scrambled in.

7

When Betsy reached home, the apartment was empty. Lee's things were strewn around the living room.

Betsy sat down and lit a cigarette. She wished Lee were there to talk to. Why wasn't Sharon back? Wasn't she due in from Paris? To check, she dialed the number for flight arrivals. The long roster of Flightways' trips was recited.

" . . . from Paris, delayed on ground. Please call again later for further information, or call . . ."

Betsy put down the receiver. There was no point in checking further.

Still, being alone felt unbearable. She began pacing up and down. She had to banish Mike and his bitter words from her mind. She had to think about something else. Of course! Lee must be at the party in 20A she had been talking about that morning.

Betsy stubbed out her half-smoked cigarette. What she needed was company—distraction—anything to chase away her black mood. She decided to look in at the party.

She could hear the noise as soon as she stepped out of the elevator on the twentieth floor. Rock music and the sound of many voices surged through the open door of the apartment.

Betsy stepped into the smoke-filled living room. The lighting was minimal and every inch of space seemed occupied.

"Excuse me, excuse me . . ." Betsy pushed through the crush of bodies. She had visited the apartment before, so at least she was able to find her way through the semi-darkness.

She peered through the gloom to see if there was anyone she knew.

Half a dozen people were dancing in the center of the room, their bodies moving rhythmically to the throbbing music. Betsy recognized the girl in the see-through blouse as one of the stews throwing the party. Then she saw another stew she recognized, who was reclining on the floor, a young pilot beside her.

"Hi, Sue!"

"Hi, Betsy!"

She began to feel glad she had come. It was a relief to be with people she knew, people from her own world.

"What're you drinking?" The young man who greeted her also worked for Flightways. Not flight-crew; Betsy had a vague memory of having seen him in the Sales Office.

Whoever he was, he handed Betsy a glass of wine. The wine tasted good. Must have been brought back from Europe by one of the girls, she thought. When she looked up, the young man had disappeared in the crush. Since there was nowhere else to sit, Betsy lowered herself to the floor. The din of the party surrounded her, dancing feet hemmed her into her dark corner. Betsy was content not to be alone any more. In the smoke and hubbub, there was no chance to think about anything sad or serious.

Another man was bending over, holding out a hand. Betsy took the hand and allowed herself to be pulled to her feet. She began to dance with her unknown partner.

"You a stewardess?" the man wanted to know.

Betsy smiled. Funny, how men always wanted to know that: it seemed important to them, for some reason she could not fathom.

"I haven't seen you around before," he said.

She shrugged. The man came close, held her tightly.

"I'd've remembered you if I'd seen you before."

Betsy laughed, swung away in time to the music.

"What's your name?"

"Betsy. You?"

"I'm Chuck. Great party, isn't it?"

They danced until Chuck suggested they find themselves a quiet place where they could talk. The overwhelming noise was beginning to get to Betsy, so she was glad to agree. Chuck appropriated a bottle of wine and two glasses. And they found a corner in the hall that was less noisy.

"Tell me about yourself," Chuck said, pulling Betsy down beside him on the shag rug.

Suddenly, she felt bored with the whole thing—with Chuck, the party, the whole getting-to-know-you game. It was a game that she had played too many times before.

"Tell me about yourself, first," she parried. "What do you do?"

It took Chuck a long while to explain and while he did, Betsy drank several glasses of wine. She began to feel decidedly light-headed. Chuck made a joke: Betsy found it uproariously funny. She laughed and laughed, she couldn't stop laughing. She felt she was floating . . .

Betsy didn't come down to earth until some time later when a girl shook her and said:

"Make up your mind—do you want to come or not?"

With some difficulty, Betsy focused on the girl. It was Lee. Her blonde hair tousled, her eyes bright, Lee was asking her something.

"What?"

"Listen," Lee said, "Pierre and I are going on to a discotheque. This party's just about finished. Do you and Chuck want to come along too?"

"Count us in," Chuck said.

"Not me," Betsy said quickly.

"It's a real fun place," Lee persuaded.

"Sure is—we'll have a great time," an older man put in. He spoke with a French accent and Betsy figured he had to be the Pierre Lee had mentioned.

"Come on, let's have fun," Chuck urged.

"Oh—I'm going to throw up!" Betsy put her hand to her mouth and rushed out of the room before anyone could stop her. She made it to the bathroom, locked herself in, then sat down on the edge of the bath and giggled. She didn't feel sick at all. But it had seemed the only way to get out of going to the discotheque.

There was a lot of banging on the bathroom door, but eventually Lee and Pierre and Chuck must have decided to go on to the discotheque without her. When things quietened down, she let herself out.

There were fewer people in the apartment now, but it was a lot smokier and the music seemed louder than ever. She made her way over sprawled bodies, to the door. Then she took the elevator back down to her own floor.

8

As Betsy stepped out of the elevator she saw, stretched full-length across the threshold of the apartment, the recumbent figure of Mike.

"Oh, so you really were out." He grinned at Betsy. "I didn't get any answer and I figured you were pretending not to be home. So I settled down to wait."

"Mike, don't be ridiculous! For God's sake, get up off the floor."

"Actually, it's comfortable down here. Cosier than the loft . . ."

Betsy stood, waiting. She could not get to the door until Mike moved. Looking up with simulated innocence, he inquired:

"Are you inviting me in?"

Betsy realized, with a stab of irritation, that she had no alternative.

"Get up and stop behaving like an idiot," she hissed. "And don't talk so loud or you'll rouse the whole building." All she needed was for someone like Mrs. Shumway to see Mike on the floor.

Inside, Betsy faced Mike, furiously.

"What the hell do you think you're doing here, in the middle of the night? I don't want you here!"

"You've been drinking," Mike observed, "My, My, little Betsy Sunshine is on the sauce."

Betsy lammed out and struck Mike across the face. He staggered backwards, taken by surprise. But his recovery was quick. Before she could move away, he lunged forward and grabbed her.

"You're going to listen to me, this time," he told her, "and you can save the karate till later. I'm going to have my say, first."

He marched her to the sofa and gave her a push so that she sat down, hard.

Betsy sat quite still. There was something about Mike that made her almost afraid. She had never seen him in this strange mood before. It struck her that he had never come to her before, after they had quarrelled. She had always been the one to take the first step, to patch things up. But this time it was different.

"Okay, so you said your piece earlier," Mike began. He was pacing nervously up and down the room. "Now I'm gonna say mine. Because I don't agree with what you said. I don't believe our affair is finished; there's too much goddam reaction when we get together, for anything to be 'finished.' You may not like the way it is—hell, *I* may not like the way it is—but there's something too strong between you and me to be ignored or told to go away."

He swung round angrily. "Do you deny that?" he demanded.

Betsy saw that his face was pale and his eyes had a strange glitter. It crossed her mind that he had to be high; but high on *what*?

"I don't deny anything," she said. As she spoke, she was casting round for something to calm him, something to persuade him to go home, leave the arguments till morning.

"You tried to say it was all over, finished, when you were at my place," he repeated. He shook his head, as if puzzled. "You can't say that, Betsy. You just *can't*."

"Mike, why don't you sit down, let's talk this over calmly."

"That's what we're doing, or so I thought!" Mike resumed his uneasy pacing. "How about that pilot guy?" he asked, suddenly.

"What pilot?"

"You know goddam-well what pilot!" Mike's voice rose excitedly.

"I didn't say there was anyone else involved," Betsy chose her words carefully. "Truly, I didn't Mike. It was *you* who invented the pilot."

He stopped abruptly, before the sofa. "Level with me, tell me who it is," he commanded.

Betsy wavered. She could see that Mike refused to believe that there was no other man involved; he couldn't accept it. And in his present strange mood, she felt it would be foolish to arouse his anger further.

"There's—someone in London," she murmured.

"A *limey*?" Mike sounded astonished.

"Yes."

"How did you meet him?"

"On the flight," Betsy lied.

"What does he do?"

Betsy looked up at Mike's taut figure. "Does it matter?" she asked wearily. The pleasant effect of the wine she had drunk had worn off and she was aware of a pounding headache.

"Tell me what he does!" Mike insisted.

"He's—he's a businessman."

"Liar! Lying little bitch!"

Betsy saw the blow coming, and ducked. Mike missed her and stumbled so that he fell onto the sofa. She leapt away but he recovered and came right after her.

"Tell me, tell me the truth!" Mike had seized her and was shaking her like a rag doll.

Betsy felt her knees give under her. She would have fallen if Mike had not had such a firm grip on her. He sensed her collapse and stopped the crazy shaking.

"Betsy! Are you okay?"

He was holding her in his arms now, his voice worried.

Betsy was hardly aware of how she got back onto the sofe, but the next thing she knew, she was lying down and Mike was kneeling beside her, his anxious face peering into hers.

"Betsy, Betsy . . ." he was saying.

"What happened?"

Her head was pounding and the room seemed to be going round.

"Take it easy." Mike stood up. "I'd better get you something. D'you want a drink?"

Betsy said nothing. She lay still and wished that Mike would go away. She felt she had had all she could take.

Mike however, showed no signs of leaving. He sat at the end of the sofa, subdued, staring down at the rug and smoking. Betsy gave a sigh and closed her eyes.

"Look—I'm sorry." His voice was gruff. "I know I haven't behaved very well, by your standards. But what you said earlier—it kind of freaked me out. I—I wasn't prepared for it. I mean, I figured you and I had something good going between us."

With an effort, Betsy said, "The good things come to an end sometimes, as well. It doesn't always work out, Mike, you know that."

He shrugged. "I don't fucking well know anything any more," he muttered.

Betsy closed her eyes again. She longed to escape into sleep, away from the turmoil of emotion and pain. Then she heard Mike's voice saying, "God, it feels like the top of my head is coming off." He was clutching his head desperately with both hands.

"Try some aspirin," Betsy suggested.

He gave a wild laugh. "Aspirin! Christ, here I am with the screaming meanies and she says aspirin—baby, those chalk-pills don't do a thing against the flaming dragons that are burning up my skull."

"Mike—what have you taken?" Betsy asked.

He turned and glared at her with bloodshot eyes. "Mind your own goddam business."

Betsy sat up. She put one leg to the ground.

"Stay where you are!" Mike ordered.

"But, Mike . . ."

"Stay there, I say!"

She was close to tears; it was only by great effort that she kept them in check. She controlled herself mainly by remembering that Mike would probably become further enraged if he saw her cry. He hated to see her crying and usually it made him get mean.

Suddenly she heard a rasping sound. A key in the door of the apartment! Lee, she wondered?

In a moment, Sharon's voice called out, "Hi! Anyone home?"

"Sharon!" Betsy jumped up and raced to the door. "I'm so thankful that you've come. Please, Sharon . . ."

Sharon, neat and trim in her uniform, dropped her bags and looked around in surprise. "What's the matter? What's going on here?"

Mike rose from the sofa.

"I'm the matter," he said, belligerently, "and don't you interfere in what doesn't concern you, or I . . ."

"Shut up!" Sharon snapped. She turned to Betsy. "What's going on?"

Tears began to roll down Betsy's face.

Sharon's determined little figure stamped over to where Mike stood. "Out!" she said, pointing a finger to the door. "Out, this instant!"

Mike started to grin. Sharon gave him a hearty push.

"I said *out*," she repeated in a steely tone. "Any trouble and I call the cops, *vite, vite.*"

Betsy saw that Sharon, who barely reached Mike's shoulder, was literally propelling him out of the apartment. Within seconds, the door had slammed behind him and Sharon was holding her arm, talking to her gently.

"Come along, you should be in bed, you've had a rough time."

Sharon put the tray down on the bedside table.

"Drink this," she ordered, handing Betsy a cup.

"What is it?"

"Camomile tea. It's very good for the nerves."

Betsy smiled. Sharon sounded just like her grandmother used to when she made special *tisanes* for sick members of the family.

"It'll help you sleep, too," Sharon said. "I would suggest a sleeping pill but I don't know how long you have before you go out on a flight."

"I don't want a pill, anyway." Betsy sighed. "If I don't sleep—well, just too bad."

"Mike seemed very strange," Sharon remarked. "Was he drunk?"

Betsy shook her head. "It wasn't alcohol," she said. "But he was high on something. In fact, he was sort of coming down, when you walked in. Before that, he was really wild."

"Did you know Mike was on drugs?"

"No-o. Well, I don't think he's on *hard* drugs."

"Yet," Sharon said, grimly.

Betsy lay back against the pillow and wished her head would stop thumping.

"Sorry," Sharon said, "I didn't mean to pry. But he looked so weird—he must've been in a peculiar state, for me to be able to push him out like that."

The memory of Sharon propelling Mike, who was nearly twice her size, brought a faint smile to Betsy's lips.

"Good you arrived when you did," she murmured. "Things were getting rough."

"Did he hurt you?"

"No—but I was scared. He seemed so excited, as if he were poised on the brink of violence. I was afraid I might do or say something that would push him over!"

"Poor Betsy. It must've been horrible." Sharon's round eyes were full of sympathy. "I know how you feel about Mike, and it's hard to see someone you love in that state."

"I don't love him any more."

Sharon smiled disbelievingly. "Don't worry about it now—think it over in the morning. You'll feel different then."

Betsy was surprised. Sharon's attitude was totally unexpected.

"I won't feel different in the morning," Betsy said.

"Is it really over between you two?" Sharon did not hide her surprise.

Betsy nodded. "Yes, it is. That's what all the fuss was about. I told Mike we were through—and he refused to accept it."

"Maybe he'll accept it now," Sharon said.

A sudden thought struck Betsy. "Look, you're the one who should be getting some sleep," she exclaimed. "You've just come off a long and delayed flight, and here I am, burdening you with all my problems."

Sharon gave a small laugh. "It's okay. I'm always available for throwing unwanted visitors out of the apartment." She busied herself with the tray. "Do you want anything else? Can I bring you some more tea?"

"No thanks." Betsy put a hand on Sharon's arm. "I think you should have some camomile yourself," she said.

"Yes, I will." Sharon picked up the tray. "Goodnight, Betsy. Sleep well. See you in the morning."

It was a funny thing about Sharon, Betsy thought, as she tried to compose herself for sleep. She had reacted splendidly, getting Mike out of the apartment without any fuss or trouble. Afterwards—well, frankly, Betsy had anticipated one of her lectures. Instead, Sharon had been gentle and kind, careful to say nothing hurtful.

You could certainly count on Sharon as a real friend when the chips were down. It more than made up for the times when she acted so persnickety.

9

Sharon woke early, despite her late night and the disturbing scene with Mike and Betsy. There were too many chores she wanted to do to allow herself another hour's sleep. Besides, it would do better to get everything done and go to bad early tonight; Tom was going out of town on a business trip, anyway.

She made herself some breakfast while she waited for his call. When she went into the living room to get the phone, she saw with distaste that Lee—only visible as an untidy heap of bedclothes on the converted sofa—had littered the whole room with articles of clothing. She would have to speak to Lee; it was embarrassing to walk in with Tom, when the room was like that.

Sharon tiptoed around the room, gathering all the scattered clothes and laying them over the back of the chair. At least that way they were all together; perhaps Lee would take the hint when she woke up and saw them.

Then Sharon picked up the phone and took it into the kitchen with her, giving the extension cord a gentle tug and getting it to allow the phone enough range to reach the kitchen table. Tom's call came through right on schedule. She sat sipping coffee and eating her breakfast as she chatted with her fiancé. He was leaving for Cleveland on a noon flight and would be back the next day.

After she had hung up, Sharon finished her breakfast with quiet deliberation. However rushed her schedule, she always ate regularly, as she was sure that her calm nerves and good health were due to well-balanced meals. Snacks might be fun—but they didn't give you the proper amount of vitamins. All the girls were prepared to admit that flying was an exhausting job. Physically exhausting—and nerve-wracking, too, when delays caused passengers to be fractious and peevish. What few of them were prepared to admit was that eating properly made it easier. And, at times, dosing with vitamins. She had managed to convince some of her fellow stewardesses—Betsy among them— that Vitamin C did help prevent the colds so often suffered by flight personnel.

Sharon's thoughts returned to the scene when she had come in the night before. It had been an ugly one. Even she had felt a momentary flutter of apprehension. Mike had looked so wild, so tightly-coiled and ready to spring.

Poor Betsy. She had been so smitten . . . but then, she was very foolish to tangle with a guy like Mike in the first place.

Finishing in the kitchen, she tiptoed into the living room once again, and went over to Thomas' tank. He peered hopefully up at her.

"I bet no one's fed you," Sharon murmured at him, and returned to the kitchen.

"Here, fella, make do with this," said Sharon as she returned with the turtle food. He snapped the food and plunged eagerly into the water, a morsel clamped between the serrated edges of his overbite.

Sharon returned to the kitchen and made a few more notes on her shopping list. Then she went to get her coat from the front hall closet. Passing Betsy's room, she saw her sound asleep. Sharon closed the door quietly. With any luck, she would sleep for a good while.

Ready for the cold weather outside, Sharon opened the front door of the apartment and almost tripped headlong over the recumbent form stretched full length across the entrance.

"Oh, no," she groaned, staring down at Mike. "Oh, *no* . . ." For a horrified second or two, Sharon just stared.

Mike lay, deeply asleep, stretched out on the edge of the hall carpeting. A copy of the New York *Times* and a huge cellophane-wrapped bouquet of flowers reposed on his chest.

Sharon snatched up the paper and the flowers. They

194

were from the florist down the block who, knowing the girls were stewardesses who kept odd hours, never rang the bell when he delivered anything to them.

Sharon glanced at the note pinned to the bouquet. *Miss Lee Pickering*, the envelope said. Resisting an urge to read the card inside, Sharon opened the apartment door quietly and put the flowers in the small hallway. Beside them, she placed the newspaper. Then she closed the door once more and faced the problem lying prone at her feet.

I wonder what the florist thought . . . Just wait till this little story makes the rounds . . .

Sharon relieved some of her growing fury by stirring Mike with her foot.

"Come along, wake up!" she commanded.

He opened his eyes and groaned, loudly. His face was very pale and he looked sick.

"You'd best get home as fast as possible," Sharon said, briskly. "Get up and I'll help you downstairs."

"I'm dying," Mike croaked through parched lips.

"Serves you right," Sharon retorted. "Now move yourself, I'll get you to a taxi."

"No money for taxi," Mike mumbled. He was trying to stand, but could only get to his knees.

Sharon hooked her hand under his arm and pulled.

"Get up, damn you, get up," she said, heaving determinedly at Mike's dead weight.

In the evening, all three roommates were home.

Betsy was stretched out on the sofa; Lee sat cross-legged on the rug, next to the hi-fi, which was playing her favorite records. Sharon was bustling in and out of the kitchen, preparing a dinner that smelled exceedingly good.

Betsy still felt slightly light-headed, as an after-effect of the scene the previous night. She felt removed from the present, as if she were living in a dream and thus was removed from events around her.

"What happened next?" she asked Sharon.

"I got him downstairs and into a taxi," Sharon said. "I told the driver to deliver him to his loft."

"Thanks, Sharon, you were very kind."

"That's five dollars you owe me," Sharon said with asperity. "I had to give it to the driver before he'd agree to take Mike, and of course, Mike didn't have any cash on him."

Betsy smiled. Sharon sounded more like her usual self.

Lee stopped the phonograph and put on a new record.

"I got this one on my last trip," she said. "See if you like it. I think it's great."

It wasn't very often that the three of them were home together, Betsy thought. She couldn't remember the last time she had spent an evening with both Sharon and Lee. She smiled at Lee.

"How was the discotheque?" she asked. "You were going on from the party with someone called Pierre, as I recall."

"Mmmm." Lee nodded her head in time to the music. "Pierre is sweet. He's in New York with the French mission to the U.N. All very top-echelon stuff. I like Frenchmen, don't you? Those flowers are from him," she added with a wave of the hand at the bouquet, now standing in water.

"Depends on the Frenchman," Betsy replied.

Sharon appeared, wearing a large striped apron.

"Is Pierre married?" she asked.

"Probably. Who cares?"

Sharon sat down on the rug. "You're a fool," she told Lee, and in the next breath she announced: "Dinner will be ready in exactly twenty minutes."

"You're sure it won't be nineteen minutes, or nineteen-and-a-half?" Lee enquired sarcastically.

"Let's have an aperitif," Betsy suggested. "Who wants what?"

"I brought a bottle of Dubonnet from Paris," Sharon said. "I'll have that, it's my favorite at the moment."

"Campari for me," Lee said.

Betsy, who still had the lingering remains of a headache, poured herself plain tonic water.

The girls sipped their drinks while Lee manipulated the music.

"I wish you'd let one record finish before you change it," Sharon remarked. "What's the use of playing an album if you keep stopping and starting?"

"I only want to listen to the best parts," Lee replied. "Anyway, I'm the one who does the work, so I don't see what you're complaining about."

"Talking about complaining," Sharon retorted, "I wanted to ask you *not* to leave your clothes scattered all over the room when you come in. Especially your underwear! It doesn't take long to put your things away and the chest *is* right next to the divan."

Lee began humming to the music, loudly.

Betsy lay back on the sofa and grinned. Things were returning to normal, at last.

The telephone rang and Betsy started up. Lee beat her to it.

"Hello?" Lee said.

Betsy waited, holding her breath.

"Hello, Pierre!" Lee cried. "How do you feel? Have you recovered? The flowers are *magnifique* . . ."

Betsy felt a stab of disappointment. For a wild moment, she had thought that perhaps David Fleming was calling.

Sharon asked, "Did you think that was Mike?"

"No, I didn't," Betsy snapped.

"All right, I was only asking." Sharon looked injured.

"I don't think I'll ever hear from Mike again. At least, I certainly hope I won't," Betsy remarked. "After what happened last night, he *has* to realize that it's all over."

"I wouldn't be too sure." Sharon frowned. "If he's on drugs, he may not be thinking too logically. Honestly, Betsy, you do pick up with peculiar types. Why can't you settle for someone decent—someone like Tom?"

Betsy could think of no reply that would not offend Sharon, so she kept quiet.

"I'm going out," Lee announced to the room at large. I won't be in for dinner after all."

"After all my trouble, cooking a special meal!" Sharon cried, "now there'll be too much, I made enough for three generous portions."

"Oh, I'm sure you'll think of something clever to do with the left-overs," Lee said, with a teasing smile.

Betsy was hardly listening to her roommates bickering. She was wondering if David Fleming would be considered 'decent' by Sharon? Yes, she was sure he would.

And yet, he was different. He would have to be, she thought ruefully, otherwise she would not have been attracted to him. It seemed her fate to get involved with men who were out-of-the-ordinary. However much she tried, she could not take the easy, conventional path in anything. Something in her rebelled against things that seemed too simple. It caused her an awful lot of trouble— but she was convinced it brought her the greatest rewards, as well.

10

The easy path in Betsy's life would have been to marry Jay Marshall and settle down at home. Home was the same place for both of them, a town small enough to allow everyone to know or at least know of practically everybody else, and big enough to support three supermarkets, two late-night groceries and one open-all-Sunday deli that made the best hoagies in the state.

Betsy had been biting into a hoagy the day she told her parents she wanted to become a stewardess. Or, more specifically, the day she told her mother. It was a Sunday, late in the evening, and Dr. Blair had two patients in the local hospital he'd "just feel better if he dropped in to see." Dr. Blair always had patients who affected his feelings in this manner, and he had gone off in his "doctor car," as they called the sober dark blue automobile, as opposed to the dusty station wagon driven by all three members of the Blair family.

"You see, Mother, I'd like to travel." Betsy dealt with some of the onion overflow from her hoagie with a frown. "And it seems better to be paid for travelling than have to pay *for* it, right?"

Mrs. Blair, who knew that there was more coming, made a noncommittal sound.

"I'm not good at any one thing. I mean, I'm not musical, or prima ballerina material, or the poet the world is waiting to hear ..."

Her mother, who loved Betsy dearly, smiled in agreement. Fond as she and her husband were of their only child, they were intelligent people and intelligent parents. Betsy was also intelligent, but she was not specially gifted. Betsy's life, her parents hoped, would be one of contentment, of knowledge and self-knowledge, of understanding and love.

". . . and if I'm just going to take any old job I might as well get an interesting one, don't you think?"

The girl paused, and looked up at her mother. It gave Mrs. Blair the opportunity to ask the question that had been in her mind since Betsy had begun talking.

"Have you talked to Jay about this?"

Betsy looked away and shook her head.

"No, I haven't. Not yet. I wanted to talk to you and Dad first." There was a brief pause, and then the words came tumbling out. "And he's another reason . . . I think I should be away, on my own, before I make up my mind . . . I don't really want to marry him, even though I know everyone thinks it'd be fine, and . . ."

Instinctively, Mrs. Blair reached out and touched her daughter lightly on the arm.

"Betsy, don't let unimportant things push you into taking major steps in your life. The only reason big enough to make you marry Jay is if you love him and want to marry him."

They talked into the darkness of the summer night, and presently Dr. Blair came home and joined the discussion. He listened to his daughter's plans, leaning back in the creaking wicker chair and sipping the tall drink he took from the table in front of him from time to time. Beyond the porch railing, frogs called against the hollow of the night.

"Sounds sensible enough to me," he said, when his opinion was eventually requested. "It took a war to get me overseas for the first time. Much more sensible to do it when it's quiet."

"Well, I don't think I'd get an overseas run right away," said Betsy dubiously. "Something tells me you have to work your way up the list. I'll probably be flying within the country for quite a while at first."

"There's a great deal to see here, too, you know," her father commented. "But, tell me, Betsy, how're you going to go about getting a flying job?"

Betsy told him, explaining how she planned, with her parents' permission, she added with a small grin, to write to several of the airline companies, asking about their hiring requirements and training programs.

"I guess I'll let them take it from there," she concluded. "I'd imagine you have to go for interviews, and things like that."

Betsy's guess was right. She wrote several letters, received answers to all of them. Not all the companies she wrote to were hiring at that time, but she pored daily over the brochures, routes and bases of the ones that were before deciding which ones she would continue to correspond with, since there were several steps to be taken. For one thing, she had to submit some more data on her education, health, and physical appearance.

For another, she would have to be told where and when the next interviews were to take place. Many of the airlines, Betsy discovered, set up specific interview dates in the bigger cities across the nation, and it was up to interested candidates to travel to the nearest city. Then maybe they'd be hired.

Maybe.

The *maybe* part of it was very much in her mind during those weeks of late summer. Maybe she was too tall ... too short ... too plump ... ("Nonsense!" said Dr. Blair) ... not the type ...

"Think positive," suggested her father. "You have only one head, you're healthy, and you can walk across a room without knocking the furniture over ... at least, I think you've finally mastered that."

"Oh, Dad!" Betsy smiled at him, knowing that her worrying was worrying him, too, although perhaps not in precisely the same way.

"Be reasonable," her mother said. "They said an extra language was an advantage, and you have two."

"Only French," Betsy murmured, "thanks to you and Grandmère."

"And Spanish," her mother reminded her. "It would come back in no time if you had to speak it, you know."

And then everything began to speed up. The letters telling her of interviews and appointed times, the trips to several cities, the meeting with other candidates, the airline personnel who interviewed them, the sudden drop into

201

a suspended vacuum after each interview, had she said the right thing, been well-groomed, spoken French correctly, made the right impression ...

Just as suddenly, it was over.

"Mother, I've got it!" she shouted, flying up the path to the front door from the mailbox. "Mother! It's *here* ..."

It was the letter she had so hoped for from the airline she most wanted. Several days later, the local newspaper carried the following item in its "Here 'n There" column:

"Miss Elizabeth Ann Blair (Betsy to her many friends), daughter of Dr. and Mrs. Edgar M. Blair, 29 Marigold Lane, will be leaving for Miami, Fla., shortly where she will spend six weeks at the Flightways Training Center preparing for a stewardess' career. On completion of the course, Betsy will be handed her well-earned wings at an official company ceremony, after which she will enter the ranks of the glamorous girls of the air."

The Blairs were not the first to see it. A neighbor called Mrs. Blair shortly after eight a.m.

"What item? No, I haven't seen the paper yet. I'll call you back, Mary, the eggs are burning."

Betsy, who could both hear her mother on the phone and see that no pan was on the stove said, "What was all that about?"

They saw as soon as they opened the newspaper at the woman's page.

"Could *Dad* have put it in?"

"I doubt it."

The phone rang again.

It did not stop ringing all day. The moment they put down the receiver from one call, another one came through. During the morning, Betsy and her mother found out that the newspaper had received the news item from the airline itself.

"I guess they always do that as part of the hiring routine."

"Well, they sure saved us the job of telling the world," Betsy grinned. She let her mother handle most of the calls from other parents for many appeared to be shocked. Betsy, who could only hear her mother's side of the conversation, thanked the heavens silently for giving her sensible parents.

"No, of course she didn't sneak off and join," she heard

her mother say. "Really, Carol, how can you say such a thing? I don't care *what* the Davis girl did, this is a respectable job. It pays very well, too."

Good for you, ma! That'll get Carol Blandings, super snooper, right where she lives—in her tight little pocketbook.

At lunchtime, Dr. Blair came home.

"You seem to have set the town on its ear," he told his daughter. Then he rumpled her red hair, a family echo of his own, in a gesture he had not used in years.

"Good for you, kiddo," he smiled. "They're mostly good folks—but we all need a little stir here once in a while."

Many of the callers were enthusiastic; they were the ones who asked specifically to speak to Betsy to give her their congratulations. The others Mrs. Blair fended off, but Betsy could see her mother was provoked by late afternoon.

"Regret?" she heard Mrs. Blair say. "Yes, I most certainly do regret something about this. I regret I'm not a generation younger, so I could join Flightways, too!"

When she hung up, her cheeks were flushed and her eyes angry.

"Oh, Mother, I'm sorry."

Mrs. Blair waved Betsy's words aside.

"No, dear, there's nothing to be sorry about ... unless it's the stuck-in-the-mud attitude of some of our neighbors."

Dr. Blair was home for dinner; Betsy suspected he had deliberately changed his office hours to spend the evening with them, after the hectic day. They talked about the phone calls, and the different reactions to the news. When Betsy told her father of Mrs. Blair's fighting words, he reached over and held his wife's hand on the white tablecloth.

Later, Betsy sensed her parents wanted to be alone, and she went off on her own, watching them go and sit on the old swing on the porch. She decided to make some coffee later, and took it out to them. They were conversing quietly; she saw they were holding hands.

"You're too old for romance," she joked as she set the coffee tray on the wicker table.

"One is never too old to be in love," came her father's voice from the shadows. "Always remember that, Betsy. It can make a big difference in life, if you keep that in mind. Choose what you really want and whom you really love, and stick to your guns. Always."

"I'll try, Dad." She said it lightly, but she knew her parents had lived by this philosophy, and it had worked for them. She lay awake for hours that night, excited by the turmoil of the day and touched by her father's quiet words. Even if it meant swimming upstream, it was worth aiming for what she really wanted.

Betsy forgot the whole incident in the weeks that followed, as she was bombarded by one new impression after another. Travel, training, relocation, the whole airline world, independence, graduation from the Flightways course, getting a bid, starting to fly, keeping house with another stewardess in their first apartment—life was full and challenging.

But now, much later, an experienced stewardess with the longed-for overseas bid well behind her, Betsy began to dovetail her ideas and see the jigsaw of her philosophy of life take shape.

"Choose what you really want . . ."

Her father's words echoed across time into the New York apartment on the sixth floor.

Did she really want David Fleming, Betsy wondered. And, much more to the point: would he ever want her?

Part 3

Flightway International 410
JFK/LHR

The bright impersonal calm of the East Side Terminal was a welcome oasis after the bluster outside. Betsy put down her suitcase as soon as she got through the doors; her fur hat, knocked askew by the gust of wind careening down 38th Street needed adjusting.

She felt secure again after she had pulled it back to its usual snug angle, and a deft flick of her fingers replaced an escaping strand of hair.

The weather, windy and clear, was being caused by the sizable high that had moved in the night before. Betsy had heard the television weather report and, adding to it her own knowledge of airline meteorology, knew the chances for good weather for the first portion of the flight were encouraging.

She picked up her suitcase and made her way to the heart of the terminal. Linda was nowhere in sight. There were few people in evidence at all; with any luck, there would not be many out at the airport, either. After all, not many people were eager to travel to Europe in the middle of November, what with the legends about European weather and Thanksgiving just around the corner. Tours were generally off-season; it was far too late for summer, still too soon for Christmas. An in-between season all around, now she came to think of it, because it was also too cold for mothers with infants or toddlers, and out of the question for families with school-age children.

No, the chances were that tonight's flight would be one

of the quiet ones, with the majority of the passengers seasoned and knowledgeable travellers, professionals at continent-hopping . . .

Betsy smiled at her rambling thoughts.

Now just watch fate prove me wrong . . we'll probably have a rock group, two stowaways and a birth on board . . .

That was all part of the enjoyment of being a stewardess. You never really did know what to expect, and the challenge was constant. Rock musicians today, a yeshiva group tomorrow, princesses the third day and celebrities the fourth. And it was up to you to make them comfortable, at ease, happy with their trip. Why hadn't she ever been able to explain to Mike exactly how it was, how it felt?

Well, she had never been able to explain it to anyone outside of the airlines satisfactorily. Her father had perhaps come as close to understanding as anyone, but he saw it strictly from the helping others point of view, just as he saw his own profession most of the time. But no—perhaps he had understood more than she realized, Betsy admitted to herself. He knew about that undefinable communication that could exist, if only for a few hours, between passengers and cabin crew members.

"Yes, I think I know what you mean," he'd said when she'd originally tried to explain it to him. "And then, the moment they leave the office, they forget all about you—until they have to come back."

Office or airplane—it was really all the same, a world of its own only tenuously connected with the outside world for the duration of the trip.

Like love, Betsy suddenly thought, with surprise. But I guess it is a form of love, to be in love with your job.

Still, even lovers had to acknowledge the existence of an outside world, if they wanted to continue to exist. Betsy decided that it was time to get a newspaper and bone up on the news. Maybe if she knew what was going on, she wouldn't feel so cut off from people who weren't in the airlines. Or, at least, maybe they wouldn't accuse her of being cut off; she still found it hard to convince herself she was really missing anything.

She walked over to the newsstand and bought a paper.

She checked her watch and then glanced at the clock on the wall; it was time to head for the bus.

The man at the doors leading where the buses were parked was saying, "Next bus to Kennedy Airport, stopping at Braniff, Sabena, Transworld and Flightways . . ."

Seeing Betsy, he smiled and nodded. "You picked a nice day for a flight, eh?"

She smiled and nodded back. He was one of the nice ones. There were a couple of old grouches, too; she saw one of them on duty at a door further on. But this one always had a pleasant remark to make, and he always said hello.

Strange, she thought, going towards the bus—strange the many different people we greet, or smile at, or exchange remarks with, and yet never really know at all. I don't even know that man's name, and yet, in a way, he's part of my life, a fleeting one, perhaps, but still, a connection, a voice.

Reflecting on names, she got into the bus and sat down. She was thankful for the warmth as she sat down; although the bus door was still open, its interior was protected from the chill.

Betsy stared out of the window. Names. Names don't mean that much, do they? After all, I know David Fleming's name. And yet I don't know much else about him. Not really. Just the surface things. And some of the facts in his life. His career, his tragedy, what he looks like. But not the insides of the man. Not the things that make him David Fleming. Why—I don't even know what he thinks of me . . . he probably doesn't think of me very much at all.

Suspecting this to be true, but not wishing to acknowledge it, Betsy leaned back in the seat and let herself daydream. The newspaper lay in her lap, folded and untouched. Still no Linda; obviously, she was not taking the bus out today. A wheeze of air brakes releasing signalled departure time, and moments later the bus emerged into the fading city light of the November day.

The muted roar of traffic in the Midtown Tunnel made a pleasantly protective cocoon of noise. Betsy toyed with her images of Fleming; had he thought about her at all, since that brief kiss? More importantly: *what* had he thought of her? And the kiss?

He was such a strange man. Betsy couldn't quite put her finger on why. Was he secretive? Well, yes, in a sense, but only by contrast to the other pilots, who tended to be far more talkative. But it wasn't really fair to call someone who was uncommunicative really secretive, was it? And yet . . .

Also, his moods were hard to fathom. One moment, he'd be old stone-face himself—and then, the next . . . well, how about that ride in from the airport? And then again, the kiss . . . She wondered how he'd be today; back to the company stone-face image, she imagined.

And yet . . .

I know he's human, a voice cried out inside her, and its pain was something she had not expected. I know it, I can feel it, I want to hold him close to me and know he's warm . . .

Betsy sat up straight and seized the newspaper on her lap. Daydreaming was all very well, but letting it get the upper hand was just plain silly.

Resolutely, she looked at the front page, reading without absorbing. Knowing she'd come to the bottom line, she opened the paper and looked at the inside pages. On the third one, a headline jumped out at her: 'BRESSANOVITCH DISAPPEARS, it said.

Why did the name seem familiar, she wondered, reading through the story beneath the two-column head. Armand Bressanovitch, age 55, a well-known banker who operated in international financial circles, had apparently disappeared without leaving any clues. Foul play was not suspected, although the police said they could not rule out the eventual possibility of . . . people connected with the missing man had been questioned and had said that . . . (they hadn't said much, Betsy noted in passing) . . . spokesmen for Mr. Bressanovitch's office stated that . . . investigation was continuing, etc., etc.

Bressanovitch. Betsy looked at the name again, but no recollection came to her. Still, she was sure she'd seen the name before. Glancing through the rest of the story, she saw he was an important and powerful, if little-known, man.

She flipped the page. Nothing caught her eye.

It was useless to pretend; she let the newspaper drop back into her lap. There wasn't anything in the news that interested her at the moment, so it seemed silly to push it. She allowed her thoughts to center on the tall enigmatic captain, and again she found herself comparing him to Mike. And to Jay, her long-time suitor and still good friend.

It dawned on her Mike didn't always make complete sense. Not the way Jay did; Jay had steady, secure ways that were obvious or easy to discover. But when Mike said something, he did make sense.

Did David?

Her thoughts rose to his defense at once. Well, he probably would make sense—complete sense—if she knew all the facts. If she did, she felt sure he'd always make sense. Look at the way he handled a flight, or an aircraft. There Betsy could see he made sense, every inch of the way.

But in private life?

From what little she knew of him, it was impossible to tell, although, she told herself, it would seem likely that the cool, level-headed attitude he displayed in the cockpit would likely hold over into his personal life. Or was that cockeyed reasoning? Betsy suddenly realized it might well be. After all, she told herself, I'm a reasonably good stewardess, and I do my job properly—which is more than I can say for the way I'm running my personal affairs right now. *Running* them? It's more like being run *by* them. Or running them straight into a wall. But whatever it is, it isn't the same confident feeling I have when I'm working.

She thought of the other crew members, and wondered about Linda. Perhaps she'd taken another bus out to the airport—or, more likely, had been driven out by Carl Masden. Such a strange girl.

But in Linda's case, there was no telling which was the more untidy, her work life or her personal life. The latter sounded as though Linda knew how to get what she wanted.

I guess that's the difference . . . knowing what you want . . . and I don't think I really do know that, yet. Perhaps I'm beginning to have an idea.

Her thoughts rambled on, and before she realized it, the open and flat expanse of Kennedy International Airport was stretching out before her in its ribboned crisscross of roads and runways.

211

2

"Did you see the paper?"

Linda's brushing aside of Betsy's greeting when the two girls met in Operations was typical of her offhand behavior. The newspaper was in her hand, folded back at one of the inside pages. Betsy saw it was the same one she herself had bought at the East Side Terminal.

"Yes, I've seen it. I just sort of glanced through it on the ride out. Why? Was there anything special?"

"Special? I'll say there is." Linda began unfolding the paper to hand it to Betsy. "It's our passenger; he disappeared. Just like he told me he was going to."

"What?"

Betsy, in spite of herself, felt the pull of interest, and reached for her own paper, which she'd pushed under the strap of her suitcase for easier carrying. "No, I have my own here. What page?"

"Here. I'll find it for you." Linda reached over and took Betsy's paper from her. "See? Right there."

Just as Betsy was registering the fact that Linda meant the story on the banker who had disappeared, the man whose name had seemed familiar to her when she'd read through the story on the bus, Rudi Becker came through the doorway.

"Ah, good evening, girls. How nice to see you both here on time." He smiled maliciously and looked at his watch. "No—actually early. Well, well. How unusual for you, Miss Kesnik."

"Oh, come *on*, now, Rudi." Linda sounded impatient, but unperturbed. "Don't be a pain in the ass. Besides—I have something to show you. Did you see the paper?"

Moments later, all three cabin attendants were poring over the disappearance story.

"He told me he was going to disappear, you know," Linda repeated. "I thought he was kidding, even though he was making sense. And he was cold sober," she added with quick emphasis.

Betsy noticed her heightened coloring, the flush in her cheeks indicating her involvement with the incident.

Rudi finished reading the story and handed Linda her paper again.

"Very interesting," he drawled. "Did he tell you where he was going?"

"No, not exactly. But we talked about all sorts of things."

"Oh?" Rudi's tone was barbed. "And did he ask you to disappear with him?"

Linda shook her head.

"No. No, he didn't. You see," her voice cleared slightly, "you see, it wasn't as simple as that at all."

Linda clearly remembered Armand Bressanovitch. He had struck her as an interesting looking man the moment she had seen him coming on board. Distinguished-looking, in a grey suit. Late forties, early fifties, she quickly reckoned, well-travelled.

Well-heeled.

He had greeted her with the polite familiarity of the frequent traveller and settled himself into a seat with the ease of long practice. Then other duties had claimed Linda, and her attention had been distracted.

It was after she had served the pilots their dinners that Bressanovitch had entered the picture again.

"There was that goon air marshal with us last time, if you'll recall," Linda went on. "What was his name? The one in front with us."

"Hadley?" Betsy supplied.

"Yes. Him."

Rudi nodded. "Yes, I remember. Did he give you trouble?"

"Well, not exactly trouble, but he kept asking loaded questions, and making insinuating remarks. You know the type."

The purser said, "You should've told me, and I'd have straightened him out."

"Oh, come on . . ."

"Well," he persisted doggedly, "I *am* in charge of the cabin, and if anyone like that gets difficult . . ."

Suppressing a smile at the thought of Rudi Becker bringing a braggart air marshal under control, Betsy said, "Rudi, let Linda tell about the passenger. Did he say anything to the marshal?"

"No, he didn't say anything. He just caught my attention, and called me over . . ."

"Yes, sir." Linda wore her professional smile. "May I get you another drink? Or"—seeing the distinguished passenger shake his head—"some coffee? Tea? Cocoa and biscuits?"

"No, no. I didn't want anything, really. Other than an answer to a question. That man who was—ah, *talking* to you there—although I think I'd rather use the word *pestering,* if you don't mind. Anyway, that man, he's one of the air marshals, isn't he?"

Linda tried to look blank, but even before she had a chance to make a noncommittal remark, Bressanovitch had nodded in understanding.

"I know. You're not allowed to tell me, are you? Well, never mind. It's just that, when one has flown as much as I have, one begins to recognize types of people. And I enjoy playing my little guessing games. You will forgive an aging man his innocent pastimes."

"Oh, I don't think . . ."

"And don't tell me you don't think I'm old," Bressanovitch interrupted. "Because I know how I feel inside. Now, run along and finish all those innumerable tasks I know they give you on these flights. Then perhaps you'll come and talk to me."

"Yes, of course, sir." Linda figured he'd forget all about it. They usually did.

But Armand Bressanovitch didn't.

"And then?" Rudi demanded, for Linda had fallen momentarily silent. She looked at him blankly for a split second, and then seemed to return from a faraway reverie.

"Well, as you know, I *did* sit down and talk to him for a while."

"Quite a long while," Rudi reminded her.

"Yes," Linda said absently. "Yes, I guess it was. He did most of the talking."

Again, she fell silent.

"But what was he talking *about*?" Betsy was puzzled.

"Mostly his life, I guess. And all sorts of things—how foolish people are, and how we waste our time on stupid things, and how little we understand. Things like that."

"Sounds like a philosophy professor."

Linda smiled. "Yes, I guess he does. But he wasn't dry or boring, or anything. It was like he was trying to describe a search for something. A search for reason in his life."

Rudi gave a short laugh.

"For a banker, that's really funny. He must've been putting you on, Linda."

"That's what I thought, too," she agreed. "Especially when he then told me he had decided to disappear."

"He *told* you this?" Rudi sounded incredulous.

Linda nodded. "That's right. He told me he was going to retire from the world. That was exactly the way he put it. Retire from the world. And he said he felt the only way to do that was to disappear—that if he tried to live a private life in the normal way, it would be impossible."

"There's always someone trying to invade your life, or your privacy, or your thoughts," said Armand Bressanovitch. "No, I'm going to do it differently. The proper way. That way, I'll leave *all* of them behind."

"All of them?" Linda echoed softly. He seemed miles away already, surrounded by his thoughts.

Despite this, he heard her. "Yes, all of them," he asserted. "My ex-wives, my children, my business associates, all of them. I have provided for everything, and everybody. Now I want to live the rest of my life in my own manner."

"You must've been very unhappy," Linda said, "if you want to leave everyone ilke that."

Bressanovitch looked at her for the first time in several minutes.

"You're a very lovely girl, you know," he said unexpectedly. "It's a shame I didn't meet you years ago. It might've made all the difference."

Then he smiled and shook his head. He reached up and switched off the light.

"No, that's not true, and it's foolish to try deceiving myself. It would not have made any difference. The final decision lies inside me, not anywhere in the exterior world. I didn't find, because I cannot give and, even worse, I am incapable of receiving."

Linda frowned. He was talking in a form of verbal shorthand that somehow touched a vulnerable point within her.

". . . but now it's too late," Bressanovitch was saying. "Now I know the path I'm taking, and I know it's the right one for me."

"Oh, you'll change your mind," Linda said airily, trying to lighten the conversation. "You wait. When we land in London, things will look different. They'll look normal again, and you'll know you'll be happier if you go back to your usual way of life. You know," she continued, warming to her subject, "one always thinks one's going to make the big change, take the big plunge. And then, somehow or other, it turns out that life goes on much the same."

Feeling she had not quite expressed what she meant, she went on, "I don't mean that one never makes any big changes. But even when one does, there are sort of general things about life that continue."

"Not always." Bressanovitch was quiet, but emphatic. "There are times when huge changes occur. But they're the ones that occur inside yourself. And when something like that happens, something clicks into a different place. And then, life even *looks* different. Or at least, that's what's happened to me this time."

His tone lightened as he finished talking.

"I still say you'll feel differently when we get to London," Linda smiled. "You wait and see. And then you'll fly back to New York, after you've attended to your London affairs, and . . ."

"No, I won't." He was smiling at her, but his words were measured. "But, since you don't believe I mean what

216

I'm saying—why don't you call me, at my office, when you get back to New York. Then you'll see for yourself." He handed her his business card.

Later, while she was fixing her hair in the bathroom shortly before landing, it occurred to Linda that it was one of the most original ways she'd ever had a man proposition her, or at least inveigle her into calling him. She smiled; he certainly had practice. And finesse.

And money.

And he was nice. Or at least, he seemed so. She had to admit it; he seemed like a genuinely charming man.

". . . and so I guess all those things made up the reason why I decided I *would* call him," Linda explained. "After all, what harm could it do? So the day before yesterday, I figured I might as well try the number."

Still in her bathrobe, the greyness of the dull midmorning a monochrome framed in the window behind her, Linda dialed the Manhattan number engraved on the business card.

"Bressanovitch Associates," a receptionist's voice said in her ear.

"May I speak to Mr. Bressanovitch please?"

A slight pause. Then: "Ah—just one moment, please."

A click. Another woman's voice came on the phone.

"Yes? May I help you?"

"I just told the receptionist—I'd like to speak to Mr. Bressanovitch, please," Linda repeated impatiently.

"May I ask who is calling, please?"

"Mrs. Smith," said Linda sweetly, long practised at the art of calling married men at their offices. "Mrs. Clarence Smith."

"Mrs. Smith—may I ask the nature of your call?"

Linda was beginning to feel annoyed.

"If Mr. Bressanovitch is in a meeting, or something, I can always call later."

"No." The woman's voice interrupted with undisguised urgency. "No, Mrs. Smith. That's not what I meant. Are you a business associate of Mr. Bressanovitch?"

Linda hesitated, then told the truth.

"No, I'm not. This is just a personal call. Mr. Bressanovitch had asked me to ring him, and . . ."

"When was that?" the voice interrupted.

"A few days ago," Linda found herself answering.

Before she could think any further, the voice asked, "Where was it you last spoke to Mr. Bressanovitch, Mrs. Smith?"

"In London." The moment the words were spoken, Linda regretted having said them. What the hell was this third degree, anyway? She heard a sharp intake of breath at the other end; then the voice began speaking again, very sweetly this time.

"I wonder, Mrs. Smith, whether you would like to drop by the office some time today? Any time that would be convenient for you, of course."

"What time will Mr. Bressanovitch be there?"

The woman evaded the direct question.

"Perhaps, Mrs. Smith, the best time would be during the early afternoon."

As the woman talked, Linda became more and more convinced that Armand Bressanovitch was not there, and that the woman, whoever she might be, only wanted Linda to appear in the office to pump her for some kind of information. Playing the game, Linda said she would be in around three, gave the Bronx Zoo number as her home phone number, and hung up. She sat motionless for a long time, staring out of the window and feeling the world gone empty.

". . . and then, today, I saw the headline," Linda finished. "He *did* do it after all. So that woman's questions and insistence make sense. The office was looking for him, too, and they thought I might know something."

"D'you think he meant to kill himself?" Rudi inquired, beginning to gather up the papers they would have to go through during the briefing.

"No, I don't," Linda said shortly. "That wasn't the way he sounded at all."

"Ah, well." Rudi rose from the chair. "I think I'd better start getting things organized."

"What *do* you think he did?" Betsy asked. She could see that Linda was still all wound up over the mysterious man.

"I don't know. I wish I did. It's like seeing a portion of a movie, and then never getting to see the end, or how it all works out. But then, that's what our flights are like, I guess. A piece of a movie. And we never do get to see the rest of the story, do we?"

Betsy considered the comparison, and then said, "Well, sometimes we do. How about young James?"

"I guess." Linda seemed to lose interest in the conversation, and Betsy watched her as she put a hand up to her forehead, as though in pain. Linda, despite her excitement about Bressanovitch and his disappearance, looked drawn and peaked. Now that the flush she had exhibited earlier seemed to have faded away, Betsy thought the older girl appeared paler than usual, if anything.

There's something almost transparent about her, Betsy realized. As though, just beneath the thin surface, she's terribly vulnerable, and very fragile.

On impulse, she said, "Linda, do you feel okay?"

Linda took her hand away from her forehead with a quick, brusque motion and said, "Of course I do. Why d'you ask? You're *always* asking me that!"

"I'm sorry—I just thought maybe you looked a little pale, as though you didn't get enough sleep, or something."

"Maybe I didn't—but what's it to you?" was the snapped retort. "Come on—Rudi's signalling to us." And Linda stood up, cutting the subject and the conversation.

A prattle of voices at the door announced the arrival of Marianne and Judy.

Betsy's last thought on the severed conversation was that it was stupid of her ever to try and understand Linda. Any gesture one ever made in her direction was either ignored or misinterpreted, so why try?

And yet for a while, when she was telling us about Bressanovitch, she seemed like a different person. But her moods change so quickly . . . and anyway, it was probably because she figured him as a potential husband, or something. It was just so hard to tell with that girl. Was it even worth trying?

3

Something in her throat made a funny, thumping movement, but Betsy managed to say, "Good evening," without
any undue inflection in her voice when David Fleming
walked in. He was closely followed by Carl Masden, and
Larry Johnson brought up the rear. The door closed
behind them.

"Are the marshals here yet?"

"They'll be in right away, Captain."

The three men disappeared into an inner office. Betsy's
attention returned to Rudi and his instructions; next to
her, Marianne Lund was chomping loudly on a candy bar.

Becker interrupted his flow of information on the flight
conditions with a terse, "I hope you don't plan on chewing
that as you work the cabin."

"It's not gum," Marianne protested.

"Whatever it is, finish it now," came the order. "You've
been warned before, Marianne."

The shapely girl stuffed the rest of the bar into her
mouth as best she could. Rudi went back to reciting
pre-flight information.

". . . as I said, six in first, just like last time, forty-six in
coach. No special meals . . ."

Betsy heard she'd guessed right on the weather. Good
all the way, with no problems expected. And, from the
sound of it, the passengers probably were the kind she
had envisioned, well seasoned travellers. No groups, no
tours. No small boys travelling solo, either. The solemn

expression and deep blue eyes of James came to mind, and she smiled to herself.

Judy Fransella was saying, "No, it wasn't the ovens, Rudi—it was the trays that held me up. I kept upsetting them."

"You're probably jerking them out of the module instead of sliding them. Easy does it," Linda explained. "That way, you won't upset the stuff on them, and then you won't have to waste time rearranging everything."

Judy's smile was one of admiration and gratitude, and Betsy knew how typical the attitude was for a stewardess right out of training. She remembered from her own early days on the line, when all the book knowledge had to be translated into reality, and how hard it was for those first few flights.

The group of cabin attendants around Rudi listened to the last details of the briefing. As it wound down, Betsy became aware of David Fleming coming towards them.

"Ready, Becker?"

"Yes, Captain."

The whole crew got together and the two men serving as air marshals for the trip were introduced.

"This is Mr. Bradshaw," Fleming said, and the tall, heavy-set man in his mid-thirties said, "Clive Bradshaw. How do'you do," in a voice that identified him as a Southerner.

". . . and Mr. Thornton."

Mr. Thornton just nodded. He was younger, and fatter, and, Betsy guessed, newer on the job.

"Now, let's go through the signals . . ."

The buzzer signals from the cockpit remained the same. As seating arrangements would be ample, it seemed unlikely the air marshals would sit next to any other passengers, so the pretense of "Here's your whiskey and coke, sir" could be omitted.

"If there's trouble up front, you take the marshals a straight shot."

"Whiskey," interposed Clive Bradshaw.

"They know that," Captain Fleming said quietly.

The discussion of signals continued.

". . . suspicious behavior of passenger, or anything you consider untoward, take the marshal the Airlines Guide, and tell him the information he wanted is on page so-and-

221

so. Make the page number the number of the row where you want him to check. Then he can take it from there."

"I guess that's about it," said Captain Fleming. "Any questions?"

There weren't, and the group rose to leave. The marshals left to join the passengers waiting in the hall, and Masden made his way out with them en route to his checking duties on the outside of the aircraft. Fleming and Johnson stood by the counter, and Fleming signed the flight release.

"Come girls—let's go."

Rudi rounded up his cabin crew with a sweeping gesture of his arm. Betsy slung her bag over her right shoulder and followed the chief purser to the door.

4

"Flightways International announces the departure of Flight 410 to London, Paris, and . . ."

Some people rose as the announcement started; others leaned forward in the wide leather seats to arrange their hand luggage, or button up a child.

". . . now boarding at Gate . . ."

The movement began to shape its way toward the waiting door. Clive Bradshaw walked slowly, a drab tan raincoat folded over his arm. A woman with three small children made her way directly in front of him.

"Flightways International announces the departure of . . ."

The voice spoke the message for a second time, altering some of the phrases as suggested by the manual on public announcements. Several businessmen, soberly dressed, held briefcases in one hand and their Coach Section boarding cards in the other; two young girls, travelling together, giggled nervously as one of them dropped the square of pasteboard that was her entry to the aircraft.

". . . now boarding at Gate . . ."

A thin, expensively dressed woman with sharp features and two emerald rings on her right hand held her Vuitton bag in her left. She was of indeterminate middle age, and her dark eyes moved restlessly with a piercing brightness, almost matching the fire of the diamond pin on the lapel of her designer suit jacket. A matching coat, fur lined, was

223

draped over her shoulders. She, too, went towards the door, a first class boarding card in her possession.

The man behind her, also alone, was slack-jawed and tall and in his mid-thirties. His large tweed hat, did nothing to mask his petulant expression.

"Last call for passengers boarding Flight 410 . . ."

Bringing up the rear was the second air marshal.

They all moved through to the corridors and down the stairs to the boarding level. At the outer door, a blast of the windy November day met them through the opened exit. Beyond, the gleaming Flightways Boeing 707 was waiting.

Carl Masden, who had already done his clockwise tour of the aircraft's exterior, was busy inside the airplane cabin with his pre-flight checking duties. He noted the proportions of Marianne Lund's breasts while he checked the coach section life vest supply, and gave Judy Fransella a quick once-over between the positions of the portable oxygen bottles.

Satisfied that all equipment was on board and functioning, the flight engineer walked the length of the cabin up to the flight deck door. His path crossed Linda's in the first class galley, but neither of them said a word.

Betsy, busy with the blanket count, noticed the pointed non-meeting out of the corner of her eye.

Rudi Becker walked by hurriedly. "Linda, I think there's a mistake in the cordials count."

In the back galley, Judy Fransella was trying to get herself organized and not feel flustered. Her nervous motions were frequently interrupted by Marianne's casual wanderings in and out of the galley area.

"If you'd just move a bit faster, Marianne."

Rudi was back again, his voice nasty behind his smile. Judy said, "I can't open the top oven, Rudi," and the purser clicked his tongue with impatience as he strode over to see what was the matter.

"Okay. Everything ready? The passengers are about to board."

The ground man, having made his announcement, scurried back down the ramp. In the front galley, the flight deck bell dinged.

"You get it, will you?" Linda said to Betsy.

"Okay."

She pushed her way through the flight deck door and clicked it shut behind her.

Carl was already in his seat. He looked up at her and smiled, visibly relieved it was Betsy who had answered the call. Larry Johnson was looking at the flight plan on his lap. David Fleming turned around, microphone in hand.

His thumb felt the mike switch.

"Ah, yes, Betsy." His half smile was pure professional courtesy. "There'll be a slight delay. Traffic's heavy. We'll have to wait for a takeoff position—so would you advise the passengers?"

"Yes, sir."

Larry Johnson looked up, opened his mouth as if to say something, thought better of it and restricted himself to a quick conspiratorial grin at Betsy. Then he returned to his work. Leaving the flight deck, Betsy heard the litany continuing behind her.

"Pitot heat . . ."

"Check and Off."

". . . recorders . . ."

"Passenger oxygen . . ."

"Normal."

"Seat and smoke . . ."

"On."

Yes, and I'd better check, thought Betsy.

She stepped into the cabin, closed the door and noted the lights were indeed working. Seeing the passengers coming toward the boarding ramp, she placed herself at her greeting station inside the entry door.

"Good evening, sir . . . good evening . . . good evening . . ."

A handsome, elderly couple made their way through the door.

"Ah, good evening." The husband greeted Betsy. "How nice to see you, young lady. We've travelled with you before."

The wife also smiled, and Betsy dimly recollected having had them on a flight some time back. She'd have to check their names from the manifest.

"Hello." She smiled and said, "It's so nice to have you with us again."

A thin woman with a fur-lined coat was the next one

225

through the door, and then came one of the men she'd been introduced to at the briefing.

"Good evening, sir."

No hint of recognition crossed her face as Thornton walked through, and the air marshal played it the same way.

"Yes, ma'am, this seat right here. May I take your coat for you?"

Betsy took the fur-lined garment with care and hung it on one of the individual hangers. She noticed Rudi stopping by the coat's owner, exclaiming with pleased surprise and receiving a similar greeting in return. When he came abreast of Betsy, she said, "There's a delay. Heavy traffic, and the Captain says to announce it."

Rudi nodded and said, "I'll have the time when I take up the passenger count," and continued on toward the aft section.

By the time the passengers were settled in, the four stewardesses had taken up their positions in the different sections of the cabin, ready to begin demonstrating the life jacket procedure. Rudi, standing in the aft galley, picked the microphone off its holding hook and got ready to speak.

"Good evening, ladies and gentlemen. Welcome aboard Flightways International . . ."

5

Betsy flipped the vinyl smock around her and snapped the tab belt into place over her hips. Linda, already garbed for the meal service routine, was setting up the bar cart and the hors d'oeuvres.

She's fast and she's good when she wants to be, Betsy thought, watching Linda's practised movements in the confines of the first class galley. Let's hope this mood lasts all the way across.

Rudi came through the divider that blocked off the coach section in the rear. He grouped the extra alien landing cards into a neat pile in his hands and slipped them into the document case.

"Ready, Linda?" He cast a quick and expert eye over the contents of the bar cart. "I don't see the olives—oh, yes, I do. And the swizzle sticks?"

"To the left of the ice . . ." Linda spoke without turning around, her attention on the hors d'oeuvres platters.

Rudi made the clicking sound he always did when irritated.

"The holder is supposed to be on the other side."

"It's broken. I used a tumbler instead."

"Oh, I see." Rudi took over the bar cart. "Betsy, you follow me with the hors d'oeuvres . . ."

As if I didn't know, Betsy thought belligerently. Betsy suspected Rudi was trying to appear extra efficient for the sake of the woman passenger he had greeted so effusively.

"Okay. They're ready," Linda announced, turning her

attention from the hors d'oeuvres to the next trolley that would be needed. She was already beginning to set up the appetizers as Betsy, her smile automatically lighting her face, began making her way down the aisle.

The elderly couple she had met before were on the left. During takeoff, Betsy had managed to look their name up on the passenger manifest. They were Dr. and Mrs. Farnsworth, and on seeing their names, she was able to recall the earlier trip she had had with them. They had been returning to New York from a medical convention in Paris. Dr. Farnsworth was a pediatrician, and Betsy had mentioned her own medical parent.

"Are you on your way to another convention?" she smiled as she offered the couple a choice of tidbits.

"Yes, that's right, young lady," said Dr. Farnsworth. "In Paris again."

"D'you go all the way with us?" his wife wanted to know.

"No, I get off in London."

"Oh, that's too bad."

On the right, a row further down, the sharp-faced female who was known to Rudi sat by the aisle in solitary splendor.

"Ah, thank you," she murmured, a glass of champagne balanced in her hand. She had a definite foreign accent. Not French, Betsy knew, and not Italian, either; perhaps German, she wasn't sure. She'd have to hear her say more than *ah, thank you* to be able to guess.

"Hi, there!" The male passenger on her right grinned and winked. "Won't you sit down and have a drink with me?"

Oh, Oh. One of *those*.

"I'm sorry, sir,"—she beamed warmly. "We have our full dinner service coming up."

"Well, maybe your girl friend up front'll be more friendly." He gestured with his glass towards the galley. Linda could be seen moving back and forth as she continued setting up the dinner trolley. Betsy noted the man's loose mouth and somewhat petulant expression. She also took a look at his drink. It was whiskey, but she decided he wasn't drunk. Just dumb; she knew the type.

Still smiling, she retreated gracefully. He was still staring at Linda.

Betsy returned to the galley. Rudi, already there, said, "Betsy, I think you'd better go back and help out in coach. With only six passengers here, Linda and I can handle dinner easily. Keep an eye on Judy. She's clumsy in the galley."

"If Marianne'd move her ass a bit more, Judy might find it easier," Linda snapped, as she loaded the coffee machine. A timer dinged softly, and she shut off two of the ovens.

On her way through to the aft cabin, Betsy was greeted by a loud, "Hey, there, sweetheart! You coming to have dinner with me?"

She smiled and said, "I have to work in the aft cabin now." The moment she was in the coach section, she almost collided with Marianne, who was bending over a seat on the righthand side. Seeing Betsy, she straightened up, and appealed to her for help.

"Betsy, this little boy's gotten himself all tangled in the seat belt," she explained.

The child's mother, in the middle seat, was tending a small baby in the window seat and seemed uninterested in her toddler son. He looked tearful, but was not uttering a sound from the awkward, pinned-down position caused by the jammed strap.

"Here, let's see what I can do." Betsy squatted down beside the boy, bringing her head to the level of his.

"Supposing you move over slightly." She tried to make her voice sound as soothing as possible. "Yes, that's right, just a bit more."

The child's wriggling enabled her to get her hand under the strap and onto the catch. A firm grasp was all that was needed.

"There!" The fastener clicked open. "Now, if you'll just sit up straight for a moment, we'll see what happened to the full length of the strap."

Marianne, who was still standing behind her, watching, said, "There now—I'll bring you your dinner right away," to the mother, and walked back to the aft galley.

Linda's right, thought Betsy, adjusting the seat for the little boy before making her way to the galley herself. Marianne could move a bit quicker.

"Oh, Betsy." Judy looked at the senior stewardess with

relief when Betsy arrived in the galley. "What *is* it I've done wrong? This blasted catch . . ."

"Don't pull it—push it in instead."

The recalcitrant container door snapped open.

"They don't teach you things like that in training." Judy was already next to the trays and Betsy moved in easily to work at the counter.

"No, they don't," Betsy agreed. "But you can pick up the tricks fast enough." She checked the ovens and switched on the coffee. "Where'd you like me to fit in?"

"Could you help me here till the second trolley?"

"Surely."

When the major part of the passengers had been served their entree, Betsy left the galley area with the aisle trolley. Working with Marianne, she helped speed up the serving side of the meal. Judy was managing very well, she noted, her early nervousness completely gone.

Most of the passengers appeared to be businessmen, bored but uncomplaining and long-used to travel. The one who had turned down his entree was already asleep. A sleeping pill taker, almost for sure. They usually did the same thing: eat an exceptionally light meal and get to sleep as soon as possible. The reading light made a pale round pool on his face. Betsy leaned over and switched it off. The passenger didn't even stir when the light beam vanished.

"Miss!" A man in a dark blue suit was beckoning to her. "Could I have some more coffee, please?"

"Does the movie start soon?" This from a young girl further back.

"I've changed my mind. I *would* like a headset."

"I'd like my coffee now."

"Where's the john?"

The answers came easily and rapidly, just as smooth and practised as the coffee-pouring routine.

Less than a quarter of an hour later, Rudi came through the cabin on a total length check before starting the movie.

"Why don't you go up front and eat, Betsy? The girls can manage on their own here from now on. Captain's been fed. He's eating now."

"Okay." Betsy finished setting up a snack tray with coffee. "I'll just take this up to the man in twenty-five."

Not even in conversation with Rudi did she acknowl-edge he was air marshal Bradshaw who, for the time being, had moved into a seat across the aisle from his assigned position.

Returning up front to the first class cabin, she found Linda in deep conversation with the tall man with the loose mouth. They were standing near the galley, but Betsy managed to slip by them without disrupting their talk. She heard the man saying, ". . . and then I know a great little place . . ." and was thankful it was Linda who had attracted him now. He shouldn't have any trouble getting a date out of her, Betsy decided, setting up a tray for herself with just a steak and a glass of milk. He presumably had money enough to entertain Linda and besides, if she and Carl had quarrelled, she'd be at loose ends when they got to London.

Taking her tray along with her, Betsy settled herself on the cabin attendant seat by the door and, her tray bal-anced on her lap by a pillow, made quick work of the meal.

Linda, she noted, was still talking to the passenger. He took out a notebook and handed it to the stewardess, and Betsy saw her write something down in its pages.

She returned her tray to the galley, placed the empty back into the carrier and disposed of the leftovers on her plate. The slack-mouthed man had gone back to his seat, looking smug; Linda was talking to the Frenchman in front of him. She came back bearing his champagne glass.

"He wants *une coupe*," she reported. "He's said it so often even I'm beginning to learn what it means."

While she poured out a fresh goblet of champagne, Linda said, "By the way, if that yuk in the brown jacket asks you what hotel we stay at in London—tell him the Dorchester, will you?"

"What on earth for?"

"To get him off my back. I'll explain in a moment."

Linda zipped off to give the Frenchman his *coupe de champagne*. When she returned, she elaborated, "It's easi-er that way—I mean to give the yuk a wrong hotel. Otherwise, he'd pester me all night. This way, he figures he's as good as scored, and he'll leave me alone."

The flight deck buzzer sounded. Linda picked up the

phone, and Betsy could hear Larry Johnson's voice coming over it.

"Be a good kid and bring me my chow, huh? Now that the Captain's *finally* finished ... I tell you, Linda, I'm starved—wasting away to a mere shadow of my former self."

"Okay, okay." She sounded impatient, but Linda was smiling. "Steak, right?"

"Ko-rrect," came the answer.

"Be right up." Linda replaced the receiver and turned to Betsy.

"Would you?"

Betsy nodded and began setting up Johnson's meal.

The dome lights were out and the movie well in progress. As far as Betsy could see, only Mrs. Farnsworth, the air marshal and the pest in the brown jacket were making any attempt to watch the screen or use their earphones. Dr. Farnsworth was fast asleep, his head back against the headrest, his glasses in his lap; Rudi was chatting with the lady with the accent; and the Frenchman had disappeared. On her way up front with Johnson's tray, Betsy shot an automatic glance at the lavatory. Sure enough, the Occupied sign was on. Having accounted for the sixth passenger, she went through the door into the cockpit.

"Hi, Betsy." As always, Carl was smooth and pleasant.

"Do I hear food?" Larry's large face looked around and beamed with delight. "My God—but you're a sight for sore eyes, Blair. To say nothing of an aching empty stomach."

Fleming turned around and smiled at Betsy, lifting the tray out of his lap and handing it to her.

"You know, David," Larry commented, tucking the napkin into his collar, "if I were younger, you'd be hauled into court on charges of cruelty to children. Making me *wait*."

Fleming smiled and pointed toward Masden's cigarettes on the engineer's table. He said, "Betsy, how about a smoke? You can put that thing down on the floor."

Gratefully, she accepted his suggestion. Fleming's next remark was addressed to his co-pilot.

"If you were any younger, Larry, I'd put you on a diet."

Johnson's fork stopped, poised in mid-air.

"Did you *hear* that, Betsy?" he appealed. "A *diet*. David"—his voice filled with mock reproach—"could you do that to a friend, a real buddy?" The fork continued its trajectory. "Yeah, I guess you could. The trouble with you is you have no heart." The words were somewhat muffled by Johnson's mouthful of food. "No heart at all. A *diet*." He groaned and dug into another piece of steak. "There is no justice in this world . . . what with you in the left seat and the missus at home . . . it's a wonder I survive at all."

Betsy leaned against the door and smoked in silence. When she finished, she picked up Fleming's tray, murmured "See you later," to no one in particular and returned to the cabin. Rudi was in the galley.

"Johnson eating?"

"Yes, he is."

"Okay. I think I will, too."

"Go ahead."

The flight wore on along with the night. The movie glow flickered light on the faces of the watchers and the heads of those who turned away, either to sleep or stare at magazines until they, too, dozed off. In the first class section, the Frenchman had another coupe de champagne, and then another, but kept himself very much to himself; the brown-jacketed Don Juan, satisfied with his prowess and the planned conquest of Linda in London, watched the movie for a while until sleep overcame him. Then he sprawled untidily across two seats, one foot over the armrest and sticking out into the aisle.

Betsy edged her way around it and went back to coach. The small boy who had tangled with the seat belt was sleeping across his mother's lap; the little baby also slept, on the seat beyond.

On the way down the cabin, Betsy snapped off a few reading lights here and there. The young girls travelling together were all watching the movie; so were several of the many businessmen on board. A few were catching up on their paperwork.

"Would you like some coffee, sir?" she asked one of them who was sifting through a deep pile of what appeared to be office letters and memoranda on his lap.

The passenger asked uncertainly, "Well, if you have some tea . . ."

Betsy picked up a few more orders for coffee along the

233

way. Where was Marianne, she wondered, when she saw her sitting on the galley jumpseat, her tray on her lap, her jaws working steadily.

Pity Larry isn't single . . . he and Marianne'd make a great eating team.

"Hi. We have customers." Betsy reached for the snack trays. "One tea, four coffees and an orange juice."

Later, when she returned to the first class section, Betsy could feel her tiredness beginning to sap her strength. Her eyes had already started feeling scratchy; it was time to take measures. Repairing to the bathroom with her hand-bag, she soaked a paper towel in cold water and applied it to her face. The cold surface felt refreshing after the dry atmosphere of the cabin. Without towelling off the mois-ture, Betsy got out her eyedrops.

Once her eyes had been attended to, she reapplied her makeup. When she emerged she saw Rudi was going on a full length cabin check, and his shape disappeared into the aft cabin.

She found Linda in the galley, talking to the sharp faced woman.

"And do you like your job, dear?" the woman was saying.

"Oh, well—you know how it is," Linda answered airily, in a tone of voice Betsy had learned to suspect. It usually meant Linda was answering whatever was most conven-ient. "It sometimes lacks whatever I'm looking for that day."

"Perhaps you're really still looking for whatever it is you want," the woman replied.

"Oh, I'm sure I am." Still the same airy tone.

"And then, of course, there are things that pay much, much better." The woman looked at Linda with signifi-cance. Then, noticing Betsy, she greeted her. "Ah! Here's your attractive co-worker. I was just asking Miss Kesnik how she liked flying, and whether she ever tried applying her—er, talents to other forms of endeavor."

Betsy censored her immediate thought and smiled at the passenger. "Well, some of the stewardesses run two jobs, but it depends on how much free time you get. I know one girl who . . ."

"Oh, but of course, I understand," the woman broke in. "Tell me, do you girls spend much time in London?"

234

"Depends on the schedule," supplied Linda. "Sometimes a day and a half, sometimes three days. It all depends."

"Well, next time you're in London, and you feel bored, I tell you what you do." The woman opened the handbag she carried over her arm and produced two cards. "Here's my name and my phone number"—she handed each a card—"and I'd be more than happy to drop by the hotel and pick you up. There are all sorts of exciting things to do in London—with all sorts of exciting people."

With that, she gave a quick, staccato laugh, closed her handbag and nodded at them. "You won't forget, now, will you?"

She turned and went back to her seat before either of them had had time to answer. Instead, they looked at the cards.

"Madame Isabelle de Courcy," Linda read aloud. "And just the phone number. No address. I wonder what kind of a crazy set-up she's running?"

"We can ask Rudi. He seems to know her."

"Okay, let's. My bet is she's a lesbian. What d'you think?"

Betsy shook her head. "I honestly don't know—but Rudi's sure to."

Linda laughed. "Yeah—right up his alley, isn't it?"

Betsy grinned, but did not answer. Instead, she glanced at her watch.

"Hadn't we better set the breakfast ovens?"

The time-gap was closing; only just after midnight by New York standards, it was early morning in Europe, with breakfast right around the corner. The first tinges of a dawn were already beginning to lighten the sky; Betsy could see the changing heavens in the small squares of the first row windows. She was glad she'd put the eyedrops in, to be ready for the dawn. Otherwise, the light would only further irritate the scratchy feeling.

"Let's feed 'em up front," Linda was saying. "I'll be damned if I want to start fooling around with crew coffee once breakfast gets started."

"Okay. I'll go up and ask them." Betsy was glad of the excuse. She wondered whether David would say anything—now, or later in London. After all, they'd have two days there, or anyway, almost two days. And it hadn't been a

235

rough flight; a couple of hours' sleep was all she'd really need.

Indulging in a small daydream, she went through the flight deck door. A few feet in front of her sat Captain David Fleming—and less than two hours' ahead lay sprawling London.

6

The crew car slid through the London traffic and came to a halt in front of a crossing. A girl in a bright purple coat walked in front of them, leading the rest of the pedestrians at the stop.

"Wow—look at that . . ."

It was Johnson who made the appreciative remark, but Betsy noticed it was Carl who looked with most interest. The girl in the coat was young and showy, but Betsy felt sure that Johnson's reaction was purely mechanical while Carl's was really lustful. Not that she felt there was anything unnatural about a man looking at women that way, but somehow, with Carl, she got the impression he was incapable of much else. She supposed he was a good engineer; that side of him was hard for her to judge. But as a person—yes, that was it; never mind male or female, just as a *person*—Carl Masden seemed sadly lacking. Betsy wondered what on earth it was that Lee had ever seen in him. Or Linda, for that matter. She glanced at her out of the corner of her eye.

Linda's eyes were closed and the pallor that usually came with tiredness was more accentuated than Betsy had ever seen it before.

Linda opened her eyes, straightened in her seat and turned to Betsy.

"Did you show Rudi the card?"

"What card?" Rudi asked.

In answer, the two girls started rummaging around in their handbags.

They both handed the cards over to Rudi at the same time.

He took them both, looked at them and handed them back, nodding.

"Yes. Madame de Courcy. She often travels with us."

"Who is she, Rudi?" Linda enquired.

"Does she run a business, or something?" Betsy added.

Rudi sniggered.

"I'll say she does. Originally, she's Bulgarian, I think. She linked up with the Allied soldiers somewhere in the last months of World War II, and got to London."

"Yes—but what does she do now?" Linda persisted.

"Runs a specialty outfit." Rudi sniggered again, as though pleased with his own words.

"Is it a boutique or something?" Betsy asked. "Because that might explain why she thought we could be of use."

"What?" Rudi's tone changed, and he swivelled around in his seat to look directly at Betsy.

"Well, when she gave us the cards, she told us to ring her sometime."

". . . if we were bored and wanted excitement," finished Linda. She yawned. "That doesn't sound like a boutique to me." With another yawn, she added, "If we don't get to that hotel soon, I'm going to fall asleep right here."

But Rudi was not listening to her any more. His face darkened with rage.

"Of all the scheming snakes . . . if she ever does anything like that again . . . filthy bitch . . . don't either of you girls even think of calling her . . . I'll see to it that she doesn't get on our aircraft again . . . blacklisting . . ."

"Rudi." Betsy tried to break through his furious monologue. "Rudi—you haven't even told us what she does."

"Must be a madame, in every sense of the word," Linda said. "Is she, Rudi?"

"Of course." His voice was tight and cold now. "Isa runs one of the most exclusive call girl operations in London. In the world, probably. I know she's contacted potential clients on our flights, because—well, because I've seen her do it once or twice myself," he finished shortly. "But trying to rope you in . . . oh, no. That, she's not

238

going to get away with. I've half a mind to call her today and . . ."

"Oh, leave it alone, Rudi." Linda sounded wearier by the minute. "You know you can't stop her."

"I can have her blacklisted."

"Maybe, but what good does it do you?"

"But she was trying to get you to work for her." His voice heightened with anger.

"We understand that." Betsy attempted to calm Rudi. "But we're not going to call her, so what's the problem?"

Rudi muttered "Such nerve, trying to recruit stewardesses right under my nose," but his anger had somewhat subsided.

"It's the same old story, and you really should be used to it by now." Linda tucked her feet up onto the seat and under her, settling back against the side of the crew car as she did so. "The image of stewardess as swinger is with us now as it was always. *Everyone* knows stews sleep with *everyone*. So from Madame de Courcy's point of view, why not turn it into a profitable business? Especially," added Linda, the gleam of malice entering her eye, "since she has the set-up going so well already."

Rudi said, "But she should know better than . . ."

Betsy interrupted him, saying, "In a crazy way, I guess it's flattering. She must've thought we'd be worthwhile." Linda laughed, Rudi looked annoyed and the rest of the ride was more or less silent.

At the hotel, the desk man said, "There's a letter for you, Miss Blair," and handed Betsy an envelope.

Betsy did not recognize the handwriting. There were two sheets of paper inside, one with an untidy scrawl, the other with the careful printing of a child.

"Oh! It's from James . . . James Murray."

She spoke to everyone in general, but David Fleming was standing right behind her.

"And one from his father, too, I see." David's voice was noncommittal.

"Yes." She could see it was an invitation to dinner, but she put the two letters back into the envelope. She'd read them later, when she got upstairs.

Betsy felt the sinking sensation of disappointment as she walked towards the elevator with Linda and Marianne. She'd hoped David would say something, perhaps suggest they go out to dinner together. But he had done nothing of the kind; he had merely inquired whether there were any messages for him. The desk man had said, "Just a moment, Captain, I'll go and see," and disappeared into the inner office. Just then, Linda had said, "Oh, goody, our room's ready. Come on Betsy, let's go," and there had been no way to get out of it.

Later, in their room, Linda said, "You know, Rudi was really mad about that de Courcy female."

"Yes, he certainly was." Betsy, already in her slip, pulled off her pantihose and wriggled her toes in relief. She bent down to massage her feet; they weren't too swollen this time.

"I'll bet it was only because he figured he wouldn't get a percentage," Linda went on, hanging up her jacket. "Rudi'd forget all about morality for a small fee."

Betsy giggled. "Ol' Ten Percent Becker."

"More like fifteen." Linda disappeared into the bathroom.

Betsy went over to the phone. "Shall I order breakfast for you?" she called out.

"Just coffee, thanks," came from the other side of the closed door.

"Are you sure? Don't you want something to eat?"

"No. Just coffee. I don't feel . . ." The rest of Linda's sentence was drowned out by the gushing sound of the shower turned on full blast.

Betsy frowned, wondering whether Linda was feeling ill. All the girls found they slept better after a flight if they ate something before going to bed. But there was no arguing with Linda, so why try?

"Room service, please."

While she waited for the tray to arrive, Betsy read James' letter.

"Dear Betsy, Please come and have tea with me today. I have a new train and lots of toys to show you. Love from James."

Andrew Murray's message reiterated the tea invitation, explaining he would not be there but that he hoped she would stay on and have dinner with him as well. Perhaps a little London night life would be pleasant afterwards?

She had just finished reading through both letters for

240

the second time when Linda emerged from the bathroom, stark naked.

"Here—let me help you." Betsy reached for the other side of the sheet and pulled it loose as she saw Linda doing her usual trick. She watched as Linda draped it around herself. "Don't you ever feel cold?"

"No. It's warmer to sleep directly under a blanket, anyway."

A knock on the door announced the arrival of Betsy's room service order.

"Are you sure you won't have anything, Linda? There's plenty here for both of us."

"Quite sure. I told you I don't feel like eating."

Betsy spread marmalade on her toast and poured herself a cup of tea. To order coffee in England was madness. Out of the corner of her eye she saw Linda take a small phial out of her handbag and shake a capsule into her hand.

I wonder what on earth she's taking? Could it be a sleeping pill? Medicine of some kind? But she says she's not sick. And I can see for myself she's tired. So why would it be a sleeping pill?

But it was no use asking. Linda was not in a confiding mood. Betsy wondered whether she ever confided anything to anybody.

When she was through with her breakfast, she put the tray outside in the corridor. Linda was already under the covers, either asleep or pretending to be.

Her usual quick post-trip shower and some sleep would pick her up. And then, when she woke up, who knew what might happen. David Fleming might even call her.

That thought kept her intrigued all the way through her shower, and she was still turning it over gently in her mind when she got into bed and fell asleep.

7

When she woke, it was two o'clock. Eight o'clock, New York time. That was two in the afternoon, local. Yawning and stretching, she decided to get up. Had David left a message for her downstairs? It was worth getting up to check.

She looked across at the other bed. Linda was deeply asleep, the dark rings under her eyes accentuating the fragility of her fine-boned face.

No, it wouldn't be fair to wake her by calling down to ask whether there were any messages. Betsy felt sure Linda was not well, no matter how much she might deny it.

Or maybe it was an emotional low, because of Carl.

Betsy felt a hot surge of anger. Oh, boy, that Carl Masden. She moved quietly around the room, putting on fresh clothes from the open suitcase.

Downstairs at the desk, the disappointment was sharp and brief.

"No, Miss Blair, no messages for you."

Well, of course, Fleming might still be sleeping. Betsy turned away from the desk just in time to see Larry Johnson push his way through the hotel entrance with a heavy shopping bag in each hand.

"Hi, there, Blair," he greeted her loudly. "See the similarity between me and a pack mule? All I need is saddle bags—and for God's sake, don't tell the missus, or she'll go right out and get some."

"Here—let me help you," Betsy offered, but Johnson shook his head.

"No, no—I gotta keep in training. You know how it is; first I'll let you carry something, and then it'll be Masden, and the next thing you know, I'll be handing packages to Fleming . . . You see the risks involved?" He lowered his voice and whispered, "They say the penalty's shooting at dawn—the only punishment stern enough for handing a package to a four-striper." Then in his normal voice he continued, "Not that I'd get much of a chance here in London. That chief of ours was out before I was today. I don't know whether he got any shut-eye at all."

Betsy's hopes sank completely out of sight, and when Larry went off to the elevator to take his first shopping haul upstairs, she walked over to the telephones and took James' letter out of her pocket. There was still time to accept his invitation to afternoon tea, even though it did mean giving up her planned shopping.

But I don't much feel like going shopping. In my present mood I'd probably get all the wrong things, and spend money on things I won't like when I get back. Besides, I really would like to see James again.

She began dialing.

Less than half an hour later, the Murray limousine was outside the hotel, with James jumping up and down in the back.

"Do hurry up, Betsy," he called out as she emerged from the hotel entrance. "I've got *so* many things to show you!"

When she got in beside him, James said, "Look at my tooth," and opened his mouth to display the thin serrated edge of new tooth in the front recess of his upper gum. From then on, he chatted about his new electric train, and when they arrived at the Murray mansion he almost dragged Betsy up the stairs and along a passage to what he called his "day nursery." Beyond it, Betsy could see a room that was obviously his bedroom, but only toys and games and two sets of table and chairs—one full size, one miniature—occupied the day nursery.

The afternoon passed quickly and pleasantly; tea was served at the bigger table by a pleasant-faced, uniformed maid. Betsy noted details she knew would interest her parents and she fully intended to give them a full description of six-year-old James and his mode of life. The maid calling him "Master James," for example; that was the sort of thing she had only read about in books before.

Despite the way he was addressed, James was, in most respects, exceedingly like many other six-year-old boys Betsy had known. His thrill at the new train, an elaborate affair mounted on a board, was more in the showing it off rather than in the playing with it. Fathers buy their sons electric trains because *they* want to play with them, Betsy decided.

James turned to his crayon box when they finished tea.

"I've got paints, too," he told her, dragging out a selection from a toy chest. "Let's draw pictures, Betsy."

So intent were they both on their drawings and paintings from then on, that both of them jumped slightly in their seats when Andrew Murray said behind them, "Well! What a lovely picture, I must say."

"Hello, Mr. Murray." Betsy rose and shook his outstretched hand. "How are you?"

Murray touched his forehead briefly, letting the palm of his hand slide back over his thinning hair.

"Just a few headaches left, thank goodness. All the rest of it's gone. The doctors said I was jolly lucky, after such a nasty fall."

Then, smiling with his practised expression, he said, "And you *are* staying for dinner, aren't you?"

"Oh, I'm so sorry, Mr. Murray,"—Betsy managed to sound genuinely apologetic—"but I can't because the crew members have all arranged to go to a show together."

Murray argued and cajoled, but Betsy was able to persuade him of her totally fictitious plans.

"In fact, I'd better get going right now," she lied, looking at her watch. "Goodness—it *is* late."

Promising she would come back on another trip, Betsy deliberately avoided acknowledging the look of disappointment in Andrew Murray's eye, and descended the big staircase with James at her side. He escorted her to the waiting car outside, and as she stepped in, he suddenly yielded and threw his arms around her neck.

"You're nice, Betsy," he whispered as he hugged her tightly. Then, perhaps embarrassed by his unaccustomed show of emotion, he ran all the way back to the front door, paused briefly to turn and wave farewell, and disappeared indoors.

"The hotel, miss?" the chauffeur enquired, and Betsy nodded, sinking back against the seat as the limousine started.

The cushioned calm felt wonderful. Betsy felt she could easily fall asleep right then and there. A fantasy involved her: she was very rich, and the limousine was hers—one of several limousines that always carried her to and from airports.

Interrupting the daydream, she found herself smiling at her own stupidity. If she had a car like this of her own, she wouldn't be flying any more, would she? But what would she be doing? It didn't seem to be an envisageable part of her future; a nice car, yes, certainly, but hardly a chauffeur-driven one. She imagined David Fleming in the back seat behind a chauffeur, and almost laughed out loud at the thought. David would never let someone else drive his car. Any more than he'd ever let someone else take command of his aircraft.

David. Where could he have gone off to? It sounded from Larry as though he'd had an appointment to keep. Why, oh why, did everything about him have to be so mysterious?

Betsy's thoughts returned to young James, and the afternoon she'd just spent with him. Such an appealing little boy.

The soothing purr of the limousine engine subsided, and they came to a halt at a traffic light. Still feeling like a pampered celebrity, Betsy looked out of the window. A taxi drew up alongside; idly, she glanced at its occupants.

She felt her heart skip a beat in the split second of her reaction. There were two people in the London taxi, a man and a young woman. Surely the man couldn't be David Fleming?

She leaned forward to get a better look. At that same moment, the young woman in the taxi leaned forward, too, and, as she was on the side next to the limousine, she hid the man sitting on the far side from Betsy's view. All she could see was the man's hand and arm as he raised it, presumably in conversational gesture, and then let it drop to his knee again.

But that was David's hand. Betsy was sure she recog-

245

nized the well-proportioned, strong lines. Her heart was pounding so hard she could feel it in her ears; the lovely feeling of calm luxury had fled, totally forgotten. She sat, stiff and still, bolt upright on the seat.

The forward motion of the limousine moved her back against the leather upholstery. In the same moment, the taxi also started forward, and for a brief second, the girl shifted her position. David Fleming's face was visible in the corner beyond.

The street divided beyond the light; the taxi sped off toward the right, the limousine glided left, continuing along the broader thoroughfare.

Betsy felt herself go limp against the back of the seat. Her heart gradually stopped pounding. Why should she react so violently? After all, it was more than likely that David Fleming had friends in London, even if he had never mentioned them.

But the wrenching feeling was still there, no matter how sensibly she might talk to herself. Who was the woman? Betsy had noted that she was young and pretty, with long dark hair and a wistful expression.

Betsy leaned against the seat back, motionless in her bewilderment, until the limousine drew to a stop outside the hotel door.

8

As Betsy was still under the impact of having seen David
Fleming with the young woman in the taxi, she didn't
immediately grasp the scene that greeted her when she
returned to the hotel room. Linda, wearing most of her
uniform, was stuffing a pair of shoes into the suitcase on
her bed. She turned as she heard Betsy behind her, said,
"Oh, hello," and disappeared into the bathroom.

She returned with her toothbrush and cosmetics case in
her hands.

For a moment, Betsy stood and stared at the other girl.
Feeling somewhat unreal, she finally asked, "We don't
have to leave now, do we? I mean, we only just came in
this morning. I thought that . . ."

"*I* have to leave," said Linda briefly. She continued
packing.

"This *evening*?"

"Today's flight was delayed—which, I guess, is lucky for
me." Linda gave a short and hollow laugh. "Some lucky
. . ."

Betsy sat down on the edge of her bed. Of course their
own schedule was for the next day's flight, and they had
no standby assignment here. Linda's departure must mean
some sort of emergency.

"Linda—what's wrong? Something must've happened
. . ."

Linda finished closing the zipper on her overnight bag
before replying.

247

"My mother's sick," came the reply. "I'm deadheading back."

"Oh, Linda—I *am* sorry . . ."

All the cobwebs gone, Betsy rose from the bed.

"Here, let me finish that for you," she offered, reaching toward Linda's suitcase.

"No, that's okay. I'm just about finished, anyway."

"Well, can I call the bellboy for you?"

"I already did," came the answer. "He'll be here any moment now." Linda slipped on her jacket as she spoke.

Betsy tried once more.

"Surely I can do *something* to help you?"

"No," said Linda shortly. "Nobody can."

She returned to the open suitcase on the bed and snapped it shut. Then she looked at Betsy.

"But thanks anyway," she said in a slightly softer tone. "You're okay, Betsy Blair—you know that?" Her voice reverted to normal and she said, "One of the Paris girls is being sent over to replace me on tomorrow's flight. I didn't get the name, but I think she's a new-hire."

There was a knock on the door.

"That's the bellboy . . . Come in!"

"Try to get some sleep on the plane," Betsy urged, watching Linda pick up her handbag. "And—I hope things work out okay."

"Yeah. Sure." Linda grabbed her cape. "See you around."

The bellboy had the bags, and Linda followed him out. The room felt oppressive in the sudden silence. Betsy sat down on her bed again and realized she was close to tears. Why did life have to be so horrid all of a sudden?

Disliking herself for indulging in what she suspected was self-pity, she stood up and went to wash her face.

There was a knock on the door. The handle turned before Betsy had time to reply and Marianne appeared.

"Hi."

Betsy stood in the doorway of the bathroom, towelling her face.

"Hi, there. Been doing much shopping?"

Marianne flopped down onto the bed that had been Linda's.

"Not much. I didn't get up until four, by the time I'd

248

had lunch, it was kind of late. Judy was out, though. That girl had energy."

Marianne shook her head in wonderment. Betsy smiled.

"You have to remember she's a new-hire, Marianne. After all, this is only her second trip to London. Remember how you felt, those first trips you took?"

"I guess." Marianne did not sound too convincing, and Betsy found herself wondering whether Marianne ever moved with any speed unless the theater or fashion were involved. Or food.

As if in answer to Betsy's thoughts, Marianne took a Cadbury chocolate bar out of her pocket.

"They really do make the greatest chocolate around here," she observed, peeling the foil off the bar. "Want some?" she offered, gesturing with the chocolate in Betsy's direction.

"No, thanks. I'll be having dinner soon."

"That's what I came by for." Marianne spoke through a mouthful of chocolate. "Judy and I are going to dinner and then a movie." She went into long detail about the starring actress. "It's her technique, you know. She has this great style. I've seen every movie she's made, and I think she is just the greatest. Well, maybe not as great as Kara Lane, but almost. Anyway, Judy and I thought you might join us."

Betsy's immediate reaction was to refuse. She felt low enough not to want to listen to Marianne burble all night about her acting career. But then common sense prevailed; after all, both she and Judy would be good company.

"I'd love to. Where d'you plan eating?"

"There's an Indian restaurant quite near here," Marianne said. "We figured we'd try it." She rose. "We'll be ready in about half an hour. Does that suit you?"

"Sure. Fine."

When Marianne left, Betsy brushed her hair and let it hang loose, and re-did her makeup.

There was still a fifteen-minute gap left.

I might as well write a postcard to Mother and Dad.

"Dear everyone," she wrote on one of the hotel postcards, "X marks the spot and, believe it or not, it isn't foggy in London-town. At least, not today. Love and kisses," and she signed it with a rapidly-traced B.

Having finished, she felt her depressed mood descend once more. She glanced back at the card; how easy it was to deceive with words. The cheerful message looked perfectly natural; no one would guess that she had been feeling miserable as she wrote it.

Oh, boy, there I go again, feeling sorry for myself. Anyone would think I really had problems. After all, there are plenty of people with *real* problems. How about Linda? Sure, she can be unfriendly, and she certainly seems to lead a crazy sort of life. And yet, she's really got a problem now—a mother sick enough to require her going home.

Betsy wondered whether there were any other members in Linda's family. She'd never heard Linda mention anyone at all. She so seldom said anything that gave any clues, any real clues, as to what she was really like, or to what her private life was like.

It was time to go. Betsy gathered up her handbag and the card for mailing. Her thoughts were still on Linda as she went out of the door to go and join Judy and Marianne. Betsy hoped things would work out okay, knowing that it was unlikely she'd ever hear about it at all. Despite all her idle chatter, Linda was close-mouthed about the big things, the things that counted.

Betsy wondered how Linda was feeling at that very moment.

9

Linda was numb as she climbed up the steps and entered the first class section of the aircraft. The coach section was almost full, the station agent had informed her; she was to deadhead in first class, having been given priority over any other possible deadheads because of the emergency nature of her recall.

Fortunately, there had been no problem about getting a seat. Another company employee, someone from the sales section at the head office, was also on the flight, but since there were only five first class passengers, no clash of interests had occurred.

Thank God, thought Linda, slipping into a window seat in the last row. I don't need any trouble or argument right now. I'm going to have enough of them when I get back home. I wonder what the hell she's done *this* time.

And then another thought crept in, unbidden:

I wonder if she's going to die . . .

She viewed the thought dispassionately, now that it had appeared. The answer came.

No, she isn't. She's going to get better, and be allowed out again—so she can make another real mess of everything and ruin all my chances of ever getting straightened out. No, she's not going to die. She's not about to do anything as easy or as simple as that. Besides, there's too much left of me for her to destroy. Why should she quit now?

Aware of the bitterness of her thoughts, Linda took off

her fur hat and slung it into the overhead rack. She pushed her overnight case under the seat, sat down and fastened her seat belt.

And they'd better not ask me to help out tonight, either. I don't feel like working—and I have too much to face tomorrow.

The two girls working the flight, who had been in the galley section checking equipment when she boarded, greeted her as they went by. Linda knew them both by sight, but had never worked a trip with either of them. The purser, who appeared through the divider, was an old friend, Ramon Gonzales.

"Hi, Ramon."

"Hey, there, Linda. They told us you'd be on board." He paused at her seat. "And they also told us why. I'm sorry to hear things are rough."

Linda shrugged. "Yeah. Well, you know how these things go."

If there was one thing she didn't want, it was sympathy. People who gave it tended to ask questions. Why couldn't they just mind their own goddam business?

"What I mean is—I forbid you to do any work." Ramon was smiling at her, and Linda realized that, in his own way, he came close to understanding. "Get some sleep."

"Thanks. I intend to. And if there's one place I can sleep—it's on an airplane."

They both grinned at the reference to her habit of sleeping on flights.

"You let me know if there's something you want, okay?"

"Thanks, Ramon."

He went on up the aisle and Linda watched him until he disappeared into the cockpit. He was okay.

She'd almost slept with him some time ago. It had been on an unexpected overnight in Philadelphia, when New York had been below limits during their scheduled arrival time in the evening, and then stayed that way all night. The captain had landed at Philly, and they'd gotten to the hotel so tired they were almost in a giggly mood. She and Ramon had felt the pull of attraction all the way through the flight, so that when the hotel was finally reached they'd considered getting together. But it had been one of

252

those things that just hadn't panned out. Maybe that was why there was still some kind of warm feeling between them now.

Whatever it was, this was not the time to be thinking about it, Linda decided. If she could just tank up on a lot of sleep . . . There was going to be so much to do . . .

Opening her handbag, Linda checked the small bottle of pills tucked into a side pocket. If she took another sleeping pill just before she had dinner, she should be ready for sleep by the time she finished her meal. She'd discovered a long time ago that taking a sleeping pill before a meal made it work faster and better. If you waited until afterwards, the food seemed to slow down the pill's effect.

She'd wait till after takeoff and then take the pill. With any luck, she'd snooze before her tray was handed to her, too. Meanwhile, she'd just lean back and close her eyes and try, somehow, to relax. It wasn't going to be easy, but then, nothing ever was.

The noises of the cabin drifted around her. She could hear the quick footsteps of the flight attendants in their incessant trips up and down the length of the airplane.

I wonder what Mother managed to do this time, before they caught up with her . . .

Linda didn't even try to tell herself she should not worry in advance, that it would be better if she waited until she got home. There never had been a time, as far back as she could remember, that the worry had not been there.

I wonder what Mother's done this time . . .

She heard the agent's voice at the door.

"They're coming on . . ."

The passengers embarked, and Linda opened her eyes. It might be better not to appear sprawled and asleep. Ramon was okay about things like that, she knew, but one never could tell what shit engineer might be on board. Or the captain might come back for something, and see her. All she needed right now was another bummer of a report.

She watched the familiar routine without seeing it. The passengers got settled down, the door was shut. The whine of Number Two engine starting up began.

"Ladies and gentlemen," Ramon's voice came over the

253

p.a. system, "welcome aboard Flightways International ..."

She closed her eyes again. The plane began to move. Its taxiing made her drowsy and she drifted off to semi-sleep once or twice while they stood at the end of the runway, waiting for takeoff clearance. Then she felt the power surging and the takeoff run began. They were off.

The moment those lights go off, I'm going to get some water and take a pill ...

She hunted in her bag for the small phial, and tipped a capsule into her hand. Both the no smoking and the fasten seat belts signs were lit.

Goddammit, you schmuck—hurry up with the lights ...

Moments later, the lights went off and Linda rose from her seat. She slipped past the galley to the drinking water spigot, took a paper cup and half-filled it. A swallow of water, and it was down. There. That was done. Now to wait for its blessed effect to take over. She went back to her seat and closed her eyes again.

Oh God ... it was all such a mess, such a hopeless mess. Linda could feel her taut nerves jump in her body. In a few more minutes, the sleeping pill should help things calm down; she took a deep breath, willing the ease to come.

From time to time, Linda opened her eyes to check what stage the service had reached. By the time the second round of cocktails had been served, the barbiturate had begun to take effect.

Things go better with pills for sleeping
Things go better with downs

Linda sang in her mind, the words fitting the commercial jingle and making her smile. That's what was nice about the pills; they made it easier, and then gave you the sleep you needed to be able to cope with the next day. Her heavy lids weighed her down, and she drifted off into momentarily light but dreamless sleep.

"Linda."

The voice spoke her name softly. Linda woke, surprised she had been asleep. Ramon was bending over the aisle seat toward her.

"You want to eat now?"

Linda sat up. "Shall I come and fix it myself?" she asked, taking care not to let her speech become slurred.

Not that she thought Ramon was the type to report her for having sounded drunk, or drugged, but because she wanted no questions.

The purser shook his head.

"Nah. You stay here. What'll you have?"

"Not much." She didn't want to blunt the pleasant effect of the barbiturate. "Don't bother with the entree—just the accompanying garbage."

She picked at the food he brought her, knowing she had to eat something, but hardly tasting what she sampled. She felt better now; the tight feeling was distant, a feeling she knew was going to return, but which she was thankful to be free from for at least a few hours. She took another mouthful.

Just another mouthful, Linda-winda, that's a good girl . . . The voice echoed to her out of the distant past, and in her present slightly drugged state, Linda saw the similarity. Just another mouthful, there's a good girl . . . so's you can grow up to be big and strong and take care of all the problems your shit mother doesn't want to face or handle or do anything about . . . *there's a good girl, just one more* . . .

And one more and another time and yet another one around. Linda put the tray aside on the seat next to her before rising to get a blanket. She moved with quiet deliberation, neither disturbing the barbiturate's effect nor signalling its presence. Dumping the blanket onto her seat, she picked up her tray and returned it to the galley.

"Thanks," she smiled at the stewardess standing there. "I'm going to sleep from now on. Would you do me a favor and wake me before the rush on the blue rooms starts?"

Back in her seat, she settled herself comfortably under the soft folds of the blanket. It felt like the effect of the pill, a temporary padding, but marvellously comfortable nonetheless. Tomorrow I'll take care of tomorrow, she thought drowsily and without pain. Right now, I don't have to do anything but sleep and forget.

The waves of sleep washed over her.

10

*"one more mouthful, Linda-winda, just like a good girl
..."*

Mommy was using her funny voice and it made Linda
feel afraid. Mommy was being silly-funny, not funny-
funny, the way Daddy could be. Daddy was big and
strong and safe, and could pick up little Linda without
hurting her or letting her fall, and he laughed with his big
white teeth showing and he let her pull his hair and ride
on his shoulder.

But Daddy wasn't here now, and it was Mommy who
was shoving the spoon at Linda's face. She was still
crooning the phrase, over and over, and Linda could see
that Mommy's mouth looked like it might fall off her
face. When the spoon reached Linda's mouth, it tipped
and jabbed her in the gum beneath her upper lip. The
warm food splashed down onto her pink dress.

"Oh, Linda-winda, just look what you did . . . you're a
naughty little Linda-winda . . . always giving your poor
Mommy such a hard time."

Little Linda Kesnik burst into tears.

There were other troubles, too. Linda heard the phrases
shouted on weekends, hissed at table, barked from the
bathroom, snarled in the dark reaches of the frightening
night.

"The goddam trouble with you is you've never
amounted to anything, and you never will."

256

"You and that fucking bottle! Can't you even wait till the sun goes down?"

"What's it to you, mac?" Her mother's voice was taunting, but this puzzled Linda, because her father's name was Paul, not Mac.

"Cecilia, I'm asking you for the last time . . ."

"You shut your big fat Pollak mouth, Paul Kesnik! After you've taken the best years of my life, and me, who gave up everything to marry you."

"You call a chorus job in feathers *everything*?"

"Shut your goddam mouth!"

"Cecilia—keep it down, will ya? The kid'll hear."

"She won't. She's sleeping. Besides, she's too small to understand."

Linda didn't understand why her Daddy wasn't there. She knew it was Sunday, because the church bell had rung so many times. Sundays were nice days, with Daddy home to feed her things that tasted nice instead of burned or nasty the way they were when Mommy cooked. But now he wasn't there.

"Mommy—where's Daddy?"

Mommy was lying down on the bed. Linda stood next to it, her feet stumbling on the bottles beside Mommy's slippers.

"Linda, go and play outside." Mommy's voice sounded very tired. "Leave me alone."

When she got hungry, Linda went into the bedroom again.

"Mommy, I . . ."

"Get out of here . . . let me sleep, goddamit."

The lady from the house next door found Linda crying on the steps, and asked her what was the matter. After that, the lady took her into her house and made her some sandwiches. They tasted more like the Daddy ones than the Mommy ones.

It was dark when Linda went home again.

"Where the hell have you been?"

When Linda told her, Mommy slapped her across the face, very hard.

"Dirty little bitch, telling stories to the neighbors! Don't you ever let me catch you doing anything like that again, you hear?"

257

From then on, Linda learned to find her own food alone.

They went away, she and her Mommy, and they went to stay in a big, dark house with an old lady who spoke words Linda didn't understand. There were lots of other people in the house, too; each one seemed to have a separate room and a separate life. The old lady and her Mommy quarrelled a lot, especially when Mommy came home late at night. Linda was supposed to be asleep on the small sofa between the windows.

"Hush up! The kid's asleep!"

"What the fuck do I care?" That was a man's voice one night, and after that, there were other men, and Linda knew what they did with Mommy on the day bed against the wall.

They left the big house and travelled by train. In later years, Linda wondered how many towns she had been to as a child. It was useless asking her mother; Cecilia Kesnik would never remember. She'd give one answer one day, and another the next. The only true statement, Linda knew, was that they had lived in Cleveland. Her birth certificate showed this.

They went through Cleveland again, several times, and on one occasion, Linda met her father again. At first, she did not recognize him, but then the memories came back.

They were both ill at ease, sitting in the little-used front room of her grandmother's house, a grandmother she had only met this trip back. Her mother had sent her to the address.

"I suppose she wants money," Mr. Kesnik said. His mother, a white haired woman in a black wool shawl, said nothing. Linda stared down at her own feet.

"Yes." Linda didn't know whether to call him Father or Daddy, so she called him nothing at all. The atmosphere of the room was closing in on her; the only way to manage was to tell the bare minimum.

"That's all I can spare." He handed her some bills. "My luck hasn't been too good lately."

"It never was," Linda's mother snorted when Linda gave her the money back at the cheap rooming house and

258

a brief account of the afternoon. "A no-good wastrel bum, that's all your father is."

Linda saw her father again that week. They bumped into each other near the railroad station. Somehow, the anonymity of the neighborhood made the meeting easier.

"Let's go get a cuppa coffee." For a moment, her father seemed almost boyish, despite the heavy jowls and the hang-dog air.

The coffee shop was warm and filled with people. They found an empty booth for two way in the back. Linda said, "Just milk, thank you," and saw her father looked relieved. The thought he'd given her all his money for her mother flashed through Linda's mind.

"What about school, Linda?"

"I do okay." She didn't think it worth telling him the time the authorities caught up with her mother, and the way she'd been told it was either Linda to school or Mrs. Kesnik up before the court. "We've moved around quite a bit, so I've been to lots . . . but I do okay."

"Linda Kesnik!"

Her name was called out at the beginning of the class, and everyone heard she had to stay after school to give an explanation for what she had put in the social studies test.

"Ohhh, Linda, what'd you do *this* time?"

The boys taunted her across the play yard.

"Nothing." Defiantly.

"You gotta stay in after school, yah yah!"

"So what?" Linda shrugged and turned her back.

"Linda." The teacher's voice was quiet, her face tight. "Just what do you mean by this answer?"

They were alone in the bleak classroom. All the other children had left. In the distance, Linda could hear their voices fading through the halls and into the street.

"What answer?" There was still some defiance left over from the play yard.

"You know perfectly well which one I mean." A paper rattled under Linda's nose. "This one!"

Linda read through her own words. She handed the paper back in silence.

"Well? Have you nothing at all to say?"

Linda made a last attempt. "But it's true. San Francisco, Miami and Boston *do* have whorehouses."

"How can you *say* such a thing?"

"Because I've seen them. My mother pointed the places out to me when we went by in a bus . . ."

Carnal knowledge had been hers ever since she could remember; carnal contact happened after her fifteenth birthday.

He wasn't nice but he was good-looking; she didn't particularly care for him, but it was better than going home right then and there, and anyway, he was good to her and he spent money on her for the movies and later for hamburgers and french fries. In a way, he reminded her of her father; there was something in his face that was reminiscent of the hang-dog expression she remembered.

She discovered later he'd told the other boys that "Linda Kesnik'll do it with anyone," and shortly thereafter she realized that the "just like her mother" phrase was being tacked onto her. They moved again that summer, but not far enough. Hearsay followed them.

So did the cops.

". . . for wilfully and maliciously destroying private property while under the influence of alcohol . . ."

It was not the first time it had happened—not the first time Linda had seen her mother hauled into court for unseemly and destructive behavior. But the incidents became more frequent, after that summer's move.

Linda was not yet sixteen the day she returned to the miserable shack where they were currently living and found flames engulfing the kitchen and her mother dead drunk in the hall.

She'd managed to drag her out of the front door. Leaving her on the sidewalk, Linda ran for help.

She never heard the end of it in the years that followed. "Leaving me there, right by the fire . . . I might have died . . . Oh, Linda-winda, why aren't you kinder to your poor dear mother? Why doesn't anyone ever treat me right? And to think that I gave you life and brought you into the world."

It was easier for Linda to give her money, and stay away from home.

She was out of school more than she was in it. If it wasn't a court summons, it was now a hospital visit. Mrs.

Kesnik, approaching her forties, was beginning to reap the results of an abused and insulted hepatic system.

"Miss Kesnik." The head nurse was waiting for her outside in the hospital corridor. "Is there no one else in the family?"

There was not. Sometimes Linda felt as though there never had been, either. Time and distance protected her father. And there was no one else.

I can't leave her in the street, to die . . .

But she was found lying on the sidewalk, on several occasions and in several towns. They moved, and moved again. Linda, an old hand at part-time, after-school jobs, finally rid herself of her scholastic obligations to the state and found herself full-time employment. In a drugstore. In a dime store. As a typist. At least school had given her *that*.

But what good was a quick mind and an aptitude for picking up the everyday skills of life? For if there was one thing Linda was well trained to do, it was cope with life on both a day-to-day and an emergency basis.

It did not look impressive on an application form.

"If I was young and pretty like you," Cecilia Kesnik was saying, "I'd try to make something of myself."

Linda sat next to the hospital bed, hearing the sound and discounting the words. Similar encouragement had been voiced many times before by a shaken, sober and recuperating Mrs. Kesnik.

Her mother went on talking but Linda was no longer listening at all. Her thoughts had turned back to those months they had recently spent in Chicago; a big chance had really come her way there—just the kind of chance her mother was talking about now. Of course, there had been a man in the deal, but the introduction to the drama coach was legitimate. So was his enthusiasm.

"You've got what it takes, and you photograph well," he'd told her after the first few tests. "It's a great combination; if you know how to work hard as well."

Linda had worked hard. Even the coach had been impressed. Life took on a different hue under the pressure of the classes and the harsh critical appraisal mixed with steady encouragement that kept coming from the man in the turtleneck sweater and chinos.

Then came the chance of a bit-part and the nerve-wracking tryout. Linda never knew the results of her test; the cops were waiting for her when she got back to the two rooms she shared with Cecilia Kesnik.

"Miss Kesnik? Would you mind coming with us, please?"

Linda nodded dumbly even before the policeman had finished saying, "We have your mother down at the station and she keeps yelling for you."

As if she could read her daughter's thoughts, the woman in the hospital bed leaned forward and grasped Linda's hand. For one brief and searing moment, Linda saw the light of recognition and horror in her mother's eyes.

"Linda," the older woman implored in a tone Linda had never heard her use before, "Linda, whatever you do—don't ever, ever be like me."

"If I was you, I'd be kinder to my poor mother," sobbed Cecilia Kesnik, her head cradled in her arms, her arms resting on the stained wooden table. The Jersey night was damp and foggy; the noise of traffic from the nearby highway was dulled by the opaque humidity.

"Mother, it's only a six weeks' training course," Linda repeated. "After that, the airline says I'll be based in New York. Which means I'll be home almost every night. I'll only be flying to other cities in this country, Mother," she added. "Not to the other side of the world . . ."

"But you're leaving me alone, all alone," her mother wailed. "You're just like your father—no good, all of you . . ." She broke down again.

Linda felt her sense of purpose stiffen with anger.

"Mother, I'm going to do it." She said in a quiet, low tone. "The pay is good, and so are the benefits." She did not feel it was the moment to mention how good the medical facilities would be both for herself and members of her family. Flightways, Inc. had its own medical center, she had been informed, and there was full medical coverage in the employment contract.

"Besides, Mother, just think of it—I'll be able to get liquor off the planes for you . . . for free . . ."

When eventually the chance of international flights came up, the promise of duty-free bottles brought in had kept Mrs. Kesnik quiet. But she still tried to gnaw through every constructive effort Linda made. Often, she partly succeeded.

Linda managed as best she could. There had been a good stretch for a while, when Mrs. Kesnik had stayed sober and held down a job for close to a year. Even after she'd fallen off the wagon that time, there'd been another long dry period after a two-month stint of trouble.

But in recent months, things had been going from bad to worse again. Another fire, another fight with her fists in a saloon, another incident of being found asleep on a sidewalk on the far side of town.

And now . . .

"Linda." The voice was quiet and kind. "Linda."

She struggled through the lingering mists of the pill and opened her eyes. Ramon was smiling down at her.

"You wanted us to wake you."

She managed a smile; the vestiges of her chemical euphoria made it easy and real.

"Thanks, Ramon. You're a doll."

She stretched under the warm cover and savored the last few moments of relaxation. And freedom. In a moment, she would go wash up and then get herself some coffee. New York was only an hour away. The company message lay in her handbag.

Local police inform Cecilia Kesnik hospitalized stop Return New York asap replacement stewardess enroute.

Linda walked slowly up front to the lavatory.

I wonder what in hell mother has managed to do this time . . .

Part 4

Flightway International 411
LHR/JFK

1

Heathrow Airport lay in pale sunshine, the sun's weak rays temporarily breaking through the gathering clouds. Activity was at its peak during the early afternoon hours and the jet roar rose and fell with every takeoff and landing.

At Flightways, the outgoing crew had begun the preflight ground procedures. Flight 411 from Paris, would arrive within the next half-hour.

David Fleming, courteous and remote as ever, went through his duties as commander with practised ease. Larry Johnson, irrepressible, could not let the chance go by.

"You know," he said, standing by Fleming as the captain signed the flight papers in Operations, "you four-stripers are grossly overpaid. What the hell else d'you ever do, except look smart-ass, sign a bunch of papers and grunt a lot?"

Fleming grinned, said nothing, and finished signing the papers.

Carl Masden, apart from his duties, had interests of his own. There was a new stewardess in the group, the replacement for Linda Kesnik who had been called back to New York the evening before. The new arrival was now listening to Rudi Becker, who was going through the passenger list and assigning duties for the flight. The crew had learned her name in the crew car on the way to the airport—Mireille Arnquist. She was tall and willowy with thin blond hair and a generous sprinkling of freckles.

Rudi was saying, ". . . and in that case, we'd better reshuffle. Betsy?"

Just then, Marianne Lund gave a small gasp and looked up from the passenger list she had been studying.

"Oh, Betsy—*please* take the galley!" she begged.

Before Betsy could answer, Marianne had thrust the passenger list into her hands.

"See? Right here! It's Teodoro Tagliamini . . . he's on board!"

Rudi looked over Betsy's shoulder.

"You mean he's getting on here. That's not the intransit list."

"That's right," Marianne bubbled. "And he's on his way to make a movie in Arizona. I read all about it in the columns last week . . . oh, please, Betsy, be a sport. Let me work the cabin, okay? Maybe he'll notice me—I know he's casting."

"Fine with me," came the answer.

Marianne beamed with gratitude.

"As for you two," Rudi turned to Judy and the new-hire, "I think Judy had better work the cabin . . ."

Mireille Arnquist's round green eyes held a worried expression and she gestured nervously as she began to speak.

"Oh, dear, I hope I can do it . . . it's all those ovens . . . I can never remember which is which, the ovens or the cold compartments."

"You'll learn," said Judy, not unkindly. "You have to start sometime."

"But it's my very first working flight. I was only observing from New York to Paris, and I was going to do a similar flight back. Then they said I had to replace someone in London," the green eyes looked more worried than ever, "and they sent me over last night, and . . ."

"And you'll do just fine," Judy told her. "Besides, Rudi'll help you—won't you, Rudi?"

Rudi, who had just been handed another list, looked at it and frowned.

"We're all going to have to help each other out," he said in answer. "There's damn near a full load."

Much of that load was milling around in the departure section of the airport building. A tour group was gathered untidily around a set of leather chairs centered by a table; their hand luggage festooned the area with souvenirs of their trip. A casual observer could have charted the course of the trip merely by noting the raffia-covered bottles of Chianti wine from Italy, the bright woven woolen sack-bags (Greece), the red-on-black rayon shawls with impossibly long fringes (Spain) stuffed into hand-made string carryalls from France.

More passengers kept arriving; a sleek limousine with a custom body slid to a stop outside the entry. The chauffeur descended to open the door of the Rolls for the two occupants of the back seat. The eclectic blonde with no eyebrows was the first to emerge, her furs a cocoon of luxury around her, her frizzy hairdo an exclamation to her face. Behind her, an immensely tall and emaciatedly thin man unfolded onto the sidewalk; the small round head atop the long boney body was an incongruous detail.

"This way, signor Tagliamini." A Flightways representative escorted them into the building, where they went directly to the second floor and the exclusive Fly Club bar. Several people noticed their passage and a few of the more knowledgable movie fans among them whispered to each other.

In the quiet hush of the Fly Club, the tables at the observation window were mostly occupied, and a range of men were standing around the free-form bar. Few were looking at the view beyond the window, where jets, sleek and silver, rose like weighty arrows into the thickening grey of the sky. On ground, more jets were parked and waiting and, within full view of the window, an empty space awaited the incoming Flightways aircraft.

The deplaning stewardess said to Betsy, "Oh, yes, and one more thing. The coffee maker is on the blink. Started right outside Beirut. It works, most of the time, and no one seems to know what's wrong with it, but it keeps going on the fritz when you least expect it."

We tried to get it fixed in Rome, but it was no go, and Paris didn't have a spare," interposed another girl as she struggled into her cape.

"A loose connection someplace," the deplaning purser

269

offered, his cap already on his head. "Are you ready, Margie?"

His teammate nodded, continuing to talk to Betsy. "So what I found worked was a tremendous wallop. Try banging it with your fist. If that doesn't do it—well, I used the hot-cup."

"Okay, I'll remember," Betsy smiled, already busying herself in the galley area.

"Right, then. Have a nice flight."

The stewardess and purser left, their pace down the ramp indicating their weariness. Betsy continued with her duties, her mind busy.

She thought: This is going to be one of those on your toes flights, I can feel it. Only one seat empty up here, and only a few in Coach. I only hope that new girl manages to keep her head above water. It might've been better to have her up here, and let me go back to help out.

But no. That was what seniority was all about. Part of the privileges earned with time. Still, it wasn't very efficient.

Moving around the galley, she caught sight of Marianne in the middle of the front cabin. She was moving at something akin to a snail's pace, a distant and soulful expression on her face. Betsy knew it would be funny if there weren't quite so much work to do. She watched the star-struck girl for a moment, and then turned back to her own tasks, momentarily forgetting all about Marianne.

Marianne was far away, remembering all the Tagliamini movies she had seen, over and over, the movies whose titles always started with T. She'd been telling Betsy about them and the famous director as they'd come out to the plane—how his T trademark stemmed not only from his initials but also the T-shape he stood in when directing a particularly vital scene, his feet together, his legs and torso straight, his arms stretched way out wide as though in supplication or, possibly, crucifixion.

She had also started telling Betsy the plot of his latest epic, but then that mean Rudi had come by and insisted she start working, and so she had been forced to quit halfway in the script. Betsy didn't know much about Tagliamini, she'd said to Marianne, although of course she'd heard of him. *Everybody* had. He was just so famous, so important in the movie world—the international movie world, the one that really counted for so much in an artistic career . . .

Marianne started down the aisle again, remembering half-way down that she had forgotten to replace the chewing gum and candy in their serving containers. She turned around to go back and do it, only to see that Betsy was bent over the kit, getting out the serving boxes. The packages of gum were behind her on the galley.

Gratefully, Marianne flashed her a wide smile as Betsy straightened up and the girls' glances met. Betsy was wonderful to work with; she was such an understanding sort of person. Marianne figured that her favorite to work with was definitely Betsy Blair.

Betsy thought: . . . and this is just the start. She's going to forget half of everything if she's in such a dreamy mood. Now Linda, lazy slob that she can be, Linda wouldn't do a thing like that. Not forget, anyway. She'd be more likely to con someone else into doing part of her work.

I certainly wish she were here now . . .

The thought caught Betsy by surprise. It was some switch, after all the mental griping she'd done about having to be teamed with Linda. But then, that had only been right at the beginning; she realized the teamwork between them had been good once they began to get used to each other.

Strange. After all, they were so different in type and character, and yet, they worked a flight well together. Linda never bumped into you in the galley, could actually work with you, side by side, and never be in the way. She had a lot of good points, the more one thought about it, but the trouble was, that bitchy exterior was the part one saw first, and it was the part that was the most obvious. Always. The real Linda was just about hidden from view. And she said so little about herself when it came to the things that really counted.

Just like David Fleming . . . not a word, not a hint of a girl friend in London . . . the Loner . . . oh, boy, what a misnomer *that* was . . .

"Ready?" called Rudi from the first class cabin doorway.

Betsy gave the working surface a quick once over.

"Yes," she called back.

"Good." Rudi positioned himself at the door. "Because here they come."

271

2

The afternoon departure from London on Flight 411 meant that tea service was offered to all passengers immediately after takeoff. This was followed by the drink and canape services, their extent differing in scope and price from first class to coach. Meal service got underway even as drinks were still being enjoyed, one service flowing smoothly into the other.

From a cabin attendant's point of view, it was a busy flight.

This view deepened to dismay whenever the flight was carrying a full load of passengers. Under such conditions, the schedule provided no time for breathing.

"It's going to be one of those flights," Rudi said in an aside to Betsy as the passengers boarded. "There'll be turbulence on takeoff, until we get through the clouds, just to make it worse for us."

"I thought so," Betsy murmured, having heard the meteorological data and seen the clouds thickening around the airport.

On this particular flight, with its multiple meal service, turbulence on takeoff meant a highly inconvenient delay in getting these services started. Inevitably, this meant a certain amount of rush afterwards. Like Rudi had just said—it was going to be one of those flights . . . turbulence on takeoff, a full load—and Marianne enraptured by Tagliamini's presence . . .

None of these thoughts showed in Betsy's expression as

she smilingly greeted the boarding passengers. The announcements, the pre-takeoff routines and the life jacket demonstration all went smoothly.

Then came takeoff, and the subsequent ascent through the turbulent rain clouds was as uncomfortable as Rudi had predicted it would be. Both the seat-belt and no-smoking signs remained on, thus indicating that the cabin attendants should stay seated, too, but Betsy soon unbuckled her belt and made her way along the aisle.

"No, ma'm, it won't last long," she assured a tense and pale woman. "We'll be up and out of the clouds very soon ..."

Further along, a middle-aged man reached over and touched her arm.

"My wife doesn't feel at all well."

Betsy went back to the galley and got an anti-airsick pill from the flight kit. She splashed a minimum amount of water into a paper cup from the spigot and took cup and pill back to the queasy wife.

"I should've taken one before ... this always happens when I fly," the woman murmured. She had the sicksack out of the seat pocket and in her lap, at the ready, but she swallowed the pill and lay back against the seat, closing her eyes. Betsy herself hoped it would be over very soon; there was too much service to be gotten through within the next hours to allow for all this heaving around.

Finally, it ended, and they broke through the layer of clouds, coming up into the empty dome of sky. By this time, Rudi and Marianne were on their feet, too.

"Don't count on me for anything up here," he told Betsy and Marianne as the three of them congregated in the galley to start the afternoon tea service. "I'll be back for the bar service as usual, of course, but Judy and Mireille have their hands more than full."

Marianne went off down the aisle, the tea cart rolling in front of her.

"And if Marianne doesn't move fast enough, push her!" Rudi exclaimed to Betsy.

"Don't worry, Rudi," Betsy assured him. "We'll manage."

She said it with a smile and turned back to her work. There wasn't going to be much time for chatting on this trip. The counter in front of her awaited service refills; she

273

worked quickly and efficiently with tea cakes, china, the coffee machine, switches . . .

Marianne returned with the trolley, needing a refill of cakes and two orders of champagne. The dreamy expression was gone from her face and the beginnings of a frown were clouding it instead.

"Just my luck," she grumbled, replenishing the tray from the layout Betsy had ready on the counter. "The greatest director in the world on board . . . and there isn't going to be one free minute from here to Kennedy."

Betsy peeped down the cabin. She suppressed a grin as she said, "Well, I don't think he's going to have much free time, either—so you'd better concentrate on the service, and give your acting career a breather."

Marianne's frown deepened. She, too, had noticed with chagrin that Teodoro Tagliamini appeared deeply engrossed in his young companion. The fur cocoon had been removed—Marianne had surreptitiously stroked its splendor when she hung it up on a hanger—and now the eyebrowless face with the frizzy hair was snuggled down in the window seat with a tight-fitting playsuit and over the knee boots for cover. The bare patch of thigh between shorts' end and the boots' beginning served as sensory drawing board for the circles described by Tagliamini's long and bony fingers. His motions were as abstract as the shapes they drew, but he seldom seemed to stop talking in a low tone.

Marianne's increasing frustration was only held in check by the ceaseless demands made upon her by both the service and the passengers themselves.

A bell dinged in the galley. A passenger was calling.

"Oh, hell!" Marianne struggled with the reloaded trolley. "Can't they just wait a minute. . . ?"

"You wanted to be cabin girl." Betsy, who wanted Marianne and the trolley out of her way, couldn't resist the dig. Then, to make up for it, she added, "You'd better remember to smile, Marianne. After all, Tagliamini just *might* look."

The curvaceous stewardess went back into the cabin. Betsy pushed a stray strand of hair off her forehead and went on with her tasks. Rudi would be back any minute; he would need the drink tray set up and the bar equipment ready. After that, dinner would be in full swing.

Heating ovens on. Cooking ovens ready. Coffee machine ... looking at it, Betsy saw the indicator light had gone off. Well, she'd been warned. She hit it with her fist, and the light came on again. So far, so good.

Marianne came back with the used tea and coffee cups, and the remains of the sandwiches and cakes. Automatically, Betsy interspersed her setting-up dinner duties with the various tasks involved in getting the tea service items out of the way: plates off, garbage thrown out, china back into used china racks, more paper into the garbage, re-set the coffee machine ...

The cockpit bell rang. Betsy reached for the interphone but Rudi Becker's arm materialized from behind her.

"Yes, Captain?"

The usual touch of unctuousness in his voice. A pause, then: "Yes, sir. Just coffee and a sandwich. Be right up." Rudi replaced the receiver. "Betsy—better take Fleming his food. All he wants is coffee and a sandwich. Chicken, if we have 'em, he said."

"We have."

"Good. I'll take over here for the time being."

When Betsy got up to the cockpit, Fleming said, without any preliminaries, "You may have to hold back dinner. You haven't started yet, have you?"

"No, not yet." Betsy maneuvered the tray across to his lap.

"Well, I tell you what. I'll be through with this in about five minutes. At that time, you come back up with Larry's chow ..."

"Yippeeeee!" came from the right hand seat.

"... and I'll be able to tell you more then. There's a report of clear air turbulence up front, and we may have to go through a slice of it."

Betsy took Larry's order, returned to the cabin, told Rudi what Fleming had told her and began setting up the co-pilot's dinner tray. Rudi groaned.

"All we needed, another delay in the service, if this sort of thing keeps up, we'll still be serving food as we land at Kennedy."

Just as Betsy was leaving for the cockpit with Larry Johnson's dinner tray in her hands, Rudi said, "Betsy, if you want to take a cigarette break now—go ahead. Later, I may need you around nonstop."

"Okay. Thanks."

The sharp crackle of receiver static was emanating from the head sets as Betsy re-entered the cockpit. She stood holding the tray for a moment, seeing Larry intent on taking down the radioed information. Eventually, after acknowledging the message, he said "Ah, shit," and pushed back his earphones.

Seeing Betsy waiting, he reached out for his tray and said, "Thanks, hon," taking the food tray out of her hands and settling it down on his lap. He slid his clipboard out from under, made another note and hung it on its peg.

"You'd better hold it back there," he informed Betsy, picking up a fork and digging into his meal. "We should go through it in about fifteen minutes' time."

"Would you buzz Rudi and tell him?" Betsy asked. "He said I could take a break now."

"Sure thing."

The cabin crew were advised by the intercom of the upcoming clear air turbulence while Betsy took her cigarettes out of the pocket on her vinyl smock and Carl reached up to her with his lighter.

"Thanks, Carl."

For a moment, there was silence between the four people in the flightdeck of the 707, a silence filled with the roar and whine of the sleek silver machine and punctuated by the clicks and cracks of open radio and electronics. It was David Fleming who reintroduced the human element into the melee.

Turning slightly in his seat, he said, "And how was your dinner with Andrew Murray?"

He was smiling as he said it, but there was something in his general attitude that stung Betsy to the quick.

"I didn't go to dinner with Mr. Murray," she retorted, trying to sound as calm as possible and feeling she only managed to sound prim again. "I had tea—English afternoon tea, with James."

"Oh, I see." David's smile was still there. It seemed to indicate that what he saw was nothing of the sort.

Betsy continued, "He asked after you. Wanted to know whether you were on this trip."

"Nice of the kid," grunted Johnson from his seat, the words filled with vichyssoise. Fleming said nothing, but Betsy thought she saw his jaw line tighten.

276

"Then he showed me his electric trains, and his tropical fish, and . . ."

"Yes, of course," the jawline managed. "And then Andrew Murray just happened to come home and invite you for cocktails."

"Yes, but I didn't accept!" Her rising anger made her flush. "Just because there's a party doesn't mean you have to go."

"Hey, Betsy." Johnson's voice interrupted. "That reminds me. D'you know what a layover is?"

Flustered, Betsy said no, she didn't.

"It's an extra girl at a party."

Carl Masden groaned.

"So help me, Larry—if you don't get a better selection of jokes, I'm going to bid another schedule."

"Ah, well, it takes talent to appreciate art," was Larry's answer. "You want to go fly with the farmers, Carl, you go ahead. Come to think of it, they might suit you."

The banter between them continued; so did the tension between Fleming and Betsy.

"So there was a party, too, was there?" Fleming said. "You remembered, I hope, that twenty-four hours before a flight."

"I know the rules." Betsy ground out her cigarette in the paper cup she'd brought up as an ashtray, her fingers stiff with anger, her voice controlled. "But I don't really see why my having tea at the Murrays' should cause so much interest." An extra burst of anger flared through her, and she found herself adding, "After all, I wasn't the only one who went visiting in London."

Fleming frowned. Betsy saw the jawline tighten again. He turned back to the front panel without a word and she saw his hand reach out to tap one of the gauges. But she observed it all through a fog of fury and, turning on her heel, she opened the cockpit door. There was no point in staying just to get herself angry. She stepped into the cabin.

It was at that moment that the airplane gave the first heave.

3

"Would you help out back in coach, Betsy?" Rudi asked. "I think the girls would be thankful to have you. And besides," he added in lower tones, "I can get more work out of Marianne if I stay up here."

The turbulence was over and it hadn't been too bad up in the first class section; even the lady who had felt queasy before appeared to have weathered it without resorting to the sicksack still in her lap. Betsy had her doubts about Tagliamini's girlfriend, whose face now had an ominous green pallor.

It seemed so peculiar, Betsy mused, to be serving what amounted to a dinner service in the middle of the afternoon. But with the time differential between London and New York, it was a necessity. Those whose lives had been on European time were ready for dinner now; that they would reach Kennedy in the middle of the afternoon, Eastern Standard Time, was one of the quirks of contemporary flying.

The seat belt sign was still on, indicating that the pilots still expected a flutter or two before the clear air turbulence area was left far behind. It would keep the passengers in their seats while the cabin attendants cleared up and set up. Up front, there was no tidying to do to speak of, and Rudi was working the galley while he goaded Marianne into greater speed.

Betsy stepped through the partition into coach. A sea of untidiness greeted her. Judy and Mireille had apparently not been able to get all the snack trays back before the turbulence had started, and there were discarded trays and cups all along the aisle.

Betsy bent down to retrieve the first two she encountered then straightened up and smiled reassuringly at the first few rows of passengers.

"There won't be any more," she told a thin girl in an aisle seat, fervently hoping it was true. We don't have time for weather, she told the fates in a mental message. We have a full dinner to serve. You can't do this to us.

As if in answer, the plane moved again, but it was a minor ripple of motion with no punch to it at all. Betsy went on walking, collecting trays.

At the back of the plane, Betsy cast a quick glance around the galley, and she noticed that everything was secure and in place. Mireille, looking somewhat pale, was struggling with her smock. Her freckles seemed more obvious than ever.

"I'd leave it on, if I were you," admonished Betsy. "This is just the time you'll get things spilled on you."

She looked at Mireille carefully. She looked a bit green, too.

"If you don't feel too well," Betsy added, "go take a quarter of an anti-airsick pill . . ."

Mireille Arnquist looked at her, startled.

Betsy nodded. "Yes, I know—you're thinking about the rules and the no-pills bit. But just a quarter isn't enough to make you sleepy and it will settle your stomach, so you'll feel much better and be able to work."

"Okay . . . and—thanks . . ."

Betsy didn't add that, for a first working flight, it was far better to be sleepy and working than feeling sick and helpless in a seat. Or for any flight, for that matter. But it was usually in their early flights that cabin attendants felt the weather.

After that, I guess we get our air legs, just like sailors get their sea legs . . .

Judy came back, bearing a sicksack.

"Kid's sick," she explained, disappearing to dispose of the sack. When she reappeared, Betsy said, "Rudi told me to stay back here for the meal service. Shall we start in?"

"Oh, goody." Judy's face radiated relief. "We really need three today. Yes, sure, let's set up."

They did indeed need three, thought Betsy, grappling with the mechanics of the galley while the other two girls sped back and forth along the aisle on the seemingly endless trips. A full cabin, fractious children and a full service already behind schedule meant all three of them working flat out. Mireille Arnquist was certainly getting a full-fledged initiation into a stewardess life and work.

A faulty cream carton shot a jet of liquid down Betsy's smock. While she was cleaning it all up, Judy came back.

"Kid's been sick again," she announced. "This time, all over the floor. "I'll need those towels . . ."

Mireille continued to serve dinner while Judy coped with the now-quiet child and Betsy managed the galley at full speed. Mireille returned and reached up to open one of the food container doors; an inadequately secured milk carton inside tumbled out and broke against the galley.

"Oh, *look* what I've done now . . ."

"It's nothing, Mireille . . . happens all the time . . ."

They cleared it up and went on serving. Judy rejoined them and worked the service, too. The overloaded refuse container tipped and spilled forward just as they reached the coffee end of the meal. Mireille took out the coffee tray and Judy checked continuing returns; Betsy mopped the galley floor and glared suspiciously at the resecured refuse container from time to time. She broke a nail on a tray holder and heaved the rolling tray module back into position.

And they call this job glamorous . . .

Her thoughts bordering on the savage, her muscles beginining to ache, Betsy changed places with Judy and took the coffee seconds up and down the full length of the aisle.

"Some more coffee, sir?"

A bell was ringing from the seat up front; more coffee was wanted there, too. Suppressing a desire to snarl *wait your turn!* Betsy poured and offered cream and sugar. Another bell rang: the little girl needed a pillow . . . could the mother please have a pill, too? Now she was not feeling well . . .

Betsy suggested an aspirin, as it was no doubt the tension from the little girl's upset. Pill and cup of water. Another trip up and down. It went on endlessly, with that eternal feeling of time pressing, right behind her.

Suddenly Rudi was by her side saying, "Go on up front, Betsy. I'll take over here."

Gratefully, she went through to the first class section. At least, it didn't feel so crowded up here and she could see at a glance that the passengers were sated and comfortable. Then she noticed the exception: Miss No-eyebrows, next to the Italian director. She looked more extraordinary than ever, her face sunken and white behind the shadow-coloring around her eyes, and the frizz of her hair looked weary. She was lying back with the seat reclining, her eyes closed, a blanket drawn up under her chin. Betsy guessed she had thrown up. Tagliamini, apparently unmoved, was leafing through the script on his lap.

No one appeared to need anything. Marianne was talking to a couple in the first row. Betsy smiled at her as she went through to the galley. The moment she got there, the cockpit bell rang.

"Who's that? Betsy?" It was Johnson's voice.

"Yes, Larry. It's me."

"Come get my tray, will you?" came the request. "It keeps vibrating on the floor and Carl's bitching about it keeping him awake . . ."

Why on earth hadn't Marianne picked up that tray ages ago? Or Rudi, for that matter. She noticed the coffee machine light out again, and she hit the metal with anger. Feeling harassed, she stormed through the cockpit door.

But the moment she shut it behind her, and became part of the tiny dark cave with all the hundreds of instruments, she was soothed by the noise and the intimacy of the atmosphere. Larry Johnson's voice boomed:

"Oh, it ain't gonna rain no more, no more
No, it ain't gonna rain no more.
And how in the dickens can the cat have chickens
When the bulldog lives next door—ohhhh . . .
It—ain't gonna rain . . ."

He sang loudly, stopping only when Betsy bent down to get the discarded dinner tray.

"Hey there, Blair," he called out cheerfully. "Didn't know I could sing, did you?"

She smiled at him, warming to his mood. He was a welcome change from the pressure back in the cabin.

"Gave up a great career when the missus forced me

into flying," the rotund co-pilot continued. "Loverboy Larry, the Tuneless Crooner, they used to call me."

"Tuneless is right," interjected Carl, but Betsy did not stay to hear any additional banter. The break had been nice, but now she felt she could go back. She also wanted to tidy herself up and refresh her makeup. She also knew her hair could do with a quick repinning.

Resolutely, Betsy stepped into the tiny cubicle of the rest room, where she efficiently began to repair the damage.

4

". . . and he never even *looked* at me," Marianne repeated in a despondent wail. "Not even when that stupid girlfriend of his was sick all over me, and thank heavens I had my smock on, or she'd have ruined my uniform skirt."

The unhappy stewardess turned to Betsy.

"You just don't know how lucky you were, being sent back to coach like that, by Rudi. It was horrible up front, absolutely *horrible*." Her eyes rolled upward to give dramatic emphasis to her statement. "And to think that after all that, he never even *looked* . . ."

"Marianne," rumbled Larry Johnson, a few paces behind her. "Do me a favor—do us all a favor: shut up. We're all pooped, too."

"But it's not just because I'm tired," she answered. "Although I am. I'm absolutely *exhausted*. But after all I did for them, all the attention I gave him and his girlfriend, he . . ."

". . . never even looked at you," Carl Masden mimicked.

Tears welled in Marianne Lund's eyes, but before she could say anything, Rudi's voice cut in.

"But that's what you're paid to do Miss Lund, remember? If you don't like the job, you can always quit." The purser's tone was edged with steel. "You were supposed to be working a flight—not auditioning for a sex movie."

"He doesn't make sex movies!"

Rudi ignored the outburst and continued, "Next time, Marianne, you might remember to spread your charms and attention further in the cabin."

And if they don't all shut up, thought Betsy, her head pounding, with exhaustion, I think I may just scream.

The whole crew was walking along the labyrinthine corridors that took them through the official departments. They trailed from Health, to Immigrations and then on to Customs. The distances seemed endless, the flooring extra-hard.

It really had been a brute of a trip. Betsy's feet, numb inside her boots, protested at every step she took. She shivered, and pulled her cape closer around her. I must be tired, she realized, for the building's warmth had been a welcome relief from the cold open space between the aircraft and the entrance to the building.

She kept on going through the motions, her movements those of an automaton. Card for Health. Passport for Immigrations. More walking. Then her suitcase.

Behind her, Marianne found a new audience in Judy and Mireille. In front, the tall figure of David Fleming strode in and out of view as he went through the same formalities in the company of Larry and Carl.

It wasn't just her feet, Betsy knew—her legs felt numb as well. The ache in her shoulders was beginning to superimpose itself on the rest of her discomforts; the effort she made to haul her suitcase onto the Customs counter made her acutely aware of her back.

"Nothing this time, eh?" The man in uniform on the other side of the counter was smiling at her. She smiled back, and shook her head.

"You look beat," he went on, helping her close the suitcase. "Better get home and get some rest."

"Oh, I will," Betsy assured him. "See you next time."

She picked up her overnight bag in one hand and her suitcase in the other. Thank heavens my bags aren't heavy this trip, she thought.

Marianne Lund caught up with her as she neared the exit door.

"My feet," Marianne was saying, "my poor feet . . ."

The cold air outside was raw and unpleasant. The rest of the crew were already on the sidewalk.

"Wow! but it's cold!" Larry stamped his feet up and

down. Then: "Well, I gotta be getting on home to chow and the missus. See you all next time."

"See you."

"You going on the bus, Betsy?" Marianne wanted to know.

"Yes, I . . ."

"No, you're not!" The harsh voice was out of place, unexpected, and Betsy felt it like a slap in the face. She whirled around.

"Mike!"

She could hardly believe it. This was not his world, nor had it been hers with him. What was he doing here? And why was he so angry?

"You're not going on any fucking bus." He seized her arm. "You're coming with me."

"Mike . . ." Betsy struggled to keep her overnight bag from slipping out of her hand. Her suitcase was beginning to weigh heavily in the other, and Mike's movement had bumped into her shoulder bag. "Mike . . . I'm exhausted. I need to go home and get some sleep."

Maybe if he realized she was deadbeat he'd stop shouting at her.

"No, goddamit, I want to talk to you now!"

Marianne, flustered by the sudden intrusion, said, "Don't you think that . . ."

Mike turned on her. "You shut the fuck up!"

Marianne gasped.

"It's all right, Marianne," Betsy started, but she could feel the people around them beginning to stare. Everyone. Passengers, baggage masters and—oh, God—maybe even company personnel, if there were any walking in and out of the terminal, which there usually were.

"Mike." She turned back to her irate ex-lover. "Not now. Look—there's my bus." She could see the vehicle parked over by the covered walkway. "We can talk later. Tonight, okay?"

But he wasn't listening. She could tell that by the expression in his angry, flashing eyes. His hair, matted and curly, bounced with every energetic movement of his head.

"Dammit, Betsy, I said now. I've got a right to know what the hell's going on. We can get some coffee and . . ."

Feeling weak with exhaustion, and helpless against

285

Mike's barrage of words, Betsy realized that the only way to quiet him was to do as he said. Otherwise, he'd be sure to create one of those appalling scenes, or one of those ugly one-sided shouting matches that were so much a part of his nature. She was just about to acquiesce when another hand pushed Mike's away from her arm and held her firmly by the elbow.

"Ah, Betsy, there you are. I'd lost sight of you before. Let's get right over this way—see you next flight, Marianne. My buggy's parked right over there in the lot."

Ignoring Mike completely, and moving as smoothly as his sentences, David Fleming steered the bewildered Betsy away from the sidewalk and across the road. On the other side he said, "Let me take that," and took her suitcase from her. They went on walking along the outside of the car park until they came to an entrance for it. Betsy was too upset to say a word until they were within the lot's confines.

Then she said, "Thanks, David. I really didn't know *what* to do."

"So I noticed," he observed drily. But that was all he said, and since Betsy couldn't think of anything else she should or could explain, they walked along in silence until they reached the Captain's bright red sportscar.

Fleming unlocked the trunk and tossed his own suitcase in first, placing Betsy's on top and relocking the trunk again. Then he unlocked the door for her, and said, "You can sling your overnight bag in the back seat if you want." Moments later they were gliding out the airport exit.

Betsy leaned back against the comfort of the contoured seat and the welcome support of the head rest. At first, she closed her eyes and let the heavy thrum of the engine blank out her thoughts, but soon she realized that the smoothness of the ride was liable to make her drift off to sleep. So she opened her eyes and glanced at David.

Even in the harsh light of day, after a night of intense vigilance, he was still a good-looking man. The tiredness could be seen in the tension around his eyes, but he did not have the dragged and sallow look so many of the pilots developed after a nightflight.

"This really—is a—fantastic automobile," she said finally, looking around the fitted interior and shifting to a more upright position within the confines of her seat.

"Thank you." He looked pleased. "I enjoy it very much myself."

"You love mechanical things, don't you?" Betsy said. "I mean—it's in the way you handle the wheel, and the same when you fly."

Fleming said nothing, so after a while Betsy went on: "I'd even guess that you like machines better than people— at least, cars and airplanes."

The moment she said it, she regretted her statement. How could she be so callous? She bit her lip and wondered what she could say to make her former statement sound better.

But to her surprise, David Fleming laughed, a short, self-amused laugh that eased the tension between them.

"You're probably right, Betsy, but it may be because I understand them better—or anyway, most of them. Automobiles and airplanes, I mean. They're much easier to figure out, you know."

"Oh? D'you always try to figure people out, too?" Betsy asked, feeling she'd stumbled on an unsuspected side of David Fleming's nature.

He retreated as quickly and unexpectedly as he had warmed.

"No, of course not," came the reply. "People are people. They belong to themselves. What they do is their own business." It seemed like a final statement, a cut-off point for the conversation. Rebuffed by his answer, Betsy sat in silence.

What you're really saying, Betsy thought to herself, is that you belong only to yourself, and I shouldn't ask questions that get too close to you, David Fleming. I wonder what you're afraid of?

And then her thoughts took her back to the tragedy of his family's death, and it seemed to answer her unspoken question.

It was Fleming who broke the silence.

"You know, thinking of people," he began, "that's some fan club you've collected for yourself."

Betsy blushed.

"Oh, you mean Mike," she muttered, "the young man at the airport. He's not really that bad, it's just that . . ."

"I wasn't just thinking of him," Fleming continued. The club's downright international, what with Andrew Murray in London."

"Now that's just not fair!" Betsy exclaimed defensively. "I told you—it was James who invited me to tea. I went to see him, not his father."

"But you saw Mr. Murray while you were with James ... and he did extend an invitation."

Betsy couldn't think of an immediate comeback. After all, it was true: she had seen Andrew Murray later in the afternoon.

"Well, yes, but ..."

She saw Fleming's self-congratulatory smile. Ohhh, but he was smug. For a wild moment, she wanted to shake him. Then another thought riveted her attention: if David was making comments like this, was it possible he was jealous? After all, why would he notice where she went or who she spoke to if he were not at least a bit interested himself?

Emboldened by her insight, Betsy considered asking a question of her own. It was not really her business, who he saw in London, and she knew it. On the other hand, it wasn't really Captain Fleming's business whether or not she saw Andrew Murray, was it?

She sat toying with the idea for a while. Outside, the heavy brick buildings of Queens lined the road. Again, Betsy shivered, and felt the world weighing heavily on her.

"Are you cold? Shall I turn up the heat?"

Her shiver had been such a small motion on her part, and yet David had noticed. He certainly was a thoughtful man. Tired as he was, he had still noticed.

"No thank you, David. I'm not really cold at all. I guess it's because I'm so tired."

"I can imagine. It was a rough flight for all of you back there, wasn't it?"

"Well," Betsy made a small gesture. "You know how it is sometimes. When it's actually going on, you don't notice it, but afterwards, when you sit down, the tiredness kind of floods through you. Luckily we'd all had a good night's rest in London."

Fleming did not say anything, and in the short silence that ensued, Betsy decided to take the plunge.

"By the way, David,"—she tried to sound as nonchalant as possible—"unless it's a state secret, where do you disappear to every time we get to London? We always see all the other crew members in and out of the hotel. But even Larry says you're up and out like a flash. And then nobody sees you until we meet downstairs to take the crew car back out to Heathrow."

After a slight pause, Fleming cleared his throat and said, "It's all somewhat complicated to explain. But there's a ... well, a friend of mind, you might say. In London, I mean. And, er ... my friend is sick, and I ... I usually go straight there ... to visit ..." Another pause, and then the same hesitant tone continued. "That's why I bid the London flight for this month, because ... well, because of circumstances."

He turned briefly to Betsy and, just as briefly, smiled.

"You see, it isn't all that interesting, is it?"

The sinking feeling she'd felt before sank a bit further in the pit of Betsy's stomach. Of all the weak-sounding excuses. Why didn't he come right out and say it was none of her business, if he felt it was so private? Anything would've been better than that unconvincing set of mumbled sentences and excuses.

It was so disappointing. She'd expected more from David Fleming. Whoever the "friend" in London might be—and Betsy noticed he didn't even have the guts to say the friend was female—whoever she might be, she certainly hadn't looked "sick" the evening Betsy had seen them together. Visiting a sick friend implied sitting by a hospital bed. Well, that wasn't what Captain David Fleming had been doing, and Betsy knew it.

Betsy leaned back against the headrest again and stared straight in front of her. There didn't seem to be any point in trying to say anything more. Fleming chose to drive over the top level of the Queensboro Bridge, and she could see the buildings of Manhattan against the winter skyline. Once they were in Manhattan, it didn't take long to reach her apartment building, and as they came to a stop in front of it, Betsy leaned over and got her overnight bag from the back seat.

"I'll get your suitcase for you."

She was on the sidewalk when Fleming handed her the bag from the trunk of his car. On impulse, she said,

"Won't you come up for a quick cup of coffee? I'm sure it'd do you the world of good."

For a moment, she saw him hesitate, and her hopes rose. Then he shook his head.

"Thank you, Betsy—but no. Not this time. Much as I'd like to, I think I'd better not."

Somehow goaded by his manner, Betsy said, "Why on earth not?"

"Well ... I guess I have ..." his voice trailed off, and he avoided her eyes.

Something inside Betsy flared out of control.

"Oh, for heavens' sakes," she burst out, "why do you have to make such a mystery of everything? The way you play it—your whole life is just one big secret after another!"

"I'm sorry," was his quiet reply, but she didn't wait for any more. She took her bags and rushed into the lobby of the building. Fortunately, the elevator was waiting, and she hurtled into it and pushed the button. Her last glimpse of David Fleming was of him getting back into his car, but then the doors closed and besides, her vision was blurry.

The tears were hot and stinging, but somehow, they were a relief.

5

"Of course, I should've guessed," remarked Sharon. She deftly removed the plate from in front of Betsy and substituted a bowl of fruit salad.

"I don't think I want anything more, thanks." Betsy's voice was muffled behind her handkerchief. Her head was throbbing and her eyes still stung. "I'd better get straight to bed."

"Try to drink some of the milk," suggested her busy roommate as she went on around the table, removing the remains of the evening meal they had shared. Lee's plate lay untouched; she was still on the phone. Sharon made a "tsk, tsk" sound and left it in place.

"Yes, I know—to help me sleep better." Despite her discomforts, Betsy couldn't help smiling. "I use that one on passengers, too."

"But it works." Sharon sat down and started in on her fruit salad. "And it's good for you. And you need the rest. But really, Betsy," she returned to the subject that had been her topic before, "to fall for the Loner is just *insane*."

Betsy said nothing. It was bad enough that the girls had found out. Both Lee and Sharon obviously knew as much as there was to know. And that's the trouble, she thought miserably, there isn't even all that much to know about it, is there? Except that I think he's marvellous and intriguing and . . .

Lee crashed back into the room again, knocking over a

ceramic salt cellar on the table as she sat down. She caught it and replaced it, murmuring, "Oops! Sorry," and she pulled in her chair with ease, ignoring Sharon's glare.

"If you'd only watch where you're going . . ."

"It's my feet, Sharon," Lee said with a shrug that indicated effort on her part was futile. "They're so big, they get to places before I do."

"You could at least try." Sharon was always convinced that trying could solve anything. She turned back to Betsy.

"If I were you, I'd try and get him right out of your mind," she went on.

"Who?" Lee demanded. Then, remembering, "Oh, you mean Captain Fleming."

"Of course. I was telling Betsy it's useless mooning over him."

"Sometimes, that's easier said than done," Lee observed mildly, stretching her long legs out to one side of her chair.

"That's because you're just as bad," was Sharon's retort. "Why you and Betsy can't pick nice sensible fellows is beyond me."

"By the way," interrupted Lee, "that nice sensible fellow from the party the other night keeps asking about you, Betsy. Chuck. Remember him? I told him you'd be back today. He rang a couple of times, so I guess he'll ring again."

"Okay."

"And Jay's called, too," Sharon said. "Now, *there's* a nice guy."

"Yes, I know." Betsy was beginning to feel like a talking doll. Press me in the right place, and I say yes, or no, or okay. But none of this is coming from me; it's just these buttons, these training buttons, I guess, that people keep pressing . . .

"Betsy! Go to bed." Lee's tone was kind, but exasperated. "You're falling asleep into the plate . . ."

Grateful for the impetus given her by Lee's words, Betsy rose from the table and went to the bedroom. Everything ached, her head, her feet, her whole body. Bed was a wonderful refuge she thought, slipping between the covers.

Her toes slid down to the bottom and found the warm surface of Sharon's heating pad. How typical, thought

Betsy, before she fell asleep, how typical of Sharon to blast her about Fleming . . . and then lend her the heating pad to make sure she was comfortable.

The next morning, there were a couple of phone calls for Betsy while the girls were enjoying a late breakfast and a relaxing morning. The nice sensible Chuck called, and wanted her to join him for a two-day skiing trip. Betsy had already accepted Jay Marshall's invitation for a date that same evening.

Jay had called quite early.

"They're letting me off my chain here," he told Betsy, "so I thought we'd make the most of it, while the going's good. Next week, I'll be back on night duty . . ."

So Betsy said yes, and they arranged to meet after six. But when she replaced the receiver, she regretted accepting the invitation. And yet—why not? It was something to do. And she liked Jay; he was always good company. But . . . but . . .

Lee, sitting cross-legged on the alcove sofa, looked up from her task of painting her nails and said, "Are you sure you feel all right, Betsy? You look kind of white."

Betsy smiled at the description. "I feel kind of white," she admitted, "but I think it's just that I'm tired. You know, that draggy feeling."

Sharon appeared out of her bedroom, her arms loaded with laundry.

"You should be over that by now," she said.

"I'm fine. Just lazy."

Sharon did not look convinced, but she let the matter drop and said, "Well, I'm going down to the laundry room. If Tom calls, tell him I'll be right back, will you?"

"Sure." Lee watched Sharon's small figure bustle out with the laundry. "Be careful, now, that you don't wash the patterns off."

Betsy ignored the jibes between roommates and drew her fingers through her hair. "I guess I'd better snap out of my lazy mood and go do something about my hair. If I'm going to wash it . . ."

She left the sentence unfinished, reflecting ruefully that long hair was a chore.

Lee put the cap back on the bottle of nail polish and began waving her hands in the air, drying her nails.

"Go ahead. I'll wash mine later," she said. "I should've done it before I painted my nails. Why is it I never remember things like that? Sharon always does. Sharon always does so many things, laundry, her hair, her Christmas list, and everything on time. And in the right order." Lee wavered between admiration and exasperation.

"That reminds me—are we planning anything for Thanksgiving?" Betsy asked. "I mean, who's in, and are we inviting . . ."

Lee was already shaking her head.

"Sharon and I talked it over last night, while you were asleep. I'm scheduled for Rome—boy, can you imagine that? Thanksgiving in Rome! Chicken and that yellow stuff, polenta, and no pumpkin pie."

"And Sharon?"

"Need you ask?" Lee struck an attempted pose but was out of balance and sank back onto the sofa. "It's Tom, Tom, Tom all the way, and the family wingding."

"It's very nice for her, Lee. I don't quite see why you make so much fun of family outings. They can be very enjoyable." For a moment, Betsy's thoughts flashed back to the smell of her own home at Thanksgiving; there were good times at many of the gatherings, particularly when Dr. Blair was along, left alone, miraculously, by his patients for the day.

"Not in my family," came the answer. "But I suppose in Sharon's case . . ."

"In Sharon's case, what?" came Sharon's voice from the door.

"We were talking about Thanksgiving," Lee said quickly, a hint of guilt underlying her otherwise innocent phrase. Sharon shut the front door and looked at her roommate with disbelief.

"Well, Thanksgiving or not, in Lee's case—I wish you'd keep your laundry out of mine." And she flung two pairs of pantihose across the room at Lee.

"Sorry." Lee scrambled to pick them up and walked to the bathroom with them.

"And while you're there," Sharon continued, "you might change your toothbrush. I have a new one if you need it."

"But . . ."

"Yours is on the floor where you dropped it this morning. And it looks like a chrysanthemum."

Lee paused in the bathroom doorway.

"You know something, Sharon? You're going to make someone a marvellous mother-in-law."

"I only meant it . . ."

". . . for my own good," Lee finished. Then, with another attempted pose, she pronounced, "That's what they all say," and disappeared into the bathroom. The splashing sound of water started at once; Betsy hoped she'd be finished soon. It was so like Lee to forget, from one moment to the other, that Betsy wanted to wash her hair.

"I just don't understand her," Sharon was saying. "I didn't mean it harshly."

Betsy heard the words through the beginnings of what she realized was quite definitely a headache. The sniping between her roommates was almost more than she felt she could bear.

Her headache was still with her when Betsy got home after her date with Jay. It was almost two a.m. when she got into bed, but tired as she was, sleep refused to come. Her head felt hot, along with the pain, and somewhere inside her she felt miserable and low. It didn't make any sort of sense at all, but the thumping in her head was the worst part of it.

She lay in the dark of the familiar bedroom, reliving parts of the evening she had just spent with Jay. She had thought it would be fun, but it hadn't been really, if she was going to look at it honestly. Not that he hadn't been his usual attentive and pleasant self; it was something in herself that made it off-key.

Maybe I'm sick, she thought. Her forehead did feel hot and throbby.

But most of all she felt low. Low in spirit, low in energy, just generally low. A tear trickled down her nose, and then she felt another one following it. Everything seemed so dismal and dull. Why, oh, why couldn't she somehow get herself together and feel right again?

Betsy sat up and snapped on the light. There was a box of tissues on the night table and she gave her nose a good hard blow. Perhaps if she thought through some of the advantages she had, she'd feel better. It was an old childhood trick, taught to her by her mother, and there were times Betsy found it worked, or, at least, it helped.

Sitting up in bed, Betsy reviewed her friendship with Jay, and his interrupted courtship of her. There was so much to be said for him. He was nice, he was kind, he understood her, or most of her anyway, he was dependable. Her parents liked him; his parents liked her. Their backgrounds were certainly compatible. Maybe she should marry him. Certainly they would have everything going for them.

No!

It was like an explosion within her, the vehemence of her rejection almost a surprise. But that was what was wrong with the whole idea, the *should* part of it. Much more to the point was, why should she feel obligated to marry him? That was another misplaced *should,* Betsy felt sure.

No, to marry Jay was all wrong. And yet . . . and yet . . . Marriage to Jay would solve so many problems. And be so easy. She knew he'd be a good husband. He'd always be there when she needed him.

The trouble is: do I love him?

No, she didn't love Jay Marshall. Liked him, yes. Respected him, admired him in many ways, enjoyed his company, trusted him—all these things, positively yes. But love him? Unfortunately, no.

And yet it seemed so silly. Why not?

That side of it had her stumped for a while. After all, if she openly admired all his many good qualities, and was willing to admit he was the nicest young man she knew—wasn't this pretty strong liking? And anyway, wasn't liking more important than loving, in the long run?

So?

So nothing . . . but I still can't help it . . . much as I like him, I do not love him . . .

Why not?

Back to that old question again. Why not, why not? The words made a one-two punch in rhythm through her thoughts. Jay had all the necessary qualities for a husband in the kind of marriage Betsy knew she wanted. A marriage like her mother and father's.

The mental image of her father came to mind. Alongside, she placed Jay's. What was the difference? If she wanted a marriage like her parents', why wasn't Jay the husband for her? Again, she considered her mother and father—but then, of course, her father was special . . .

There. That was it. Her father was special and, whereas Jay was nice, it wasn't enough. Not for her. No doubt Jay would be special for someone else. But Betsy wanted a man who was special to her just the same way her father was for her mother. It was that gleam, that something, that added spark that made all the difference. Being special for someone. That was it. Nice was not enough. Nice could be good and kind and thoughtful, but that wasn't special, and only special was the answer.

Another image formed.

David.

He was special. To her, anyway. Betsy hugged her knees and felt more miserable than ever. But hiding from her thoughts wasn't going to help, and her thoughts of David were there for her to see. He was maddening at times, and enough to make her want to scream with frustration when he became secretive. Or maybe he wasn't secretive, but merely an unusually private person. She had to admit she admired him for it. Grudgingly, perhaps, but she knew that was because she longed to know what it would be like to share that privacy with him, to be part of the life of David Fleming, the life he shielded so carefully from the world.

But of course, it was a hopeless dream. No one ever got close to the Loner. Everything pointed toward that fact.

Including her two roommates. They'd been berating her on the subject ever since she'd arrived home that trip. Especially Sharon. She'd heard the story on her return from Paris, although she wouldn't say from whom. Not that it mattered, and anyway, it was typical of Sharon to have heard whatever talk was going around. Maybe Linda had mentioned something to someone on ground. Or Carl Masden. Or even Larry Johnson. No, that seemed unlikely, as he never appeared to take an interest in anything outside of food and flying. But there was Rudi, and the other girls on the trip; gossip travelled so quickly on an airline, it was impossible to guess who had said what.

And Sharon always heard everything; Lee once told her she should have picked a career as a gossip columnist. Sharon had been peeved by the remark, but Betsy had seen Lee's point. Not that Lee was an innocent, either; she said she'd also heard about Betsy's falling for Fleming, but she was not the one to bring up the subject in the first place. It had been Sharon.

Betsy's thoughts chased each other round and round her aching head. Her headache was getting worse. With an effort, Betsy turned and put off the light. She lay back on the pillow her eyes filled with tears, but the heaviness in her head, she knew, would eventually turn into sleep.

6

The day of her flight Betsy woke up to face the unmistakable fact she had the flu. Her head was pounding, her throat sore and her nose was stuffed.

"Perhaps it's just a cold," she hesitated, knowing her statement to be a lie.

"Nonsense. It's flu, and you'd better get back into bed immediately." Sharon was busy at the stove. "I'll make you some tea, if you'd like it."

Betsy opened the refrigerator.

"Isn't there any juice? I'd rather have that."

Even the cool orange juice tasted peculiar, but Betsy forced some down.

"Nothing tastes right."

"Then I'll make you some honey and lemon. At least that'll help your throat."

"That's okay, Sharon, I'll . . ."

"Oh, for heavens' sake!" Sharon whirled around. "Go back to bed, will you? It'll only take me a moment."

Betsy left the kitchen and, seeing that Lee was awake, sat down by the telephone. If it was flu, she'd never make her flight. She knew Lee was her stand-by, so she'd tell her first, but all the same she had to advise Crew Scheduling that she was sick.

Lee sat up in a tangle of bedclothes and said, "Hello. What's up?"

"I think I've got flu."

Lee rubbed her eyes, then stretched her long arms above her head and yawned.

"That means I'm it for your flight today."

"Do you mind very much?"

Lee looked at Betsy in surprise. "Hell, no. Why should I?"

Betsy started dialing. When the company switchboard answered, she said "Crew Scheduling, please," into the receiver. Then, looking up at Lee, she said, "I just thought you might have a date or something."

Lee shook her head and went on stretching, her legs sticking out from beneath the covers. She rubbed her eyes again, slid her feet onto the floor and padded over, barefoot, to the kitchen.

A voice spoke into Betsy's ear.

"Crew Scheduling."

"Good morning. This is Stewardess Blair. I'm scheduled for 410 tonight . . ."

"Yes?"

". . . and I have the flu. Lee Pickering is my standby, and she's also my roommate, so I can tell her."

"We'll have to give her official notice, Miss Blair."

"Yes, of course. D'you want to speak to her now? She's right here."

"No, we'll call back."

Betsy was reminded once again of how cool and impersonal the office always sounded on the phone. And yet, if one went there, the atmosphere was always one of energy and involvement.

"Okay—and I'll get to Medical as soon as I can."

"When do you think that might be?"

Betsy considered the question and her thumping head at the same time. The old rule flashed through her mind: two days to get it, two to have it, two to send it away. But she figured she had it, having been incubating it over the past several days, so tomorrow would be the bad day, and then the worse would be over.

"Maybe the day after tomorrow. If not, I'll call in."

She was glad to have the phone conversation over and to be able to lie down in bed again. She could hear the girls talking in the kitchen and hoped fervently they wouldn't bicker. Not today. She didn't think she could take it, and then the very thought made her realize her

300

feverish state. Otherwise, why should she care whether they bickered or not? Sometimes they could be quite funny to listen to if one wasn't involved.

But not today. Her head felt too clogged up to be able to take any discord. She turned over onto her side, trying to find a more comfortable way to lie.

She dozed off, woken by Sharon's entrance.

"I'll just put it on the night table for you. But do try to sip some of it, if you can."

The hot water and honey mixture did make her throat feel better, but Betsy found she couldn't drink it all in one go. Sharon stood by the bed, watching her drink a portion of it. When she put it aside, Sharon said, "You'd better try to get some sleep."

Betsy saw the rest of the morning in layers of wakefulness between her naps. An early layer was the phone ringing and Lee's voice in answer.

"Yes, I know and yes, I'm ready for it. What's check-in time? Okay. Thank you."

Drifts of sleep covered the subsequent sounds; when she awoke again, Betsy knew she had been dimly aware of further phone calls and long-familiar sounds, the thump of suitcases, the click and clack of the opening and closing front doors, signalling her roommates' routes, and the old and familiar ones, to the dry cleaners', the laundry room downstairs. Another well-known sound had reached Betsy: the ironing board being set up in the living room. That must've been Sharon, she knew, for if it didn't wash and wear, Lee wouldn't think of wearing it, let alone washing and ironing it. Sharon, on the other hand, was an excellent ironer.

Through half-closed eyes, Betsy saw a shape in her doorway.

"Hi, Lee . . ." Her voice was croaky.

"Could you face some soup? We're both going to have a snack, so we thought you might like something."

Both girls came in and sat with Betsy as she downed a cup of soup, tasting little but glad of its warmth. All three would sleep through the afternoon; Sharon's flight left later than Lee's, but the early lunch timed out well for both of them.

"What time is it now?" Sharon leaned over to look at Betsy's clock. "Oh, good. It's still early. That means I can

301

pack and then get to sleep. I have to finish my list, though."

"What list?" Lee wanted to know.

"My shopping list. I've decided to divide my Paris list into three sections. Otherwise, I'll lose too much time, going from one place to another. So I'm going to concentrate on one list per trip ..." and Sharon was off on a long explanation of her complicated plans. Betsy heard it through a haze; it was easy enough to nod and murmur and let Sharon keep on explaining.

"But you can get those here," Lee interrupted. Sharon had been itemizing again.

"But not at a *discount*. And anyway, the selection's much, much bigger there."

"I suppose." Lee was not interested. "Want any more soup, Betsy?"

But all Betsy wanted or needed at that point was more sleep. The other two girls drifted out of her room, taking the remnants of the lunch with them, and once again sleep made the headache recede.

Lee's alarm clock woke her; she lay groggily in bed listening to the sounds and glimpsing the occasional sight through the door of Lee preparing for what should have been Betsy's flight. If only she didn't have this stupid flu bug, she and not Lee would be going out on 410 with David Fleming.

Turning over onto her side, Betsy realized it was nose-blowing time again. For her to be jealous of Lee was stupid. For one thing, Lee had never evinced any interest in David, and for another, it dawned on Betsy that Flight 410 would hold problems of its own for Lee, because of Carl Masden. However flighty Lee might seem, Betsy knew perfectly well that Lee had cared for Carl, and it was going to be difficult for her to be on the same flight with him.

Besides, Betsy thought, he's such a bastard, that Carl. He's bound to make it worse than necessary for poor Lee. If he's chasing someone else, he'll make it good and obvious. And if no one else takes his fancy, he's just as likely to try making out with Lee again.

Betsy was almost sure Lee would fall for it, too. For all her seemingly uninvolved way of living, Lee was vulnerable and easily hurt.

Fully dressed, but without her hat and jacket, Lee appeared in the doorway, looking longer and slimmer than ever in her uniform pants.

"Yes, I'm awake." Betsy turned on the lamp.

"I just came in to see whether there's anything you want from London."

"No, thanks, Lee. I hadn't planned anything special. Is Linda Kesnik back on the flight?"

Lee shook her head. "She's still out. Scheduling told me. Becker's still on, of course. Lucky me."

"Rudi's not too bad, Lee. He doesn't ride you if you work, and he's a whizzbang worker himself, which helps." Betsy could not bring herself to say anything about Fleming. Besides, she wondered, what could she say?

"Okay, I'd better go now." Lee smiled down at Betsy on the bed. "Try to get better, Betsy. You sure you'll be all right on your own, after Sharon leaves?"

"Quite sure."

"Well, anyway, I told the girls upstairs, so if you need anything, they expect you to call."

"Thanks, Lee. Have a good flight."

No sooner had Lee clattered herself and her bags out of the front door than Sharon's alarm rang in her bedroom. Again, the routine sounds began; the shower, the thump of the big suitcase, the neat tearing of the zipper on Sharon's overnight bag, the quick precise steps, dulled by carpeting, as Sharon, now dressed, did her final tasks.

She wore her uniform skirt as she always did; vanity and common sense made her admit she was a shade too short for pants suits. Besides, she had well-formed, small feet and liked them visible in the sleek-heeled shoes. Betsy saw her trot across the living room and disappear into the kitchen; the kettle whistled shortly thereafter, and Sharon came into Betsy's room, a steaming mug in her hand.

"Here's some more honey and lemon. D'you feel like eating anything? I'm about to make myself an omelette."

Gratefully, Betsy took the mug of hot sweet liquid, but declined any food.

"You'd better have something," urged Sharon. "No aspirins on an empty stomach, remember?"

"Okay. But just a piece of toast, if I must."

In the end, she simply had a glass of milk with the aspirins. The thought of solid food was nauseating.

"You're at the worst point," Sharon observed. "D'you want me to get one of the girls from upstairs?"

Betsy shook her head. "I'll be okay. Besides, Lee already told them I'm sick. All I need to do is sleep. This," she waved her hand at the now almost empty mug on the night table, "is just what I needed, thank you. Nothing more."

She lay back against the pillows, the effort of drinking and swallowing and talking having drained her. Her head no longer thumped, but it felt full and hot and her eyes, red and stinging, wanted to close in sleep.

"I'll bring the phone in, as close as I can." She took the phone off its table in the living room and brought it into Betsy's bedroom. She laid it down on the floor, went back outside, brought in one of the phone books and put the phone on top of it.

"There. That way, it won't be too shrill," she said, adjusting the bell down to low. "And if you need anything, it'll be close at hand."

"Thanks, Sharon." Betsy felt close to tears; everything seemed too much to take, whether it was her roommate's thoughtful kindness or the imminent solitude that was about to face her the moment Sharon went out on her flight.

It was dark outside. Sharon closed the venetian blinds in Betsy's room and drew the drapes over them with a quick impatient gesture. She glanced at her watch.

"Goodness, I'd better run . . ."

She paused once more in the bedroom doorway, her uniform complete, her hat snugly on her head.

"Is there anything . . . ?"

"Not a thing, Sharon. Thanks again, and have a nice flight."

The front door banged shut for the second time in two hours. Betsy, low with flu, was now truly alone.

7

The next morning when she woke up she felt exhausted and limp. She told herself the worst must be over, that the fever must have broken, but the aftermath of the flu's high point was hardly pleasant in itself. Besides, she felt so dreadfully weak, discovering this fact when she made her way, knees trembling, across the silent living room and into the bathroom. Looking at herself in the mirror over the sink she could see the effects of the flu. There were no two ways about it: she looked like all hell.

The thick and heavy-headed feeling of the day before had now been substituted by a light and shaky sensation. She made her way carefully from the bathroom to the kitchen. All tasks seemed to take greater concentration than she remembered them to need; the refrigerator door felt far heavier than usual, the cold from its insides made more impact than before.

She saw that Sharon had mixed up a fresh batch of juice for her. Propped up against the bottle was a note saying DRINK THIS, in Sharon's neat handwriting. Betsy smiled, remembering Lee's jibe about Sharon practising to be a mother-in-law. Well, maybe—but before that she'd probably be an effective mother and have healthy children. At least they'd be well cared for. They might rebel at the neatness, though; Betsy didn't think children would conform too easily to Sharon's idea of what a room should look like.

Betsy poured out a glass of orange juice and was

pleased to find it tasted pleasant—a far cry from the way it had tasted the morning before. So she must be over the worst of the flu. If only her knees felt more reliable . . .

But they didn't. Betsy sat at the kitchen table and realized she was trembling. She couldn't control the involuntary shakes; they kept coming and going, rippling through her body at uneven intervals. Perhaps going back to bed for a while would be a more sensible move. Then, later in the day, maybe food would have more appeal.

The weakness flooded through her when she got back to bed, and within a short while Betsy discovered her feeling of recovery had been a mirage. She only just made it to the bathroom in time, and the retching continued even after she had vomited all the orange juice. When it was over, she sat on the edge of the bathtub for a long while, her head leaning against the comforting cold of the basin's edge, her heart pounding against her rib cage and her head echoing the beat.

Back in bed, she felt the fever return, but she let it take its course uninterrupted, too sick to try getting herself some more milk for the aspirins, and not really caring. She dozed fitfully on and off, losing all track of time and ignoring the phone that rang on several occasions.

When she woke fully, it was midafternoon. She sat up hesitantly, then decided she would be able to make it to the kitchen again.

After a glass of milk and two aspirins, she returned to bed, feeling better physically, but low in spirit. The loneliness of the empty apartment weighed heavily upon her. There was nothing she could do, no way she could make the time go faster. Her eyes and head hurt too much for reading, her energy was zero. Even standing up was an effort, and she didn't feel like doing it for long, anyway.

The loneliness, she began to realize, extended further than the boundaries of the apartment. Betsy felt cut off from the general flow of the world around her, alien to the majority of people who lived in the building and the neighborhood. It was almost as though she lived on one space-time level in the place, and all the rest of the people lived on another. All except the other stews, of course. It was the apartness of the airline world, coming home to roost.

And it *is* different, she reflected, a really separate

world. It's not only our hours, and schedules. After all, factories work split shifts and midnight shifts and goodness only knows what-all kinds of times and shifts. But ours is so ... so different. So out of kilter with the rhythm of the rest of the world. Why, we even take dysrhythmia as an everyday affair. And most of the rest of the world has never even heard of it, and if they have they call it jet lag and don't know what it's all about, anyway.

Or, worse still, they think they know all about it, and don't realize it's still being studied. Or ...

Her thoughts whirled as untidily as the swirl of bed-clothes around her. Both began to feel uncomfortable; Betsy decided to allay her physical distresses first. She got up, unsteady but determined, and remade the bed.

Maybe I could eat something now ... or at least wash my face and run a comb through my hair ...

She made herself some soup and a slice of toast and managed to eat both. Afterwards she left the dishes in the sink and went back to bed.

The clock by her side ticked the empty minutes away. Evening came; Betsy woke surprised to find that she had indeed been asleep and knew that, this time, she was really over the worst. The weakness was one of spent fever, the aftermath of ill health, but underneath she felt steadier. Of body, if not of mind.

No, not of mind. The depressed feeling of before now had new dimensions. The loneliness, uncluttered by nausea, was more real now. She wanted someone to talk to, now that she felt like talking again. Before, it was the idea of background people, rather like background music, that had appealed to her.

Her thoughts jumped. Poor Thomas the Turtle! Lee had fed him before she left but he must be really hungry by now.

Thomas seemed unperturbed about her forgetfulness, and he accepted his turtle food with alacrity, snatching the piece of meat out of her hand and whipping under the water. She watched, smiling, at his greedy enthusiasm. The recognition of another living being in the apartment, even if he was a small and greedy turtle, made the emptiness seem less, somehow.

Having slept all afternoon, Betsy knew she would not be able to return to bed immediately and go right back to sleep. Besides, she felt like moving around; it was a good sign. But it would be nice to talk to someone. Maybe she could call someone on the phone. Not the girls upstairs; although they were great as neighbors, she didn't have a close friendship with any of them.

Who was there that she could chat with? Again, the sense of alienation hit Betsy with force; it would have to be one of the other stewardesses, because an outsider would not be able to understand her particular brand of solitude.

Linda.

Now why on earth, Betsy wondered with amazement, should Linda's name be the first that popped into her mind? Of course she knew she was still in town. But all the same, they were hardly friends.

Maybe it was because she had wondered how Linda was getting on, when Lee told her the day before that Linda was still off-schedule. Yes, she would call Linda.

She went back into the bedroom to look at the clock, but she saw it was too late to call the office for Linda's number. Then she remembered that some months back, Sharon had had to call Linda because of a flight swap she'd wanted to make. Knowing Sharon and her meticulous ways, the chances were high she'd written down Linda's number in their telephone book.

Betsy slipped her finger under the K section of the indented alphabet of the book. She scanned down the page—Kraft, Koenig, Koster—sure enough, there it was in Sharon's neat script: Kesnik, Linda.

Betsy dialed. The phone rang twice. The voice answering was not Linda's.

"Is Linda Kesnik there, please?"

"She's still out in Jersey, at her mother's. Would you like the number there?"

"Oh, yes, if you can give it to me."

Moments later, Betsy dialed the telephone number given her by Linda's roommate. It rang several times, and Betsy was beginning to think no one was home when she heard the phone was answered.

"Hello?" Linda's voice sounded strained, wary.

"Hello, Linda?"

"Yes. Who is this?"

"This is Betsy, Linda. Betsy Blair."

308

"Oh." She sounded as though she were disguising her reaction. "How are you, Betsy?" And then, with a surge of interest, "How come you're in town?"

Betsy felt tears welling. It was turning out to be an evening full of self-surprises. What on earth was the matter with her? Just because Linda sounded more friendly.

"I—I have flu, and Lee took my flight," she stammered, feeling caught in a trap of her own making. Why on earth had she called Linda anyhow? The room swam around her; she moved from her perch on the chair arm into its cushioned seat. The room cleared; so did her eyes. Linda was talking.

"You sound funny, Betsy. Are you alone?"

"Yes." It was the smallest *yes* Betsy had ever heard herself say.

"Did you want me to come over? Are you feeling terrible?"

Overwhelmed, Betsy let the tears flow.

"Oh, no, it isn't that, Linda. I'm okay by myself, truly I am. It was just that . . ." The tears were running freely now. "Just that, oh, well, I wanted to talk to someone, just for a minute. You know how silly one gets when one has flu. I'm sorry." Betsy paused. But it didn't matter any more; she didn't care if Linda realized she was crying.

"If you want me to come over, I could try to be there in about an hour."

"Oh, no. *Really* no. I mean it." Betsy managed to be firm. "I called because Lee told me you were still in town and not going on 410 this trip either, and I wondered how things were with you, and whether your mother . . ."

"Everything's more or less under control." Linda sounded infinitely weary. "It takes some doing, though, which is why I'm still here. But how about you, Betsy? Are you sure you're okay enough to be alone? I know how godawful it is to be alone. I hate it, myself."

"No, really, Linda, I'm beginning to feel pretty stupid about having broken down like that."

"That's silly." Despite the words, Linda was kind. "I tell you what you do. Suppose you give me a list of groceries, or whatever you need, and I'll drop by to visit you tomorrow morning. I have to go into the city anyway."

"Oh, Linda, would you? I'd really like that."

"Sure." Offhand. Then more intently, "If you're sure you don't need anything tonight."

"I don't even need anything tomorrow. Sharon and Lee got groceries before they left. But I'd really like your company. Maybe I can fix us a sandwich, or something."

"Coffee'll be all I'll need. How about aspirins, or cough medicine? You need anything like that?"

Betsy assured her that she didn't, adding that she felt better already, knowing she'd have a visitor on the next day.

"Well, don't overdo it on the strength of the idea," came the reply. "But I'll see you tomorrow, okay?"

When she hung up, Betsy found she actually did feel better for the brief talk and the anticipation of a visit the next day. Later, when she went back to bed after another light meal, Betsy realized she was looking forward not only to Linda's visit, but to seeing Linda herself. For herself.

Linda was so defensive about herself, and difficult to get to know. Who would have thought she'd offer to bring in groceries and be as nice as she'd been on the phone?

But then, who would have thought that it would be Linda Kesnik that she would think to call?

8

"You didn't really have to come into the city, did you?"

It was a sudden thought.

"What makes you say that?" Linda looked at Betsy obliquely, her lashes lowered halfway to cover their expression.

"I'm right, aren't I?" Betsy persisted, sure of her guess now.

Linda shrugged and drank some more coffee.

"You know how it is," she finally said when she put the cup down into its saucer again. "There's always something one needs from the stores, and out where my mother is, the selection just isn't the same."

Betsy let it pass, but she knew her intuition was right.

"I think it's very sweet of you, that's all," she murmured. "Is your mother better now? Can you take the next flight?"

The two girls were sitting in the pale morning light entering through the windows of the living room. The light was harsh and unflattering, and it spared neither girl. Betsy felt she must look a mess, her hair pulled back with an elastic, her terry robe worn but comfortable.

Linda looked fragile and weary, but nonetheless intriguing in an unusual way. Betsy thought it was a shame Mike could not see her as she looked now. Linda was wearing almost no makeup, and her long eyelashes accented the striking eyes with the blue-toned shadows smudged beneath them. She wore a simple but elegant beige pants suit that made her look more stylized than ever. Betsy knew that someone like Mike, who saw in terms of shape and line, would be interested in the high-cheekboned girl who sat opposite her on Lee's convertible sofa. For a wild moment, Betsy considered trying to introduce Linda to Mike, but she dismissed the thought the moment it came to mind. At this stage of the game, Mike would be nothing but trouble, all the way around.

Linda said, "You don't mind, do you?" and kicked off her buckled shoes. Then she tucked one foot underneath her and sat on it, stretching the other leg along the sofa cushions. Her movements reminded Betsy of Lee, also long and leggy, except that Linda moved with a fluid grace that was utterly beyond Lee Pickering's capabilities.

"My mother is never going to be better," Linda said suddenly after a short silence. "Oh, it's a long story," and she waved a hand as if to stave off concern. "There's nothing new in the situation. It's just that, while I was in London, she had a—well, I guess you could call it a bad turn." She ended her phrase with a short harsh laugh.

"I see," murmured Betsy, who didn't, but figured a direct question about Mrs. Kesnik seemed inappropriate at this time. "Did you bid London again for next month?"

"Yes, but I'm not taking it. I'll probably end up with a standby slot for the second half. Just my cruddy luck, with Christmas and all. Not that I had any definite plans, or anything, but still . . ."

"Standby? With your seniority?" Betsy was amazed. A fifteen-day slot of permanent standby was the sort of thing only a very junior girl pulled down, and Linda was senior to Betsy and a Flightways stewardess of long standing.

"With my consent, is the point." Linda's smile was bitter. "My choice, in fact. You see, I need the first half of December to get my mother straightened out. As straightened out as she can ever get," she went on, more to herself than to Betsy. "But maybe at least under control."

Her head turned and she looked directly at Betsy.

"You see, my mother's an alcoholic."

Her head turned again, and she was no longer facing Betsy but looking off into the distance.

"Oh, I'm so sorry." It was all Betsy could think of to say.

Linda shrugged. "Don't be. It's just the way it is. And there are worse things, I guess. For families, I mean. Because they're the ones who go through the hell." She said softly, her voice heavy with irony, "People like my mother make sure of that."

Her tone sharpened again, and her eyes blazed with anger.

"You know what brought on this latest bat? I mean the binge she went on that landed her in so much trouble they called me back from London?" Linda stabbed herself in the middle of her chest with her index finger. "Me. It's all my fault. Because I moved out. I couldn't take it any more, and I worked out a deal to share an apartment with two girls on the West Side. It's no palace, but at least it makes life halfway normal for me."

There was nothing Betsy could say at all, so she sat still and waited. Betsy felt sure more was coming, and she was also almost certain that it was the first time in a long time—perhaps ever—that Linda had talked to anyone about her mother, at least in this manner. She realized with surprise that Linda Kesnik was a friend.

"It wasn't just all the godawful scenes with my mother," Linda was saying. "It was the place, the *feel* of the place, too. Living in New Jersey is one thing. Living in the asshole area my mother had chosen—and with my mother, at that . . . Shit, it was a bad deal all around. So when I hit the new pay scale, I worked out a deal with two of the domestic kids. My mother didn't believe me when I first told her, so I just packed up and left."

Betsy listened intently as Linda went on to describe her mother's reactions.

"I tried everything. I really did. Going back at least once a week to see her, to reassure her I'd pay some of her bills like I always have. Everything. But no. We had to have the big dramatic scene every time, about how I didn't love her and was abandoning her in her old age. Shit—she's not even that old. She just looks terrible, because of the booze."

Linda's words tumbled out faster when she spoke of her mother, only to slow down when she referred back to herself.

"But it was worth it, for the peace and quiet of the girls' apartment. There was no shouting at the neighbors

313

over nothing, no hassles over who was going where, no need to worry about fires . . ."

She broke off, glanced at Betsy and then let her shoulders sink. "Yeah, that's another of her cute tricks. She sets fires."

Betsy felt her eyes widen involuntarily.

"But can't you . . . ?" she began.

"Lock her up? Oh, sure. We've been through that one. Many times. That's what's going on now. She set a beauty when I went to London. Got hurt this time, too, but not too badly. Oh, it's all happened before, Betsy, so don't sit there looking shocked."

"I'm sorry. I didn't mean . . ."

"No, no, I know you didn't. Forget I said that." Linda put her hands up to her face, and for a moment Betsy thought she was going to dissolve into tears. But instead, she rubbed her face and forehead, hard, with her long thin fingers, running them back into her hair and pulling her scalp so taut it slanted her eyes.

"I'm so tired of it all," she eventually said, leaning over to her bag and pulling out her cigarettes. "Sometimes, I think I'd just like to lie down and sleep for a month." Her lighter snapped a flame. "But my mother'd find a way to wake me up." A small smile formed around her cigarette.

She lay back against the alcove, shoving a pillow into the small of her back.

"To bitch up my life, anybody's life—along with hers, of course. That's all she seems to aim for. And then she uses the goddam bottle as her excuse. But she's not the only one. That's the worst part of it. Because it seems like *everybody* uses it as an excuse for her. Poor Mrs. Kesnik," Linda's voice went high in imitation. "Must have been soooo beautiful when she was young . . . but soooo sick," dropping her voice to a whisper, "an alcoholic, poor thing, just can't help herself, it's an illness, they say . . ."

Linda sat up. "Illness, my ass. Why don't they just call her a goddam drunk? Because that's what she looks like from where I sit—and believe me, I've sat pretty damn close." Her words were angry. "It's all a big excuse, anyway, a crutch with which she can lam out at the world . . ."

So this is the real Linda Kesnik, Betsy thought. She must have had a terrible childhood. No wonder she considered James over-privileged and spoiled. It explains so much about her.

Aloud, Betsy said, "And your father?"

"He copped out years ago. And I don't blame him. I just wish I could, too."

Before Betsy could think of anything to say in the sudden silence that fell after Linda stopped talking, the telephone rang. Grateful, Betsy rose and answered it.

"Hello?"

"Betsy!" Jay's voice was startled. "I was just calling to find out what time you'd be back from London tonight. What're you doing home?"

"Lee took my trip. I was sick." And Betsy explained her bout with the flu.

"But, look here. Why didn't you call me?" Jay demanded. "I could've given you something to pull you through it."

Betsy laughed. "Thanks, Dr. Marshall, but I'm doing okay on—guess what? Honey and lemon, the old wives' standby."

"D'you still have fever?"

"I don't think so. I feel much better."

"Well," Jay sounded unconvinced, "I'll be over to see you in a half hour or so."

"With your little black bag and all your pills?"

"Of course."

He sounded serious, but Betsy knew he was smiling. She said, "There's really no need for you to come, Jay. I'm doing fine. By tomorrow, I'll be completely over it."

But Jay was insistent, so finally Betsy said, "Okay, but only if you let me give you coffee instead of you giving me pills."

Betsy saw Linda rising from the sofa.

"If you're having company . . ."

"Linda, please don't go." Betsy said it urgently, and she meant it. "It's a friend of mine from years back, and I'd really rather you stayed, if that's okay with you. Unless, of course, you have something else you have to do."

"Well . . ." Linda looked uncertain.

"Oh, come on," Betsy urged. "Besides, we need a sandwich. And when Jay comes by, he can join us for coffee. He's a doctor," she explained, "nothing to do with the airline. But he tries to understand."

"About the life, you mean?"

Betsy nodded. "Yes. He doesn't always succeed, but he tries. It's so difficult to explain, isn't it?"

Linda nodded, said, "You sure it's all right if I stay?" and, reassured by Betsy, sat down on the sofa again. "Is he your boyfriend, your fiancé or your lover?" she wanted to know.

"No, nothing now. Our parents know each other. It's one of those things from way back."

"But you don't want it." Linda was observing her keenly.

"That's right. Come join me in the kitchen, will you? I know we've plenty of sandwich fixings."

Over their impromptu lunch, the girls went deeper into the question of the great divide between the airline world and everyone else.

"I find myself thinking, oh, what's the use of saying it, they won't understand anyway," Betsy said. "Or else they think you're bragging, which is even worse."

"I know exactly what you mean. The tone of voice they get when they say, 'My, aren't you lucky, going to *Paris*'— like they were really saying 'going to *hell*'."

Betsy laughed. Linda had a talent for mimicry. Her acting training, Betsy supposed. Or natural talent, which was why she'd tried acting in the first place.

"Or else they say something like, 'That's nice, dear', when you've been telling them about some crazy kook of a passenger, and the next thing you know they're asking you did you see the TV spectacular last Wednesday. Or asking you when you're going to settle down and find a *real* job. That's the one that gets to me." Linda bit into her sandwich with more enjoyment than Betsy had ever noticed her show toward food before.

Without asking, Betsy poured some more milk into Linda's glass, saying, "And how about the ones who ask if you aren't tired of all the moving around?"

"Mmm. I usually find that asking them whether they aren't tired of just sitting in the same old place finished *that* conversation off fast." Linda said between bites of her sandwich.

"And yet, I guess one does eventually get tired of it, don't you think?"

"I guess. I don't know yet. Even after the time I've flown, I still get restless if I stay in one place too long."

"Perhaps it all depends who one is around," Betsy said slowly, speaking more from theory than experience.

"It could help," Linda agreed. "Now, if someone were to cover me with diamonds and furs, no doubt I could consider staying in one place, too."

Betsy grinned, and was about to make a similarly flip remark when the door buzzer sounded.

"That must be Jay," she said, rising. "No, don't get up. He'll come into the kitchen with us. I'll just go let him in."

9

Well, thought Betsy, closing the door behind Linda and Jay. *Well.* Of all things.

She leaned against the wall for a moment, weak and slightly dizzy. The living room, though silent, seemed to buzz with the echoes left over from the animated conversation that had filled it just before. Betsy felt the apartment's emptiness in something akin to a physical sensation for her body. Perhaps that was why she felt so weak—a reaction to the past couple of hours.

But of all things . . . who would have thought . . .

And she had noticed it right from the moment it started. When Jay had walked in through the front door, he had looked at Betsy with concern, and questioned her about the flu while they went towards the kitchen. Then he had seen Linda.

"Linda, I'd like you to meet Jay Marshall—*Dr.* Jay Marshall, but he's okay once you get to know him," Betsy said with a teasing glance at Jay. Her longtime childhood friend was staring at Linda.

Linda did look exceptionally pretty, prettier than Betsy had ever seen her look before. Perhaps the relaxation of the previous hours had helped untangle her usual tension, and maybe talking about her own problems had relieved Linda in some emotional way. She did not look drained, as she often did on flights, and the smudges beneath her eyes were only slight shadows, accenting her features rather than detracting from them.

"Hello, doctor . . ." Linda's eyes smiled, too.

"Hello. I see you've been taking care of my patient." Jay regained his composure. He put his small black doctor's bag down on the kitchen table. "All the same, Betsy, I think you should take some of these . . ."

All the way through his instructions on how to take the capsules he had brought her, Betsy felt that he was really talking for Linda's benefit. And it wasn't that he looked at her too often; on the contrary, Betsy felt that he and Linda were almost avoiding each other's eyes, as though it was too much to look directly into each other's eyes. For a moment, she came close to feeling angry; did Linda really have to make a play for every man she met?

But then she watched Linda's face. Linda didn't seem to be playing; there was none of that too-bright smart-alecky air about her at all.

That was while they were all in the kitchen. Later, they'd gone into the living room again, and sat around talking and playing a few records.

"I really must get going," Linda said eventually, and Betsy immediately said, "In that case, I'm throwing you out, too, Jay, because I've some household chores to attend to before Lee gets back."

Linda glanced at her watch. "That's right. She should be in soon. I'm glad," and she smiled with genuine warmth at Betsy. "That way, you'll have someone here with you tonight."

Jay rose from the armchair. "Don't overdo it, Betsy," he warned. "Flu can leave you weak as a kitten."

"I'm not planning to scrub floors, or anything, just fix a few things for Lee, that's all."

"Good girl." Jay went to the hall closet and retrieved his coat. "Is this yours?" he asked Linda, drawing out a fleece-lined suede coat. "I don't recognize it, so it must be."

"Yes, that's right." Linda eased into the garment as Jay held it for her and Betsy felt she could almost see the currents of attraction between them.

After they had gone, and after her slight dizziness had disappeared, Betsy picked up the coffee cups and took them back to the kitchen. She called the number with the recording of the flight arrivals and departures; Flight 411 from London was slightly delayed. Good. That gave her time to clear things up and have a shower before Lee arrived home. She didn't plan on getting dressed, but a clean nightgown along with a change of sheets on her bed might be a good idea now her flu was almost over.

Betsy remade her bed, finished the washing up in the kitchen, loaded the percolator with fresh coffee and took out another nightgown from her chest of drawers. As she performed the tasks, her thoughts revolved around Jay and Linda. There were twinges of jealousy, she knew, that irked her in two different ways. They made her angry because she knew that if she didn't want Jay for herself (and she didn't), she should at least be able to wish Linda well with him. But she could not help feeling somewhat discarded, like an old hat, by her longtime suitor. Where was all that faithfulness he'd been promising her through the years?

You idiot, Betsy told herself fiercely. You're the one who kept telling him it was no good, that you'd be his friend for life but never his wife—so what did you expect? Did you think Jay'd stay a bachelor forever just because you turned him down?

Still, it piqued her. It piqued her doubly because she knew it shouldn't. She managed to wash much of her unreasonable mood away under the shower, and the clean nightgown felt smooth against her skin. She put on her bathrobe, and then returned to her bedroom and combed her hair. It was still early; Lee wouldn't be back for at least another half hour. Betsy felt the need for a short rest. Jay had been right; the flu had left her weak.

She lay down on the bed, still in her robe, and curled her arm under her pillow. She could feel herself sinking into sleep at once. I'll just doze, she thought, until Lee gets home . . .

"Betsy? Are you decent?" Lee's voice broke into her consciousness. Betsy struggled with sleep.

She opened her eyes. Lee was in the doorway.

"Hi, Betsy. I've brought you a visitor."

But Betsy had already seen Fleming standing there, too

10

Betsy sat up, blinking and feeling foolish. David was smiling at her from the door, his lean height making him tower over Lee.

"Oh, hello . . . I didn't expect . . ."

Lee came up to the bed, her long legs making the passage in three steps. She sat down on the end. Fleming remained in the doorway.

"Hello, Betsy," was all he said.

"I told him you were ill, and he asked so many questions, I thought I'd better bring him back to see how you were for himself." Lee rattled on, peering at Betsy as she did so. "But you're better, aren't you? You certainly look better."

Betsy pushed a strand of hair off her face and nodded, smiling first at Lee and then up at David.

"Oh, yes, much better, thank you."

She covered her confusion by making much of getting her feet over the edge of the bed and finding her slippers.

"I have the percolator set up, and there's eggs and bacon, if you want, and . . ."

David Fleming started to protest. It was Lee who stopped him.

"Oh, come on, Captain—coffee isn't going to kill you. And you weren't going anyplace. You drove me here, didn't you? Well, coffee is the payment. For a tip, you might even get food."

Lee stood up and Fleming moved out of the way so

that she could go through the doorway to the kitchen. He and Betsy looked at each other until she dropped her gaze.

"It's very sweet of you to have come."

"I wanted to see how you were. Lee's description of you when she left sounded grim." Beneath his light tone, Betsy sensed genuine concern. If only her heart would stop thumping so loudly; she felt it could be heard clear across the room.

"Are you sure you're well enough to get up like that?" David asked when Betsy finally located her slippers and stood up in them.

"Of course I am." Surprisingly, all that heart-thumping did not affect her voice. "Come on, let's go into the kitchen and I'll fix you and Lee something to eat."

They had to avoid Lee's boots in the doorway of the bedroom and her jacket halfway across the living room floor. Betsy grinned seeing David notice them.

"She's our strip tease artist," she explained, pointing out the fur hat near the front door. "If you weren't here, she'd have another layer off by now."

Lee was standing by the refrigerator, but Betsy pushed her aside.

"I'll do it, Lee. Honestly, I'm fine."

Lee sank into the nearest chair and waved a hand at the chair opposite. "Come on, Captain, take a load off your feet. Ohhh," she stuck her legs out in front of her and wriggled her toes. "I think mine are on fire."

David remained standing; Betsy set out plates and got the food started at once. Outside, the dark winter sky seen through the window over the sink had the bleak cold look of late November.

"Eggs and bacon? A ham omelette? Pheasant under glass? What'll it be, folks?" Betsy looked around to get food orders.

"Cyanide," was Lee's request, given with a sigh. She swerved around in her chair and added, "You know, Betsy—you and Sharon are absolutely right. I never learn, do I?"

Betsy sensed that, underneath the clowning, Lee was hiding a new hurt. Carl, no doubt. But it couldn't have been too bad, or Lee would not be clowning it as easily as she was.

"Food requests first, crying towel afterwards," was Betsy's reply. "And how about you, Captain?"

They stayed there, the three of them, warm and easy in the kitchen's homey atmosphere. From time to time Betsy or Lee would get up from the table and get some more toast, or another round of coffee; the conversation centered on the flight, which had been a relatively easy one from both cockpit and cabin point of view. They had been close to full in coach on the way back, hence Lee's aching feet, since she had been doing much the same as Betsy had on her last flight, skipping from one section to the other.

"But you were right about Rudi. He really works."

"I told you so."

David Fleming leaned back in the straight kitchen chair, listening and occasionally adding his comments to the girls' chatter.

At last, Lee pushed her cup into the middle of the table and said, "I've had it with food. If you'll excuse me, I'm going to go and lie in a tub until all the transatlantic trotting soaks right out of my poor feet." She looked at them again, shaking her head in mock wonder. "How could *anything* in the world grow so big and still be so sensitive to being walked on?"

Laughing, David Fleming pushed his chair back and began to rise. "I'd better be going, too."

"Certainly not—I didn't say I was going to take a bath as a hint for you to leave." Lee put out a hand and placed it on his shoulder, pressing him back into his chair. Betsy was surprised at the calm way Lee made the gesture, but David seemed grateful for the invitation to stay.

As soon as Lee was out of the room, Betsy rose and poured some more coffee.

"Let's take it to the living room," she suggested. "The chairs out there are more comfortable."

And, she reasoned, since Sharon was out on her Paris trip and would not be back until the following evening, Lee didn't need the alcove sofa to sleep in. She could always use Sharon's room. Betsy hoped she'd remember to keep it more or less tidy, and then decided it would be easier to help her tidy it tomorrow, before Sharon returned, than to remind her about it now. The thing was, Lee appeared to be physically incapable of pinpoint neatness, an attribute that seemed to come naturally to Sharon. As go-between, Betsy always found it simpler to pitch in than to remind.

She and David Fleming walked into the living room, and a short silence fell between them as they sat down. David did not look too tired, she noticed, so there was no need to feel guilty about keeping him from his sleep. Besides, she sensed he wanted to stay, miraculous as it seemed.

"And how was London?" she managed brightly, filling the momentary quiet.

"London was Londonish, as usual. Not too cold, fortunately. And I think Larry must've bought out the food department at Harrods."

"Does his wife really insist on him buying all those things?" Betsy wanted to know. "Or haven't you ever met her?" she finished quickly, not wanting to appear knowledgeable about his friendship with the Johnsons.

"I've known her for years," was the reply. "Myra's an okay kid. You'd like her," David said surprisingly. "And she knows Larry through and through. They complement each other very well. As to the food shopping he says she forces him to do . . . well, you should hear her side of the story on that one."

It seemed to Betsy that the great silent Loner was talking more than anyone could ever have guessed he was capable of doing. She listened with interest as he described Myra Johnson's cooking expertise and Larry's appreciation of both her and her talents.

The sound of water cascading into the bathtub ceased, and after some splashing noises that Betsy knew to be Lee clambering into her bath, a shout of "Hey, Betsy! I forgot my robe" came from behind the closed door.

"Excuse me." Betsy rose and went to the bathroom door, opening it and slipping through into the steam-filled space with the dressing gown she'd seized from the arm of the chair.

"Here you are." Dimly, she could see Lee through the billowing clouds. "Wow! Isn't that water burning you?"

"It's absolute bliss," breathed Lee, her eyes closed. She was lying as flat as she could get in the porcelain tub, a chantilly of bubble bath blanketing the surface of the water and rising around her neck. Her eyes opened, and a hand came out from under the froth. She beckoned to Betsy to come closer, placing a finger on her lips to signal silence.

"Listen," she whispered when Betsy was near, "he's interested, really interested. I may be a fool when it comes to men for me, but boy, can I recognize a guy who's interested elsewhere."

Lee was still whispering. "He wanted to come and see you in the worst way. That's why I brought him, and tried to make it as easy and nonchalant as possible."

"Thanks, Lee," Betsy whispered back. Louder, she said, "D'you need anything else?"

"Just a new pair of feet," groaned her immersed roommate, sinking further under the water. "No, nothing else, thanks Betsy."

When Betsy left the bathroom, there was much splashing going on behind her.

"Sounds like she needs water wings," remarked Fleming who, Betsy saw, was now standing over by the bookcase and flipping through magazines. "Who's the theater fan here?"

"I am, sort of," Betsy murmured.

"Why sort of?"

"Well, I mean I enjoy seeing plays, but I'm not totally involved."

"But you're interested enough to get a magazine like this." Fleming held up the one he meant.

"Not regularly. I picked that up on a newsstand," Betsy told him. "But I did find it interesting—to see the theater world from the inside, sort of thing. That's what they call a trade magazine," she went on, "written more for show business people themselves than the audience."

"I know," David Fleming interrupted. "It's the one my sister works for."

"Oh." Betsy felt slightly embarrassed.

But the tall captain was not listening. He was flipping through the magazine.

"Her name's on the masthead, I think," he was saying. "She's been with them for years. Loves her work. Travels for it, too."

Struck by a sudden possibility, Betsy found herself asking the question before she had had time to consider it.

"Does she often go to London? Was she the girl I saw

325

. . ." and then her voice died away. Of course that could not have been his sister; she had been married several times, David had said. And the young woman was certainly still in her twenties somewhere, hardly likely to be multi-married. Betsy bit her lip; why, oh, why didn't she think before she spoke? Perhaps David hadn't heard.

But he had. Closing the magazine, he asked, "What girl, Betsy? What girl did you see?"

They faced each other across the room. The sound of more water being run into the tub splashed through the closed door of the bathroom. Its gurglings seemed extra loud in the sudden hush of the strained silence between them.

"What girl are you talking about?" David Fleming repeated.

"Uh, nothing, I . . ." But she knew she wasn't going to get away with it. His eyes were looking directly at her; Betsy could almost feel them boring right into her thoughts. And anyway, so what? She hadn't done anything wrong, or sneaky. All she'd done was see him in a taxi. And there had been a girl there, too.

"In London," she said, avoiding his gaze. "In a taxi. I know I saw you . . . it was when I was coming back from having tea with James . . . at a red light . . ." She sat down on the sofa.

"So that's what's been bugging you." He said it softly, almost to himself. "Well, I guess it won't do any harm if I explain it to you."

And the next thing Betsy knew, David was sitting down beside her.

11

Fleming lit a cigarette and looked at Betsy.

"I assume you know I'm a widower, and how it all happened," he said.

For the second time that day, Betsy searched for words and found there were none. None that fitted, none that would sound right. First with Linda, and now with David, she had discovered the terrible lack. How could one ever say the right thing—how could anything be right to say when you wanted to say something to a person whose life had been torn apart? Linda's disastrous, alcoholic mother, David's tragedy and loss—what could she possibly find to say that would make them know how she felt for them?

"Yes. Yes, I do," was all she could think to murmur. "I'm so terribly sorry . . . I don't really know what to say . . ."

But before she had finished her sentence, David's gesture, an impatient wave of the hand, made it clear he did not want or need any words from her at all.

"It all happened several years ago, and the pain has gone, now. I guess it died, slowly, as time passed. You know they say time heals all wounds." He looked at Betsy again. "Well, that's almost true. Now, the incident is a bad memory that comes back from time to time, but that's all."

Betsy watched his face as he spoke, and got the impression that what he was saying was close to the truth. She also felt that, whatever it was Fleming wanted to tell her, he would brook no further interruptions while he talked. Apparently the silent Loner, when he made up his mind to say something, wanted to have his full say without distraction.

"So if you know the story," he was saying, "you've doubtless heard the part about my wife and our son being killed. What you probably don't know, because few people do—and even fewer remember—is that there was a third person in the car that day. And she was not killed.

"Marta was little more than a kid herself at the time. She had come to us from Portugal to help with both the child and the house. She loved it here in the States, and was full of plans and ambitions. Meanwhile she was living with us, of course, and doing more than her share of work. The contract was she'd stay with us for at least a year. I don't know whether you know or not, Betsy, but there are a number of people who used to come into this country that way, do domestic service for a while, and then go on to other things."

"Yes, I know," Betsy nodded. "Wasn't there even a famous case when a girl who came in as a maid married the rich boss' son?"

David grinned. "Yup, that's right. But anyway, getting back to Marta—she, too, was in the car that day. In the back seat, and it saved her life."

He paused for a moment.

"She was in pretty bad shape, though. They wouldn't even let me see her at first, and then, when I did get to visit her, she was in casts and covered with bandages. All I could see were her big black eyes. No, that's not quite so," he corrected himself. "The rest of her face showed, too, although it was bruised at first. Even her nose had been broken."

Betsy shivered. Despite the dispassionate tone in which he was telling the story, she could feel its impact and got a glimpse of how Fleming himself must have felt those years ago.

"I was really the only person she had here in the States, and she hasn't much family back in Portugal, anyway. Besides, as her employer, I was of course responsible for her. And luckily there was insurance to cover everything. Because, after she had gotten over the worst of it, we found out there'd have to be operations."

Fleming paused again. "Like I said, there had to be operations. Marta had several of them here. In between, she'd have to wait until she healed."

It had been a long and complicated process, he explained, with the retraining of muscles taking up much of the time between trips to the hospital itself.

"Eventually, all the major muscles and bones and things were working okay again. But there were smaller things that were still wrong, smaller muscles that had been torn and hadn't mended right. That sort of thing. Some experts said it was just a question of time, but then we heard about this surgeon in England . . ."

David had bid a series of London flights sometime back to go and talk to the London doctor who did operations to correct conditions similar to Marta's.

"I was very impressed with the guy, and the things he told me and showed me. So when I came back, I told Marta all about it, and she said yes, she was willing to undergo more surgery. Anything to get back to a totally normal life."

With the insurance on one side, and the cooperation of Flightways on the other, Fleming was able to get the young Portuguese girl to London and into the English surgeon's clinic.

"She's been there ever since, and now, thank God, the actual operations are all over."

"And have they been successful?" Betsy found herself asking eagerly, by now deeply involved in the occurrences David was recounting.

"Yes, completely." David looked at her again and smiled, his expression one of relaxation and relief. She could see how much the surgical success had meant to him and understood, in a burst of empathy, the emotional reprieve it must be for him personally.

Almost as though he had heard her thoughts, Fleming said, "I felt as though a huge burden had been lifted off my shoulders. Not that I was responsible for the accident and, yet, in a way, I couldn't help but feel guilty about it. Guilty that somehow it had been my family had wrecked the life of a young and lovely girl. But that's all over now, too. Or almost. Marta still has to do some therapeutic stuff, but, by comparison to what she's been through, the rest is child's play."

"And she's going to be perfectly all right again."

"Miraculously enough—yes, she is. When you saw me with her in London, we were going back to the clinic after spending about as normal an afternoon as Marta has spent in years. I took her shopping," and again David Fleming smiled. "You don't know me well enough, Betsy, to understand how unusual that is for me."

"But I can guess," Betsy grinned. "Still, under the circumstances, I'm sure you enjoyed it."

"Very much," David agreed. "Marta only wanted to buy presents for her family. She's going back to Portugal next month, to spend Christmas with some cousins, and so she bought all sorts of things to take back with her."

"So that's why you bid the London trip," Betsy said.

"That's right. I wanted to be around when the results of the operation began to show. I was there for the surgery itself—took time off from the company to be around, in case anything was needed."

A small silence settled between them, sealing the things that had been said more than any words could have done. It was Fleming who broke it by saying, as he leaned back against the alcove wall and closed his eyes, "Phew! I suddenly feel as though all the energy I had left has drained out of me. I guess I really *am* tired."

"Maybe it's getting it out of your system—I mean, telling me all about it," Betsy murmured.

"You're probably right. I don't often mention it at all. But you—you're easy to talk to, Betsy, you know? And I think I wanted to tell you, somehow, right from the beginning, though I don't understand why."

Unexpectedly, as he opened his eyes, he stretched his hand toward Betsy's face. His fingers touched her, lightly, and brushed aside a strand of hair that had fallen forward across her cheek. There was electricity in the touch, and Betsy felt it throughout her body.

"You're lovely, too," she heard him saying. "There's something so restful about you, Betsy, I . . ."

Suddenly, he moved back, and looked at his watch. It was as though he was deliberately pulling away from the moment, the special something that had just happened between them.

"My God—it's late."

"Yes, I guess it is."

"I must get going."

Where did the impulse come from? Betsy never knew. But she heard herself saying, "Oh, come on, now, you don't want to drive again before you sleep. Look—why don't you take my room? Sharon—our other roommate—won't be home till tomorrow night. I can sleep in her room. I often do."

If I tell him I'll sleep on the sofa, she thought, he won't stay. But Sharon's room . . .

"Well . . ."

Betsy was already steering him across the living room toward her door. "The sheets are clean, because I just changed them today, and I'll get you a towel from the linen closet, and you can just go to sleep right now."

Looking as surprised as Betsy felt, David Fleming allowed himself to be led into the bedroom.

"Here." Betsy handed him a towel. "Now—would you like anything else before you go to sleep?"

"No, thanks, Betsy, just some more coffee, if there is any."

"How about some warm milk instead? It makes you sleep better."

"That'll be great."

Betsy closed the bedroom door behind her thinking that she seemed to live in a constant round of hot milk for sleeping.

The bathroom door clicked open in front of her.

"Lee!" Betsy had forgotten all about her roommate.

"Is it okay to come out now?" Lee whispered, looking cautiously around the room.

"Yes, of course it is. Why didn't you come out sooner?"

"Because I didn't want to disturb you. Things seemed to be going so well . . . Where is he?"

"In there." Betsy gesticulated. "He's going to sleep."

"Hey, great." There was admiration in Lee's voice. "You take Sharon's room, okay?"

Betsy shook her head. "Nothing doing. You're the one who's just come in from a flight. You take her room. I'll take the sofa."

"You sure?"

"Positive."

"Wow. I'm really water logged." Emerging from the

331

steamy doorway, Lee stood, clad in pyjamas, her robe and clothes over her arm. "That was more than a super-sauna." She moved toward Sharon's room. "I guess now I really understand how Thomas the Turtle feels."

12

Betsy, holding a mug of warm milk in one hand, knocked softly on the door of her bedroom with the other.

"Come in."

David was still fully dressed.

"Betsy," he began, "I don't think I'd better stay. I was thinking it over, and . . ."

"For heavens' sake, why not?" Boy, but he was an unpredictable man. "You're dead tired, the bed's there for you, clean sheets and all." She stood there, feeling exasperated, the hot milk in front of her.

"Put that down, Betsy, and listen to me."

Automatically, she obeyed the quiet-spoken command, placing the milk on the bureau. When she turned around, David was standing directly in front of her. She could feel his closeness.

"If I stay," he said, and his hand again reached out to touch her face, "you know as well as I do that it isn't a question of which bed or clean sheets or anything else."

For an enormous second, she was aware of nothing but the two of them standing there. Then his arms reached out for her and the heat of his body was hard against hers and his mouth closed down directly, demandingly over her mouth. She clung to him and gave and felt her own body demanding, too.

His hands tangled her hair and he spoke her name over and over through the thick strands before he gripped her back, pressing her closer and closer to him. She felt dizzy with delight.

The steps to the bed were awkward but once taken seemed inevitable. Buttons, shoes, clothes, all fell away. The sheets felt silken smooth, welcoming the tumult of emotion between them. Then David ceased calling her name, until she called out his, and an answering groan reassured her. The rush of force carried her along with it, unresisting and wanting David, and David, and David again.

Afterwards, they were silent. He kissed her shoulder and she placed her hand along his face. For several moments they lay there, quiet under the soft light of the bedside lamp.

David was the first to speak. "It's not right, you know. It's no good."

"What's no good?"

"Us. This."

Betsy snuggled closer, only half-hearing his words.

"It's not right," he repeated.

This time, she reacted.

"Why?"

"Because . . ." and then he hesitated, as though uncomfortable with his thoughts.

"David Fleming!" Betsy sat up and looked at him. "You're not going to give me a long, over-thirty type lecture about nice girls not doing it, are you?" She opened her eyes wide in mock horror. "Heavens to Betsy—Betsy *does* it!" she falsettoed. "Land sakes alive!" Back in her normal voice, she added, "Well, Captain? Is that what you're going to hassle about?"

"No, of course not." He looked more pained than amused.

"Then what?"

"Well—look at the age differential, for a start. There's almost a generation between us."

"There *is*?" Betsy looked and sounded skeptical. "You could've fooled me."

David hardly listened. He was saying, ". . . and I feel as though I'm almost old enough to be your father."

Betsy giggled. "To do that, you'd have to have been a *terribly* precocious little boy."

"No, but *really*."

334

"No-but-*really*," she imitated. *"Really*, David ... now honestly, don't you think you're making a big deal out of something that's just a big nothing? Why—the way you talk, you'd think you were 90!"

"I'm ..."

"I know exactly how old you are," Betsy interrupted. "Crew manifest, remember?"

"Then you realize why I think it's pretty foolish of a man my age to fall for a young girl like you."

Betsy, seeing how serious he was, stopped trying to make light of the subject.

"What I realize," she said slowly, "is that it's pretty foolish to generalize like that. At least, that's what my Dad always maintains—and he *is* old enough to be my father."

It was David's turn to smile, somewhat ruefully.

"He's a doctor," Betsy continued, "and I've always considered him pretty smart about people. He'd say it's up to the individual, and I feel the same way. It depends how each person feels."

"Maybe." Fleming still sounded doubtful. "It's just I've always figured it should be to each his own generation."

"To each his own *choice*," Betsy corrected, rephrasing the thought.

". . . and youth with youth . . ."

"And do you truthfully feel all your youth is behind you?"

"Well, not exactly, but . . ."

"But nothing, Captain Fleming ... and please stop pulling rank on me."

"It was you who said Captain."

"David." Her eyes glowed.

"Betsy ... I ..."

They kissed, and their passions matched again. Afterwards they slept, and towards dawn Betsy woke and watched the sleeping man beside her and hugged her knees with joy.

They breakfasted alone. Lee remained behind the closed door of Sharon's room. Betsy and David sat in the kitchen, sharing their new secret.

Over their second cups of coffee, Fleming said, "It's almost Thanksgiving, isn't it?"

"Day after tomorrow," Betsy nodded.

335

"You going home?"

"No, not this year. I usually do, but this time, what with my bid—I'm scheduled out the next day."

"I know," David smiled. "I am too."

In a soft voice, Betsy said, "I know. Isn't it wonderful?"

"We'll have London together. But what about Thanksgiving."

"Oh. Yes. Well, my schedule makes it sort of stupid to rush off for the day and then rush back again. So I'm staying here."

"Tell you what." He leaned toward her across the table. "Why not come with me to my crazy sister's? If you'd like to, of course," he added hastily, drawing back again as though suddenly aware of possible rejection.

"*Like* to? I'd *love* to!"

They smiled into each other's eyes.

"Fine. I'll call you tomorrow sometime, to let you know when I'll pick you up on Thursday, okay?"

"That'll be lovely."

"But I must go now, Betsy, I really must." He rose. "I have things to attend to . . ."

Catching himself in midsentence, he stopped, then said, "But I can tell you now, can't I? I have to go to Boston, to see one of Marta's doctors and pick up some records they need in London. I'll take the shuttle, and be back by tomorrow evening. Or maybe I'll drive, if the buggy's working."

Betsy sensed the barrier he'd just vaulted, being able to tell her where he was going, and doing so without regret.

"I'll be out during the middle of the day myself," she told him. "You know, reporting to Medical, about the flu."

"Well, then I'll either call you early in the morning or after I get back sometime, okay?"

David kissed her goodbye and left. He closed the front door without a sound. Betsy stood for a moment in the middle of the living room, lightheaded with joy and anticipation. It was a marvellous sensation, and it stayed with her, like a big beautiful bubble buoying her no matter where she went or what she did for the rest of the day.

13

Sharon did not return from Paris until late that night, but she insisted on staying up until she had heard Betsy's news. Betsy, although she had talked to Lee about nothing else all day, was only too happy to have an excuse to tell the story all over again.

Lee kept interrupting, supplying the parts that had occurred before Fleming's arrival at the apartment.

"I *knew* he wanted to see her," Lee told Sharon. "So I more or less cornered him into driving me home. And the rest was easy . . ."

"Well!" Sharon exclaimed. "Well I think it's just . . . almost unbelievable! The *Loner,* of all people . . . he must be very *serious.*"

Betsy started to protest.

"He's never looked at another girl before," Sharon pointed out, sticking to her opinion."I think it's wonderful, if it can all work out. And it could, you know." She eyed Betsy speculatively.

Betsy blushed, and kept silent not wanting to expose her private dreams out loud.

"Oh, you never know," she said. "We'll have to wait and see. One never knows what may happen. He may never even call me again."

"He will." Sharon was definite. "If he said he will, he will. He's not the type to break his word, or stand you up . . . unlike some other men around here whom we all know."

Her glance across the table made Lee say, "Oh, come on, now Sharon, let up on me, will you? I *know* I pick the wrong men. I always have." She looked down at the floor reflectively. "I wonder whether it has anything to do with having big feet?"

They all laughed and went back to the subject of David and Betsy until Sharon said, "I must get to sleep. There's so much I have to do tomorrow before Tom picks me up in the afternoon. We're going to spend Thanksgiving with his folks," she explained, as she had several times before in the preceding weeks.

The next morning's first phone call was David Fleming, and it was Betsy who answered. She felt awkward and clumsy and thrilled, all in one. David's call was brief and almost drowned out by the sounds of automobile engines behind him.

"I decided to drive and just came by the garage to get the buggy, so I thought I'd better call now. Can you hear me?"

She struggled to hear his words over the roar of a racing engine.

"Yes, David—just."

"Fine. About tomorrow—I'll pick you up around five thirty, okay?"

"Fine," Betsy breathed, "lovely."

She heard her own words being drowned out by another revving motor.

"What's that you say? Sorry, Betsy, I can't hear you."

Then why did you call me from such a crazy place? Betsy thought, but shouting, she said, "Fine. Great."

"Okay. See you then." He hung up, leaving Betsy with a slight feeling of frustration. But I suppose that's the way he is, she realized. I'd better get used to being called from noisy places filled with engines.

The next call was Tom for Sharon. They spoke for ages, arranging and rearranging their plans for Thanksgiving. Lee, who had been roused by the phone calls, remarked that they spent so much time and effort talking about what they were going to do that they risked not having enough time to do it, and Sharon threw her a look. When she finally got off the phone, she said, "At least I can *rely* on Tom."

338

"I guess." Lee yawned, unwilling to start bickering. Betsy was glad to see the potential friction die down; she felt so happy she didn't want to see her roommates at odds.

The phone rang again; it was the girls upstairs to say that they were having a Thanksgiving party, and would Betsy, Sharon and Lee like to come? Lee accepted with alacrity, and became even more enthusiastic when she heard a whole new crowd was going to attend.

"A group that Sonia met last weekend," Lee explained after the phone conversation was over. "She says the guys are really great."

Sharon's "Hmmph," audible as she unpacked one of the excelsior-padded cartons she had brought off the flight, was tempered by Betsy's "Well, at least you won't have to go far in this cold weather." Then she added, "Okay if I use the bathroom first? I have to report to Medical."

"Sure, go ahead," the other two chorused, and Betsy showered and dressed warmly, bundling herself up against the chill November weather outside. She went straight to the Flightways Building, and came right back after her appointment with one of the company doctors, stopping only at a nearby drugstore to fill the prescription she had been given.

"Just to help build you up properly," the doctor had explained.

She swallowed one the moment she got home. Both the other girls were out; Sharon had left with Tom for their Thanksgiving holiday, and a note from Lee, attached to the icebox door, explained "Out till late. Dinner out, too." Lee had apparently done the household shopping before she left, as the groceries were in bags on the counter.

Betsy was in the midst of putting them away when the phone rang. For an awful moment, she thought it might be Jay, inviting her out for Thanksgiving. He had told her he wasn't sure whether or not he'd be able to take any time off for it, but that it was faintly possible.

It was not Jay. Linda's "Hello, Betsy, how are you today?" was happy-sounding.

"Much, much better, thank you—fine and dandy, in fact."

"You *sound* much better. Your voice is normal. Can you take the trip?"

"Yes. Medical okayed me today."

339

"Oh, good—because I am, too."

Her mother, explained Linda, was better and being properly taken care of in a special hospital section for alcoholics.

"The doctor on the case, he's just great—even Jay said the things this guy had done were tops, and that's why it's okay for me to take the trip."

Betsy caught the reference to Jay with slight surprise, and smiled wordlessly. So Linda had been seeing Jay, had she? That was interesting.

Linda said, "What are you doing for Thanksgiving?"

After only a brief hesitation, Betsy told her.

"Wow!" Linda's admiration was clear. "The Loner!"

"Yes, but Linda—please don't tell anyone." Betsy almost regretted having told Linda until common sense made her realize it was impossible to keep anything hidden on an airline, and Linda would have found out soon enough.

"Oh, I won't, if you don't want me to. But Betsy, face it—we're going on a trip together, right? And there are other crew members who'll be along . . ."

"Oh, I know, I know, but, well . . ."

"I understand. And anyway, it makes it easier for me, because there was something I wanted to *ask* you. Now, I guess I only need *tell* you." Linda stopped, sounding almost shy.

"Go ahead." Betsy was intrigued.

"Well, it's just that Jay asked me to spend Thanksgiving with him—he has those crazy hours, you know, so it won't be a real date, or anything—and I wondered if it truly was okay with you. I mean, your having been his girlfriend—practically his fiancée, and all . . ."

Betsy laughed, her genuine pleasure mixed with relief.

"Oh, of *course* it's all right! In fact, I think it's wonderful. Think of all the things we'll have to tell each other on the flight."

The two girls, each delighted with her own and the other's news, chatted briefly for a few more minutes before ringing off with "Happy Thanksgiving, and see you the day after tomorrow," and "Meet you at the bus." That way, they would be able to swap all their holiday news on the ride out to the airport.

Putting down the receiver and returning to the kitchen,

340

Betsy again reflected on how funny life could be. Fancy turning out to be good friends with Linda Kesnik. Had someone mentioned the possibility to her less than a month before, Betsy would have found the idea ridiculous.

But then, she also noted, stacking cans in the cupboard, who could have guessed that she was going to spend Thanksgiving with Captain David Fleming.

Betsy smiled. No, she wouldn't have believed that one, either. And yet, there it was, all perfectly true.

Tomorrow, David was coming to pick her up at five thirty.

14

"I'm not even going to ask you whether you want seconds, David, because I know you do. Just pass me your plate."

Margaret Rasmussen stretched a plump bangled arm across the table to her brother, and Betsy watched David hand over his plate. Candles flickered over the colorful centerpiece of fruit and autumn leaves, dancing flames reflected on the polished silver bowls and heavy cutlery. A glow of color and contentment seemed to suffuse the room. Betsy smiled at David.

The fourth occupant of the table, Eric Rasmussen, offered Betsy some salad.

"Oh, no thank you—I don't think I could . . ."

"But you do still have some room, I hope, for the dessert that's coming?"

Betsy was about to answer her hostess when David said, "You'd better have, Betsy. Margaret's famous for her desserts—and equally famous for her violence when people don't eat them."

"Hangs visitors who refuse them by their thumbs from the chandelier," said Margaret's husband in his quiet, behind-the-scenes sort of voice. Betsy giggled at the thought, and decided that Eric Rasmussen, his wife and her brother David made an extraordinarily close-knit trio, warm and friendly to outsiders like herself. They had made her feel part of the group the moment she had arrived.

David had picked her up as arranged, and they had

driven across town through Central Park to the large West Side apartment building.

The heavy wooden door to the Rasmussens' apartment had been opened by a uniformed maid, but a second later Margaret Rasmussen had appeared through a doorway at the far end of the high-ceilinged hall.

"Darlings! How wonderful."

Betsy saw a plump energetic redhead coming swiftly towards them, both arms outstretched in greeting, her multiple bracelets jangling.

"David—you must have speeded both ways. Betsy, I'm *so* glad you could come."

There was something about her hostess and her home that made Betsy feel at ease immediately. The high-ceilinged hall had not been intimidating, and neither had the vast living room into which she and David were led after they had handed their coats to the maid.

A large shaggy sheepdog rose from in front of the sofa; simultaneously, Betsy saw a rotund man, his pink face framed by a circlet of pale grey fuzz, rising from an armchair opposite the dog.

"My husband, Eric Rasmussen."

While the introduction was performed, Betsy thought her host would make a lovely Santa Claus. The grey fuzz, she saw, was a combination of his muttonchop whiskers and what remained of his hair; a long white beard, she decided, plus a red cloth cap was all he needed to make him the hit of Macy's during the Christmas season. Keeping her thoughts to herself, she sank comfortably into the chair David indicated. A glowing fire added to the cheery atmosphere, and the sheepdog, having inspected Betsy and found her acceptable, stretched out on the hearth and went back to sleep.

Drinks were served and Margaret Rasmussen perched on a sofa arm. Talk flowed easily, mostly directed by the hostess, but, Betsy realized, adeptly primed every once in a while by her twinkley-eyed husband. His subtle charm complimented his wife's vivaciousness. Perhaps it's the good currents between them, Betsy thought, that make this place so pleasant.

"Mrs. Rasmussen, do you . . . ?"

"Margaret, *please*. Absolutely *nobody* calls me Mrs. anything."

"It's true, you know," Eric Rasmussen said before Betsy had time to rephrase what she had wanted to ask. "Even the super of this building calls her Miss Margaret. Sometimes, I get confused, and wonder whether we *did* get married after all."

"Do you write for the magazine?" Betsy asked, skipping the question of names completely.

"Oh, heavens, no! I can't write a line. It's all I can do to get my name right on a check."

Eric Rasmussen leaned over toward Betsy and, in a clearly audible whisper, said, "She can't spell."

His wife smiled fondly at him. "It's true, you know. I'm one of those word-blind people."

"Lazy, is more like it," said David.

"Thank you, baby brother. That's what I call family loyalty. But to answer your question, Betsy—no, I don't write. I'm on the business side of it."

"She keeps track of how many more issues are possible before they go bankrupt."

Margaret nodded. "Right again. *And* what's what in the financial world of the theater, don't forget that one, David."

"Uses an abacus." Rasmussen's conspiratorial aside made Betsy smile. "After she runs out of fingers . . ."

"That's not true," Margaret Rasmussen protested. "In summer, if I have sandals on, I *always* use my toes before the beads."

The friendly joking enveloped Betsy and she forgot all her initial shyness and eventually she found herself telling anecdotes about passengers which seemed to fascinate the Rasmussens.

"All we ever hear from David are all those technical things," Margaret told her. "I've always known there were people on board, but to hear my brother talk about his job, you'd think it was nothing but metal and electronics."

"Up front, that's about all it is."

At dinner, served in a large dining room with panelled walls referred to by Margaret as "our mausoleum," Betsy was able to observe her hostess more closely as the conversation fell off in favor of food. Margaret Rasmussen was probably in her late forties or early fifties. Betsy was sure the red hair was courtesy of a hairdresser, but was probably the woman's original color, for it matched both

344

her skin tones and temperament. A natural redhead herself, Betsy always felt personal interest when meeting another redhead.

Totally unlike her brother physically, Margaret was also poles apart temperamentally. David was cool and detached. Margaret Rasmussen was movement, sound, color. Interestingly enough, Betsy noted she had married a man who, although physically quite different, was nonetheless very like David Fleming in his air of quiet assurance.

The brothers-in-law obviously got on well together. As dinner progressed, Betsy discovered they shared a passion for mechanics. Rasmussen, a specialty importer, dabbled in mechanical construction.

"He even knows how to take music boxes apart—and then put them together again so they'll still play," his wife explained to Betsy.

After the meal, Margaret Rasmussen led Betsy to her dressing room "so we can freshen up a bit." The room was totally feminine; the walls were lined with built-in closets and there was a long dressing table whose surface was covered with expensive perfume bottles. A professional makeup mirror stood in the middle; a tall, three-way glass took up one corner of the orange-carpeted room.

"Oh, it's marvelous," Betsy breathed.

"I must confess I love it too," her hostess smiled. "One of the many advantages we saw in getting this enormous place. But it suited so many of our purposes. David had just become a widower, and it just seemed easier all around for him to come and live with us. We hardly even know he's here. His rooms are off on the other side of the hall. Go on, Betsy, help yourself to anything you want. The bathroom's over there."

The bathroom, done in pink and orange, was a glamorous and perfect extension of the dressing room itself. When she emerged, Betsy found Margaret pulling a comb through her casually coiffed hair. Without stopping her task, she said, "So you're in love with David."

Betsy blushed, taken aback by the unexpected and direct quality of the remark. She sought Margaret's gaze in reflection through the mirror.

"I ... I don't really know," she finally managed to murmur, lowering her lids and dropping her attention to the carpet.

"Well, *I* do," declared David's sister. "And I think it's wonderful. You'd be very good for him, you know. There!" She gave her hair a final swipe, and swung around on the dressing table stool.

"Now, don't worry," she went on, looking at Betsy directly, "I shan't say anything."

Betsy, remembering the things David had said about his sister's eagerness to push him into marriage, said breathlessly, "Oh, no—please don't!"

"Of course not. This time, I really think there's something in it, so I shan't try to push him at all. David takes a long time to make up his mind, you know. He's always been like that, ever since he was a little boy."

Betsy smiled, trying to visualize David as a small boy with Margaret, his plump older sister, trying to get him to do something.

"We spent a lot of time together as kids," the older woman was saying. "That is, I was often left in charge of him, because our mother died when he was still a baby. And then early in his teens, he got to be taller than I, even though I was so much older." Margaret Rasmussen laughed softly at her memories. "They used to call us 'the long and the short of it' in those days. But by that time, of course," she continued, "I was no longer minding the baby—because the baby was all grown up . . ."

She broke off, and replaced the comb on the dressing table.

"I still say he's as stubborn today as he was when he went around in diapers," was her closing statement on her brother. "But, although I promise I won't say anything, Betsy—I just want you to know, I'm on your side."

Her hand reached out to the younger woman's, and Betsy seized it impulsively. Their quick, warm handclasp sealed a bond between the two redheads. Then Margaret Rasmussen rose and said, "Well, let's get back to the boys before they snooze off in front of the fire."

They rejoined the men, finding them comfortably seated in the big chairs in front of the fireplace, the sheepdog at their feet. When she and Margaret entered the room, Betsy felt a physical thrill as she realized that David was rising from his chair and smiling at her in exactly the same manner as Eric Rasmussen was at his wife.

Perhaps, someday, she and David . . . if only . . .

Was it possible?

After all, why not? And her eyes met Margaret Rasmussen's across the room, and the warmth of her reception enveloped her.

Epilogue

Less than twenty-four hours later, her eyes still heavy with sleep, Betsy methodically packed her bags for her flight. The pale sunlight was fading outside; soon she would wake up properly under the shower, and then get dressed in the uniform presently lying on her bed.

She put the last few items into her suitcase and closed its cover, snapping the locks into position and carrying it out into the living room. There. That was done. She returned to pack her overnight bag. From the rest of the apartment came sounds made by her roommates. Lee was talking on the phone to someone she had met at the Thanksgiving party upstairs, while in the kitchen Sharon was whipping up a light supper for all three of them. Betsy could already smell the coffee.

"Lee! Are you eating with us?" Betsy heard Sharon call.

"Just a moment, Jimmy—no, thanks, Sharon. I'm going out in a while." Then Lee's voice was directed into the receiver once more. "Yes, she's my roommate ... now, where'll I meet you ... ?"

Betsy checked her handbag and slung it over the back of the chair. She hesitated a moment, and then slipped into her bathrobe. Dreamily, she made her way towards the bathroom where, under the cascading warmth of the shower, she projected her thoughts forward to the hours that lay ahead—Flight 410 to London, on board with the man she loved.

THE BIG BESTSELLERS
ARE AVON BOOKS!

Jonathan Livingston Seagull Richard Bach	14316	$1.50

Open Marriage
    Nena O'Neill and George
    O'Neill
	14084	$1.95

Ringolevio Emmett Grogan	14449	$1.50
The Barracudas Keefe Brasselle	14639	$1.50
Net Net Isadore Barmash	14621	$1.50
The Stewardess Julia Percivall	14456	$1.50
The Fatal Friendship Stanley Loomis	14118	$1.50
Moorhaven Daoma Winston	14126	$1.50
The Call Oral Roberts	W364	$1.25
A Raging Talent Jack Hoffenberg	14027	$1.50
The Real Isadora Victor Seroff	J147	$1.50
Don't Look Now Daphne Du Maurier	W343	$1.25
The Khaki Mafia Robin Moore and June Collins	J142	$1.50
The Flame And The Flower Kathleen E. Woodiwiss	J122	$1.50

The
#1
Bestseller

AVON

$1.95

Open Marriage

A
New
Life
Style
for
Couples

Nena O'Neill and George O'Neill